"Let me tell you about this case," Kate said, feeling her control slipping into heedlessness. "Nobody cares about this case. My male partner hates this case because Teddie Crawford was gay. Male officers in my department hate this case because the witnesses are gay — they did toss-off interviews and toss-off reports to prove it. The male pathologist hates this case because Teddie Crawford was gay, and you saw his autopsy report."

"The men in this office hate this case too," Linda Foster said quietly. She pulled off her glasses, tossed them on her desk, looked at Kate with intense gray-green eyes. "I have no illusions why it was assigned to me."

Kate said, "There won't be any press coverage at the prelim or the trial — who cares about a dead gay man? Teddie Crawford is a throwaway human being, this is a throwaway case. Nobody gives a good goddamn."

"Nobody but you and me," Linda Foster said. "Let me refill your cup and let's talk about our witnesses at the prelim."

Praise for
THE BEVERLY MALIBU
Lambda Award Winner, Best Mystery

"Ms. Forrest's Los Angeles homicide detective Kate Delafield makes a strong impression . . . for the smartly professional but still compassionate manner in which she investigates the murder of a crusty, elderly film director . . . The author tells an interesting story about the bad old days of the Hollywood blacklist, and her detective plies her trade with admirable efficiency and more hard-to-come-by integrity."
The New York Times Book Review

"An absorbing procedural . . . An intelligent, complex series heroine . . . Forrest has created a restrained and compassionate portrait of a turbulent period in American history. Movie buffs as well as mystery fans will enjoy her book."
Publishers Weekly

"Fans of earlier Kate Delafield mysteries will welcome the return of the gutsy lesbian cop. She is a well-rounded, expertly developed character, both on and off the job. Her blossoming romance with the young and sensual Aimee provides a sexually explicit, emotionally powerful subplot . . ."
Booklist

"L.A. policewoman Kate Delafield has been the most acclaimed of the lesbian detectives, and this enthralling account of murder in a rent-controlled apartment building shows why . . . Forrest has a talent for characterization, and she manages to incorporate both explicit (but not gratuitous) sex and some consciousness-raising political history without losing command of a well-constructed whodunit plot."
Ellery Queen Mystery Magazine

"As politically intelligent as this book is, Forrest keeps the murder investigation primary. She is pleasingly deft in giving an insider glimpse of little-known movie crafts; evoking the quality of evil at work in the murder scene; and developing the powerful attractions that threaten Kate's grip on her solitary, workaholic life."
Ms. Magazine

"The best feature of *The Beverly Malibu* is its exploration of the effect of HUAC and the loyalty investigations . . . Forrest neatly juxtaposes the feeling of that time with the treatment afforded gays and lesbians to this day."
The Drood Review of Mystery

"Forrest moves far beyond the narrow confines of an ordinary suspense novel. Skillfully combining the wiry tenacity of a homicide investigation, the sensuality of making love, and the moral perspective of a political critique, Forrest has come of age as a writer on the national scene."
The Advocate

"This, the third Kate Delafield mystery, is the best of the lot, with Kate becoming increasingly well-drawn . . ."
The Gay Community News

"Kate Delafield is a classy cop, but one conceived in a very real and complex manner by Forrest . . ."
The Bay Area Reporter

"I liked *The Beverly Malibu,* but then I knew I would. I like Kate Delafield, and I feel that I know her."
The Lambda Rising Book Report

MURDER BY TRADITION

KATHERINE V. FORREST

NAIAD
1996

Printed in the United States of America on acid-free paper
First Edition   June, 1991
First Trade Paperback Edition   January, 1993
Second Printing June, 1993
Third Printing February, 1995
Fourth Printing July, 1996

Cover design by Catherine Hopkins
Typeset by Sandi Stancil

Library of Congress Cataloging-in-Publication Data

Forrest, Katherine V., 1939–
Murder by tradition / by Katherine V. Forrest
   p.   cm.
   ISBN 1-56280-002-7
   I. Title.
PS3556.O737M84   1991
813'.54—dc20   90-21994
                                                           CIP

Acknowledgments

To Detective Supervisor Mary F. Otterson, Madison, WI. For the incalculable value of her advice, her patient communication of the realities of police work. For her precious friendship over the years. For her own integrity which more than anything has given me Kate's reality, has helped me understand the essential truth of Kate Delafield. And especially for giving me the truth of this case to see and understand, and a love for a young man whom I never met but will always mourn.

To Gretchen Hayward, senior prosecutor in the District Attorney's Office, Dane County, Wisconsin, for her real life example and practicing belief in the ideal of equal justice for *all* Americans.

To Jo Wegner, blood spatter expert for the State of Wisconsin. In memoriam. I am grateful that she saw the manuscript of this novel, and knew that our hour together gave me the authenticity for the character of Charlotte Mead.

To the Third Street Writers Group, respected and highly talented colleagues who have become, over the years, my trusted friends:

Gerald Citrin, Montserrat Fontes, Janet Gregory, Jeffrey N. McMahan, Karen Sandler, and newcomer Vicki P. McConnell.

Added thanks to Jeff and Gerry for vital moral support.

To Michael Nava for advice on several legal intricacies, and for his honest friendship and the inspiration of his own work.

To Barbara Grier, an editor's editor, for her advice, for her clear perception of this novel and all my work.

BOOKS BY KATHERINE V. FORREST

CURIOUS WINE

DAUGHTERS OF A CORAL DAWN

AMATEUR CITY
A Kate Delafield Mystery

AN EMERGENCE OF GREEN

MURDER AT THE NIGHTWOOD BAR
A Kate Delafield Mystery

DREAMS AND SWORDS

THE BEVERLY MALIBU
A Kate Delafield Mystery

MURDER BY TRADITION
A Kate Delafield Mystery

FLASHPOINT

To the real Teddie Crawford
And his own Kate Delafield:

To Ivan

and

To Mary

PART I

— 1 —

Detective Kate Delafield drove down Third Street, past five black-and-whites clustered beside an expanse of yellow police tape fluttering in a mild breeze. She parked the Plymouth around the corner on Harper Avenue. Detective Ed Taylor, yawning audibly, climbed out of the car and stretched; he knew from many past investigations how deliberately she preferred to approach a crime scene. Pulling her notebook from her shoulderbag, Kate recorded the date, Feb. 4, 1989, the time, 7:35 a.m., and the temperature, approximately fifty-five degrees in the

city of Los Angeles. She strode back around the
corner, Taylor dawdling in her wake.

At this early hour on a Saturday morning, auto
traffic moved smoothly along Third Street, slowing
only momentarily at the site of the police activity.
The block was devoid of pedestrians. She walked
past a liquor store occupying the corner of Harper,
its vertical neon sign reflecting down the two
intersecting streets. Then came Indigo Restaurant,
Minassian Rug Company, a Christian Science
Reading Room, John Atchison Beauty Shop, a
laundry. Then Tradition.

The mid-block restaurant, its taped-off perimeter
patrolled by Felix Knapp and Chris Hollings, was
scarcely wider than a storefront. Kate nodded to the
two officers, pleased with the positioning of police
tape which would help to keep media coverage well
back from the crime scene.

Taylor ducked under the tape; Kate moved past
it and looked in the window of the adjacent
business, Andria's Hole in the Wall — a
contemporary clothing shop with garments in its
window that she would not wear to a Halloween
party. Next came Mariana Custom Cleaners. Then a
small office building, and on the corner of Sweetzer
Avenue, a mini-mall with a half-dozen shops. Across
the street a 7-Eleven dominated a matching
mini-mall. The next building was Taj Soundworks,
then a vacant storefront, a shop called Objects,
Pacific Printing, Classy Nail, a yoga center, and
Banner Packing.

After recording all of this in her notebook, Kate
walked back to Tradition and past the tape to study
the restaurant.

White shutters decorated the lower half of the front window, tapestry curtains the top half. A small puff-shaped canopy, dark blue, sheltered a door, the window in the door decorated by tapestry matching the curtain in the larger window.

Sergeant Fred Hansen, with Taylor beside him smothering another yawn, stood sentry in the doorway, watching her, one hand resting on his gun belt, the other clutching a clipboard.

She nodded. "Morning, Fred."

Hansen returned her nod. "How are you, Kate?" Somberly, he consulted his clipboard. "Victim's Edward Ashwell Crawford, white male, goes by Teddie, T-e-d-d-i-e, according to his partner." He gestured behind him. "Nice little neighborhood restaurant with takeout, catering, too." His stolid expression softened. "Nice little business. Wouldn't mind having it myself." The softness was replaced by impassiveness. "Except for what's in the kitchen. Real scenic in there. His partner slid all over the place getting to the victim to see if he was still alive."

"Great," muttered Taylor. He unbuttoned his plaid jacket, tugged on its sleeves, shoved his hands in his pockets.

Kate recognized Taylor's fidgeting as preparation, a bracing for what awaited them. "Anything else?" she said to Hansen with a brusqueness that came out of her own tension, a familiar tightening inside her, a necessary girding.

Hansen shook his head. "The partner's too freaked out, couldn't get much out of him." He gestured to a black-and-white parked off to the side of the yellow police tape; a figure sat in the rear, his bowed head in his hands. "Pierce and Swenson, Foster and Deems are canvassing but everything on the street's closed except the 7-Eleven. There's an alley behind the restaurant, we're working the neighborhood over there. The victim's been dead a few hours, I'd say. Some of the mess is drying."

"Thanks, Fred," Kate said.

Hansen opened the door of Tradition.

A counter with an old-fashioned ornate cash register occupied the front of the long room. A refrigerator display case along the adjacent wall was empty of its usual contents, but neat tags in script lettering announced what had been planned for the case: lemon pasta with herbs, grape leaves, chicken breasts dijon, shrimp salad, vegetable bouquet.

Visible in the murky depths of the room were eight small tables on a faded Oriental carpet, with tablecloths and delicate wrought iron chairs with tapestry-covered seats. On the walls three impressionist prints of nature scenes seemed dream-like in the shadows.

Taylor, glancing around, scratched the bald spot at the back of his head, pulling his lank blond hair back over it. "Very frou-frou," he pronounced.

Kate liked the place, its gentility amid the prosaic commerce of the street. She suspected that it attracted loyal customers who appreciated the unpretentious charm. She moved to the counter and stooped down to read a card in a small wicker basket.

TRADITION
Catering for the Discriminating

She stood up straight. Squaring her shoulders, she walked toward the doorway behind the counter. Standing on the threshold she took in the scene in one encompassing glance that included the ceiling, then carefully focused her gaze.

The kitchen was compact, with a double stainless steel sink and Formica-topped counters, a built-in refrigerator — all surrounding a large table for food preparation. Immaculate, Kate thought. She would trust anything prepared in here. She lowered her gaze slightly, examining the room in patterned sections like a camera lens. The cabinet and walls were pristine white, except for a considerable area near the sink where a design of bright red arcs and splatters extended several feet high on the wall. Low on the wall was a smear of red as if a hand had swiped at the stain.

"This guy can't have an ounce left in him," Taylor grunted from behind her in the doorway.

She lowered her gaze to the polished tile floor. Blood had pooled into the channels between the white tiles for several feet around the body of Edward Ashwell Crawford. Other individual puddles and trails of blood defiled the floor, as well as bloody footsteps, several of them skid marks where someone had slid through the gore. The dead man's black pants clung wetly to his legs. Patches of white skin were visible through a torn and shredded shirt fouled crimson and plastered to his body; only from a portion of the collar could Kate tell that the shirt had been white. Teddie Crawford's arms were crossed over himself as if to staunch the blood draining from his body. His dull brown stare was fixed on the ceiling.

"Swiss cheese," Taylor said. "Somebody turned him into fucking Swiss cheese."

"You never realize how much blood the body holds," Kate murmured.

"One hell of a good-looking young guy," Taylor offered.

Wondering how he could tell, Kate looked more closely at the body. The head lay in a pool of blood, and the tousled hair, dark and thick, was saturated with it; the face, bleached out, was measled with red droplets. Even so, the head and its features were finely made. Long eyelashes thickly fringed the staring dark eyes, the nose was patrician, the mouth, even in the slackness of death, was sensuous, the torso slender and well-formed. The bloodied hand nearest to Kate had long tapered fingers. In a scene of such carnage, she was amazed at Taylor's perception. "Yes," she agreed. "Very good-looking."

And gay. She sensed it with gut-deep certainty.

She craned her body over the threshold, studying the dead man's hand which was nearest to her; it was turned palm down, the little finger angled unnaturally. She needed to get more information from this room, and quickly. She said impatiently, "Not a damn thing we can do till the coroner and the technicians get here. We can't even go in."

Taylor pointed at the maelstrom of blood and bloody footprints. "How can anybody mess this up?"

"Let's not make it worse," Kate said flatly. As the D-3 on this case, she was in charge; essential crime-scene decisions were hers. "We need Shapiro and Napoleon Carter here before anybody else goes in."

"See that?" Taylor was pointing to the table.

A piece of glass glittered under the fluorescent light; a powdery residue coated its surface.

"Coke," he said.

She shrugged. "Probably."

"A party that got out of hand," Taylor said. "Way out of hand."

"Maybe," Kate said, staring at the dead man's fixed gaze, knowing she was being irrational as she hoped that this beautiful young gay man had not lost his life in a party that had gotten "out of hand."

— 2 —

"My whole life's in that place," sobbed Francisco Caldera. "It's gone, it's nothing without Teddie . . ."

The rail-thin Latino was slumped sideways in the back seat of a black-and-white, feet dangling out of its open door, arms crossed in a clutching of his own body. Kate stood beside the squad car with Taylor.

"When was the last time you saw him?" she asked. With difficulty she kept her gaze focused on the grief-ravaged young face turned up to hers. After a single glance at Taylor, he had not taken his eyes off her. Even the knowledge that this man was a suspect, that killers often exhibited as much or more grief as anyone else, did not diminish an almost compelling need to soothe him, to stroke his thin, fine-textured dark hair.

"Last night," he said, brushing away tears. "We closed up at eleven."

"Was that as usual?"

He shook his head. "Big catering job tonight. We made marinades, sauces . . ." He lifted a hand, dropped it into his lap in a gesture of futility. He wore a white cotton jacket over a lime green shirt; his pants were gray and voluminous.

Kate asked, "Who left first?"

Briefly he closed his eyes. Moisture glistened on his dark lashes. "He did. Gloria picked him up." At Kate's questioning look he added, "Gloria Gomez. His roommate. They have an apartment over on Crescent Heights."

A female roommate. Kate felt no shift in her certainty that Teddie Crawford was a gay man. And that Francisco Caldera was a gay man also. Possibly the female roommate was a lesbian. She said, "Where did they say they were going?"

"Malone's. A bar in West Hollywood." He added in bitter self-reproach, "He wanted me to go. But me, I had to get some sleep. I go to that bar with him, he might be alive . . ."

Kate thought about Joe D'Amico at the crime lab and his constant gossip about the gay bars in West Hollywood and Silverlake; she didn't recognize the

name of this one. Could it be new? Or perhaps not a
gay bar? She asked casually, "Does Malone's have a
particular clientele?"

"A mix. Gloria likes it. She was seeing some new
guy she wanted Teddie to meet."

So Gloria Gomez apparently was heterosexual.
And Malone's Bar attracted an assortment of sexual
orientation and ethnicity, judging by Gloria Gomez's
affection for it.

"This Gloria," Taylor said. "How'd she get along
with Teddie?"

"Like he was her brother. Everybody loved
Teddie."

"Somebody didn't. Tell us what happened to him
last night."

Warily eying Taylor, Caldera shook his head.
"After he left here — I don't have clue."

Kate observed Taylor with weary annoyance. His
knee-jerk behavior toward men in any way distinct
from himself was always heavy-handed assertion of
authority. Francisco Caldera might have been born
and bred in middle-class American culture, but he
was Latino, and that was all Taylor saw.

Taylor said, "You actually see Gloria Gomez pick
him up?"

"She honked from the alley. She drives a Honda
Civic, I know the horn."

Hitching her pants to put a foot up on the floor
of the squad car, Kate leaned over to be closer to
Francisco Caldera, a hand not quite touching him.
She said gently, "Tell us when you got here this
morning and what you saw."

"I came in the place about seven o'clock —" His
dark eyes awash and fixed on Kate, again he crossed

his arms over his chest in an effort to control his shudders.

"Which door?" Taylor was busy writing.

"Through the alley door like always. I saw Teddie . . . lying there. I had to see if . . . I ran to him, I slipped all over the place . . ."

He lowered his head and sobbed. He pointed a tremulous finger at his white Nikes. "It's Teddie's bl . . . it's Teddie's bloo —" He dissolved into gulping sobs.

Taylor asked, "Did you touch him?"

"I don't remember, sir." The voice sounded as if it were bubbling up through water.

"Turn him over?"

Caldera shook his bowed head. "I was so scared, I got to the phone and then the police came."

"Why were you scared?"

Taylor's voice was mild, but Caldera jerked his head up. "I never saw anybody dead before. It was *Teddie*. My friend, the best friend I ever —" Another paroxysm of tears.

Taylor said, "You knew why this happened to him, that's why you were scared, right?"

Jabbing tears off his cheeks with his fingers, Caldera stared at him. "Man, what are you *talking* about?"

Taylor, Kate conceded, was asking good questions. But she entered the conversation. "What can you tell us about his associates?"

"He knew everybody. All up and down the block. Everybody in the neighborhood where he lived. Everybody."

"His family," Kate said, "what do you know about them?"

He slumped further down in the seat, a hand across his eyes. "Joe and Margaret will just . . ." He shook his head.

"Joe and Margaret," Taylor said, writing in his notebook.

"An aunt and uncle. They raised him. They live in a trailer park in Lancaster, but Teddie sees — saw them every chance he . . . got. God . . . he's *dead*." Again he burst into tears.

Kate watched him with an emotion she recognized from witnessing bereavements and having gone through her own. People were either sheathed by shock and behaved calmly, almost normally, as she had, or they were swallowed up by agony. Difficult as it might be to witness, agony at least meant that grieving was already in process, and recovery closer.

"I'm sorry," Kate said. "I know this is very hard for you. But we need to get information as quickly as we can to find out who did this." She asked, "Did Teddie have enemies? Anyone at all you can think of?"

"No. Not a soul. I tell you, everybody loved Teddie."

"Everybody's got enemies," Taylor stated.

Caldera answered with quiet dignity: "Not Teddie.'"

"Who was his girlfriend?"

"Girlfriend?" Caldera looked at him. "Teddie was gay. We're both gay."

There it was. Kate marveled at Francisco Caldera, at the ease of it. She asked, "How did the two of you get along?" Before Caldera could answer she rephrased the question more bluntly: "Were you lovers?"

"Never happened." To Kate the tone carried a strong vibration of regret. "He was more than a partner, he was like a brother. We both put everything we had into this place. But he was the one who really made it work. I can't do anything without him."

Taylor said, almost idly, "You're both young guys. How'd you get the money to start up?"

"My money. But he had the brains. Teddie was born knowing how to do this. And he charmed the customers, the business was just starting to —"

"Okay," Taylor said, "how'd *you* get the money?"

"Insurance."

Kate, although she surmised what was coming, waited along with Taylor.

"A friend died, okay?"

"I'm sorry, Mr. Caldera," Kate said into the silence.

Caldera shrugged. "Call me Francisco. And I've lost many friends . . . many."

"Francisco," she said, and smiled at him. "Did Teddie have a lover?"

His face softened as he looked at her. "Nobody serious. Not since Carl."

"Tell us about Carl," she said.

He shrugged. "Nothing to tell. He's been history over a year now."

Taylor said, "Where can we reach him?"

"He's in the book. Carl Jacoby, in Silverlake. But he didn't have anything to do with this. He broke up with Teddie when he tested positive."

"Teddie tested positive?" Taylor's voice was suddenly animated.

"No, Carl did."

"Your friend Teddie gave it to him," Taylor said. "Right?" He gestured so imperiously at Tradition that Kate had to resist looking around at the restaurant. She stood with her back to it, as if to block out images of its blood-drenched kitchen.

"No, Teddie was negative."

Taylor shook his head. "I don't get it."

"Carl was freaked at the idea he could've given it to Teddie. So freaked he checked right out of Teddie's life." He was looking at Kate as he spoke. "It happens. You test HIV-positive, you look at everything differently. Everything."

Criminalist Napoleon Carter and his team had arrived, along with blood spatter expert Charlotte Mead and photographer Ted Carlton. As had Shapiro, Wilshire Division's photographer.

Kate said, "We'll have more questions later, Francisco." Then she asked quietly, "How old was Teddie?"

"Twenty-three," he said, and again began to sob.

Every angle and dimension of Tradition had been photographed. The body of Teddie Crawford, no longer strobe-lit, would nevertheless lie on the floor for hours longer, Kate knew; Charlotte Mead and Ted Carlton would now begin work in this room that in the awakening warmth of the day was filling with the rich coppery scent of blood.

"Ed, Kate," Charlotte Mead barked from beside the double sink.

Kate smiled at the tall, lanky, blue-smocked woman. They had worked together on other homicides when blood spatter analysis was necessary. Charlotte Mead was brilliant at her difficult, painstaking, eccentric profession.

"Come on over here, you two," Mead commanded. "Hands in your pockets, you touch anything, you own it. Ed, you watch where you put those elephant feet." She indicated a route that skirted the gore on the floor.

Taylor stepped over the threshold. "Believe me, you're gonna see a real twinkle toes." He stuffed his hands in his jacket pockets, as did Kate — routine safeguarding of a crime scene; he and Kate would not touch anything, even accidentally. But Kate also understood that a deeper concern underlay Taylor's caution: the dead man was gay, and this room was awash in blood.

"Your assailant's been cut," Mead told them. "See this nice single round drop of blood?" She pointed with her pen at a red globule on the counter near the sink. "We got a swimming pool on the floor but this drop's all by itself. So it hardly came from the deceased. And over here, blood's on one of the faucet handles. And on this bar of soap. No question we'll find blood in the drain. Your man tried to clean himself up."

Mead's weathered face was sharp with eagerness, her professional interest whetted by a crime scene only minimally despoiled. All too frequently, police presence — hands and feet altering evidence — cast ambiguity onto the reconstruction she was required to create for the benefit of a jury.

Kate looked at Charlotte Mead with deference and a touch of envy. Her expertise — and that of all the criminalists — was the one purely impartial aspect of a homicide investigation. Mead was on the side only of her scientific findings, and her testimony in court could be the despair of the prosecution just as well as it could the defense. The best course of action always was to find out exactly what she knew.

Kate said, "Anything else you can tell us right now?"

Mead indicated the wall and cabinets behind the corpse of Teddie Crawford. "There's a castoff pattern." With her pen she described an arc corresponding with a faint pattern of red droplets rising high up on the white surfaces. "Your man threw blood in the act of stabbing. His own blood. No question he's cut. Check the hospitals and clinics."

"We'll get right on it, Charlotte. No sign of the weapon, I take it."

"Come on, Kate. He'd put his pecker back in his pants, wouldn't he?"

"Just checking, Charlotte." Kate grinned at her. A familiar tenet among law enforcement professionals held that multiple stabbing was a form of sexual pathology.

Mead's blue eyes fastened onto the body on the floor. She shook her head. "Look at him, just look at him. Such a beauty."

Kate joined Mead's contemplation of Teddie Crawford. Twenty-three years were all he had known. The rest had been taken from him. What else was important?

"You be real careful in here, Charlotte," Taylor said. "The guy's gay, you know."

Kate looked at him balefully.

Charlotte's voice, her face, were impassive. "Careful is my life, Ed."

Gloria Gomez had arrived at Tradition, Hansen informed Kate and Taylor.

"Take her to the station," Kate ordered. "Ed and I will be along shortly. Fred," she added, "call us the minute the coroner gets here." She wanted to be present when Teddie Crawford's body was moved. She was grateful for Charlotte Mead's information; knowing the killer was wounded narrowed the field of suspects significantly.

The media, both print and visual, had assembled along with a sizable crowd outside the yellow police tape protecting Tradition, the crowd and the television cameras settling in to wait for that hushed moment of drama when the wrapped body of Teddie Crawford would be rolled out to the waiting coroner's van.

Lieutenant Bodwin had also arrived, and entered Tradition accompanied by Kate and Taylor, who briefed him. Silent, his craggy face expressionless, he observed the kitchen from the doorway. He would be dealing with the press.

"Charlotte says our man's wounded, Lieutenant," Taylor told him. "We need somebody to get right on checking hospitals and clinics."

"Yes, well, it seems pretty fucking stupid for him to go to a hospital, doesn't it," Bodwin said, turning his back on the room where the crime lab team worked.

"Good thing so many of them are pretty fucking stupid," Kate said agreeably. She knew he understood that criminal impulses and behavior had little to do with intelligence. His remark had been reflexive, rooted in his unforgiving resentment of Charlotte Mead. Mead, who observed no niceties of status and would take on Chief Daryl Gates if it meant preserving the sanctity of a crime scene, had repaid the lieutenant's assertive entry into one such scene by isolating his fingerprint on an item of evidence and then spreading the report throughout the department.

"I'll take care of assigning someone," Bodwin said, and left to face the television cameras.

Gloria Gomez, in black jeans and a white cotton knit sweater, her shoulder-length dark hair disheveled, looked younger than her twenty years. Her delicate, almost childlike hands lay tightly clasped on the Formica-topped table in the interview room.

"I need to see Teddie," she whispered, her eyes dull black with shock. "I . . . can't do anything with how I feel till I see Teddie."

Kate nodded. "I understand," she said. Seeing Anne had been so absolute a requirement that she had disregarded every attempt to dissuade her from viewing what was in the burned out wreck on the

Hollywood Freeway. She added, "But that won't be possible for a while."

For Gloria Gomez, seeing Teddie Crawford would not happen for days, if it happened at all. There would be further violation of Teddie Crawford's body at the autopsy. Then his next of kin — presumably Joe and Margaret Crawford — would determine what happened to him next. His face appeared minimally damaged, and clothing would conceal the devastation done to his body. Depending on the Crawford family's burial beliefs, Gloria Gomez might have her wish in the form of an open casket funeral.

"Gloria," Taylor said, "we know this is hard. But try your best to talk to us. When did you last see Teddie?"

Kate flicked a glance at Taylor. He was being as considerate to Gloria Gomez as he had been impersonal with Francisco Caldera.

"Last night . . ." The young woman faltered.

"Last night," Taylor said, leaning back, crossing an ankle over a knee, his casual posture an attempt to relax her. "Tell us about that."

"I picked him up at Tradition like I said I would —"

"Where was Teddie's car?"

"He doesn't — didn't have one."

"What time did you pick him up, Gloria?"

"Right at eleven. We went to Malone's like we planned."

"Anybody with you?"

She shook her head. "I had a late date with Paul. I wanted Teddie to meet him."

"What's Paul's last name?"

"Lopez . . . Paul Lopez. Teddie liked him —

bought both of us beers . . ." Her gaze seemed unfocused.

Kate thought of Aimee, remembering the homicide investigation of only two months before, the horror of Owen Sinclair's death reflected in Aimee's unfocused eyes. She needed to call Aimee, to tell her she would be tied up indefinitely on this new investigation. And, she ordered herself, she needed to eliminate extraneous thoughts and concentrate on the brutal murder of this gay man and the important work required of her right now in this room.

"He can't be dead," Gloria Gomez said to Kate. "There's no reason . . ."

"No, there isn't any reason at all," Kate said quietly. "I'm very sorry."

"The guy he met . . . did he . . ."

Kate exchanged a swift glance with Taylor. "What can you tell us about that?"

"Not much. Teddie met this guy. They left together."

Kate recognized in the matter-of-fact voice the deep calm of shock. "What was his name?"

"Lyle . . . Miles . . . something like that. I'm not real good at names . . . I didn't hardly exchange word one with this dude."

"I take it you didn't care for this dude," Kate suggested.

"Teddie likes a different line of men than me, macho-types." The attempt at a grin distorted into a grimace. "Yeah, I didn't like him. I can't exactly tell you why."

"What did he look like?"

"Muscle-bound. The type that wears a tight T-shirt and sticks out his chest like a rooster, you know?"

Kate nodded encouragingly. "That's what he was wearing? A T-shirt?"

"Yeah. A black one. Under a bomber jacket."

"What color was the jacket?"

"Dark . . . dark brown. Maybe black."

"Do you remember about his pants?"

"Jeans."

"Regular jeans?"

"Oh yeah, I remember now, that's one of the things I didn't like about him. His jeans. Real faded. Ladders in the knees. People that buy clothes to make them look poor make me sick."

Her voice shook with a vehemence that Kate recognized as misdirected emotion. She made her own voice calm as she asked, "Dark hair? Blond?"

"Blond. Thin stuff, you know? Be bald in no time."

Kate nodded. "His eyes, do you remember what color?"

She pondered. "Maybe blue."

"How old do you think he was?"

She shrugged. "Older than Teddie. Maybe thirty? He had a moustache, I can't figure men with face fuzz too well."

"Neither can I," Kate said with a smile, adding another note on her legal pad. Gloria Gomez showed every sign of being a very good witness. "His moustache, was it thin? Medium? Thick?"

"Thick. With guys, the thinner the hair, the thicker the moustache. Right?"

Again Kate smiled. "Would you recognize him if you saw him again?"

"Yeah. Sure."

Kate turned to a new page. "Gloria, tell us everything you remember about last night at Malone's Bar."

The young woman sighed, and sat up in the metal chair. "We went in, the place was crowded, and Paul, he's at a table. I introduce Teddie, he goes to the bar to buy us some beers. I see him right away talking to this dude. Then Teddie comes back and sits with us, but I see he's still staring over at the bar, I kidded him a little bit."

Taylor looked up from the pad on which he was scribbling notes. "Paul knew Teddie was gay?"

"Sure. Paul was kidding him too. Like, saying he'd buy the next round of beers but maybe Teddie'd like to go get them."

"And did he?" Taylor asked.

"Yeah. Yeah, he did. He stopped to talk to the dude again." She leaned forward, arms crossed, the small hands clasping the inside of her arms. "He walked the beers back to the table, said he'd be back with us later. I didn't pay much more attention, Paul and I were rapping, but all of a sudden Teddie's at the table with this dude, saying he'll get himself home." The hands were again clenched tightly together, the knuckles and fingertips white. "Teddie shook hands with Paul, he . . . kissed me goodnight. I told him to be careful. But I didn't mean about . . . I never thought . . ."

Kate asked, "Did this man speak at all?"

"Yeah, I don't remember what he said."

"Did he have any sort of an accent? Anything you remember about his voice?"

Pulling at the ends of her hair, she reflected. "Uh uh."

"Gloria, will you help us out? Work with a police artist in putting together a picture of this man?"

"Yeah. Sure. Anything."

Kate said, "Tell us a little about Teddie. How you met, how you ended up sharing an apartment."

"We were in a psych class together at Cal State L.A. a couple of years ago. We helped each other out, we hit it off, we stayed friends. He and Carl split, I lost my roommate, Teddie moved in. I'm in school full time, I need all the help I can get with the rent."

"How do you support yourself?" Kate asked.

"I work nights at the Cineplex at the Beverly Center. Sometimes I help out at Tradition if they get in a bind, but I really don't like that kind of work. My brothers, they're helping with my bills, to get me through school. I'm going for my chemistry degree. Six more quarters and I'll have it," she said in the tone of someone on an unshakable course.

Taylor asked, "When did you know Teddie was gay?"

"One look." She smiled briefly. "So many gay men are gorgeous, it's the first thing you think when you see a really good-looking single man. Teddie, we talked a few minutes, I knew — and it was never a secret anyway. Teddie was proud he was gay."

"Proud?" Taylor looked up from his note-taking.

"Yeah. Proud." The dark eyes focused on Taylor had lost some of their dullness. "You got some problem with that?"

Taylor shrugged. "Some people do. Did he pick men up all the time?"

"The other way around. Teddie was . . ." Staring at Taylor, Gloria said, "Okay, he was a queen. A flirt. He was beautiful, a flashy dresser, he was smart and funny, guys came on to him all the time. But he was careful, too. I mean, I bugged him about it. You worry about every gay guy you know these days."

Taylor leaned toward her. "He much of a drinker?"

"Uh uh. He'd drink a beer now and then. Wine. He gave me a bad time anytime I drank in front of him."

"He take anything else?"

Kate knew he was thinking of that piece of glass in the kitchen of Tradition. *A party that got out of hand,* Taylor had said. *Way out of hand.*

"You mean dope?" Gloria Gomez was indignant. "Give me a break."

Taylor said disarmingly, "Lots of people take a toot once in a while."

"Yeah, and I don't see why you people make such a freaking deal out of it. But Teddie didn't. Not even a joint."

"You can't be sure about that," Taylor said with clear skepticism.

"I'm sure about Teddie," Gloria Gomez said. "Case closed."

"Gloria," Kate said, "tell us about Teddie." She felt seared by the image of Teddie Crawford on the

blood-soaked kitchen floor of Tradition. She needed
to see something else.

"The sweetest guy . . . my best friend. Francisco,
he's so good a cook he's magic, and Teddie, he
always brought food home from Tradition." Gloria
Gomez said softly, "I'd come in from work, from
school, there was always food. He'd do my laundry,
anything to help out. Teddie always took better care
of other people than he ever did of himself."

"What other people?" Taylor asked. "Who besides
you and Francisco?"

"Everybody. With me, guys come and go like ping
pong balls. But Teddie, he seemed to stay friends
with everybody he knew. Even ex-lovers. His friends
dying and he never gave in to the dying, you know?
The guy — he's just amazing. I always told him so,
told him every day . . ."

She was smiling fondly, in reminiscence, and
Kate saw in her dark eyes the depth of the grieving
to come. Gloria said, "Mrs. Sheffield down the hall.
Eighty-seven years old, Teddie looked in on her
every day, took her trash out for her — she's crazy
about Teddie. Joe and Margaret, the way he cared
for the two of them. Teddie was . . . Teddie
was . . ."

"A saint?" Taylor suggested.

Gloria Gomez looked at him and closed her
mouth, her lips narrowing.

As silence accumulated, Kate decided to conclude
this interview, if for no other reason than to gather
more information from other sources. "Paul Lopez,"
she said. "Where can we reach him?"

Gloria Gomez pulled an address book out of a
cloth shoulderbag, opened it to a page, handed the

book to Kate. Kate recorded an address on Hobart
Avenue in Hollywood and a phone number.

There was a tap on the door of the interview
room. Taylor climbed to his feet, excused himself. A
moment later he signaled to Kate from the doorway,
then disappeared.

She rose. "Gloria, we'll set you up to work with
our artist. And we'll need you to sign a statement."

As Kate walked out of the interview room with
Gloria Gomez, she glimpsed Taylor in the homicide
unit of the Detectives Squad Room, in conversation
with assistant district attorney Bud Sterling. Sterling
Silver, he had been nicknamed, for his successes in
court. Could this highly experienced prosecutor be
taking on this case?

"Detective Delafield," Gloria Gomez said as they
approached Records and Identification. Kate turned
to her. The young woman's eyes were coal black in a
face that seemed bleached of color. "You're gonna get
this motherfucker."

Kate nodded. "I'll get him."

"Two messages," Taylor told Kate as she
approached her desk in the Detectives Squad Room.
"A suspect —" He checked his notebook. "Kyle
Jensen, caucasian, blond. At Hollywood Presbyterian.
Being treated right now in ER, cuts on his hands.
They'll keep him, we got two uniforms on the way.
And Hansen says Everson's at Tradition."

"Good," Kate said. "We'll go there first. What
about Bud Sterling?"

"He heard about the case."

"So I gathered. Did you tell him we may have a suspect?"

"Yeah. I told him everything we know so far."

"What did he say?" She was exasperated by his phlegmatic responses.

He shrugged. "He says he'll follow up."

"I've always wanted to work with him." Slinging her purse over her shoulder, she tried to transmit some part of her own zeal to him. "Let's go get him a good case, Ed."

As Taylor climbed into the Plymouth, he grumbled, "I don't see why the hell we have to go back to the crime scene. We got a live suspect."

"He isn't going anywhere," she answered, sliding in behind the wheel. "I want to hear what Everson has to say. We haven't really looked at the scene. Or been near the body."

"Autopsy's Monday."

"You'll have to attend, Ed. I've got court, the Weldon prelim. Anyway, we need a good look at everything right now — before we question this suspect."

"You want to count the knife cuts on this stiff or what? What's to see?"

"His hands," Kate said, threading her way through the police vehicles in Wilshire Division's parking lot.

"Why? So what if he's got defensive wounds? Or doesn't? We know what happened."

Her patience was running out. "Okay," she said. "Why don't you tell me what we know happened."

"The same tired shit. Teddie picks this guy up,

they come back here, snort coke, Teddie wants to get down to screwing and the guy turns Teddie into his personal dart board."

"The same tired shit," she echoed contemptuously.

"Come on, Kate. They live like that, they ask for it."

Kate sped down Venice Boulevard. Be cool, be calm, she ordered herself. But the torrent of anger felt cleansing. "So Teddie Crawford meeting somebody in a bar and dying for it is tired shit. So Florence Delgado walking down La Brea at night and dying for it is tired shit. The day that taking murdering creeps off the street becomes tired shit, I quit."

"What is *this* shit? I'm a cop, you're a cop. Why are we having this conversation?"

She bit off her words: "Because you think Teddie Crawford deserved to be killed."

"Goddammit, nobody deserves to be killed. But some people fucking ask for it. You know it, Kate."

"Right," she snapped. "Justifiable homicide. The victims being tired shit and all."

"The victims being *dumb* shit," Taylor said heatedly. "The victims —"

"Deserve what they get, is what you're saying. You got it all figured out, Ed."

"For chrissakes, Kate. I didn't make the world. I don't see you with any smart answers."

"I don't have any." The curtness of her dismissal was directed at herself. Taylor was no less a blockhead today than he had been in the seven years they had worked together. What point was there in arguing with him?

The crowd had thickened in front of Tradition.

Soon they would have what they were waiting for:
the coroner's van was parked in front.

Kate pulled the Plymouth into the same parking
place on Harper Avenue that she had used that
morning. Still seething over her encounter with
Taylor, she strode down the block, Taylor in her
wake, and pushed her way through the crowd.

Everson, arms tidily crossed over his tweed
jacket, stood beside the kitchen sink talking with
Charlotte Mead.

"Christ, it smells like a stockyard in here,"
complained Taylor from the kitchen doorway.

"Charlotte's perfume," Everson said.

"Right," Charlotte Mead growled, looking up from
her clipboard. "Eau de stockyard."

Grinning, Kate made her way into the room. She
liked this deputy coroner; his personal fastidiousness
seemed ludicrous in context with the carnage of the
crime scenes he visited, but it reflected his diligence.
"How are you, Walt?"

Everson gestured to the floor. "Better than him."

"When'd he get it?" Taylor asked.

"Not before one this morning," Everson said. "Say
between one and three."

Kate asked, "He have any defensive wounds?"

Everson nodded. "Rigor's almost complete, but I
can give you a bit of a look."

Taking a fresh pair of latex gloves from his bag,
Everson snapped them on and hunkered down beside
the body of Teddie Crawford. Kate and Charlotte
Mead crouched at his side, Taylor leaning over.
Everson grasped Teddie Crawford's left arm with
both hands, and with effort managed to turn it
slightly. In the palm of the bloody hand a gash was

visibly incised. Everson repeated the process with the right hand. Its palm was also slashed, the little finger almost severed.

"Classic defensive wounds," Everson said.

"His hands need to be bagged," Taylor said.

"Thank you, Ed," Charlotte Mead said. "We dolts at the crime lab are happy to know that."

Kate allowed herself a scant moment to enjoy Taylor's discomfort. "No watch, no jewelry," she mused, examining Teddie Crawford's hands and wrists. "Walt," she said, rising to her feet, "did you notice a wallet?"

"Nope, but knowing you were coming, I didn't turn him." He leaned over the body. "Move back."

Grasping Teddie Crawford by the shoulders, Everson pulled him over onto his side. The hands and arms, stiff from rigor, did not move, but blood from multiple wounds on the dead man's back poured onto the floor in crimson gushes. Kate stared, startled, disoriented. If Teddie Crawford was still bleeding, how could he not be alive? Her mind flashed to a death investigation five months ago, a three-month-old baby left for several hours in a car on a hot September day while the parents shopped. She herself had lifted the baby from the car, a tiny blonde girl still very warm to her touch, and formula had bubbled from the baby's tiny rosebud of a mouth. Kate had thought for a wild hopeful moment that the baby was reprieved, that somehow the clock had turned back to change events, that the pronouncement of death was wrong. The coroner later told her that what she had seen had resulted from the cooking process still at work in the baby's body. And the blood now gushing from Teddie

Crawford's body resulted from its collection against open stab wounds in his back. Then or now, there would be no reprieve.

"The guy who did this must have been going for the record," Everson muttered, crouching down and studying the punctures as blood pooled into fresh formulations on the floor. "Probably close to forty wounds all told." He patted the pockets of the blood-soaked pants, sliding his gloved hand into each one. "Nothing," he said. Gently he lowered the body back into its previous position, stood, snapped off the wet red gloves and dropped them into a plastic sack. He addressed Kate. "We take him?"

"He's yours." The coppery odor in the room was overpowering, clinging to her nostrils, penetrating her clothes. Her corduroy jacket and gabardine pants had just been to the cleaners; they would need to go directly back.

As Everson picked up his tape recorder and began dictating, Kate turned to Charlotte Mead. "Anything else you can tell us?"

Mead placed her clipboard in her sample case. "Nothing you can't see. None of the blood, except for the cast-off pattern, is more than thirty-seven inches off the floor. Your man got the decedent down and that was it."

Kate pointed to the wall, at a pattern of wavy vertical lines close to the floor. "That's an odd looking pattern."

"Not if you know what it is," Mead said with only a trace of tartness. "The decedent never got off the floor but he was all over the place while he was being stabbed. Got his hair soaked in his own blood on the floor, banged his head up against the wall."

Criminalist Napoleon Carter came in to tape
paper bags around the hands of Teddie Crawford.
Two attendants from the coroner's office began the
process of wrapping the body in a new white sheet
which would afterward go to the crime lab for
separate analysis. Then came the placement of
Teddie Crawford in a body bag, loading the zipped
black bag onto a stretcher. Finally he was wheeled
out for the edification of the waiting crowd and the
television cameras.

Kate examined the room. All surfaces had been
dusted for fingerprints, the piece of glass on the
counter collected for analysis of its powder residue.

"Here's our weapon," Taylor announced, pointing
to an oak knife block on the counter between the
stove and a microwave. "Or where it used to be, I'm
betting."

Kate examined the knife block. Seven of its eight
apertures were filled. The handles of the knives had
not been dusted; they were rough-textured plastic
that would not hold a print. With a thumb and
forefinger placed carefully on the haft, she pulled out
one knife after the other. A cleaver and a serrated
blade filled the top of the block; the rest of the
well-used knives were arranged in order according to
length, and all were clean. The empty slot was
between a six- and a ten-inch blade.

"We need to collect the knife block," she said.

She and Taylor inspected the contents of the
cabinets and refrigerator. Basic foodstuffs were
neatly stocked, as was an assortment of cooking
utensils; nothing seemed out of place or in any way
unusual.

"Let's go talk to our suspect," Kate said.

— 3 —

The day was fast winding down, the hazy city washed by orange-gold from the dying sun. As Kate and Taylor drove eastward through spotty Saturday afternoon traffic toward Hollywood, upscale Santa Monica Boulevard mutated into shabby mini-malls, food stands, used car lots, film labs, an occasional porn theater, auto repair and plating shops — many of the businesses with retractable metal bars across their fronts.

In a treatment room at Hollywood Presbyterian Hospital, a thin, bearded young man in hospital

greens stared impatiently as Kate and Taylor
extended their badges and identified themselves.
"Yes, all right," he said, "I'm Doctor Mercer."

Kate said, "You treated a man named Kyle
Jensen for cut hands. We need to ask you some
questions about that."

"Can't tell you a thing," the surgeon replied
curtly. "Medical information is confidential. As you
know."

"Yeah, we know," Taylor said. His tone was
matter-of-fact. "So you tell us now or we subpoena
records and you sit in a courtroom hallway two days
waiting to testify. How did he cut his hands?"

The surgeon's narrow shoulders moved in a slow,
weary shrug. "I never talked to you, agreed? He says
he cut them on an open ham tin."

Kate said, "And did he?"

Mercer shrugged again. "Could be. Open ham tins
are so lethal they should carry labels."

"What are his wounds?"

"Severe lacerations, both hands. In lay terms, the
web between the thumb and the forefinger on the
right hand —" He held up his own hand in
demonstration, "— incised to the bone. Another
minor laceration on the outside edge of the palm.
Less trauma to the left hand — a palm laceration
and one inside the thumb. Minor cuts on all the
fingers."

"Could they be knife wounds?"

"Certainly."

Taylor asked, "Defensive wounds?"

"Could be, yes. Very deep, though. If he was in a
knife fight, it was the fight of his life, he really tore

up his hands. The stupid prick's got the pain
threshold of a bull. Couldn't understand why we
wouldn't just slap on a bandage. We had to refuse
treatment unless he checked in for surgery."

Kate asked, "Any other cuts on him?"

"Not that I saw."

"Blood on his clothes?"

"He came in with his hands wrapped in bloody
towels. I didn't see his clothes." He crossed his arms
and said with finality, "Check with Nurse Donnelly."

"We'll want you to hang onto those towels," Kate
said.

"Check with Nurse Donnelly," he repeated.

"We need to talk to him," Taylor said. "What
pain meds is he on?"

"The anaesthetic was local, he's had antibiotic,
and Tylenol with codeine. We'll give him a
prescription when we release him tonight."

Kate said, "In your medical judgment, is he in
any way impaired to talk to us now?"

Mercer checked his watch. "He had pills more
than an hour ago. Take your best shot." He strode
toward the door. "Remember, you owe me. Keep me
out of that goddamn hallway."

"Right," Kate said. But if Kyle Jensen was
Teddie Crawford's killer, Dr. Henry Mercer would
indeed be in that hallway.

The gown-clad young man sitting up in the
hospital bed was alone in his semi-private room.
Impassively, he listened to Kate identify herself and

Taylor, looked over their identification, and tersely
answered Kate's question: his full name was Kyle
Thomas Jensen, he lived at 1699 North Western
Avenue in Hollywood.

Kate scrutinized him. Muscular, with thinning
sandy-blond hair hanging down his neck, a light
stubble on his cheeks, a thick moustache that
accentuated rather than concealed sensuous, slightly
bow-shaped lips, he was a possible fit for Gloria
Gomez's description. And his first name, Kyle, was
close enough to Lyle and Miles, the names she had
mentioned. But thus far he also fit the picture of
innocence: he looked polite, a little puzzled, a touch
annoyed.

Propping a foot up on the bedside chair, Taylor
flipped open his notebook. "How old are you, Kyle?"

"Twenty-seven. Why?"

Kate asked, "How are you feeling?"

Jensen glanced at his bandaged hands as if to
judge their condition by appearance. "Okay." His
eyes, pale blue, diamond-shaped, met Kate's; they
were unreadable. "What's this about?" His voice was
a high-pitched huskiness.

Taylor replied affably, "We like to check out
people who come to emergency rooms with major
injuries. How'd you cut your hands, Kyle?"

"This is a major injury?" He waved both hands.
"It's just a dumb-shit accident."

"Needing surgery means pretty bad cuts. Tell us
about it."

Jensen shrugged his broad shoulders. "I took out
the garbage. Slipped, took a header, cut my hands

on a ham can. That's it." The twitch of his lips was rueful. "Those things are damn sharp. I bled like a pig."

Kate nodded. He was very convincing. "Where was this?"

"The apartment building. Out back."

"Anybody see you?" As Jensen shook his head, Kate continued, "When did this happen?"

"This morning . . . maybe about eight."

"When did you get here?"

"I guess maybe ten or so."

"You were injured enough to need surgery, Kyle. Why'd you wait till ten o'clock?"

"Hey, I didn't know how bad off I was till I got here. I wrapped up in towels, the bleeding stopped. My girlfriend, she freaked out, she brought me here." He poked at his hospital gown with a bandaged hand. "These bozos feed you bullshit. They make you check in just to get your money."

"What's your girlfriend's name, Kyle?"

"Shirl. Shirley Johnson."

"She live with you?"

"Sure."

"Where do you work?"

"Why? What the hell *is* this?"

"Routine," Taylor said. "We just need to make sure you're not shitting us, you're not protecting somebody who did this to you."

"Yeah, well I'm not — and I don't know what the hell that doctor did to me but right now I need another pain pill."

Kate said casually, "We do have a few more

questions, Kyle. We understand you'll be released this evening. Why don't we have a car pick you up and take you to the station, then home?"

He shrugged, lay back on his pillows. "Yeah, sure. Anything to get this bullshit over with."

Kate approached the patrol officer outside Kyle Jensen's room. "He see you, Dale?" she asked, indicating the closed hospital door with a motion of her head.

The thin young officer shook his head, grinned. "Nope."

Kate said, returning his grin, "Make sure he doesn't."

"You got it."

"And check with Nurse Donnelly about the condition of his clothes when he came in. Have her hold onto the towels his hands were wrapped in."

"You got it."

Without comment, Taylor accompanied her down the hallway to the elevator. He knew as well as she did that despite Gloria Gomez's description and the incriminating evidence of Kyle Jensen's cut hands, there was insufficient probable cause to arrest or even hold him, much less get a search warrant to obtain his bloody towels. Jensen had done them a favor by his willingness, undoubtedly unwitting, to come to the station to answer further questions. Either he believed their story that they routinely checked out major injuries at hospitals, or he was confident that he would not be linked with a

homicide, or he felt that cooperation was his best
option. Or, he was simply innocent. She and Taylor
had much more work to do. She needed to be well
prepared for the next meeting with Kyle Jensen.

* * * * *

Sixteen-ninety-nine North Western Avenue was
close by, a five-story brick building on the corner of
Hollywood Boulevard, its facade crisscrossed with
corroded fire escapes, its red brick coal-dust-grimy
from decades of air pollution. Across Western a
similar building of stucco was freshly painted pink, a
banner on a fire escape proclaiming *Se Rentan
Apartamentos.* Across litter-strewn Hollywood
Boulevard was a seedy store named Bargain Saver, a
billiard room, a hamburger stand, a pawn shop.

The small lobby of the apartment building was
tracked with dirt and reeked of cooked cabbage and
onions. Junk mail littered the cracked gray tile floor
under a row of mailboxes identified by names on
slips of paper jammed into crevices or fastened on
with tape.

"A palace," Taylor muttered.

"We've seen worse," Kate returned.

"Like I said, a palace."

His tone was curt — more indication to Kate
that he detested his involvement in this case. Screw
him, she thought. He would do his job as he was
supposed to. She would see to that.

He was inspecting the mailbox for apartment 209,
its identifying piece of cardboard held on by a piece
of electrical tape. Two names were scrawled on the

cardboard: *K. Jensen* and *B. Dayton.* He said, "Wasn't the name of the alleged live-in girlfriend Shirley Johnson?"

"Let's check out back," Kate said. "See if there's any sign of the alleged ham can."

The cracked and broken cement at the rear of the building was strewn with newspapers and shards of glass and junk food wrappers. A battered dumpster squatted at the edge of the alley; Taylor raised its misshapen lid. "Fucking shit," he said as a stench distilled from rotting garbage and alcohol fumes engulfed them. The dumpster was less than a quarter full.

"Call in for a photographer while I look around," she told him. "Priority. We'll need gloves," she added as he trudged off. "And an inventory sheet."

"Fucking shit," he repeated.

She got down on one knee to examine the cement around the dumpster. Meticulously, she inspected the path she and Taylor had taken from the apartment building's rear door. When Taylor returned a few minutes later, she pointed down at the cement, its fractured surfaces scoured and baked by years of wind and sun. "From his story, the severity of those cuts, there should be blood marks."

Taylor grunted assent. "Let's check out the alleged girlfriend. I'm betting she's as make-believe as the ham can."

The young man who answered the door of apartment 209 wore only skin-tight stone-washed jeans. Looking at the well-muscled torso, hairless save for a dark column extending down from the

navel, Kate thought of Aimee's female loveliness with
a renewed sense of self-certainty. No male chest held
any allure for her beyond objective admiration.

"I'm Detective Delafield, LAPD," she said. "This is
my partner, Detective Taylor."

The young man glanced at their identification
with an impatient heave of his naked shoulders.
"Yeah, so what?"

Kate said, "Is Shirley Johnson here?"

"Shirl?" He stared at her, his hostility dissolving
in surprise. "What the hell you want with Shirl?"

"A few routine questions," she replied. "Is she
here?"

"Nah." He leaned against the door jamb. "Maybe
later."

He's got a rap sheet, Kate's intuition told her. He
had relaxed too visibly at their apparent lack of
interest in him. She said, "Does Shirl live here?"

"Nope."

"Has she ever lived here?"

"Nope."

"Where is she?"

He replied with a shrug.

Kate said, "May we know your name, sir?"

"Sir? Geez, what a sweetheart of a cop. Dayton,
Burt Dayton. What you want Shirl for?"

Kate said, "May we talk somewhere other than
this hallway, Mr. Dayton?"

"Mr. Dayton, yet. Okay. But like I said, Shirl
ain't here." He stepped away from the doorway to
allow entry.

The sagging sofa and armchair were

mustard-colored, the carpet dirty gray and thread-
bare. The lampshade on the single table lamp was
stained yellow-brown.

"Take a load off," Dayton said, throwing himself
onto the sofa.

Taylor propped himself against the adjacent wall;
Kate remained standing. She said, "Does Kyle
Jensen live here?"

Dayton's dark eyes flashed to her. Warily, he
nodded.

"Did Shirley Johnson take him to the hospital
this morning?"

He rubbed an index finger around his lips as he
contemplated her. The lips were thick, fleshy;
sensual for the narrow sharpness of his features. "So
what if she did?"

Taylor said, "How did Kyle cut his hands?"

"I don't know. Oh shit," Dayton uttered in
disgust, realizing that he had already said too much.
"Shit," he said.

"We need to know," Taylor said, pen poised over
his notebook. "How did he cut his hands?"

"Shit, man, I don't know."

"When did it happen?"

"Dunno."

"Burt," Taylor said with elaborate patience, "do
we need to haul you in for something so dumb as
finding out how Kyle cut his hands?"

Dayton pointed to Kate. "I like her better. She
calls me Mr. Dayton."

"Mr. Dayton," Taylor said, unperturbed, "when
did you find out about his hands?"

Crossing his arms over his chest, Dayton
slouched down into the sofa, spreading his legs wide

open. Kate had always disliked such a posture in either men or women, its impudent flaunting of genitalia. Dayton said reluctantly, resentfully, "This morning."

"What time?"

"Early. Why? What's up?"

"What time, Mr. Dayton?"

"Early. Dunno what time, I coulda cared less." Looking at Taylor he conceded, "It was still dark out."

"Mr. Dayton," Kate interjected. "Why don't you just tell us about it?"

"What's to tell? I was asleep, okay? He comes in the bedroom, wakes me up, says he hurt his hands. They're all wrapped up, he wants me to help him out of his clothes. So I do it, okay? This morning he has me call Shirl. She comes over, looks at his hands, takes him to the hospital and that's all I know. Okay?"

"Let's take this one step at a time," Kate said. She moved to the armchair, gingerly positioning herself on its grubby arm. Before this day was over, she reflected, these pants might be too far gone to even go to the cleaners. Propping her notebook on her thigh, she said, "He came into the bedroom. How many bedrooms do you have?"

"This is the White House or something? One." He gestured behind him. "We got extra beds."

You had to mention the beds, Kate thought. God forbid anybody should think you're queer. "He told you he hurt his hands. How did he say he did it?"

He looked at her, his gaze vigilant. "This is big trouble, right?"

She returned his gaze. She and Taylor had to be

exceedingly careful. If Kyle Jensen was a viable suspect, it was possible that he had not acted alone, that this man was an accessory. "Mr. Jensen's injuries are quite severe," she said. "We're making routine inquiries. How did he cut his hands?"

"Said he fell, cut them on some kind of a can." His thick lips turned down in distaste. "I didn't ask for a blow by blow, ya know?"

Didn't you now, Kate thought. "Tell us what you saw when you looked at him."

He shook his head. "Nothin'. I didn't look, didn't see him. Not then. He said don't put a light on, I'd toss my cookies." He shifted uncomfortably. "He knows blood makes me puke, okay? He was so sticky wet, I almost lost it anyway. And when I went in the bathroom and washed my hands, saw my hands . . . yuchhh, holy Jesus." He sat up, crossed his arms over his chest, closed his eyes and pulled his legs together.

Kate felt persuaded, if not convinced, that Burt Dayton had had nothing to do with the murder of Teddie Crawford. "You said you helped Mr. Jensen take off his bloody clothes. Where are those clothes now?"

Burt Dayton raised a hand, and without looking, pointed in the direction to the left of Kate.

Adrenalin surging through her, Kate stared at a black plastic garbage bag, its top tied with a yellow strip, sitting on the far side of the closed apartment door.

"Kyle said throw it away," Dayton continued. "Me, I wouldn't touch it if a garbage truck drove up the stairs to pick it up. What if the bag busted open?"

Thinking about Charlotte Mead and the tests she could run on this cache of what might be uncontaminated crucial evidence, Kate released an inaudible breath.

"Kate?" Taylor said.

She looked at him, her mind racing, knowing he was questioning the legalities here, knowing she must not make a mistake.

They did not have a search warrant. In any sort of felony trial, much less a homicide trial, any violation of Fourth Amendment rights could mean the release of a defendant, no matter how compelling the evidence of guilt might be.

She and Taylor had properly identified themselves and had been invited into this apartment. Without a search warrant they could conduct a search beyond this room only with Burt Dayton's permission, but in any event they could not remove anything from the bedroom that Kyle Jensen shared with Burt Dayton. This room, however, was a common area into which they had been lawfully admitted, and potential evidence had been pointed out to them and was in plain view. She said quietly to Taylor, "Get an evidence bag. And check on that photographer."

"This is some kind of really deep shit," Dayton muttered as Taylor left the apartment.

Kate said placatingly, "We often have to do far more than necessary just to be thorough."

"Christ, don't tell Kyle I said anything or he'll fucking kill me."

"If there's no problem, then there's no problem. Right?" Kate said. As Dayton puzzled through this

platitude, she asked casually, "Is he that much of a
hothead?"

"He's okay. Unless you do something that pulls
his cork."

"Does he get his cork pulled very often?"

He looked at her and did not answer. She had,
she sensed, just run out of cooperation.

"Where can we reach Shirl? We need to talk to
her."

"Dunno."

"Where does she work?"

"Dunno."

"What's her phone number?"

"Ask Kyle."

"How long have you known Kyle?"

Studying her, again he circled his lips with an
index finger. "Long time. We came out here
together."

"From where, Mr. Dayton?"

"Pittsburgh."

"Really." She made her tone conversational. "I
understand that's a nice town."

"A dead town. Dead and buried. Here is where
it's at."

She kept her gaze on his face, wondering how
this fleabag of a place could be better than what
he'd left. She asked, "Then you've been lifelong
friends with Mr. Jensen?"

He contemplated this question as if it were a
new concept. "Yeah. Maybe. Off and on. We do our
own thing, but he's okay, you know? Whatever this
is about, he's clean."

As Taylor returned to the apartment with a large evidence bag, Kate asked, "What about you, Mr. Dayton? Are you clean?"

"I got no problems," he said, watching Taylor bag the black plastic sack and begin to fill out the evidence seal.

Kate said casually, "Okay with you if we take a look around, Mr. Dayton?"

"No way. And knock off that Mr. Dayton crap. No way, lady. You want anything more outta me, I think I'll check it out with a shyster."

"That's certainly your privilege, Burt." Getting to her feet, she pulled a card from her notebook. "Maybe Kyle doesn't have to know how we got the bag of clothes. You were supposed to throw them in the dumpster, right? If you see or hear from Shirl, have her call us, okay?"

He got up, took the card, tucked it in the back pocket of his jeans. "Yeah." He almost smiled.

Ted Carlson photographed the interior and exterior of the dumpster and the area surrounding it. Then Kate and Taylor donned plastic gloves.

Kate removed her jacket, handed it to Carlson. Steeling herself, she turned to Taylor. "Give me a lift up."

"Christ," Taylor grumbled. "Christ knows what's in there. These days you'll catch Christ knows what."

"It could be worse," she said, more to herself than to him as he locked his hands together and she fit her foot into the brace. "The city picked up the garbage no more than a day or two ago —" She vaulted up and into the dumpster.

She landed on shifting mulch and staggered, grabbing the edge of the dumpster to catch her balance. Determinedly ignoring the stench, telling herself the germ potential couldn't be fatal — could it? — she surveyed the refuse in which she stood shin-deep.

The gleam of silver caught her eye and she immediately fished out the object and passed it up and over to Taylor.

"What the hell," he said. "A *wheel* . . . from a fucking *wheelchair.*"

"Seems like it," she said, unable to even conjecture why such a thing would be in here.

Grateful for the nicety of several closed trash bags, she first passed these out to Taylor for separate inventory, then methodically dispensed to him every solid object she put her gloved hands on. He laid out the trash on the concrete around the dumpster: liquor and wine bottles and beer cans and foil dinner trays and cardboard cartons and newspapers. Finally, only a layer of refuse remained, sloshing around her shoes: chicken bones, potato peelings, egg shells, coffee grounds, rotting fruit, other unidentifiable food remnants. Bracing her hands on a corner of the dumpster, Kate scrabbled awkwardly up and out.

While Carlson photographed the dumpster's emptied interior, she and Taylor laid out the contents of the bags. She took it upon herself to inspect several sanitary napkins, identifying the rust-colored stains as menstrual blood. She was

surprised to see four broken hypodermic needles —
that they had been thrown away. Dopers risked
AIDS transmission as much through their
unwillingness to buy new needles as through
ignorance — they did not hesitate to inject their
bodies with broken needles.

"Wonderful stuff," Carlson said as he photographed from his blue-jeaned knees the array of
debris. "Maybe I'll enter these shots in competition."

"First prize," Taylor muttered.

While Carlson packed up his gear, Kate and
Taylor threw all the garbage back into the dumpster.
They had not been quiet or discreet about any of
their activities. Several people had peered down at
them from windows, but no one had so much as
inquired what they were doing.

Taylor snapped off his gloves, tossed them into
the dumpster. "So much for the alleged ham can," he
growled.

— 4 —

Kate's apartment was empty. A few dust motes spun in the slants of greenish-yellow light allowed by branches of the scotch pine guarding the living room window. The faint smell of damp earth reached Kate: Aimee had watered the plants. She smiled. That Aimee did not actually live here was becoming more and more a technicality.

Kate checked the answering machine. From its unblinking light Aimee had picked up the message about the homicide investigation that had been set into motion by the early morning call from the watch commander.

Kate walked into the bedroom, pulling off gun belt and clothing as she went. Looking at the unmade bed and its configuration of pillows, she remembered the dark tangle of Aimee's hair over the pillow that morning, the bow-shaped curving of her body under the blanket she had pulled up to her ears in slumberous protest when Kate had taken her warmth from the bed.

She and Aimee had made love last night, as they had every night during this, their first month as lovers. Even knowing that much of Aimee's passion came from sheer youthful vitality, that much of her own passion was fueled by Aimee's newness, her beguiling beauty, her frank eroticism, she luxuriated in memory — the intimate caresses that had awakened her from sleep in the heart of last night, the renewed fire of their lovemaking . . .

Kate turned away from the bed.

You can't divide your focus, she castigated herself. *You need to think about Teddie Crawford, nothing else. If Kyle Jensen is Teddie Crawford's killer, tonight may be your one clear shot at him. You need to piece together what happened at Tradition, you need maximum preparation. No distraction.*

She stuffed her discarded clothing into a plastic bag and then tossed the bag of clothing into the depths of the closet. She felt empathy for Burt Dayton's revulsion at the contents of that other plastic bag; she was beginning to sense a seeping contamination from the death of Teddie Crawford

unlike anything she had ever experienced. At least
that other plastic bag now resided in Charlotte
Mead's care. Mead's test results would by themselves
establish certain incontestable facts.

Setting the taps scalding hot, she stepped into
the shower, the scent of Aimee's lilac shower gel
invading her senses. Quickly shampooing her hair,
she mulled over the facts of this homicide case,
searching for obvious loose ends. She had assigned
officers to interview the residents of Teddie
Crawford's apartment building, and Carl Jacoby,
Teddie Crawford's former lover, as well as Margaret
and Joe Crawford. She and Taylor would go next to
Malone's Bar. For now that was all she could do.
Until she confronted Kyle Jensen . . .

Briskly toweling dry, she glimpsed her body in
the steam-shrouded mirror. She really should gain
back some of the weight she had lost in the first
weeks of experiencing Aimee. In her fourth decade of
life, a degree of huskiness seemed better suited to
her five foot-eight inch frame than the leanness of
her youth. As usual during the fast-moving early
stages of a homicide, she had no appetite for food.
She had not eaten today — but she needed to, for
the sake of her own efficiency.

She munched on a piece of cheese while she
selected fresh clothing. Authoritative clothing,
specifically for her interview with Kyle Jensen. Black
pants, a simple white blouse, simple black wool
jacket. She had just buttoned her jacket over her
gun belt when she heard Aimee's key in the lock.

"I'm here," Kate called. Walking into the living
room, she watched Aimee toss her leather jacket into
an armchair, admiring her body in jeans and a

maroon pullover. Would she ever become accustomed to her beauty?

"I have to run," she said, edging toward the door, resisting the urge to take Aimee in her arms and know again for just a few moments the actuality of her. But that would be too radical a distraction . . .

"I heard about it on KFWB." As if sensing Kate's need for remoteness, Aimee remained where she stood and crossed her arms. "You changed your clothes," she observed, the blue-violet eyes surveying Kate's body. "Kate, this killing's really bad, isn't it."

Aimee had come to know why Kate was sometimes compelled to change her clothes during the process of an investigation. Kate understood that Aimee admired her, viewed her profession with something close to awe, but that a component of that awe was the sort of dread fascination accorded by most people to morticians. What Kate told her about her cases, past or present, she sanitized. "A stabbing," she summarized, for her own sake as well as Aimee's.

"Yeah," Aimee said, stuffing her hands in the back pockets of her jeans. "The dead guy's gay, Jennifer actually knows him. She's been in that restaurant, what's it called, Tradition?"

"Yes," Kate said. Jennifer and Cheryl, whom Kate had never met, were current roommates of Aimee's in the condo they all shared in Brentwood.

"You arrest anybody?"

"We're checking out a suspect."

"Kate, you gotta get this gaybasher."

Gaybasher. Somehow she had not thought of Teddie Crawford's killing as a gaybashing.

Aimee asked, "Will you be back tonight?"

"I think so. I'll let you know if I can't. Will you
be here?"

Aimee's gaze drifted down Kate's body. She
smiled. "Sure."

Kate let herself out of the apartment. *Gaybasher.*
She felt shaken by the word. She buried her
inchoate emotion. She would exhume it later for
examination, when she was able to.

She turned her thoughts back to Aimee, but
briefly. When she came home she would make love
to Aimee. She would need to.

Malone's Bar, near Formosa Avenue and the
former Samuel Goldwyn Studios — now Warner
Hollywood Studios — on the eastern edge of West
Hollywood, stood out from its neighboring nondescript
storefronts. The clapboard front, freshly painted
white, was a virtual inducement, Kate thought, for
the legion of sprayers layering graffiti over the city.

Inside the bar, its length at least three times
that of its width, the usual beery-acid-ether smell
invaded her nostrils. But she liked the place. The
room felt comfortable, dark and cool and well-used,
even though it contained few patrons on this
Saturday afternoon — three Latinos at a table
silently drinking Dos Equis from the bottle, a fat,
gray-haired man hunched over the bar watching
television, and a young man sitting alone at a table
reading a newspaper through a curtain of straight
dark hair hanging over his eyes.

The bartender, a small man of perhaps fifty,

wore a brown leather apron over a sport shirt and pants. From the sharp-eyed glance he cast over Kate and Taylor's identification, his cautiously neutral face when he looked up, Kate surmised that he had seen police badges more than a few times.

She said, "Were you working here last night?"

"Sure," the man answered in pure tenor tones. "I'm Jimmy Malone, it's my place, why wouldn't I be here?"

Irish as Paddy's pig, Kate thought, smothering a smile. "Do you know a man named Teddie Crawford?"

The reaction was unguarded astonishment: rounded lips and rounded blue eyes. The bartender quickly recovered himself. "Can't say I do," he said.

"Of course you do," Kate said quietly. "And you need to talk to us. Teddie Crawford was killed last night."

Jimmy Malone's jaw worked soundlessly for a moment. "Teddie? *Teddie?*" The tenor tones were even higher. He slapped both hands on the bar and stared aghast at Kate. "Teddie's *dead?* He was in here just last night." He said in a stunned whisper, "He's *dead?*"

The other bar patrons, Kate noted, were looking on in alert curiosity, nothing more. She said to Jimmy Malone, "Was Teddie a regular here?"

Malone moved down the bar, Kate and Taylor following, out of earshot of the other patrons. "Just semi. A great guy. A terrific guy." He shook his head, his eyes teared with shock.

"He came in last night," Kate said. "Tell us about that."

Malone shook his head as if to clear it. "What's to tell? Gloria and him came in, sat at a table with a guy I pegged as Gloria's."

"Why?" Taylor asked.

"Teddie likes Godzilla-types. Ever since he broke up with Carl. Does Carl know about this?"

"You get a lot of gays in here?" Taylor inquired.

Malone looked at him. "I don't ask. Or care. I welcome everybody. Even you."

Feeling like cheering, Kate grinned at Malone. "And did he meet Godzilla here last night?"

"He did. The usual. Muscles, jeans, hair, leather jacket — you know the type."

"What's this Godzilla's name?"

"That I don't know."

"Ever see him before?"

"I have. A few times."

"How long has he been coming in?" Kate asked.

The bartender pondered. "Maybe a month, six weeks."

"This Godzilla, he cruise guys in here?" Taylor asked.

"Can't say I noticed that he did. Older men come here, very quiet types. So any cruising's pretty quiet stuff, you know."

Some older gays, Kate knew from Joe D'Amico, went to such bars as the Gold Coast or the Gauntlet; they did not frequent a big dance and cruise bar such as Rage, or stand and stare bars like Micky's or Motherlode. And the older, very quiet types mentioned by Jimmy Malone were undoubtedly closeted and would seek ambiguous bars like Malone's . . .

"Mr. Malone," Kate said, "has there been recent gaybashing in the neighborhood?"

"Call me Jimmy. Cops haven't been in about it." He looked at her gravely. "The men talk about it."

She nodded grimly, understanding him. Closeted men often did not report gaybashing; they could not afford to. And bars such as Malone's would be prime hunting ground. She said softly, "Describe Godzilla."

Writing in her notebook, she led Jimmy Malone through a description that had points in common with Gloria Gomez's report of the man Teddie Crawford had left with. Remembering the piece of glass on the counter in Tradition, she sent up a trial balloon. "Jimmy," she said, "we have information about illegal substances being used in here."

"For sure not," he bristled. "What is this, now?"

"Jimmy," she said, hardening her tone, "my partner and I haven't the least interest in conducting a narcotics investigation. None. We're looking into a homicide. Period. But if we find out you've withheld any information connected to this case, you'll be up for obstruction."

Malone raised his hands. "Look. Nobody I see deals in here. Nobody. But I don't control the world. Fellows come in, they pop a pill right along with their beer. What am I supposed to do? I go in the john after I close up, there's empty baggies all over the place. What am I supposed to do?"

"Did you observe Teddie Crawford or any of the people he was with take anything?"

"Teddie, Gloria, never. I don't know about anybody else."

Taylor asked, "What about the john? Did Teddie or Godzilla use the john?"

"Yes," Malone answered immediately. "They went in together."

Kate nodded. She knew from Maggie Schaeffer, the Nightwood Bar owner who had become her close friend, that good bartenders were observers who did not miss a thing. "Jimmy, tell us what you know about Teddie Crawford," she said.

He shook his head. "A charmer. Flashy dresser, too good-looking, but you couldn't help liking him." Jimmy Malone's eyes moistened again as he spoke. "He'd prance in here like a leprechaun, talk to everybody, he knew everybody. I tell you . . . well, I just liked him."

"Thank you, Jimmy." Kate gave him one of her cards. "If you remember anything else you think might help us, call me."

"That I'll do," he said sadly, tucking the card in a pocket of his apron.

— 5 —

A message lay on Kate's desk in the Detectives
Squad Room: Shirley Johnson had called at 7:05 pm,
left no number, would call again. Kate issued
instructions that she be notified immediately when
that next call came in. Kyle Jensen had been
transported to Wilshire Division by Officer Dale
Morrissey, and was waiting.

Kate preceded Taylor into the small, blue-walled
interview room with its acoustic tile ceiling and
Formica-topped table. Jensen, his back to them,
looked thoroughly bored as he lounged in one of the

metal chairs, legs outstretched and ankles crossed, bandaged hands resting on his thighs. He wore navy blue sweatpants and dingy jogging shoes; sandy-blond hair hung not quite to the collar of a gray sweatshirt that outlined the musculature of his shoulders and arms.

Kate studied the dressings on his hands. The right hand was entirely swathed, while a thinner bandage covered the palm and thumb of the left, with tape on the fingers. Were these the hands that had plunged a knife over and over again into the body of Teddie Crawford?

Gaybasher. Kate's unwilling mind became an echo chamber for the word. Looking away from Kyle Jensen, she gripped the cold metallic back of a chair.

If you have ever been objective and professional, be that now. If this man is a killer, his conviction will hinge on your professional conduct in this room right now.

"How you doing, Kyle?" Taylor asked cheerfully, unbuttoning his jacket, pulling out a chair and settling himself into it.

"I'm okay, man," Jensen answered, his gaze drifting over Taylor. "Goddamn waste of a Saturday, I just want to get home."

Kate took refuge from her tension in an uncharitable assessment of Taylor's apparel. He too had gone home after the rummage through the dumpster, and had changed into brown pants and a blue-yellow plaid jacket over a canary-yellow shirt and blue-patterned tie. By this time she knew that any time Taylor's attire coincided with her own view that clothing should reinforce one's stature as a police officer, it was purely by accident.

"Kyle," she said, to draw the young man's gaze. She had remained standing, and used her height to look down at him. "We tape-record interviews as a matter of routine. Any problem with that?"

The light blue eyes fixed on hers were expressionless. "No problem, I'm cool."

Naive cool, she thought, making herself comfortable at the table. Kyle Jensen lacked the hard-won smarts of a career felon — the criminal history check on him had come up negative — and in all probability he also lacked knowledge of both the capabilities and limitations of police work. Burt Dayton, on the other hand, had two priors, both in Pennsylvania, one a 1987 for shoplifting, sentence suspended, the other a 1988 for bad checks, sixty days plus probation, the jail time impetus, probably, for his decision to leave for California.

"What's your situation with pain medication?" she inquired. "Feel well enough to talk to us?" She knew from Head Nurse Donnelly at Hollywood Presbyterian Hospital, via Officer Dale Morrissey, that the pain medication given Kyle Jensen would allow questioning.

"Yeah." Jensen waved his hands. "This wasn't brain surgery, you know."

"Pretty serious, though." Her tone was sympathetic. "Ever had a serious injury before?"

"Nah." To her surprise, the diamond-shaped eyes filled with regret. "If Dad could see how okay I was with this . . . I didn't have a war to fight like he did, you know. All I ever heard was how he got his ass blown off in Korea, how it was two days before they could get him out and he never said shit about the pain."

"I was in Korea too," Taylor said, grinning. "Got my ass shot at, but not off."

"Dad really did get his ass shot off," Jensen said, grinning back at Taylor. He brushed his left posterior with the undamaged fingers of his left hand. "One side of him all gimpy, looked funnier'n hell. Grenade blast took off a pretty good-sized chunk. Dad took out the slope-head shit that did it, though. Two more besides."

"Right on," Taylor said.

Repulsed by this exchange, Kate was nonetheless pleased by its tenor. To have either herself or Taylor establish rapport with this suspect would be an advantage, and Taylor appeared to be succeeding in that. Taylor said conversationally, "Your dad live in California?"

Jensen shook his head. "Been dead five years and two months. Lung cancer."

"Sorry," Taylor chorused with Kate.

With the fingertips of his left hand, Jensen fished a pack of Marlboros from a pants pocket. Taylor took the pack, shook out a cigarette, handed it to Jensen, lit it for him. "Dad got lung cancer from the goddamn steel mill," Jensen said, the smoke he expelled through his nostrils partly dissipated by his thick moustache. "The goddamn smelter, not cigarettes."

Sure, Kate thought, imagining how that moustache must reek of smoke. She pushed the ashtray toward him. "Steel mills — I take it you're from Pittsburgh." When he nodded she followed up, "How long have you been in L.A.?"

He studied the cigarette he held between the taped thumb and middle finger of his left hand. "I guess . . . more than a year now. Took off last January."

He knew to the month how long his father had been dead, yet had to reflect over how long he had lived here . . . She asked politely, "You still have your mother, I hope?"

"Maybe *you* hope — I don't. Yeah."

His tone closed this off as a topic of conversation. She asked, "What do you do, Kyle?"

He sat up a little straighter. "Deliver for Green Haven. Know them?"

"Can't say I do."

Taylor said, "Aren't they landscapers for rich people?"

"Yeah. Yeah, man." Jensen turned to Taylor, the high pitch of his husky voice amplified. "They do lawns, plants, even trees — I mean *big* trees. I deliver shit you wouldn't believe. Arabs buy up these Beverly Hills mansions, the sand niggers rip out everything. Green Haven comes in and next day there's this perfect lawn and palm trees and hedges and rose bushes like it's been there a century already. Unreal, man. Movie stars do it, too. I was at Warren Beatty's house once. He was doing this party . . ."

He trailed off, watching Kate write on her legal pad. "Look, what do you want from me? I just want to get the hell outta here."

Kate felt a coiling tension. "Let's get a few standard questions out of the way," she said. She took his name, address and phone number again, and his date of birth.

"Ever been arrested?"

"Nope."

"What hours do you work at Green Haven?"

"Days. I work days. Why?" The tone had grown distinctly hostile.

Kate selected her words. "We're checking out a serious incident that occurred last night. Before we can say any more about it, or ask you any relevant questions, we need to tell you what your rights are."

His shrug was impatient. "I watch TV, I know all that shit."

"We need to tell you anyway, Kyle." Taking a card from her pocket she read him his Miranda rights. "You can decide at any time to exercise these rights and not answer any questions or make any statement," she concluded. "Do you understand each of these rights as I have explained them to you?"

"Yeah. What bullshit."

"Having these rights in mind, are you willing to talk to me and Detective Taylor now?"

"Yeah. What bullshit," he repeated.

His ignorance of the power of his constitutional protections, typical of most citizens, was to her and Taylor's benefit, and his arrogance would enhance their advantage. He had apparently lost awareness that his words were being recorded, a not uncommon occurrence during interrogations. She would not remind him. She tucked the card back into her pocket and said pleasantly, "Now tell us again how you cut your hands."

Jensen's sensuous lips became distinctly bow-shaped as they curved slightly upward. "You keep your part of the deal first. What's all this about?"

"A young man was stabbed last night in West Hollywood."

Instantly he said, "That's got nothing to do with me."

"How did you cut your hands?"

His chest and shoulders moved in a visible, if inaudible, sigh. "Like I already told you, I took out the garbage this morning. Tripped, took a header, landed on an open ham can. That's it."

"What time was this?"

"Like I told you, this morning, about eight."

"Anybody see you do it?"

"How the fuck should I know? Sorry," he said, softening his irritation. "Not that I know of."

"What did you do after you fell?"

"What do you mean, what did I do?"

"Did you bleed?"

"What am I, made outta wood?" He shook his hands at her. "Shit yes, I bled."

"A lot?"

"Like a fucking pig."

Obviously he was no longer concerned with the niceties of language with her. She said, "So, what did you do about the bleeding?"

His nose twitched, apparently from an itch caused by his moustache; he pawed impatiently at it. "Wrapped my hands up in towels."

"When was this?"

He stared at her. "A week later. For chrissake lady, right away. I was *bleeding*."

"Then you bled right away, as soon as you were cut?"

Continuing to stare at her, he said with deliberate slowness, as if communicating with a simpleton, "Yeah, I always bleed as soon as I'm cut."

"So you bled down at the dumpster?"

"Yeah."

"You bled on the ground?"

"Sure."

"In the hallway, on the way to your apartment?"

For the first time he looked at her warily. "Well, hey, I don't remember it all that well, I was, you know, I was pretty pissed off, I don't remember exactly how I bled, who would?"

She pursued him. "Did you bleed on the floor of your apartment?"

"Dunno. I guess."

"Did you get blood on your clothes, Kyle?"

"Yeah. Some." His tone became hostile again. "Why do you need to know all this shit? Who got killed, the pope?"

Kate stopped to write down his exact words, then asked, "Did you change your clothes?"

"Sure."

Kate pointed to his hands, the cigarette held awkwardly because of the bulk of the bandage. "If you had your bleeding hands wrapped in towels, how'd you manage to change clothes, Kyle?"

There was no hesitation. "Shirl helped me."

"Shirley Johnson, right?"

"Yeah."

Kate finished making another note on her pad. "Where can we reach Shirl?"

"What the fuck for?"

"Is there some problem about her verifying what you've told us?"

Again Jensen pawed at his moustache. "You people fuck around for no reason. You got my phone number, right?"

"Yes. What's her number?"

"That's her number."

"You're saying she doesn't have a phone?"

"I'm saying that's her number."

"Are you saying Shirl lives with you?"

"Yeah. I told you before. Yeah."

"Where were you last night, Kyle?"

His eyes, glittering pale blue ice, traveled from her to Taylor and back again. "You're trying to fuck me over, the both of you."

"Where were you last night?"

He sat up at the table. "With Shirl." The husky tones were forceful.

"Where?"

"At her place."

"I thought she lived with you."

He shrugged. "Yeah, well, sometimes she does."

She said commandingly, "What's her phone number, Kyle?"

For a moment he contemplated the corner he had backed himself into. "I ain't gonna tell you," he said. "You can just fucking lay off her."

"How long were you with her last night?"

He shrugged again. "All night."

"Can she verify that?"

"Maybe not." He grinned at Taylor. "Maybe I fucked her brains out."

Recognizing this as a diversionary tactic, Kate sat back, confident that Taylor would now pick up the interview.

Grinning back at Jensen, Taylor reached to the

ashtray, snuffed out the cigarette that Jensen had smoked down to the filter. "So okay, you were with Shirl last night. Did you leave at any time?"

"Nope." Jensen shook another Marlboro out of the pack, stuck it in his mouth.

Taylor lit the cigarette. "You feel okay? Anything you need?"

"I'm okay, man." Smoke streaming from his nostrils and through his moustache, Jensen surveyed the room. "You oughta pipe music in here."

Taylor looked at Kate and rolled his eyes. He asked with ironic politeness, "Any special kind?"

Jensen knocked ash from his cigarette. "AC-DC, Poison, White Snake, stuff like that."

"My youngest son is nuts about Metallica," Taylor offered.

"Yeah, they do real good shit."

Kate was looking at Taylor in wonder. He grinned back at her. "Kyle," she said, picking up the questioning again, "did —"

There was a knock at the door. Taylor got up, left the room, returned a moment later. "The call you've been waiting for," he said.

Shirley Johnson. Kate walked from the room, then hurried to her desk and picked up her phone.

"Ms. Johnson, this is Detective Delafield —"

"Yeah. Burt Lancaster talked ta me, I figured I oughta call."

"Burt Lancaster," Kate said, confused.

"Yeah, you know, Burt Ding Dong Dayton." The woman on the phone sounded as if her mouth were stuffed with cotton. "Lissen, whatever you got Kyle

for, it's got nothin to do with me, unerstand? Burt
Lancaster phones this morning, says Kyle cut his
hands real bad. So I come over and take the jerk to
the hospital cause Burt Lancaster don't drive."

Kate could hear chomping, the distinct snapping
of gum. The woman continued, "Burt Lancaster's a
jerk too. I unerstan not havin a car, but can you
believe livin in this town and not bein able to
drive?"

"Hard to imagine," Kate said, enjoying Shirley
Johnson, gum chewing and all. "Ms. Johnson, what's
your relationship with Kyle Jensen?"

"*Relationship?* Uh oh." The snaps of gum
resembled the back-firing of a car. "What's he tellin
ya?"

"You're his girlfriend, you live together off and
on."

"*What?* The asshole. The *turd*," she shrieked,
adding a furious punctuation of gum snaps.

Grinning as she made notes, Kate asked, "What's
the truth of the matter?"

"We went out *once*. Okay, twice. I been over to
his pigsty *once* before today. He calls me, I talk to
him, but I ain't inerested. Somethin weird about
him."

"But you went over this morning to help him
out."

"Yeah, well, what can you do?"

"I know what you mean," Kate said. She liked
this woman. "Other than today, when was the last
time you saw him?"

"Two, three weeks ago."

"You didn't see him last night?"

More gum snaps. "Nope. Me and Monica went to this movie, rotten movie, lemme tell ya —"

"Did you help him change his clothes this morning?"

"Fuck no. You kiddin?" The chewing sounds ceased. "Burt Lancaster says this is serious shit. That right?"

"It could be, yes," Kate said. "I'm not at liberty —"

"Hey, I don't even wanna know. I'll check things out later with Burt Lancaster."

Some instinct nudged Kate into a curiosity question. "Why do you call him Burt Lancaster?"

"Walks around with that naked chest of his stickin out, thinks he's gonna be an actor, the dipshit. Struts like he's Bruce Willis. Kyle, he's a muscle-builder, so he struts too. You ask me, those two guys strut for each other."

Kate understood this last remark to be in the same vein as the observation that women dressed for each other, but she found it interesting. "You've been very helpful, Ms. Johnson," she said. "Would you give me your phone number and address? We'll bother you as little as possible."

"Yeah, okay. Kyle's a turd, but I hope he's not in bad trouble."

Kate returned to the interview room fortified by her contact with Shirley Johnson. As she took her place at the table, Jensen was still talking about music. Taylor greeted her in mute relief.

It was time to get to the guts of this interrogation. "Kyle," she said, and waited until he turned to her. She asked without preamble, "Ever been in a bar named Malone's?"

Jensen's gaze moved away from her, upward, to contemplate the acoustic tile of the ceiling. "It don't ring a bell," he said.

"How about a bartender named Jimmy Malone? Know him?"

"Nope."

"That's odd," she said. "Because he claims to know you."

He shrugged. "I ain't responsible for what some nut claims."

"Do you know a man named Teddie Crawford?"

Still gazing at the ceiling, Jensen shook his head. "Don't ring a bell."

"Ever been in a restaurant called Tradition?"

"Can't say I have."

"Do you know Burt Dayton?"

His glance at her flashed away; he returned his gaze to the ceiling. "Bullshit. This is just bullshit."

Her fingers tightened on the pen she held; she felt tension clamp onto every muscle in her body.

Everything they had learned so far pointed to this man. He fit the description of Teddie Crawford's late night companion. He had transparently lied about how he had cut his hands. He had no alibi for the time when Teddie Crawford had been killed.

But no one had directly identified him. Any competent lawyer would discount the fact that she and Taylor had found neither a ham can nor bloodstains. And so what if Jensen had no alibi? Scientific evidence had yet to be developed that would place him at the crime scene. So they had nothing on which to hold him. As Taylor would put it, they had diddley shit.

If she did not break him down right now — or if it occurred to him to exercise his right to terminate her questioning or to insist on the presence of a lawyer — they had no option but to release him until they could accumulate sufficient evidence to arrest him. As if this murder suspect, this drifter, would hang around waiting for an arrest.

She reminded herself of the first rule of interviewing criminal suspects: *Make them believe you know everything.*

"Kyle," she snapped, "stop playing games."

He did not respond.

"You think Detective Taylor and I were playing games while you sat in your hospital bed all day? You can't be dumb enough to believe you could be out in this city last night and have nobody remember you. You were in Malone's and we know it. You met Teddie Crawford there and we know it. You left with him and we know it."

She got to her feet and paced beside the table, halting to stare down at him. "You say you cut your hands on a ham can. There is no ham can. You say you immediately bled. There is no blood."

He said nothing.

She lowered her voice. "But there *are* the bloody clothes you wore last night, Kyle. We have them. Bloody clothes to match the blood at the scene. All as evidence against you."

She played her final card. "The call I just took? Shirley Johnson. You said she helped you change your clothes this morning. She says she didn't. You said you were with her last night. She says you

weren't. She hasn't seen you in weeks. You've got no
alibi, Kyle."

"Kyle," Taylor said in a tone that was all the
more telling for its gentleness, "you're dead meat."

Still communing with the ceiling, Kyle Jensen
said, "You got the wrong guy. I didn't kill anybody."

Kate exchanged a triumphant glance with Taylor.
She said quietly, "That's the second time you've
mentioned somebody being killed. Who said anybody
was killed?"

His gaze jerked to her. "You did. You —" He
clamped his mouth shut.

"We never told you anybody was dead," she said.
"But you've just told us that again. You said it
because you know it — because you know it better
than anybody."

She glanced at Taylor. His nod was almost
imperceptible, but it buoyed her; her tension was
almost unbearable.

She took a deep breath, expelled it in pistol-shot
words: "Look at me, Kyle."

Standing over him, she stared down into the pale
blue eyes. "Everything you've told us is a lie. You've
got one chance left. The truth, Kyle. Tell us right
now what went on between you and Teddie Crawford
last night. The truth is the only thing that can
possibly help you. It's the only hope you have."

As seconds of silence passed, Kate walked back to
her chair, sat down. There was nothing more she
could say or do.

"I got a question." Jensen turned to Taylor. "I
want to ask a question."

"Sure," Taylor encouraged him.

Kate watched in prickling suspense, knowing that

Taylor, too, understood that Kyle Jensen hovered on
the brink of revelation.

"This is just a for instance." Jensen's husky voice
was scarcely audible. "For instance you get into it
with somebody and you're trying to protect yourself
and they end up dead. Then what?"

Taylor said, "Depending on what went down,
maybe a case can be made for self-defense."

"Like . . . meaning what?"

"Kyle," Kate said, entering the discussion to
prevent Taylor from saying anything that even
faintly smacked of a deal or an offer, "if you were
acting to save your own life . . ." She reached to
him, touched his arm lightly, briefly, as if to add the
final push to a tree ready to topple. "If you were
acting in self-defense you could be cleared."

His eyes met hers, slid away. "Yeah, well, that's
what I did."

She said slowly, deliberately, "What did you do?"

"The dude came at me. I had to take care of
myself."

"Meaning what, Kyle?"

"I took him down. To make him stop."

She closed her eyes for a moment, dizzy with the
release of tension. Struggling to control a sudden
convulsion of emotion, she said, "Tell us about it."

He slumped in his chair, crossed his bandaged
hands on the Formica-topped table, stared down at
them. "Malone's yeah, okay, I met him there. Yeah,
okay, he had some coke, we scored a couple of lines.
Real good stuff. He says he's got more back at his
restaurant. So I say okay, let's go. We get there and
the place is all closed up, you know? But I figure

what the hell — and like a dumb shit I go in with him."

His voice dropped. "He comes at me with a knife, a big motherfucking knife. Man, I was scared shitless. Even when I got the thing away from him he didn't back off an inch. I cut him, I had to, he fought like hell. I lost it, I just fucking lost it. I didn't know if the dude was alive or dead, I just got the fuck outta there."

Gaining control of herself, Kate spent time over her shorthand notes until it was plain that nothing more would be forthcoming. "Kyle," she uttered softly. Her objective now was to have him view her as an ally, to have him talk as much as possible. "We need to understand how you got yourself into this mess. Let's take this one step at a time. When did you first see him?"

He said earnestly, "He came in with this Mexican chick, I was looking at her, not him. Next thing he's at the bar getting some beers. Then he's back at the bar and we're shooting the shit, he says do I want to go to the john, he's got real good coke."

She was interested in his insistence that he had looked at Teddie Crawford's female companion, not Teddie Crawford. And she was intrigued by his voluntary admission of sharing cocaine. In her experience, such an admission was tactical: See how forthcoming I am when I don't have to be — why would I lie to you about anything else?

"So you went with him to the john," she said.

"Yeah. He rolls up a bill and we score the stuff."

"How many lines?"

"Two."

"Two each? Or altogether?"

"Each."

"Anybody see you?"

He shook his head. "We were in a stall."

"Let's back up. When he first came up to the bar, what was said?"

"He said how're you doing and I said just trying to get fried, how about you, friend. He just grinned, said he'd drop off the beers and be back."

"Did he introduce himself?"

"Said his name was Teddie."

"Just that?"

"Yeah. Just that. I said my name was Kyle. You got a problem with that?"

"Of course not, Kyle. I'm just trying to get a complete picture of what happened. He came back and then what?"

He shrugged. "We got into the usual shit, what we did for a living, all that. He was nosey, wanted to know a lot of stuff about me. I told him I like to go to the beach and work out and ride around on my bike — I'm a dirt biker. You know, just shit like that."

"What did he tell you about himself?"

He cocked his head as he reflected. "Not a whole hell of a lot, now that you mention it. Mostly he yakked about his restaurant."

Making rapid notes, she asked, "What did he say?"

"How hard he worked but he liked it, and his partner was the best thing that ever happened to him, and the catering part was really starting to take off. He told me some stories, funny stuff he saw at parties he worked."

"When did you leave the bar?"

He shrugged. "Late, I don't know, before last call."

"Did you talk to anybody else while the two of you were there?"

"Nope."

"When you left with Teddie, how did you get to the restaurant?"

"I took us. On my bike."

"You went directly to the restaurant?"

"Yeah. No, wait a minute, I stopped at the 7-Eleven on the corner to get some smokes."

"Did you both go in?"

"Yeah."

"You mentioned you were uncomfortable that the restaurant was closed, you said you were a dumb shit to go in. Why did you think that, Kyle?"

He shifted on his chair. "Nobody was around, I didn't like it. I hardly knew this dude."

She looked him over, wanting him to notice her scrutiny of the breadth of his chest and shoulders, the dimensions of him. She asked, "Why did being alone with a much smaller man concern you?"

"Hey, lady, it didn't. Not till he pulled the shiv. That's when I saw I was a dumb shit."

"Let's go back a minute. You arrived at the restaurant. What door did you go in?"

"Back door. We came in through the kitchen. I took my jacket off, he right away lays out lines of coke, we score it."

"Then what?"

"I get this big tour. He tells me about every stupid thing in the place. Like napkins — how he got a hundred of 'em, a dime apiece, from some

fancy French restaurant that went belly-up. Then we
go back in the kitchen and finish off the rest of the
coke."

"How much altogether from when you got to the
restaurant?"

"Three lines."

"Each?"

"Yeah, he was really wasted."

"And you? Were you wasted?"

"Nah, I was high, that's all."

"Then what?"

"He picks up the knife. Comes at me."

"Come on, Kyle," Taylor interjected. "Let's stop
shitting around. Tell us why the knife, what he
wanted."

Jensen turned to Taylor, looked at him carefully.
"I'm guessing you already got it figured out, man."

"Maybe," Taylor said equably. "But you're the guy
that has to tell us what and why and how."

Jensen shrugged, shook a cigarette out of his
package of Marlboros. Taylor lit it for him and said
with quiet command, "Tell us, Kyle."

Jensen exhaled smoke through his nose and
moustache with an audible snort. "He was a fag,
man. He wanted to suck my cock."

"Okay. What did he say, what did he do? You
want to help yourself, you gotta tell us the detail
how you got into self-defense with him."

"Makes me sick, man."

"Sure, I know." Unbuttoning his jacket, Taylor
leaned back on two legs of his chair and hooked his
thumbs under the straps of his shoulder holster.
"But you gotta help yourself here."

Kate listened to this exchange in disgust. Taylor would say that he was playing on Jensen's homophobia to keep him talking, but she knew better.

"First I knew what he had in mind," Jensen said, "we were in the restaurant part, I'm looking at these fucking ten-cent napkins. He puts his hand here —" He brushed his upper right arm and across his chest, "feeling me up."

"What did you do?"

"I was cool. Stepped away. But he comes at me again and skims his hand down over my crotch, tells me he likes the look of my basket. That's when I say I'm not gay, not interested."

"What did he do then?"

"Just laughed, he says no problem. Says come on in the kitchen. So we go in there, do the one last line. Then he gropes me again, says I don't have to do anything, just let him suck my cock. I push him away, tell him I'm getting the hell out of there."

"I bet. Then what?"

"He yanks a knife out of this rack, stands there holding it." Jensen squeezed his eyes shut. "I can see him plain as day. 'You do my coke, I do you,' he says to me. 'That's how it works.' And I'm staring at that knife, I could vomit on him, I'm scared shitless."

"Take us through the rest of it," Taylor said softly. "Everything you remember. One step at a time."

"I turn to pick up my jacket, see him relax a little bit. I figure I can grab his wrist, get the knife away from him. Instead he jerks the knife so I catch it in my hand. He yanks it out, comes at me, I catch it in my other hand, knee him in the balls. We go down on the floor."

He sighed, stubbed out his cigarette. "I don't remember nothing more till he stopped fighting, stopped moving. I got over to the sink, grabbed some paper towels, turned on the taps, saw I was cut bad. I grabbed a couple of dish towels, wrapped myself up. I got the fuck outta there."

Kate asked quietly, "Was he dead?"

. He did not look at her. "He didn't move. I heard some . . . sound."

She said, keeping her tone even, "When you were describing him coming at you with the knife, you said you could see him plain as day. How was he holding the knife?" She stood up, away from the table. "Show us."

He got up, positioned himself in front of her. "He was about here. And the knife was like this." He held a bandaged hand up at shoulder level. "The blade was stuck right out at me."

"Yes," Kate said. "You said you were staring at it. Was the cutting edge up or down?"

"Up. I could see how sharp it was."

"Okay, I'm Teddie." She assumed a stance mimicking holding a knife at shoulder-level. "You try to take it away. Show me."

"Okay." He reached for Kate's wrist with his right hand. "But he moved and I grabbed the knife instead." She made a stabbing motion at him; bandaged palm up, he pantomimed closing his hand over the imaginary knife. "Then he slid it out and cut me." She slid the "knife" out. "He tried to stab me —" She raised the "knife" again. He grabbed for it with his left hand. "He slashed my other hand. I kneed him." He grinned at her. "I won't show you."

"I appreciate it," she said, managing to grin in return. "Then what? You said you both went down. How did that happen?"

He looked at the floor as if picturing the events. "I knee him, he buckles, lands on top of me, takes me to the floor. We're fighting like hell for the knife. That's all I remember."

"Sit down, Kyle," she said. Reclaiming her own chair, she waited until he was settled in and Taylor had lit another cigarette for him. "Did he cut you anywhere else?"

"Nope."

"Any bruises or marks?"

"Nope. He fought like a fucking cat, tore at my clothes, my hair . . ."

"What happened to the knife?"

"Took it with me."

"Why?" she asked. She remembered Charlotte Mead's words: *He'd put his pecker back in his pants, wouldn't he?*

"Fingerprints," he said.

She nodded. But his fingerprints at the crime scene, in the absence of related evidence forming a path to him, would prove useless unless they were on file in the criminal justice system. She guessed he might not know that. "What else did you take, Kyle?"

"I had some butts in an ashtray. Drank out of a glass. I tossed the stuff into one of those green plastic garbage bags. I was so freaked I even took my paper towels."

Remembering that Teddie Crawford's body lacked

any jewelry, she reminded herself of that first rule of interviewing criminal suspects: *Make them believe you know everything.* She said, "You took a few other things, Kyle."

"Yeah, well, I don't know why I did. I didn't keep any of it."

She caught Taylor's glance; his eyes glinted in appreciation. She said to Jensen, "Describe what you took."

"I don't know what kind of watch it was."

"Describe it the best you can."

"Black strap, black face, gold numbers."

"And?" she said insistently.

"The pinky ring was just . . . a gold ring."

The deputy coroner, she remembered, had not found a wallet on Teddie Crawford's body. "What else, Kyle?"

"A dinky little fruity wallet."

"Did you take the money out?"

"No," he said.

He was playing the odds that they would not find that wallet, she guessed. Making a note to double-check with Gloria Gomez and Francisco Caldera about what jewelry Teddie Crawford wore as a matter of routine, she thought of the blood-drenched kitchen in Tradition. Of the man seated in front of her tracking footprints through the blood as he gathered up evidence of his presence. Of him looting Teddie Crawford's body while the young man groaned and bled away the last moments of his life.

She did not believe that Teddie Crawford — the Teddie Crawford she had come to know from her interviews with the people in his life — had threatened Kyle Jensen with a knife, demanding sex. Far more probable was the scenario that Teddie Crawford had been the one defending himself, from a hate-filled gaybasher.

Gaybasher. The word reverberated in her.

She looked away from Kyle Jensen, knowing that while she could control her voice, she could not conceal the naked loathing that might be on her face. She said evenly, "What did you do with the stuff you took?"

"Tossed it. An alley. Don't ask me where. I just tossed it."

She did not believe him, but she let it pass; she would find that green plastic bag. Back in control again, she looked at him. "How did you get home?"

"On my bike." He raised his hands. "They really didn't hurt very much. Not till this morning."

She nodded. Cuts could be like burns, with the nerve endings temporarily numbed. "A few more questions, Kyle. Beyond what you've told us, did Teddie make other sexual advances toward you?"

"Nope."

"What were you doing in Malone's?"

He sat up. "What do you mean, what was I doing? Having a few beers. Like you do in a bar."

"Do you go there all the time?"

"Shit no. I just found it. It's quiet, I like the place."

She asked, "Have you ever been in the Gold Coast or the Gauntlet?"

"No," he said, belligerent.

"How about Rage?"

"Never."

"Micky's or Motherlode?"

He glared at her. "Why are you asking me about fag bars?"

"Have you been in any of them?"

"What the fuck is this? You calling me a fairy?"

"Have you been in any of them?" she repeated.

He half rose, shoved his face toward hers. "I'm not a faggot. I'm not a goddamn butt-fucking faggot."

She looked into his eyes, into bottomless rage. "You left Malone's with a gay man."

"*I'm not a faggot.*" The husky voice was a seething fury. He swallowed, sat back, obviously struggling for control. "Lady, you're really pissing me off. I didn't *know* he was a faggot. I didn't know till he groped me."

"You couldn't tell at the bar?"

"Shit no. I can spot fags with the best of them, and the man didn't act fruity with me."

"Okay," she said. He relaxed visibly. "We'll need to go through this one more time, Kyle." His relaxation became slumping dejection. "Then we'll have a statement for you to sign, and we'll book you."

"*What?* Book me? You said —"

"We'll book you for homicide," she said, feeling a small measure of satisfaction. "Our job is to investigate, to gather information. The degree of responsibility for what you did is something for the court system to determine."

"That's not what you told me, man," he accused Taylor.

"It's right down the line what we told you," Taylor said.

"Fuck. The fuck you did, man."

"So we'll book you," Kate said, "then place you in a detention cell."

He held his head between his bandaged hands. "I need a pain pill. Fuck."

— 6 —

Kyle Jensen, his confession signed, had been officially arrested, and incident to that arrest had been booked, strip-searched and incarcerated, had had samples drawn of his blood and urine, as well as hair follicles taken from his head and crotch — all of this to his profane displeasure. On Monday he would be arraigned and assigned a public defender. And he would remain in jail, Kate was reasonably sure, until the disposition of his case; bail of any amount appeared beyond his resources.

She walked into the Detectives Squad Room, Taylor at her side, and dropped into her desk chair, feeling as if her bones had turned into quick-melting plastic.

Taylor propped a hip on the edge of her desk, crossed his arms, and gazed down at her. "That's the best goddamn interrogation I've ever seen you do, maybe the best I've ever seen, period. Nobody else in the department could have pulled that confession out of him. We had diddley shit and you nailed him, trussed him up like a Thanksgiving turkey. Partner, you were great."

Smiling her thanks, warmed by his appreciation, she felt — knew — that she had been like an athlete in a peak performance, she had extended herself fully, used every ounce of her training, experience, instincts, knowledge, courage. She felt expended, spent.

"I figure a plea bargain, involuntary manslaughter," Taylor said.

"You're not serious," she said, gaping at him, realizing that she did have something left in her: astonishment.

"I hope we *get* involuntary. He draws a public defender that takes it to trial, he could even get off. "Hey," he said as she stared at him, "figure it out for yourself. Teddie Crawford made a pass at another guy, backed up his cock with a knife. A jury's looking at this red-blooded normal guy, they'll figure Jensen freaked out and just lost it, that's all."

"*Just lost it?*" With effort she lowered her voice. "Look Ed, I know juries are capable of anything. But we throw in the towel and take manslaughter? This red-blooded normal guy let himself get picked up by a gay man, he robbed him, he hacked and *mutilated* him to death."

"Hey, I'm on your side — sure the guy should do time," Taylor said, spreading his hands. "And maybe a jury's gonna buy it. But I say Jensen's story hangs together just enough. I say a jury's gonna look at Kyle Jensen and see a regular guy who got freaked out by a cock-sucking fag."

"Let me ask you something, Ed." She was amazed by the calmness of her voice, the coherency of her words. "*Why* do men freak out over gay men? *Why is calling another man homosexual the ultimate insult? Why* are gay men so completely disgusting to other men?"

He pinched the crease in his brown pants between his thumb and forefinger, pulled at it. "Come on, Kate. The shit they do to each other is so up-chucking putrid you can't even think about it."

She could see his tension and discomfort. She pushed on. "Why not? Please do your best to tell me, Ed," she said. "I really want to know."

"Jesus, Kate." He looked at a spot somewhere over her head. "What's to tell? They aren't men. They're faggots." He raised a hand, waved it limply. "Mincy little faggoty fake-men."

"That doesn't answer it. And not all of them are effeminate. Look at Rock Hudson," she argued, wishing she could name other virile but closeted movie stars made known to her by gay friends Joe and Salvatore. "Some of them are really masculine."

"Rock Hudson was a pervert, not a faggot. All those masculine-type guys are perverts. They use the faggoty men like some guys use sheep or a piece of liver."

She could hardly wait to pass on this piece of wisdom to Joe and Salvatore. "Ed, so what if somebody's a mincy little fake-man? Some people grow to be over seven feet tall. Some people —"

"Some people are freakish, but they're still men or women. Faggots, they want to be fucked, so they turn themselves into women. If you're a real man, then you aren't a woman."

She chose her words. "Ed, what you just said — do you realize, do you have any idea how much it shows utter contempt for women?"

His face acquiring a florid cast, he got up from her desk. "Hey, Kate. With all due respect — don't tell me how men feel about women. I'm a normal guy, I been married twenty-three years to a woman who's very happy about it. You don't understand. I don't expect you to. Just drop it."

Here it was again, his unspoken judgment that being a lesbian rendered her invalid — an outsider, a misfit. "Ed —"

"Do me a huge favor, Kate. Drop it. You're a great detective, a terrific partner. Let's not get into this other crap with each other, okay?"

Cold fury gathered within her. "Then you do me a favor too, Ed. I intend to put together the best possible case for Kyle Jensen spending the rest of his unnatural life in the cage where he belongs. What he did was not manslaughter. It was murder."

She watched in escalating rage as Taylor stood with his arms crossed and his legs spread, his face closed. "Monday I'm in court, so I need you at the autopsy." She snapped off the words. "The favor is, do only what you need to do on this case. Let me do the rest, and stay the hell out of my way."

"It'll be a pleasure, not a favor." He made a tiny, ironic bow, and turned his back on her. "With your approval, I'll leave you to sweep up and I'll just take myself on home to Marie."

Kate let herself into her apartment at 2:30 a.m., her mind still churning over details of the Teddie Crawford homicide and her anger at Taylor. She had dictated her preliminary report for transcription, then reviewed the reports generated by the patrol officers at the crime scene and by the detectives assigned to interview people peripheral to the crime. The interviews she would follow up as a matter of routine. And necessity. She had felt currents of the officers' homophobia in the terseness and the brevity of some reports that dealt with gay male associates of Teddie Crawford.

A search warrant was in the works for Kyle Jensen's apartment and his dirt bike; the bike would be impounded for lab analysis. Again she reassured herself that so far she had done everything possible to facilitate the district attorney's evaluation of the case.

Taking off her jacket, she noticed light glowing palely from the bedroom. Aimee must have fallen asleep waiting for her. Kate tossed the jacket over the back of a chair, removed her gun belt and took out the Smith & Wesson, shook the bullets out of the cylinder, placed the gun and ammunition in a table drawer. Now that Aimee spent so much time in the apartment, safeguarding the gun had become routine, just as it had with Anne.

Aimee was awake, sitting up against pillows under the narrow beam of a reading lamp, wearing the white silk sleeping shirt Kate had given her, a book in her lap. Kate loved her in the shirt, the white a backdrop for the rosy hues of her skin, the dark sheen of her hair, the blue-violet of her eyes.

"Welcome home, Detective Delafield. Did you get him?"

Aimee's voice was languid, she looked charmingly sleepy-eyed. Kate stood gazing at her with pleasure. And want. "Yes," she said. "Arrest and confession."

Aimee put her book on the night table. "Tell me."

"Tomorrow." She added gently, "I need to not talk about it tonight, okay?"

"Okay. Do you have to go in tomorrow?"

Kate sat on the side of the bed, took her in her arms. Warmth from Aimee's body radiated into her hands, seemed to flow up her arms and under her breastbone. "Yes," she said. "Early." Officers had been assigned to safeguard the search warrant site, and she would be advised when the warrant was ready so that she could be present for the search. She was certain that the green plastic bag Kyle Jensen claimed he had tossed away would be found in either the apartment or the bike's storage compartment. "Couldn't you sleep?" she murmured, wanting right now to know only the silkiness of Aimee's hair against her face. She inhaled an amalgam of shampoo, face cream, ineffable female scents.

Aimee nestled her head on Kate's shoulder. "I

dozed a few hours. You have to be too tired to move. Come sleep in my arms." Her lips touched Kate's neck, moved upward in drifting softness across her cheek, her arms sliding around Kate's shoulders.

Kate kissed her. The lips under hers were a soft welcome, parting for her tongue. Kate momentarily savored the delicate flesh between, and then Aimee's tongue met, sweetly stroked hers.

Aimee eased her lips from Kate's. "You need sleep, not this."

Kate's arms tightened. "No. I need this." And once more Aimee's lips were under hers, parting for her tongue.

Some moments later, Kate released Aimee and said thickly, "Let me shower."

Aimee had begun to unfasten Kate's clothes. "Baby, just get in bed."

She could not. Her need to shower was absolute. "I'll only be a minute."

For the third time since her day had begun she cleansed her body with scalding shower spray. The heat seemed to expand the tumult of her need for Aimee. Wrapped in a towel, she returned to the bedroom.

Aimee's reading light was extinguished, the vertical blinds open; the room was a silver wash of moonlight. Again Kate sat on the side of the bed, marveling at the gift of beauty this young woman had brought into her life, luxuriating in the sight of breasts covered by the silk shirt that glowed ivory in the silver light, the eyes and cheekbones sculpted from shadows.

Then other eyes, blankly staring eyes, intruded

into Kate's vision. Shaking her head as if that would dispel the images, she grasped Aimee's arms.

"Easy, baby . . ." Aimee's hands skimmed her shoulders. "Your back's still damp," she murmured, and undid Kate's towel and pulled it up around her shoulders.

Kate slid her hands around Aimee's back, lifting her body up into her own, acutely aware of the fit of Aimee in her arms, the configuration of the breasts and body against hers, the murmur in Aimee's throat as Kate enclosed her in her arms. She brushed a hand down over Aimee's thighs, heard the intake of breath, felt tension in Aimee's body.

"All day," Aimee whispered. "I thought about you . . ." Her arms encircled Kate's shoulders.

"I need to hear that tonight." She would answer that want, and perhaps some of her own need.

Breathing the scents of Aimee's hair, she slid her hands under the silk shirt, around her waist. Caressing the soft flesh of her stomach, she moved her hands slowly upward, filling them with the exquisiteness of Aimee's breasts, the nipples blossoming in her palms. Aimee, head back, eyes closed, sighed.

"I need to hear you," Kate said again. She heard the urgency in her own voice.

"You will," Aimee murmured.

Kate drew the shirt up over Aimee's head, Aimee raising her arms to aid her, the down on her arms outlined by moonlight. Kate ran her palms along her arms, over her shoulders, her throat, cupping her face. She kissed her throat, exploring until she felt the pulse beat; she pressed her lips hard against it.

Aimee uttered a sound, a vibration under Kate's mouth.

Kate lowered herself onto her, groaning with the bliss of Aimee's warm nakedness everywhere melding into hers. Kissing her, she pushed a thigh between Aimee's legs, her kiss increasingly passionate. But Aimee's soft warm hands slid down her back, and Kate took her mouth away, groaning again, and buried her feverish face in the cool pillow next to Aimee's head in surrender to the gentle caressing.

But somehow the scent of the pillowcase held hints of copper, and memory of a bloody room, and the smell in that room filling up her nostrils. She felt a vibration in her own throat from a sound that was like a sob, and raised her face blindly from the pillow.

Aimee's arms gripped her body. "Kate . . ."

Kate's mouth possessed hers, her tongue thrusting into her; Aimee's body thrust up into hers in equal power. Kate's hand clasped between Aimee's legs, the hair wet on her palm, the interior a velvety yielding to her fingers; she sank fingers in to the hilt.

Her mouth came to Aimee's breasts, captured a nipple. Tantalized by the faint salt taste she sucked each nipple in turn, she moved her fingers strongly in the creamy wet, greedy for more of the ecstatic gasps. She would gorge on this feast of a woman, feed herself till she burst.

She moved down Aimee's body, not quickly, breathing her, inhaling her, pressing her mouth into her, her tongue grazing the down-dewy skin. Her hands gripped firm curving hips then slid up inside

smooth thighs, clasping and feeling the tender flesh
as she spread the thighs fully open.

For a long moment she breathed in a woman
smell that seemed to go beyond woman to creation
itself. Then she claimed the woman, sucking her into
her, and stroked and drank the satiny wet, dimly
aware of thighs shuddering against her face, of
thrashing on the bed, of muffled cries, of stillness, of
soft moaning.

She raised herself. Aimee's supine body lay in
strips of moonlight from the vertical blinds. An
image of another body, slashed, splashed with blood,
filled her vision.

She clasped Aimee's hips, pulled her across the
bed, out of the moonlight, and again buried her face
between her thighs. She sucked and stroked and fed
again, the hips imprisoned in her hands sometimes
undulant, sometimes shaking; she drank until she
was spent, until the wet seemed like endless salt
tears.

She lay exhausted, Aimee's body in her arms an
inert, shapeless weight. "Baby," Aimee breathed, "let
me . . ."

"I'm okay . . . Aimee . . . I needed . . ." She
could not continue.

And then Aimee was asleep, and Kate finished
her answer from a place so dark and so desperate
that it would forever exist in silence: *I needed to feel
alive.*

— 7 —

Kate passed through security at the downtown Criminal Courts Building, and rode up in a crowded elevator to the fifteenth floor offices of the District Attorney of the City of Los Angeles. In the blue-carpeted, simply furnished outer office, she waited while the receptionist announced her to Deputy District Attorney Linda Foster.

From the few facts she had picked up from her contacts in the DA's office, she did not feel optimistic about this prosecutor. Linda Foster's six-year career had begun, as had most DDA careers, with a probationary period at an outlying court; for eighteen months she had prosecuted misdemeanor cases and handled felony prelims in Compton. Then had followed a standard one-year stint at the Eastlake facility for juveniles.

All the action was downtown of course, and she had been assigned here as a DDA-1 three years ago. She was now a DDA-2 and, except for a few assault with a deadly weapon cases, had been buried mostly in drug enforcement — little felonies, as they were referred to — because, according to several of Kate's sources, Foster had a habit of saying exactly what was on her mind, not a good idea in view of the man who was currently the elected District Attorney.

Wryly, Kate remembered her hope of having Bud Sterling prosecute this case; instead, in testimony to its status, it had been assigned to the low woman on the totem pole, one who had never even tried a homicide case.

"Kate? Linda Foster. I've heard about you, it's good to meet you."

Murmuring her own automatic pleasantry, Kate shook the cool, firm hand extended by a thin, frizzy-haired young woman in a tailored black skirt and jacket.

"So. Come on back to the office." Linda Foster turned and marched briskly off, Kate following.

Kate felt at home in the warren of utilitarian cubicles assigned to the deputy district attorneys, the worn anonymity of the cramped offices, the work-laden desks. This place always held for her the same weary yet not unpleasant ambience of entrenched bureaucracy and never-ending paperwork as did her own Wilshire Division.

In her windowless box of an office, Linda Foster kicked off her pumps, flung her well-cut jacket onto a bookcase stuffed with case files, dropped her body into her desk chair. "Feel free to make yourself equally comfortable," she told Kate, reaching to a shelf behind her desk to plug in a Farberware coffee percolator.

Smiling, Kate sat in the flimsy metallic chair across from her. "I'm okay. I have to conceal my gun in public, so I'm used to wearing a jacket."

"That's a bitch."

Kate surveyed Linda Foster with casual but acute attention, trying to evaluate the slender young woman as a jury might view her. She was in her mid thirties, and the sandy blonde frizz was a distinctly contemporary hairstyle. Stylish oversize rose-tinted glasses framed gray-green eyes intense with impatient intelligence. Her makeup was light, the delicate mouth barely lipsticked. Simply cut clothing and minimal makeup did not conceal Linda Foster's femininity, but, Kate reflected, most women could more easily exaggerate their femininity than understate it. She wore no wedding ring; Kate had learned that she was divorced, had a seven-year-old son, and lived with a college professor.

Kate sensed rather than saw a strain of toughness in Linda Foster, a trait common to good female attorneys, but a double-edged sword. Many male cops and judges, resigned to the legally mandated presence of women within their ranks, disdained more forceful women attorneys as cutthroat castrating killer bitches. Kate did not doubt that certain members of juries held the same opinion.

Foster blew a strand of frizz from her forehead,

propped one nyloned foot on a corner of the desk. "So. This is what I know. Kenneth Pritchard's a volunteer public defender."

Kate nodded. "I know a Kenneth Pritchard, but the last I heard he was a corporate insurance lawyer."

"Insurance? God, what a bore. This guy's from Butler, Steele and Simon, the snotty firm for upper-class felons. So he's slumming, he's a cowboy riding into town to defend the disadvantaged and downtrodden."

Grinning, Kate asked, "And you're not?"

Foster shrugged. "Sometimes the disadvantaged and downtrodden deserve to be. I already know from the case reports we'll have a pre-trial motion for dismissal on the grounds the cuts on Jensen's hands prove self-defense. A motion to quash Jensen's confession on whatever procedural bullshit Pritchard can concoct, aside from claiming Jensen's pain pills impaired his ability to know what he was saying. Thanks to your excellent work, that shouldn't fly a foot."

Kate nodded. "Thanks. Good," she said. So far she was pleased with what she had heard.

"So then they plea bargain. Involuntary, is my guess. What do you think?"

"Look," Kate said, sitting up in her chair. "I know plea bargains are often no worse than a jury might decide. But manslaughter doesn't fit anywhere here. By every definition this is first degree murder."

Foster put the other foot up on her desk, laced her long fingers together. "So. Tell me."

Kate took a deep breath. Everything rode on convincing this blunt-talking young woman —

everything. "You read the reports, heard the interview tape —"

"It'll make for drafting a good complaint. You should see the horseshit I get from the bozos in narcotics. I wish more detectives gave us so few procedural problems."

"I appreciate that." And she did. "This is what I think about Kyle Jensen. He's a drug user who rolled gay men from bars like Malone's because that kind of gay man can't afford to report that kind of crime. He's —"

"Can you give me that?" Foster said. "Substantiate it?"

"I'm working on it." She was not ready to admit that she had made unsuccessful trips to Malone's, and to several other bars, asking patrons and bartenders if they recognized the booking shot of Kyle Jensen. She had left a stack of her business cards, inviting any sort of information, even anonymous. But eliciting cooperation from the gay male community would be a serious problem when LAPD was viewed as homophobic, and for ample reason. Police chief Daryl Gates had fought recruitment of openly gay officers, with the dismissing comment, "Who'd want to work with one?" The department was being sued by a former police sergeant whose sexual identity had been discovered and who had been harassed into resigning for fear of his life. Gay and lesbian cops within LAPD were known only to one another — and she herself needed to be very careful what she revealed to this woman.

Kate said, "I'm certain Jensen knew Teddie

Crawford was gay. This was a man so far out of the
closet — everyone I've talked to so far says Teddie
Crawford was proud he was gay."

"Okay," Linda Foster said, making a note on her
pad.

At least she had not reacted as Taylor had —
but Kate could not tell if "okay" meant anything
more than simple acknowledgment of the fact. She
continued, "Everyone I've talked to so far says
Teddie Crawford didn't have any sort of drug habit
— which doesn't mean anything, of course, and
toxicology will tell us the truth — but the people in
his life are indicative of the person he was. And he
seems very much . . ." She searched for a word.
"Cherished. His aunt and uncle are de facto parents,
really nice people. Teddie was the center — the
bright center — of their lives." She ached with the
memory of her interview with Joe and Margaret
Crawford, their stunned faces, their numb pain and
bewilderment.

The coffee pot chuffing behind her, Linda Foster
crossed her arms and contemplated Kate. "So. You
think Jensen is homosexual?"

Kate said carefully, "A lot of us in the homicide
business think multiple stabbing involves sexual
pathology."

Foster shrugged impatiently. "Yeah, well, so
Jensen could be repressed. Or this could be a pure
and simple skinhead-type hate crime. Or maybe he
actually didn't know Teddie Crawford was gay and
maybe two men skulled out on cocaine testosteroned
it out with each other."

Irked by Foster's habit of making conclusory

judgments about her statements, Kate at the same time knew she was playing devil's advocate. But it was still difficult to control her rising agitation.

"Your last theory doesn't mesh with this crime. Teddie Crawford is far from being any sort of fighter. Jensen told us he fought like, and I quote, a fucking cat. Why would he take on somebody as big and muscled as Jensen? According to Jensen, Teddie Crawford was wasted on cocaine. Yet this wasted man, scant minutes before he died, was showing Jensen around his restaurant, explaining how he and his partner put the place together, where he bought the napkins, how many he bought, how much he paid."

Foster looked at her with a thin smile. "Yes, not exactly the cokehead type I've come to know and love. So, that leaves us with Jensen killing a homosexual — either the one in Teddie Crawford, or the one in himself."

Kate was struck by the wording of this last assessment. She said reflectively, "Somebody once said that the hater actually longs for the object of his hatred."

The coffee pot stopped chuffing. Foster got up and yanked out the plug, pulled out the strainer holding the coffee grounds, dumped the grounds into her waste basket. "So, figure this guy's repressed. Okay, I'll buy that — but I don't know if a jury will. If he's been rolling gay men, what made him kill for the first time, and why this man?"

"How do we know Teddie Crawford was the first time?"

"Good point." Foster poured coffee into two mugs of dubious cleanliness and handed one to Kate, sat down again. "You don't take cream or sugar," she said in a tone that meant no right-thinking person would. Amused, shaking her head, Kate accepted the coffee mug.

Foster sipped her coffee. "So. We still have to sell intent, premeditation, malice aforethought and beyond-a-reasonable-doubt-and-to-a-moral-certainty to Mr. and Mrs. America on the jury, Kate."

"You listened to the tape," Kate said. "He talked about sand niggers, slope heads —"

"An equal opportunity bigot," Foster said.

"Right," Kate said, chuckling. "Like most bigots." She was warming to this woman. Who served an excellent cup of coffee. "He goes to great lengths to claim heterosexuality. When he talked about the first time he saw Teddie Crawford —"

"I need us to call him Teddie," Foster interrupted. "It makes him a person to me."

Now she liked this woman. "When Jensen talked about the first time he saw Teddie, he took pains to point out he was looking at Gloria Gomez, not Teddie. He claimed Shirley Johnson was his live-in girlfriend, claimed she helped him take off his bloody clothes when it was actually Burt Dayton — he wanted no insinuations about a man helping him undress. When he met Teddie at Malone's, Jensen said they introduced themselves by first name. But men interested only in conversation with each other introduce themselves by full name. Men cruising each other use first names."

Foster was making rapid notes on a legal pad. "You're very good at your job, Kate."

Please be good at yours. "I've been doing it a long time," she said. "There's more. You heard his regret that his father wasn't around to see how brave he'd been about the cuts to his hands. Kyle Jensen is a man with a war hero father he could never measure up to, a mother he's estranged from."

"Three more cheers for the traditional American family," Linda Foster muttered.

Kate said, "For me, one of the telling moments in that entire interview was how upset he got when I asked whether he'd been in any other gay bars. I think Jensen took one look at Teddie and knew he was gay. And when Teddie told him he was a partner in a restaurant, that cinched him as a robbery victim."

"But a murder victim?"

"Jensen never had these circumstances before," Kate argued. "This was different from rolling a guy in a parking lot or in a car. Teddie had no car, and that put Jensen in control. He had a smaller man than himself as a victim, private surroundings to do whatever he wanted."

"So Teddie managed to get his hands on a knife to defend himself, Jensen got it away from him and killed him."

That scenario felt somehow wrong, but she could not argue against it. Not effectively. Not yet. She said, temporizing, "Charlotte Mead at the lab will be giving us a lot more information about the crime scene evidence."

Again she took a deep breath. "Look, Linda, I don't want this case dumped on a cheap plea bargain. Manslaughter? No way. This murder was no accident, it was not spur-of-the-moment. This killer stabbed a man thirty-nine times. I don't want him

back on the street after a few years of easy time. Do
you?"

Tapping her pen on her legal pad, her eyes
unreadable behind the reflections on her glasses,
Foster did not respond.

Kate had to convince this woman who had shown
more understanding of the ramifications of this
homicide than anyone else. "Let me tell you about
this case," she said, feeling her control slipping into
heedlessness. "Nobody cares about this case. My
male partner hates this case because Teddie
Crawford was gay. Male officers in my department
hate this case because the witnesses are gay — they
did toss-off interviews and toss-off reports to prove
it. The male pathologist hates this case because
Teddie Crawford was gay, and you saw his autopsy
report."

"The men in this office hate this case too," Linda
Foster said quietly. She pulled off her glasses, tossed
them on her desk, looked at Kate with intense
gray-green eyes. "I have no illusions why it was
assigned to me."

Kate said, "There won't be any press coverage at
the prelim or the trial — who cares about a dead
gay man? Teddie Crawford is a throwaway human
being, this is a throwaway case. Nobody gives a good
goddamn."

"Nobody but you and me," Linda Foster said.
"Let me refill your cup and let's talk about our
witnesses at the prelim."

— 8 —

"Kenneth Pritchard," Kate said, flabbergasted.

"Kate Delafield," the tall, dark-haired man returned as he stood outside the 13th floor courtroom of the Criminal Courts Building. Smiling, he reached for her hand and shook it vigorously.

"I saw the name on the arraignment report," Kate said, trying to recover her composure. "I didn't think it could possibly be the same Kenneth Pritchard."

He chuckled. "I saw your name as investigating

officer and knew damn well it was the same Kate Delafield. I'm surprised you remember me."

"Of course I remember you." With effort she summoned a smile for this handsome, well-tailored man who had so suddenly — and painfully — reconnected her to her past. "When did you leave Guardian?"

"Three years ago November. Criminal law was an old dream — I have to tell you Anne's death was one of the factors that got me off my duff. The reality's a lot different from the dream, Kate . . ." He shrugged. "But the deep end of the pool is still more interesting. I'm glad to say Butler, Steele and Simon want their attorneys to take some public defender cases."

He put his briefcase down on the plastic bench molded into the wall and looked at her with candid dark eyes. "You look well. Much better than the last time I saw you. I hope you know Anne's death was a terrible shock for me, too. There aren't that many people you call friends in the business world. It's been what, five years?"

"Six." Six years and five months, to be exact, since the day of Anne's funeral — the last time she had seen Kenneth Pritchard, corporate attorney at the insurance company for which Anne had worked. Of all people, for him to be the defense attorney for Kyle Jensen . . . Shocked by this new ingredient in the Teddie Crawford homicide, she looked blindly past him, down the wide corridor to the clusters of people waiting in resigned patience outside other courtrooms.

Pritchard said, "Anne was so very proud of you, Kate. She talked about you constantly."

"Yes. Thank you. I guess we'd better get in there." She reached to the closed double doors of the courtroom, but he moved around her and pulled a door open.

She preceded him awkwardly, galled by her feeling of defenselessness, that she should be so unprepared for an incursion into her professional world by someone who knew intimate details of her life. Her lesbian life.

She was immediately soothed by the courtroom, affected as always by its aura. The high bench and the jury box, bereft of their judges, seemed no less symbolic or majestic. The simple dark shapes of the wooden paneling and furnishings seemed to brood over the handful of people within the chamber's confines.

Inside the railing separating the court's inner sanctum from the spectator benches, Linda Foster sat hunched over her notes at the right-hand end of the counsel table, looking like a somber, perched bird in her dark jacket and skirt. A portly bailiff, who Kate vaguely recognized, sat at his desk looking through a notebook; a bald male clerk, head down, worked in his cubicle to the right of the judge's bench; a Latino court reporter waited in alert readiness at his machine.

In the aisle separating the two rows of spectator benches, three witnesses for the prosecution stood exchanging low-toned pleasantries: pathologist Brian Whitson, and Patrol Officers Jim Foley and Nancy Simmons. Ignoring them, Kenneth Pritchard pushed his way through the gate to the inner court and

placed his briefcase on the left-hand end of the
counsel table.

Kate nodded to the group, then took a seat at
the rear of the courtroom beside two other
prosecution witnesses. She smiled reassuringly.
"Francisco, Gloria, how are you?"

"Doing okay," Gloria answered for both of them,
turning grave dark eyes on Kate.

Wearing a navy blue dress with a square neck,
her shoulder-length dark hair brushed to a sheen,
she sat erect, her small hands clenched in her lap.
Francisco Caldera, in an oversize gray jacket that
looked as if it could slide off his frame, managed a
smile for Kate. They looked like children frightened
into formal behavior. Kate said soothingly, "It'll be
all right, this is routine and will be over with very
quickly."

Gloria Gomez said, "I'll finally get to see . . .
him."

"Best to get it over with now," Kate offered.

The bailiff's phone buzzed. He spoke softly,
briefly, and then said to Kenneth Pritchard,
"Bringing in the prisoner." He unlocked the door
next to his cubicle, and a few moments later
emerged with Kyle Jensen.

There was a sigh from Francisco Caldera; no
sound at all from Gloria Gomez. Kate noted that
even in the absence of an empaneled jury, Jensen, in
his prison blues, had been cleaned up for court. He
was shaven, his moustache substantially trimmed,
his hair neatly shortened to the nape of his neck.
The hands were unbandaged — but then ten days

had passed since he had been booked. He quickly sat down next to Pritchard, stuffed both hands into his jumpsuit pockets.

"Come to order," intoned the bailiff, "court is now in session."

Judge Michael Torgeson strode into the room through a door beside the clerk's cubicle, several folders under an arm. He took his place on the bench, opened his top folder. "*The People versus Jensen,*" he intoned. He looked up, his glance raking the courtroom. "Case number A9471341."

Kate watched as Michael Torgeson ascertained which attorneys were present, and the other opening particulars necessary for the court reporter's record. She knew this thin, ascetic-faced judge, knew he would be sharp and attentive in a rote performance, like an expert mechanic working on a routine brake job. This preliminary hearing was for the sole purpose of showing probable cause for binding the case over for trial; the trial itself would be assigned to another judge.

The prelim was very useful to the defense for viewing prosecution witnesses and to learn the prosecution's major evidence and general approach to the trial. For this reason, Linda Foster would present the minimum witnesses necessary. And the defense would present none at all.

"The People call Francisco Caldera," Linda Foster said in a clear, confident voice.

Francisco sighed again, a sound that was close to a sob. "It'll be okay," Kate said softly as he made his way past her.

He answered Linda Foster's opening question tremulously, seeming to shrink back from the microphone and into his chair as he identified himself and stated his address. But the impersonality of her questions about his actions the morning of February 4th gradually calmed him — until Foster led him up to his discovery of the body of Teddie Crawford. She handed him a black and white photograph taken at the murder scene. "Is this the person you found?"

He crumpled in his chair. His Adam's apple bobbing, he nodded.

Foster said softly, "Please identify this person for the record, Mr. Caldera."

"It's Teddie," he whispered. "Teddie Crawford."

"Let the record reflect that the witness has identified Edward Ashwell Crawford, also known as Teddie Crawford, the victim." Foster handed the photograph to the judge. "People's Exhibit One," she said. "I have no further questions."

"Mr. Pritchard?" the judge said.

"No questions," Kenneth Pritchard said.

Pale, trembling, Francisco Caldera left the stand. He had not, Kate observed, looked even once at Kyle Jensen.

"The People call Dr. Brian Whitson," Linda Foster said.

Kate stared contemptuously as Whitson, a husky young man wearing slacks and a sport jacket over a red sweater vest, walked through the swinging doors held open by the bailiff and took the stand.

Three days ago she had confronted Taylor with the autopsy report, waving it at him: "Who *is* this Whitson?"

"A new guy, he seems okay."

"*Okay?* He didn't probe the wounds!"

"So?"

"He *has* to probe the wounds, he's *required* to give measurements of stab wounds." Had she herself attended the autopsy instead of Taylor, she thought in fury, she would have challenged Whitson on the spot to perform the work mandated for him.

"Jesus, Kate. Who gives a crap? There was plenty enough organ damage to establish cause of death. Why poke around in the body of a guy who might have AIDS?"

Turning her back on him, she had immediately called Geoff Mitchell at USC Medical Center to determine the proper channels for reporting Whitson's professional misconduct.

"I don't blame anyone for being afraid," she had raged at Mitchell. "But you have safeguards, all the proper tools, it's his *job* —"

"I agree, Kate," Mitchell had told her. "Sorry it's too late for your case, but aside from your making a formal complaint, he's shot himself in the foot. A good defense attorney reads a pathologist's previous autopsy reports. The incomplete autopsy he did on your man will cripple him as a future expert witness in forensic medicine."

". . . a total of thirty-nine homicidal stab wounds," Whitson was laconically replying to Linda Foster's questions. "Inflicted to the upper extremities, twenty-three to the back, twelve to the chest and arms, as well as cuts to both hands and fingers, and fresh abrasions and contusions on the face and scalp."

Kate glanced at Kyle Jensen. He sat slumped in his chair, feet straight out, staring at the floor.

"Cause of death was three stab wounds in the

back, penetrating the right lung, and two stab wounds in the chest penetrating the left lung, causing massive internal and external hemorrhage, with almost total collapse of both lungs."

"Would you elaborate on the cuts to the hands," Linda Foster said.

"There's a deep cut and severing of tendons at the base of the fourth digit of the right hand, accompanied by dislocation. The palmar aspect of both hands shows slash wounds from the junction of the wrist and palm. The cuts on both hands probably represent so-called defense wounds."

"Thank you," Linda Foster said. "No further questions."

"Mr. Pritchard," Judge Torgeson said.

Kate watched Kenneth Pritchard get to his feet with the grace and confidence one might expect from a man who, she recalled Anne telling her, had been in the top ten of his class at Georgetown. Kyle Jensen, his eyes on the silk-suited attorney assigned to him, had to be pleased by his good fortune. Still, Kate reflected, it was a common misperception to believe that a private attorney was automatically superior to a public defender. PDs were cruelly overburdened, but in her experience they were canny, work-toughened, highly committed trial attorneys with invaluable courtroom and case law expertise simply because they handled so much work. Pritchard, in this case, was an unknown factor. It was impossible to gauge how capable he might be.

"Thank you, your honor," Pritchard said. "Doctor, the drug and alcohol readings?"

"Alcohol level was point oh three. Toxicology is still pending — another week, probably."

"About the wounds to the decedent's hands. You described them as representing so-called defense wounds. So-called, because there could be another explanation?"

"No, so-called because it's layman's terminology. The wounds are classic by any terminology, but yes, there can always be another explanation."

"No further questions."

Kate was not surprised that Pritchard had ignored the incomplete autopsy report. Teddie Crawford had indisputably died at the hands of Kyle Jensen, and from the defense's point of view, the extensive detail that Linda Foster would draw out at trial regarding the victim's death throes would include fewer specifics about the depth and dimension of the fatal wounds.

She watched Kenneth Pritchard as Patrol Officer Jim Foley tonelessly described his discovery of the crime scene and that he had found no evidence of forcible entry and no sign of a weapon. Patrol Officer Nancy Simmons, a wiry young woman in a crisply pressed uniform, testified to the execution of the search warrant, and the property which had been discovered in the seat compartment of Kyle Jensen's motor bike, including a bloodstained knife. Pritchard, busily taking notes, had no questions for either of these witnesses.

"The People call Gloria Gomez."

The young woman rose stiffly from beside Kate and marched to the stand as if she were wearing boots instead of high heels.

As Foster led Gomez through the standard opening questions, then asked her to identify and confirm the objects found in Jensen's motor bike had belonged to Teddie Crawford, Gomez never took her eyes from Jensen. Jensen never took his eyes from either his shoes or his attorney.

"Do you recognize this wrist watch, Ms. Gomez?"

"Yeah, it's Teddie's Seiko," she said fiercely. "Teddie's blood-soaked Seiko."

"Objection. Move to strike," Pritchard said, not looking up from his note-taking.

"Strike that," the judge said to the court reporter. "Ms. Gomez, answer the question and only the question."

Kate watched in profound sympathy as Gloria Gomez stared at Kyle Jensen in baffled, frustrated, furious hatred. The suffering from a crime of homicide never ended with the criminal act.

The questioning of Gloria Gomez ended with three more People's Exhibits — Teddie Crawford's watch, ring, and wallet — and Gomez was dismissed as a witness. As she passed the counsel table she hissed clearly and distinctly to Kyle Jensen, "You motherfucking slimeshit."

Kyle Jensen jerked upward. Pritchard gripped his shoulder and pushed him down, the bailiff rose from his desk. The judge rapped his gavel. "Ms. Gomez, any more out of you and you're in contempt. One more word of profanity and you're in jail. Do you understand me?"

"Yes, sir," she said, her tone on the bare edge of defiance. "I got nothing more to say."

Linda Foster spoke up quickly: "The People call Detective Kate Delafield."

Kate felt the familiar thrill of tension as she approached the witness stand and took her place in the chair behind the microphone. But she relaxed

into confidence as Linda Foster skillfully confined
her questions to when Kyle Jensen had been advised
of his constitutional rights, the contents of the typed
statement signed by him, and the facts in the
criminal complaint. Since every word she said here
would be evaluated and used to undermine her
credibility, any extraneous questions about the crime
scene, or any fact not in the complaint, would open
a Pandora's box of cross-examination from Pritchard
that would be used to challenge her statements at
trial.

"Detective Delafield, the man named Kyle Jensen
who you questioned and arrested — do you see that
man in this courtroom?"

"Yes." Kate pointed at Kyle Jensen. "Seated to
the left of the defense attorney at the counsel table."
Jensen looked up, but his diamond-shaped blue eyes
did not register her, as if the witness stand were
empty.

"Let the record show that the witness has
identified the defendant," Linda Foster said. "No
further questions."

Tensing as Kenneth Pritchard approached the
stand, Kate sat back in her chair to convey the
opposite.

Kenneth Pritchard looked at her as impassively
as if he had never seen her before. Kate understood
that any pleasantries between them existed in the
past. She was now the enemy. "Detective Delafield,
who besides the defendant did you talk to at
Hollywood Presbyterian Hospital?"

"I spoke with the admissions clerk, Doctor Henry
Mercer, and Patrol Officer Dale Morissey."

"Were you aware that the defendant was under medication?"

She concentrated on narrowing the focus of her replies only to what he asked. "Yes, I was."

"Who told you?"

"Doctor Henry Mercer."

"What did he tell you?"

"Objection, hearsay," said Linda Foster.

"Overruled. Ms. Foster, this is a preliminary hearing. Detective, answer the question."

Kate said, "He enumerated the medications and stated there was no medical objection to talking with the defendant."

"At the hospital, did the defendant complain of being in pain?"

"Yes. At that point I terminated the questioning."

"When you questioned the defendant in his hospital room, did you advise him of his Miranda rights?"

She said carefully, "There was no reason to."

Pritchard smiled. "When did you place him under arrest?"

"At ten twenty-seven p.m. that evening."

"Where did you arrest him?"

"In an interview room at Wilshire Division."

"How did Mr. Jensen come to be in that interview room?"

"He came in voluntarily."

"He walked in off the street, Detective?"

"He agreed to be given escort from Hollywood Presbyterian Hospital by a patrol car."

"Did he indeed. Did he complain of pain while you were questioning him?"

"Yes."

"Was he given medication?"

"Yes."

"At what point was he given medication?"

"When he asked for it, which was after relating the details of the homicide and learning that he would need to repeat them."

"Thank you, Detective." His smile contained confidence.

Foster had been right, Kate thought as she returned to her seat. Pritchard's questions had been designed to set up a motion to suppress Jensen's confession. And also to intimidate her.

"Your honor," Linda Foster said. "The People have no further witnesses. We move for bind over of the defendant for trial."

"Your honor," Kenneth Pritchard said, "the defense moves for dismissal on the grounds that the State has failed to prove the material allegations contained in its complaint."

"Your motion is noted and denied, Mr. Pritchard," Judge Torgeson said. "Based on the allegations contained in the complaint, I find probable cause that a crime was committed, and that the crime was committed by the defendant. The defendant is ordered bound over to Superior Court, for trial date —"

"Your honor," Kenneth Pritchard said, "in view of my client's inability to make bail, and a pre-ponderance of evidence in his favor, the defense requests a speedy trial."

"A speedy trial," murmured the judge. "What a concept." To chuckles from the courtroom, he consulted a calendar. "Judge Alicia Hawkins just had three weeks open up, beginning May eighth. Do I hear any objections?"

A few minutes later, the trial date was agreed upon. Court was adjourned.

"It went well," Linda Foster told Kate in the hallway outside the courtroom.

Kate nodded. A courtroom was a battleground, a setting for brutal warfare structured like a highly civilized chess game. Some moves were automatic, like the prelim, to set up the real contest.

"There were no surprises," Foster said. "I don't like surprises."

"There was one surprise," Kate said. "Kenneth Pritchard is the same one I knew from years ago, he's moved into criminal law."

Linda Foster shrugged. "Yeah, well, so what?"

— 9 —

On the Saturday two weeks before the trial of
Kyle Jensen would begin, Kate sat in her Nova in
front of Tradition at one-forty-five in the morning.
Wearing jeans and sneakers and a gray LAPD
sweatshirt, sipping from a carton of coffee she had
bought at the 7-Eleven on the corner, she
contemplated the shuttered restaurant alongside its
companion businesses, their dark windows guarded
by retractable iron grates. No other cars were parked
on the lifeless street; sparse traffic traveled
past her.

The last time she had been here was six days after the murder of Teddie Crawford. In a follow-up interview with Francisco Caldera, he had confessed that he could not enter the restaurant because the kitchen was filled with Teddie's blood; he could not bring himself to clean it up, nor could he ask anyone else to do so. "Do you have a wet mop in the restaurant?" she had asked. She had gone into the place that evening, swabbed the blackened floor, wiped down the spattered cabinets and walls, made the kitchen spotlessly white once more. This homicide was not the first time she had performed such an act.

On Monday she would meet with Linda Foster for pre-trial planning. Toxicological reports were in place; and Charlotte Mead had completed her blood spatter analysis of the crime scene. Linda Foster possessed all of these reports, as did Kenneth Pritchard, as part of the discovery process which required the prosecution and the defense to submit all written material to one another. The defense, as customary, claimed they had no written material to furnish.

This homicide investigation was the same as any other in terms of putting together the tightest possible case — except that Kate herself had done work she would have either performed with Taylor or delegated. She was still conducting background interviews, following up on a few details. And there was one other element differentiating this case. She needed to be here at this hour, on this day of the week — the hour and day when Teddie Crawford had died.

Since she was the investigating officer of his

death, he was exposed to her in an eerie intimacy that did not allow him protection or privacy. The nakedness of his body was open to her scrutiny, the contents of his home and his life hers to probe. From his family, his friends, his lovers, his possessions, she now understood that he was not a man of silences and restraint. She understood the voluble, chaotic energy of his personality, the extravagance of his style, the flash of his dress, the bite of his wit. She understood his romanticism, his generosity, his sweet optimism.

To speak with total authority to Linda Foster, and beyond her, to a jury, she needed to add one final piece. She needed to see — to understand — what had happened in the kitchen at Tradition. To understand it in her bones.

She drove down the dark alley behind Tradition, got out of the car. Restaurant keys in hand, she closed her eyes briefly. "I am Teddie Crawford," she whispered.

Then she was climbing off the motor bike she had been riding behind Kyle Jensen. Preceding Kyle Jensen to the back door of her restaurant, unlocking the door. Walking in and pridefully throwing the light switch to illuminate the immaculate kitchen. Eager to show Kyle the rest of this place she and Francisco had so lovingly built.

Kyle wants to do cocaine first. Okay. Then I'll enjoy watching this good-looking man slide that leather jacket off that broad chest. Watch his body as he lays out some lines. Okay, I'll do just a little of it, to keep him company, be sociable.

Now I get to show him my restaurant. It's so pretty from the light from the kitchen, all shadows, quiet and romantic — but let me turn the room lights on so he can see everything. Kyle, I told you how Francisco and I found this place . . . Putting it together was such great fun, we searched out the tables, the chairs, the linens . . . I picked up a hundred napkins at a bankruptcy sale, only a dime apiece, feel the fabric, isn't it fine? The customers love the impressionist paintings, they add a lot of charm to the place, don't you think?

Let me turn out the lights again. Kyle, sit at a table with me, feel the comfort, the romance in here . . . See the windows, how the street light filters in through the gauzy window coverings. Take my hand, Kyle . . .

Come on, man, don't pull this hetero-butch number, it's a bore, I don't go along with the pretense any more. Get real, why don't you? Who do you think you're kidding? You came here to do coke and do me, so don't say you're not gay. You're gay, man, you're gay as I am.

Wait a minute, where the hell you going? What do you want in my kitchen? Get out of here. Just get the hell out of my restaurant.

A terrible mistake. I've got to get him out of here, oh Jesus, he's twice my size . . .

Let go of me! Oh God this tiny kitchen . . . I'm trapped, trapped. *Wait, no . . . Take anything you want, just don't . . . Don't . . .*

She slumped down onto the cold tile of the claustrophobic kitchen, her back against the wall, seeing him frantically thrash on the floor, slamming his head into the wall as he rolled in the small room trying to protect his face and chest from the slashing knife, Kyle Jensen leaping on him,

straddling him, pinning him face down as he thrust
the knife again and again into the frenzied body
beneath him until . . .

Jensen finished, getting up, his jeans crimson.
His jeans wet and warm with blood. Moans, the man
rolling over onto his back, his arms feebly clutching
at himself to staunch his wounds . . .

She stared at the ceiling. Its white brightness the
last image in the dimming eyes of Teddie Crawford.

She rose to her feet, turned the lights out, again
lowered herself to the floor and sat with her back
against the wall in utter blackness.

She felt his fear. His terror at the ebbing of his
life. With her own sense of sight blanked out she
listened to the building as Teddie Crawford had last
known it, its creaks, the hum of the refrigerator, the
constant drone of the city, all the sounds so ordinary
to the man who had belonged here in this place
where he had felt safe, where he had found
validation, where he had been confident and proud.
Until the blood-lust of a stranger.

She got up and turned on the lights. Pulling
photographs out of an envelope in her shoulderbag,
she arranged them over the table. Photographs of
Teddie Crawford's corpse lying amid pools of blood.
Autopsy photographs of Teddie's naked body, its pale
torso studded with dark red gashes. Crime lab
photographs of the knife, bloodstained from blade-tip
to handle, recovered from Kyle Jensen's motor bike.
Another lab photograph, of Jensen's jeans, so
blood-saturated that Jensen's white shorts, the
subject of another, separate photograph, were also
soaked scarlet.

She now knew with gut-deep, settled certainty

that Teddie Crawford had never held the knife. Had never picked it up to either threaten Jensen or defend himself. It was not in his nature. It was Kyle Jensen who had come at Teddie Crawford, and with explicit intent. Kyle Jensen who had sat astride a male body and used a knife to thrust into that body until his pent-up lust was spent.

"Teddie," she murmured, picking up a closeup photo of the handsome face, "when Kyle *first* came at you with that knife, exactly what in the world happened? How did Kyle get cut?" But the knowledge was forever hidden behind the staring dark eyes fixed lifelessly on the ceiling.

She stacked the photos, tucked them back in their envelope. She was prepared to see Linda Foster — except for this one final, crucial point. Since Jensen had had the knife first and not Teddie, the defense wounds on Teddie's hands were clearly explainable. But how had Jensen come to have such severe wounds to his own hands?

"Nobody's coming in today but you, I skipped wearing the monkey suit," said Linda Foster. She finished priming her coffee pot and plugged it in.

Kate tossed a folder onto a corner of the desk, thinking that even in powder blue pants and the soft cling of a white cashmere V-neck sweater, Linda Foster looked sharp and tough. Shrugging out of her corduroy jacket, Kate said, "I'll get comfortable too."

"Do that," Foster said absently, her eyes on the thick, three-ring murder book splayed open on the desk in front of her, her long fingers running over

its index tabs. "So. I've pored over every word. I
think as a general approach we need to have Mr.
and Mrs. America on the jury see Teddie as a
regular citizen, don't you?"

Kate, settling herself in the chair across from
Linda Foster, sat up straight. "You mean play down
the fact that he was gay."

At her tone, Foster looked up. "Kate, the bottom
line is, we need to figure a way to reach the jury. It
doesn't take much brainwork to figure the scenario
Pritchard'll work up. The heterosexual defendant's
the good guy, the homosexual got what he asked
for."

"The homosexual panic defense," Kate said
evenly, commanding herself to be calm.

"Well . . . not exactly. Pure homosexual panic
needs clinical proof. Proof of psychosis, of a
breakdown into violent psychological panic — very
hard to prove. You need a certifiably loony tunes
client."

Shifting her holster, Kate sat back in her chair,
eased by the knowledge that this woman had done
some research, and could be talked to. "There was a
case last year," she said. "The killer got
manslaughter, but the judge said the gay man he
killed was responsible for his own death because of
his reprehensible act in making a sexual advance."
She had read about the case in the *Advocate*. She
decided not to mention the dismal fact that the
comments had been made by a judge in San
Francisco.

"I know the case," Foster said. "And another
really gross one in Kalamazoo where the jury came
in with not guilty even though the defendant first

beat the crap out of the victim, then came back and finished him off with a sledgehammer." She pointed to a stack of photocopies on the side of her desk. "Lots of cases, Kate, and let me tell you, the claim of homosexual advance comes up even with no evidence. The creeps think of it after they've killed. And defense attorneys take it and slip it in, figuring some dipshit on the jury will buy it and they'll get a lesser verdict and a lighter sentence."

Kate asked in a casual tone, "Would you use it?"

"Me?" Foster grinned. "Only with gay men prettier than I am. I have enough trouble competing with women. Let me tell you, I have real trouble with that defense, and I usually don't have ethical problems if an attorney isn't actually manufacturing evidence. But killing somebody is an *outrageous* response to a proposal of sex. I mean, come on. Be upset, even be revolted. But kill? I couldn't buy that from a client, they'd have to find somebody else who would."

Kate leaned forward. "Linda, what you just said — why do you think we can't communicate exactly that to a jury?"

"Because I'm no Gregory Peck."

Kate looked at her.

"*To Kill a Mockingbird*, Gregory Peck trying to reach a white jury about a black man — remember? To Mr. and Mrs. America, gay people are a different species. And let's not even talk about AIDS. If Pritchard gets his way, the jury'll think Jensen's rubbed out one of *those*, not one of *us*, and he didn't do that much of a bad thing."

"You make very good points, Linda," Kate said quietly. "But I have to tell you I think it's a mistake to try and rehabilitate Teddie into someone acceptable to a heterosexual jury."

Foster got up, poured coffee. "I'm listening."

"Do you know what the term queen means among gay men?"

"Men in drag, right?"

"Sometimes, not always. Mostly it's men who parade their feminine qualities, men who are overtly gay. Linda — Teddie Crawford was a queen."

"This is good news?" Foster handed Kate a mug of steaming coffee.

Kate smiled. "Actually, yes. If Teddie was that obvious, why was Jensen so shocked when Teddie made an advance — assuming he did? I think we *need* to state from the outset that Teddie was gay. Unashamedly gay, ostentatiously gay. And that way we set up proving that Jensen knew exactly what Teddie was, and chose to victimize him."

"Granting you that, Kate, we still have a jury that may think when it came down to really having a sex act with a man, he freaked. A jury that may think that under those circumstances they would, too."

"You want to make Teddie a regular citizen?" Kate challenged her. "Then make him exactly that. As a regular citizen he met an adult at a bar, like a lot of regular citizens do. He was led to believe that the adult he met shared the same interest he did. He left with that adult expecting to have a nice evening. When Kyle Jensen agreed to come to Tradition, Teddie had a right to believe that Jensen's expectations were the same as his own. Because Teddie Crawford was a regular citizen. A regular gay citizen."

"Sounds pretty shaky to me." Foster grinned at her. "Certainly Pritchard won't be expecting it. We still have the problem of Jensen's defense wounds."

Satisfied by Foster's response so far, knowing the strategy-discussion had not ended, Kate accepted the change of direction. She took the folder from the corner of the desk and opened it.

"There's something strange about those wounds, Linda. I had Doctor Mercer make drawings of the cuts in Jensen's hands. They aren't the kind of glancing wounds you'd expect in this kind of fight for possession of a knife. Some of those lacerations are deep and *severe.*"

Kate handed the drawings to Foster. "I've thought and thought about those wounds. They just don't make sense as defense wounds. Why the cut between the thumb and forefinger and not to the palm of the right hand? Why wouldn't a man as powerful as Jensen get the knife away from Teddie before he got a wound that almost took his thumb off? Not to mention the other damage?"

"All kinds of wounds can happen during a knife fight," Foster said. "And maybe Teddie's fear gave him more strength than you'd guess from his size. It often does, you know."

Kate said doggedly, "How did he get that wound on the outside edge of his palm? How did he get —"

"Look, I think this could be important, too. My, uh —" She looked at Kate. "What do *you* call somebody you live with? I hate the word lover, it's too personal. I barf over significant other."

"Companion or partner," Kate said, grinning.

"Companions are for old ladies. My partner's a woodworker by hobby. Why don't I get him to duplicate the murder knife out of plywood or something? Maybe we can come up with a demonstration, a plausible scenario of how Jensen got those wounds to explain it to the jury."

"I did something like that for another stabbing case I had," Kate said, remembering a death investigation a few years ago in a Wilshire District highrise.

"Did it help?"

"Nope."

"Terrific."

Kate said, grinning, "But I did get the killer."

"I'm sure you did," Linda Foster murmured, and sipped from her coffee, scrutinizing Kate over the rim.

— 10 —

The Nightwood Bar held perhaps twenty patrons at this 9:00 p.m. hour, most of them familiar faces to Kate. Four women at the back of the bar were playing Scrabble; three others lounged at tables beside the bookcase reading books; two more were immersed in a table-top video game. The others sat at tables talking or in attitudes of quiet relaxation. On the jukebox Patsy Cline was singing "I Fall to Pieces."

Kate made her unobtrusive way through the room, returning a few smiles and waves, and hoisted

herself onto a barstool. She grinned at Maggie
Schaeffer who stood behind the bar, Nike-shod feet
spread, arms crossed, her deep-set, hooded dark eyes
scrutinizing Kate, the silvery lettering of DYKE
POWER on her lavender sweatshirt picking up the
silver of her close-cropped hair. Smoke rose in lazy
curls from the cigarette in an ashtray behind her.

"The usual?" Maggie inquired in a soft voice
incongruous to the burly, assertive-looking woman
from which it emerged.

Unbuttoning her jacket, Kate flexed her aching
shoulders. "Make it a double."

A young woman wearing a yachting cap and,
despite the chill of this May evening, a sleeveless
T-shirt tucked into cutoff jeans, swung herself up
onto the barstool beside Kate. "A double *is* your
usual," she said.

Kate gave a deliberate, audible, exaggerated sigh,
then said, "Hello, Patton." She said to Maggie,
"Under the circumstances, double my usual double."

Maggie was already pouring Cutty Sark freely
over a glass of ice cubes. "Bug off, Patton. Obviously
our favorite cop's had a bad day."

A husky Latina wearing a vest and leather pants
took the stool to Kate's left. "Cop? This woman's a
cop? What the fuck you letting into our bar,
Maggie?"

"I even let in queers, Tora," Maggie said, sliding
a napkin over in front of Kate and placing the drink
on it.

Grinning, Kate turned to Tora, her palm meeting
the palm raised in greeting.

"This place has gone totally to hell," said Raney,

one of two black women who had come up behind Kate. "Maggie even lets *us* in." Audie, the other black woman, slid a plump arm around Kate in a brief warm hug.

Sitting angled to the bar, Kate smiled gladly at the five women surrounding her. She had impulsively stopped by here after a lengthy evening meeting with Linda Foster, the need to be in this place more compelling than her desire to go home to the singular comforts of Aimee. These lesbian faces, this warmth, this companionship, were exactly what she had come here looking for.

"Why the double dose of poison?" Patton asked Kate. "The murder business slowing down?"

"Never." The scotch was familiar welcome hotness in her throat, a faithful spreading warmth throughout her body, its action even swifter tonight: she had scarcely eaten all day. "The Teddie Crawford case," she said.

The five women waited in sudden stillness. They were following every phase of the case, as was the entire gay community. The *Los Angeles Times,* surprisingly, had carried an article about the forthcoming trial, and several out-of-state gay press reporters had called Kate, seeking information or commentary. She could offer nothing beyond the statement that the case was being vigorously prosecuted.

Kate said heavily, "We finished jury selection today."

"Ah," Maggie said.

"Jury selection," Patton scoffed. "You mean picking kangaroos for the kangaroo court?"

Swirling the scotch around her ice cubes, Kate closed her eyes for a moment to inhale the smell of coffee brewing on the bar behind Maggie, and a faint aroma of Aramis from Raney, recognizing the scent from a certain patrol cop who doused himself in it. On the jukebox Whitney Houston began "All At Once."

Patton rubbed her hands over her bare thighs. "Have I got this scoped out right? The kangaroos can't figure out why we need a trial over a dead fag."

"Patton, for once give it a rest," Maggie said, looking at Kate. "The woman's dead tired. The woman's told us before she can't comment on the case."

"Jury selection's a matter of public record, Maggie." She would not take the offered out. "I can talk about this."

Kate fixed her eyes on the amber liquid in her glass. "The deputy district attorney asked each person in the jury pool one basic question: Do you think a homosexual is as good as anyone else?"

"Dumb question," Tora said, hands on her hips. "Everybody knows we're scum."

Kate did not smile. Her mind filled with images of faces, faces containing not hate but earnest expressions of discomfort and a straining for tolerance. "Four people said we were mentally ill. Four more said we wouldn't have problems if we'd stop pretending we're normal and just keep quiet." Kate took a deep swallow of her scotch, seeing again Linda Foster's tense, impassive face as the young woman questioned and dismissed-for-cause one potential juror after another.

"Well, sure," Patton said. "Jeez, that nice pope says it's okay for us to love each other, so long as we just don't *touch*."

Audie ran a fluid hand over Raney's Grace Jones haircut. "That's reasonable enough, don't you think so honey? Let's never touch, what do you say?"

Raney's histrionic groan drew a smile from Kate. She continued, "One woman couldn't get it through her head why we made life so tough on ourselves when we could just go out and get ourselves cured."

Audie nodded sagely. "Just say no. You hear that, Raney honey?"

Raney groaned again. "Audie," Kate said, grinning at her, "what about this business one guy mentioned, about homos in the schools teaching kids to be queer?"

"Well sure," said Audie, a kindergarten teacher. "We call the course Queer 101."

"Listen," Patton said amid the laughter. "Let's pick a kangaroo court for Kate and get this stupid trial over with." As Diana Ross began "Where Did Our Love Go?" Patton leaped from her barstool and began dancing. "Okay, all together now, name the slimebag who's got to be the judge."

"Jesse Helms," came the chorus.

"Yeah yeah yeah," Patton crooned. "On the jury we for sure got Danne-meyer, Dor-nan, An-i-ta Br-y-ant —" She snapped her fingers as she sang and danced.

"William F. Buckley," Kate said, laughing, her

body swaying to the infectious beat of the song. "For the guy who said Buckley was right about us needing to be tattooed."

"Four, we got four," Patton said, ticking him off on her fingers as she spun.

"Patrick J. Buchanan," said Tora, dancing opposite Patton.

"Yeah, yeah, that's five." Patton dipped and swayed. "And that Cardinal back East, what's his name? Six. Hey, we got to have Phyllis Schlafly and her righteous hair spray. Seven!" she shouted. "Do I hear eight?"

"Eddie Murphy and Andrew Dice Clay," said Raney, bopping and spinning to the music.

"Nine. We need three more —"

"And two alternates," Kate said, beating both hands on the bar.

"Easy," Maggie said, who was doing her own stiff-legged boogie behind the bar. "The supremes."

"Our Diana Ross?" Raney exclaimed, stopping to gesture at the jukebox. "The fuck you say."

"No, knothead," Tora said, energetically tapping the heels of her cowboy boots as the song reached its final chords. "Those five fools on the Supreme Court that said we don't count."

"Yeah, right. There you are, Kate," Patton said, collapsing back on her barstool and dusting her hands. "A judge and jury who know all about our lives. Perfect."

As the song ended, the other patrons in the bar burst into applause for the impromptu dance, adding a few cheers and whistles.

Applauding along with them, Kate said, "Thank you all very much, that takes care of it."

Audie slid an arm around Raney. "So . . . what kind of jury did we actually end up with?" Her dark eyes added, *And what do you think about it?*

"Six women, six men," Kate said, quickly sobering, calling into her mind the faces in the jury box that she had scrutinized for every possible clue. "Two women alternates."

"More women on the jury itself would be better, I think," Maggie said softly.

Kate nodded. "The defense figured that, too." And Kenneth Pritchard had maneuvered as deftly as Linda Foster. "Of our twelve, two men and two women are black, one's a Latina, one's a male Chinese." She added, "Big city juries tend to have older citizens, they're more likely to have the time to serve. But our jury has three men and one woman under forty, two males in their twenties."

"That seems good," Raney said. "Don't you think?"

"Bigots come in thirty-one flavors," Patton said.

"Patton's right about that," Kate said.

But she did think that the jury's age composition was an area where clearly Linda Foster had out-thought Kenneth Pritchard. Foster had selected older women and younger men, subscribing to Gloria Steinem's dictum that men tended to become more conservative as they aged, while women, with their children grown and off on their own, looked around at the world and turned into radicals. Also, younger males on the jury might add balance to the jury's view of cocaine at the murder scene.

"The mix of people on the jury seems representative," Maggie commented.

"Representative of *what?*" Patton's voice echoed in

the bar; every woman in the place looked over at them. She jabbed a finger toward Kate. "Ask this woman — *ask* this woman how many gay people are on this jury!"

"Patton, I have no idea," Kate said calmly. "The question was never asked."

However, Kenneth Pritchard had used his allotment of peremptory strikes — the dismissals used by each side to disqualify potential jurors without citing a reason — very carefully. Toward the end of the lengthy selection process, two jurors accepted by Linda Foster had been dismissed by Kenneth Pritchard because, Kate was certain, they fit gay stereotypes: the woman had short hair and wore mannish pants and the male spoke in a high-pitched voice.

A slender Latina in a maroon sweatsuit came up and circled Tora with an arm. "Hi, Kate. You've all been having a great time over here."

Tora winked at Kate, then said to her partner, "I got a question for you, Ash. Do you think a homosexual is as good as anyone else?"

"Well . . ." Ash rubbed her chin. "I wouldn't want my daughter to marry one."

Laughing, the group began to move off into the bar. Patton said to Kate, "I know you need your beauty sleep for tomorrow or I'd whip your ass at pool."

"Next time, Patton," Kate said. "And we'll see whose ass gets whipped."

As Patton wandered away, Patsy Cline sang the piercing opening notes of "Sweet Dreams." Maggie said, "Speaking of sweet dreams, how's Candice Taylor?"

Kate grinned at Maggie's name for Aimee, a cross between Candice Bergen and Elizabeth Taylor, Maggie's opinion of Aimee's beauty. "For the duration of the trial you can call Candice Taylor the widow Taylor. She's still adjusting to life with a homicide cop."

Maggie caught someone's eye across the bar, nodded, took two pilsner glasses from a plastic tub. Filling them with draft beer, she said, "Kate, she'll keep on trying to adjust till you share your work with her."

Kate sighed and swallowed more scotch. "Look, she's beautiful because she's young, fresh, naive. I tell her some things, but I'm not going to come home and dump ugly all over her. Case closed."

Maggie's warm, calloused hand covered Kate's. "Katie, it's good to see you loving somebody. But the way you are with this young woman — holding back you're still lonely."

Kate sighed again and did not respond. They had had this conversation before. "I need to get home to her, Maggie. Tomorrow's a very big day."

Maggie placed the draft beers on a tray and then leaned across the bar. She said softly, "Kate, about this jury. Tell me what you honestly think. Do we have a chance in hell?"

Finishing her drink, Kate rattled the ice cubes, reflecting over the question. "I honestly don't know, there's no way anyone can ever figure a jury. But . . ." In her mind was the level, gray-eyed gaze of the strong-faced grandmother she hoped would be the jury foreperson. "Maybe we've got reason to hope . . . maybe this jury will be fair."

"Fair," Maggie repeated, picking up her tray. "Isn't that all we've ever asked on this earth?"

PART TWO

– 11 –

"Come to order, court is now in session."

At the command from the Bailiff, the murmuring conversations broke off in the fifteenth floor courtroom, Division 113 of Superior Court, in the downtown Criminal Courts Building in the city of Los Angeles.

Kate, seated in the first row outside the railing behind the counsel table, watched as Judge Alicia Hawkins, a stack of documents in one arm, entered and moved to the bench. Without a glance at her respectfully quiet audience she took her place

beneath the large gold medallion of the Great Seal
of California, sitting precisely between the flags of
the United States and California, the high back of
her modular chair extending several inches above her
dark hair. Picking up a pair of half glasses attached
to a chain around the neck of her judicial robes, she
perched them on her nose and frowned at the
contents of her folder.

Kate had been a witness in cases before Judge
Hawkins and knew she was a woman of quick if
impatient intelligence who held her courtroom under
strict control. Kate liked the formality. The casual-
ness, the laxity of other courtrooms seemed to
degrade the majesty of the laws of a society
enforcing its code of civilized behavior.

She remembered with gratitude the Judge's
handling of the pre-trial motion to quash Kyle
Jensen's confession, a suppression hearing at which
Kate had testified for three hours. The hearing had
been important to the defense because the stakes
were high: the possibility of having Kyle Jensen's
confession ruled inadmissible as evidence.

With gentility and every courtesy, Kenneth
Pritchard had gone for the jugular, deluging Kate
with insistent pin-point challenges to her every
contact with Jensen, an exhaustive process designed
to break her concentration and elicit a response
different from a previous answer. At the first
objection from Linda Foster that Pritchard was
repeating his questions, Judge Hawkins had
sustained the objection. And from then on, she had
displayed her own gift for pin-point detail,
remembering what he had asked from even an hour
before, and how he had asked it, forbidding

repetition. And she had ended the hearing by throwing out the motion to quash.

"*The People versus Jensen,*" Judge Hawkins said crisply. "Case number A9471341. Is the defense ready?"

Kate watched in a gathering of tension as the immaculately tailored Pritchard rose to his feet. "Yes, your honor." His deep voice resonated in the quiet room.

"Are the People ready?"

Linda Foster did not rise; she hastily finished a note on a yellow legal tablet, looked up and answered quietly, "Yes, your honor."

The judge focused on the court reporter seated at the desk below her, his face blank, his hands poised over his machine. His fingers danced to her words: "Yesterday we finished empaneling and instructing the jury." Her gaze encompassed the jury box. "Good morning, ladies and gentlemen." The brief smile was luminous on her thin dark face. Over their hesitantly murmured responses she continued, "Today we begin with opening statements. Are the People ready?"

"Yes, your honor."

Foster pulled the yellow sheet of paper from the legal tablet, slid it under a sheaf of notes, gathered up the notes in a black leather binder and moved to the small podium facing the jury box.

Kate assessed the conservative lapel-less navy blue jacket fitting down over the hips, the white silk blouse with a tie, the knee-length skirt, the navy blue pumps with modest heels. Foster's severely conventional clothing and lightly made-up face seemed adequate enough compensation for her stylishly frizzy hair and oversize rose-tinted glasses. And the jury would not know that she was a rookie deputy district attorney about to make the opening statement of her first homicide case.

Foster placed her notes on the podium, her long fingers straightening the pages with unstudied grace. Unhurriedly, she contemplated the six women and six men, who stared solemnly back at her. Finally, she placed both hands over her notes and leaned toward the jury. Kate too leaned forward, her pulse accelerating.

"Good morning, ladies and gentlemen." Foster smiled, and held the smile as the jury chorused its response. "For the next several days you will learn about a young man named Teddie Crawford. A bright, talented, beloved young man. A young man on the threshold of his life. You will learn exactly how this young man died. And you will learn why *this* man —" She broke off. Without turning her head she pointed behind her.

Kate's gaze, along with that of the jury, flashed to Kyle Jensen. Wearing black chinos and a blue shirt under a dark blue crewneck sweater, he slouched beside Kenneth Pritchard in easy athletic grace, arms crossed, legs straight out in front of him and balanced on the heels of his shoes; he stared at a spot on the floor in front of the jury box. Linda Foster continued quietly, "You will learn why this man, Kyle Jensen, killed him."

Foster looked down at her notes. "We will present convincing evidence of an act of first degree murder. But first . . ." She closed her notebook, concealing her notes under its black cover. "Before that, I want to speak directly and candidly."

She leaned forward, her hands extended over the podium and loosely clasped. "Teddie Crawford was a gay man." Her eyes rested on one juror after another. "Whatever you think about that, he would not want the fact minimized in this courtroom. Because Teddie Crawford had accepted his life as a gay man. He never pretended to be anything else. He lived his life — his brief life — openly as a gay man. The defense will tell you the defendant did not know Teddie Crawford was gay until moments before the defendant killed him. We will prove to you the impossibility of such a claim. We will prove to you that in the early morning hours of February fourth, this defendant —" Again she pointed behind her, "— committed first degree murder. This defendant knew Teddie Crawford was gay. This defendant knew exactly who he was killing and why."

Linda Foster leaned back and opened her notebook. "Now I'll tell you exactly what happened that night."

There was a collective sigh in the courtroom, a release of tension. Kate herself remembered to breathe. She was heady, almost dizzy with the sheer theater of what she had just witnessed. In her estimation, rookie Linda Foster had conducted herself, and the opening of her first homicide trial, perfectly.

Kate had known that Foster would take her advice about confronting the issue of Teddie Crawford's sexual identity — but she had not known how unflinchingly Foster would strip it open. And now that it was out there . . .

". . . met Teddie Crawford at Malone's Bar," Foster was saying, "a place frequented by the defendant. Teddie Crawford invited him to his restaurant. And the defendant, with every evidence — every evidence, ladies and gentlemen — that Teddie Crawford was a gay man, took him there on his motorcycle . . ."

The jury sat unmoving. The youngest of the six women, a straight-haired blonde wearing glasses, drew Kate's notice; she was slumped in her seat, her head so low that she appeared to be gazing into letters on her blue sweater that spelled PARIS.

As Linda Foster stepped over to the large sketch of the murder scene stipulated for use in the opening statements, Kate consulted her jury chart. Number four was Judy Harrow. Thirty-eight years old, a telephone operator, married to a telephone repairman, no children. As Kate watched her, juror number four raised her head, flicked a glance over the crime scene sketch, then resumed her contemplation of her sweater. Kate decided that maybe number four would be all right, she simply had her own way of listening and absorbing information.

". . . and here in the tiny kitchen of Tradition, the defendant, five-feet eleven inches tall to Teddie Crawford's five feet-eight, outweighing Teddie Crawford by forty-three pounds, overpowered him and repeatedly stabbed him, stabbed him to death. And afterward, with Teddie Crawford bleeding and dying on the floor, amid the indescribable horror and gore of this murder, he attempted to clean himself off at the sink of Teddie Crawford's restaurant. He took the watch, ring and wallet from the dying man's mutilated body. Soaked in blood from head to foot, he went home . . ."

Juror number eight, the older woman Kate thought might end up as jury foreperson, unbuttoned the gray blazer she wore over a navy blue skirt and blouse, and settled in to rapidly copy the crime scene sketch into a spiral notebook.

". . . the defendant's own admission of his crime. This defendant is guilty of murder in the first degree and we will prove that guilt to you. And we will prove it beyond a reasonable doubt."

Foster stepped away from the sketch clipped to the courtroom blackboard, moved confidently back to the podium and gathered her notes. "Thank you, ladies and gentlemen, for your attention."

Win or lose, Kate exulted, Linda Foster had come out of her corner battling for Teddie Crawford.

Judge Hawkins finished making a notation. "Mr. Pritchard," she said.

"Thank you, your honor." Pritchard closed his leather binder, picked it up, then tossed the binder back onto the counsel table. Empty-handed, he strode to the podium.

Tall and slim in his dark gray suit and gray-blue striped tie, he stood with his hands at his sides, gazing somberly at the jury as if measuring and absorbing each face. And each juror's face acquired tense self-consciousness under his gaze, Kate noted, including number four, who had raised her attention from her PARIS sweater.

"Ladies and gentlemen," Pritchard began, so softly that the jury leaned toward him. "So far this morning we've had lots of drama in this room from the district attorney." His voice strengthened. "So much drama that I'm reminded of one of those old time movies set on a Scottish moor, one of those

scenes where the special effects man —" Pritchard's
hands began motions of constructing clouds around
him, "— pumps in fog around the feet of the actors
to add lots of damp misty gray atmosphere. The
State is pumping in the same kind of special effects.
Adding billows of fog to what is, when all is finally
said and done in this courtroom, a very sad and
very simple story."

Pritchard's fine, supple hands clasped the sides of
the podium. "The State has declared this case to be
first degree murder. The State has concocted a
fog-filled scenario to dramatize its claim." He paused.
Then his voice rang in the quiet courtroom. "Amid
all the billows of fog the one *fact* is that a young
man is tragically dead." He continued, snapping off
his words, "*Why* he died is the issue before us. *Why*
he died is what the twelve of you must decide."

His voice softened. "As you listen to the State's
witnesses and the State's version of events, do not
for one moment let anything deter you from that one
central question: *why* did this young man die?
Remember that in the State's thirst for a first-degree
murder conviction, they bear the burden of proof.
They must *prove* that the young man seated at the
counsel table is guilty — beyond a reasonable doubt
and to a moral certainty — of premeditated murder."

He fell silent, his gaze again moving from juror
to juror. "We all bear responsibility for our acts," he
said, so quietly that again the jury leaned forward to
hear. "As does my client, Kyle Jensen. And, ladies
and gentlemen, as does the dead man himself, the
young man whose tragic death has brought us here
today."

Again he paused. "When the State has finished

with all of its dramatic posturing, when it has finished filling this courtroom with all of its layers of fog —" Again his hands created billowing clouds, "— you will learn the truth of what happened on February fourth. In the meantime, I ask you for an open mind. Ladies and gentlemen, I thank you for your attention."

Kate looked dismally at the sober faces of the jury. If Pritchard had been surprised by Linda Foster's decision not to minimize Teddie Crawford's sexuality, by her aggressive attack on Kyle Jensen, he had recovered quickly.

Judge Hawkins finished making a note and looked up. "Ms. Foster, do you have anything further?"

"No, your honor," Linda Foster said evenly.

"Are the People ready to proceed?"

"Ready, your honor."

"Call your first witness."

— 12 —

As a somber-faced Francisco Caldera left the stand, Judge Hawkins became involved in a low-toned conference with her court clerk. Kate glanced at her watch. Gloria Gomez, next to be called, would probably conclude her testimony before the judge recessed for lunch.

Caldera, clad in flowing black trousers and the same oversize gray jacket he had worn at the preliminary hearing, seated himself beside Gloria Gomez who took his hand and patted it, then resumed her staring at Kyle Jensen. Gomez had declared that she would not miss a moment of the trial, but had also pledged to conduct herself with restraint. Pritchard had not insisted on sequestering trial witnesses from the courtroom; Kate suspected that he wanted to portray his client as an underdog to the jury, he wanted a courtroom of supporters for Teddie Crawford in contrast to virtually none for Kyle Jensen.

Caldera had given the same testimony as before but with a calmer demeanor. In the four-month interval since Teddie's death he had become even thinner, his eyes shadowed and remote as if he had learned stoic endurance of his pain. From what Kate had heard, Tradition was failing; neighborhood customers shunned the restaurant, and gay patrons were also avoiding a scene of nightmare.

Behind Kate, Burt Dayton squirmed on the uncomfortable wooden bench, his shiny electric-blue shirt straining over his body-builder torso. Dayton, Kate had learned, made daily jail visits to Jensen; had brought Jensen the clothes he now wore in the courtroom.

Joe and Margaret Crawford were not present; Kate was relieved that they had chosen not to witness a proceeding that would flay them with repeated grisly depictions of Teddie's death. But Carl Jacoby, Teddie's ex-lover, was here, a dark, scowling, bristling presence in the row behind Burt Dayton. Jacoby had refused to cooperate with Linda Foster, refused to speak to Kate other than to characterize Officer Mark Parks, who had initially interviewed him, as "a Nazi gay-hater." Kate had urged him to file a complaint, but he had disdained both her and her advice.

No one, Kate reflected, could ever fully realize the agonies inflicted on a homicide victim's survivors. Friends and acquaintances who immediately flocked around with protestations of shock, with fervent offers of support, soon resumed their own lives, while the bereaved were left to endure an endless gauntlet — the loved one's death agonies dissected in callous detail as the case dragged its way through a labyrinthine court system that seemed more cruelly capricious than just.

Kenneth Pritchard had had no questions for Caldera, and Kate doubted that he would cross-examine any of these first witnesses. The facts of Teddie Crawford's death were not in dispute, and Pritchard's line of defense had been made clear, not only from his opening statement but also from his take-it-or-leave-it plea bargain offer of involuntary manslaughter. His estimation, obviously, was that a jury would decide no worse — perhaps even acquit his client.

If the trial went as mapped out in Linda Foster's strategy session, the patrol officers at the crime scene would take the stand, then Brian Whitson, the autopsy surgeon who had resigned from the coroner's office, so the story went, to enter private practice in Palm Desert.

Over the next few days Burt Dayton would testify, and Napoleon Carter and his lab technicians, and Charlotte Mead. And then Stacey Conlin, a prosecution witness who, Kate was certain, would come as an unpleasant surprise to Kenneth Pritchard. The strongest witness would conclude the prosecution's case — Kate herself.

Then it would be Pritchard's turn. From the

subpoenas he had issued, he would offer an "expert" on the effects of cocaine; then Kyle Jensen's mother, who was planning to fly in from Pittsburgh, undoubtedly to protest that her Kyle was really a good boy. All of this as a lead up to Pritchard's star witness: Kyle Jensen, testifying in his own defense.

And then there was Kate herself. That Pritchard would attack her objectivity as primary investigating officer she had no doubt. His unfailing courtesy and cordiality to her contained smugness, a coiled assurance. When and how would he attack?

Deliberately, she had not discussed with Linda Foster Pritchard's knowledge of her personal life, and her instinctive certainty that he would attempt to reveal it on the stand. She would tell Linda, of course, but at this point it would only distract the young district attorney from the framework of her case. And Kate herself was still mulling over the ramifications.

Over the past four months, apprehensiveness had built within her. Aimee had sensed she was troubled, but Kate had avoided all discussion. I don't want to alarm her, she had told herself.

But she knew that she simply did not want to hear Aimee's opinion no matter how much she was growing to love Aimee, no matter how intelligent and logical Aimee's opinion would be — because it would come from the perspective of a twenty-six-year-old without the life experience to truly know what was at stake. She would tell Aimee after the fact.

Close confidante Maggie Schaeffer had more than sufficient life experience, but Maggie's advice would not deviate an iota from what she had said all along: *There has to be an end to it. All of you*

*staying in the closet will never put an end to it. You
have to come out, Kate. How long can you live like
this? How long can you tolerate LAPD behaving as if
there's something wrong with you?*

The situation was hers to deal with. No one she
knew could help her. Anyone else's awareness of the
situation would serve only to distract her, just as
the knowledge of Pritchard's impending ambush
would distract Linda Foster.

But as Kate looked around the courtroom, the
knowledge of what she could lose flooded in on her.

She loved this majestic room. She loved being a
police officer. She loved that reach into herself to
find the fortitude, the sheer guts it took to protect
and to serve. She loved the intensity of touching life
in the raw. She loved knowing she was good at her
work, she loved this one area in her life where she
could operate with sureness and competence, where
she could sometimes help, sometimes make a
difference.

She held no illusions that her sexual orientation
was not a subject of conjecture at LAPD. But
conjecture was one thing, confirmation another. The
discrimination lawsuit against LAPD by former
Sergeant Mitch Grobeson was prime evidence of
what could happen to even an exceptional cop and
an exceptional career.

She could lose what she knew best, loved best. If
being a police officer was taken from her, what in
the world would she do with her life?

Looking at Kenneth Pritchard out of an im-
measurable darkness, she felt anger at Anne. How
could Anne ever have had this man for a friend?

—13—

"The People call Charlotte Mead."

Kate sat straighter in her seat in the first row behind the counsel table. She had read the crime reports, had heard detailed testimony from Napoleon Carter and his technicians, but now she would finally hear the impartial analysis that would strengthen — or critically weaken — the prosecution's case against Kyle Jensen. Jensen, in his daily attire of pants and shirt and crew neck sweater, sat in his usual posture beside Kenneth

Pritchard, arms folded across his chest, feet outstretched.

Mead, a neat sheaf of papers under one arm, wearing a navy blue V-neck dress unadorned by scarf or jewelry, entered the inner court through the railing gate held open by the bailiff, clumping her way to the stand on loose-fitting square-heeled pumps.

Linda Foster, unobtrusive in a simple gray suit and wine-colored scarf, completed her standard questions eliciting Charlotte Mead's academic and professional credentials as an expert witness, then said, "Ms. Mead, would you explain to the jury your approach to this particular crime scene."

"Certainly." Swinging around in her chair, Charlotte Mead adjusted her microphone with practiced ease, fixed her pale blue eyes on the jury and addressed them directly. "My job is evidence collection and analysis, to extract information for the court. As customary, I went through this scene with a photographer and an assistant."

Kate smiled. Mead's voice contained not a trace of her on-the-job testiness; her tone was vibrant, her gaze so sharp that even juror number four was constrained to raise her face from her contemplation of the PARIS sweater she had worn since the trial began.

"This crime scene was relatively intact because police presence had been minimal and the decedent's body hadn't been moved. The first thing I did was look at where things were in relation to the body, at whatever looked odd, and then I had the area critically photographed."

Linda Foster, having been briefed by Kate about

how Charlotte Mead preferred to conduct herself in a courtroom, downplayed her own assertive presence by standing well to the side and away from the witness stand, notebook in hand, allowing her witness unimpeded communication with the jury. She asked, "Would you explain what looked odd, and why?"

"Well, the scene was unusually bloody," Mead said, settling comfortably into her chair. "The floor was a massive pool. Scuff marks and footprint impressions everywhere in the blood, a distinct castoff pattern of blood on the wall."

"We'll get into each of those things in a moment," Foster said easily. "What docs critically photographing a scene mean?"

Her head cocked to hear the question, Charlotte Mead did not take her eyes from the jury. She said conversationally, "We work only from the scene, but we take reference photographs so we can lay the scene back together. We photograph the entire floor in sequence, the footwear impressions on the floor, the blood spatter pattern on the wall. Then we begin our sketching, measuring, documenting." She gestured with large, blunt-fingered hands. "We measure blood drops to figure the angles of where the blood had to start from to get onto the wall. And of course we take samples, critical stains, cross-sections from the floor and walls."

"What did your samples tell you about the origin of the blood?"

"The first step is called species identification," Mead told the attentive jury — three jurors were taking notes. "We confirmed all the samples were blood, and blood of human origin. We unsealed blood samples taken from the decedent and the defendant and determined that two ABO types were present, type O Positive from the defendant and type AB from the decedent. The preponderance of blood shed at the scene was type AB from the decedent, but all blood samples taken from the scene matched blood samples from either the suspect or the decedent."

Foster made a note on her legal pad. Kate knew she had paused to allow these facts to sink into the jury's consciousness. Foster asked, "What determination did you make about the footwear impressions in blood?"

"In every case they matched the footwear collected in evidence from the suspect."

"There were no other footwear prints present?"

"None."

Foster turned to Judge Hawkins and made reference and confirmation for the record to exhibits of Kyle Jensen's Puma jogging shoes. She said to Charlotte Mead, "You immediately informed the investigating officers at the scene that the suspect had to have been cut. On what basis did you make that judgment?"

"There was a single red globule on the counter near the sink. Here's this massive pool of blood on the floor —" Mead gestured for the jury as she continued, "— but this one drop's all by itself. It could hardly have come from the deceased. And blood on one of the faucet handles and on a bar of soap — the usual indications of an assailant trying to clean himself up. Plus, we had blood spatter evidence . . . a castoff pattern."

"Before we discuss this castoff pattern, what did your tests of samples taken from the sink area show?"

"All the blood from the sink area is O Positive, from the defendant, including blood we isolated in the drain. None of the blood in this area matched that of the decedent."

"Ms. Mead, would you now explain what you mean by a castoff pattern?"

"A castoff pattern occurs when an individual holds an object that's bloody and swings it back." She demonstrated, flinging her hand back. "It'll throw blood off. In this case, we determined that all the blood in the castoff pattern was O Positive from the defendant, and he was throwing blood off his own profusely bleeding hand."

"Objection," Pritchard said. "Outside this witness's area of expertise — she is not an MD."

Foster countered in an incredulous tone, "Your honor, she is a blood spatter expert."

"Overruled," said Judge Hawkins impassively.

Foster said to Mead, "How did you know he was bleeding profusely?"

"The size of the castoff drops in ratio to their height — and the position of the decedent's body."

Mead consulted the notes in her lap, and as she proceeded to give precise dimensions to the jury to demonstrate her findings, Foster looked on with a satisfaction that Kate shared. This was effective testimony, and going very well. Foster said, "There was other blood on the wall not in a castoff pattern, is that correct?"

"Yes."

"What can you tell us about that?"

"Well, we measured various key drops. The lowest drop that has an upward direction tells you everything had to take place underneath that drop."

"Ms. Mead, could you clarify that a bit more?"

"This is how it works." Again Charlotte Mead demonstrated with her large square hands. "The direction of blood flung onto a wall has to either be on its way up or on its way down. If the blood is flung up, then the assault had to happen below where the blood was flung up." Focusing on juror number seven, a young man in a gray bomber jacket, Mead said, "Let me go through that again," and nodded afterward as if satisfied that he too understood her.

"Thank you," Foster said. "Previous testimony has established that the victim's hands had wounds — the palms slashed, the little finger of the right hand almost severed. Was there any evidence of a castoff pattern from the victim?"

"No."

"Was there any evidence that the victim ever had the knife?"

"Objection," Pritchard said quietly. "Speculation."

"Sustained," Judge Hawkins said.

Foster said, "Ms. Mead, excluding the castoff pattern, which we've established as belonging to the defendant, to whom did the blood on the wall belong?"

"Entirely to the decedent."

"And how high was the highest drop on the wall?"

"Thirty-seven inches above the floor."

"So," Foster said, "this blood spatter pattern. What conclusions can you draw about it to a reasonable scientific certainty?"

"That these two people had to be down on the floor during the entire altercation."

Pritchard started to rise in objection, then subsided.

"Ms. Mead," Foster said. "We direct your attention to two People's exhibits, numbers twenty-three and twenty-nine."

Again, Kate saw Pritchard tense. He had lost his pre-trial claim that the photos, part of a photographic exhibit of the clothing recovered from the plastic bag taken from Kyle Jensen's apartment, were too inflammatory to be admissible. Number twenty-three was of Jensen's gory jeans. Twenty-nine was of Teddie Crawford's perforated and even gorier shirt.

Foster handed Mead the photo of the vividly blood-soaked jeans. "You examined these jeans as part of clothing the defendant wore the night Teddie Crawford died. What conclusions can you draw to a reasonable scientific certainty?"

"We took cross sections from all over the jeans. The blood is of human origin, and entirely that of the decedent." Charlotte Mead pointed. "Heavy staining in the crotch area is consistent with the defendant straddling the victim."

Foster took the photo to the jury box where it was hastily passed from hand to hand. Foster displayed the second photo. "You examined the victim's shirt. What conclusions can you draw to a reasonable scientific certainty?"

"We took cross sections from all over. All the blood was of human origin, and also that of the decedent."

Taking this photo to the jury box, Foster asked, "What were your findings regarding the vertical marks at the base of the wall?"

"Marks from the decedent's bloody hair. He was slipping around in his own blood as he struggled, got his head soaked, banged it up against the wall."

"Thank you, Ms. Mead," Linda Foster said with satisfaction. "No further questions."

Kenneth Pritchard unhurriedly finished making a note, turned back the page, rose and walked slowly to the witness stand and stood directly in front of Charlotte Mead.

"Ms. Mead, how much of the crime scene did you examine?"

Charlotte Mead did not look at him; she continued her direct discourse to the jury. "My sole area of expertise is blood and blood spatter. I took critical stains from where anyone bled. Off the floor, the walls, the sink area, and of course, the decedent."

"Did you examine the restaurant outside the kitchen area?"

"No, I did not," Mead told the jury.

Pritchard, obviously assessing that Mead would look at him only if he stood directly in front of her with his back to the jury, walked to the left of the witness box and leaned on it in a relaxed manner. "The only place you took critical stains from was the kitchen, you took no critical stains from anywhere else, is that correct?"

"Correct."

"You have alluded several times to the massive pool of blood on the floor. And that identifiable footwear impressions belonged entirely to Mr. Jensen. How would you explain the absence of footwear prints from Francisco Caldera, who discovered the body?"

"Could be a number of factors. The nature of his footwear — they may have been smooth-soled. The possibility that he slid in the blood, leaving only a scuff mark pattern. Or that he took more care than the defendant in how he conducted himself around the body."

"Move to strike that last remark," Pritchard said to Judge Hawkins. "Speculation."

"Overruled, Mr. Pritchard. You asked for her speculation."

Pritchard's relaxed expression did not change. "In reference to the wounds on Mr. Crawford's hands, you testified that there had been no castoff pattern from Mr. Crawford, is that correct?"

"Correct."

"But the castoff pattern you claim comes from my client — would that not have originated from my client's own wounds?"

"That's correct."

Kate mentally groaned. Charlotte Mead, neutrality personified, would answer Pritchard's questions exactly and without any regard to any shadings, however truthful those shadings might be.

"You stated that the castoff pattern indicated profuse bleeding. Is that not because the wounds were quite severe?"

Charlotte Mead nodded. "Blood like that, the defendant really tore up his hands."

Tore up his hands, Kate thought. The same phrase the emergency room surgeon had used . . .

There had to be — had to be — an explanation for
Jensen's hands, an event in the crime scene that
analysis had not yet accounted for . . .

"Ms. Mead, where exactly did you find blood that
matched that of my client?"

She consulted her notes. "On the counter. The
taps. In the drain. On the murder weapon. On the
defendant's clothing. The castoff pattern on the wall."

"Nowhere else?"

"Nowhere else."

"Ms. Mead, in a scene which you yourself
describe as a massive pool, isn't it possible that the
copious amount of blood from Mr. Crawford could
have simply masked the presence of other blood?"

She nodded. "Yes, but . . ." She hesitated, as if
she would add more, then merely said, "Yes, it's
possible."

Pritchard, Kate thought gloomily, was thoroughly
undermining Foster.

"Ms. Mead," Pritchard said, "would you repeat
your contention about the meaning of the highest
drop of blood spatter being thirty-seven inches from
the floor?"

"My conclusion, from the height of the spatter
and the bloodiness of the scene, is that these two
people had to be on the floor during the entire
altercation."

"Isn't it possible that there could have been a
fight above the floor that did not involve blood being
spattered on the wall?"

"Not much of a fight," Mead said.

"Just answer the question please. Was it possible,
yes or no?"

"Yes."

"You found hair marks on the wall. Did you find actual hair you could identify as that of Mr. Crawford?"

"No sir, we found no individual hairs. But the decedent's —"

"Isn't it true that the hair marks could also have been those of Mr. Jensen?"

"Well, only if —"

"Yes or no."

"Mr. Pritchard," said Judge Hawkins, "allow this expert witness to answer your questions."

"Yes," Charlotte Mead answered simply. Judge Hawkins smiled.

Kenneth Pritchard also smiled. "No further questions."

Kate stared at Linda Foster, anxious to see how she would reconstruct what Pritchard had damaged.

Foster, seated at the counsel table, rose but did not approach the witness stand. "Ms. Mead, was there blood in any other area of the crime scene other than what you've testified to?"

"No, there was not."

"The victim's shirt, was it uniformly soaked in the victim's blood?"

"No. Not uniformly. There was much less blood on the front. There wasn't a trace of white left, but some of the upper body areas were pink instead of crimson."

"Did you test the front as well as the back of the shirt?"

"I tested all areas on the shirt."

"Did you find any blood from the defendant?"

"Of all places I sampled on the shirt, I found no blood from the defendant."

"There was no blood on the front of the shirt from the defendant, is that correct?"

"Correct."

"About the hair marks on the wall — can you draw the conclusion to a scientific certainty that they are solely those of the victim?"

"Yes."

"On what basis?"

"Three. reasons. The decedent's hair was soaked in blood. The marks extended no more than four inches above the floor. And the defendant's T-shirt had only traces of blood on the back, meaning that if the defendant put those hair marks on the wall, he'd have had to do it bending over while he was on his knees."

Linda Foster smiled, as did Kate. "Ms. Mcad," Foster said. "In your expert opinion, where was the victim during the fatal assault on him?"

"On the floor. From all those marks on the floor and on the wall, and all that blood, he fought for his life on the floor, he never got off the floor."

"No further questions," Linda Foster said.

"Mr. Pritchard?" Judge Hawkins said.

"I have nothing further, your honor."

Linda Foster said, "The People call Stacey Conlin."

The courtroom stirred with interest. Judge Hawkins picked up her half-glasses to scrutinize a thin young blonde in black tights and black mini-skirt, pink tank top and black leather Eisenhower jacket, who teetered to the stand on spike heels that were, Kate estimated, at least five inches high.

Kenneth Pritchard rose to his feet. "Objection, your honor. This individual is not on the witness list."

"Your honor," Linda Foster said, "the importance of this witness did not come to light until after the trial began."

Judge Hawkins nodded. "Very well. You may proceed."

Pritchard sat back down and folded his arms, confident, Kate supposed, that this witness's appearance would by itself damage her credibility.

Stacey Conlin had been mentioned — although not by name — by Kyle Jensen in his recounting of how he had arrived at Tradition on the night of Teddie Crawford's death. But Kate, hard-pressed to complete work on the case without Taylor's involvement, had assigned low priority to interviewing her, never dreaming that Conlin's recollection of that night would result in incriminating evidence.

Conlin took the oath and stated her name. Linda Foster asked, "What is your occupation, Ms. Conlin?"

Conlin pulled a lock of hair back from her face and leaned toward the microphone, gazing uncertainly, shyly, at the jury box. "I'm . . . like, a clerk."

Foster nodded encouragement. "And where do you do this work?"

The voice was soft, but clear. "At the 7-Eleven on the corner of Third and Sweetzer."

"On February fourth of this year, what shift were you working?"

"Graveyard."

Judge Hawkins chose to ignore a few titters in the courtroom. Linda Foster asked, "Is that eleven to seven?"

"Yeah."

"Do you see anyone in this courtroom who came into the store during your shift?"

"Yeah. Him." She pointed a pink, inch-long fingernail at Kyle Jensen. "He came in with Teddie. Teddie Crawford."

"Let the record show that the witness has pointed out the defendant," Foster said. "What time was this, Ms. Conlin?"

"Five after two."

"How do you know the time?"

"Teddie said my watch was really neat. So, like, I looked at it. How you do when somebody says that."

Kate grinned as Conlin pushed up the sleeve of her leather jacket to reveal a red plastic wrist watch with a face only slightly smaller than a saucer.

Foster was also smiling. "Did you know Teddie Crawford well?"

"Yeah, he came in all the time."

"On the night in question, did Teddie say anything else to you?"

"Yeah. He was buying cigarettes for this dude —"

"You mean the defendant?"

"Yeah."

"Teddie bought the cigarettes?"

"Yeah."

"You're positive of this?"

"Yeah, he gave me a fifty-dollar bill and I kidded

him about it." Again the pink fingernail pointed. "He was showing off for this dude."

"Objection!" Pritchard said vehemently. "Speculation, move to strike."

"Sustained. Strike that last remark," Judge Hawkins instructed the court reporter. "The jury will disregard."

Foster said, "Tell us what happened — what was said between you and Teddie, as best you remember it."

"Okay. Like, he came in with the dude —"

"Objection," Pritchard complained. "Objection to the witness's characterization of my client."

"Ms. Conlin," Judge Hawkins said softly, "you might refer to Mr. Jensen by name or as the defendant."

Stacey Conlin held up both pink-fingernailed hands. "Like, I call all the guys dude, no offense. Anyway, they came in and Jensen says he wants Kent Lights and Teddie plunks down a fifty. So I wink at Teddie and say somebody musta died and left you this big bill. He winks back and says no, he's givin me a test how good I make change. And so I give him the change and he just stuffs it in his wallet without even lookin at it and then he says he likes my watch. So I look at my watch and say that's a real compliment comin from a queen like you. So he laughs and the two of them leave, that's it."

"A queen," Linda Foster said slowly, deliberately. "You called Teddie a queen?"

"Yeah."

"What did you mean by that?"

She fidgeted in the chair. "Like, you know, a queeny gay guy. A gay guy with . . . attitude. You walk the walk, you talk the talk. You know, a *queen.*"

Amid titters in the courtroom Foster said, "And he laughed, you said."

"Yeah."

"You felt okay calling Teddie a queen?"

"Well sure," she said. "He called his own self a queen, he was fine about being gay."

"And the defendant," Foster said. "Where was the defendant while this conversation was taking place with Teddie?"

"Right there. Right beside him."

"The entire time?"

"Yeah. The whole time."

"Thank you, Ms. Conlin. No further questions."

Kenneth Pritchard did not rise from the counsel table. "Ms. . . . Conlin," he said as if skeptical that it was her real name. "You said Mr. Jensen asked for cigarettes and Mr. Crawford plunked down a fifty. Did Mr. Jensen have an opportunity to pay for the cigarettes?"

"He didn't even try."

"Your honor," Pritchard said sharply. "Please direct the witness to answer the question."

"Answer the question yes or no to the best of your ability, Ms. Conlin."

"Uh, no."

Pritchard asked, "Did you exchange any conversation with Mr. Jensen?"

"He asked for the Kents, that's all."

"While you were exchanging witty conversation with Mr. Crawford, what was my client doing?"

Stacey Conlin drew back her shoulders, her tiny breasts outlined in the tank top. "What do you mean, what was he doing? He was standing there."

"Was he looking around at the store, looking at you, what was he doing?"

"I told you, he was standing there the whole time I was talking to Teddie."

"He added nothing to your conversation?"

"Didn't say diddley."

"Then how do you know he was listening to what you said?"

"Cause he was *standing* there."

"Can you say with absolute *certainty* that he was paying attention?" His voice rose. "That he was even *listening?*"

"I told you what went down," she said with dignity. "And that's all I got to say."

"No further questions," Pritchard said.

"I have nothing further," Linda Foster said.

"The witness may step down," Judge Hawkins said, and favored Stacey Conlin with a smile. The jury, Kate saw, had also liked this witness.

Judge Hawkins adjourned for the day.

— 14 —

"Kate, come on in." Lieutenant Mike Bodwin beckoned energetic welcome from behind his desk, gesturing her to a chair.

Closing his door, Kate took a seat across from him amid the comfortable clutter of a room pleasantly redolent of pipe tobacco. Windowless to the outside world as were all the cubicles in the Detectives Squad Room, the lieutenant's office was paneled in dark wood, but well-lighted, the walls brightened by LAPD award plaques and commendations. Papers, file folders and notebooks lay in haphazard stacks on his desk and credenza, along with family photos and an array of golfing trophies.

Bodwin leaned toward her, his broad shoulders hunched inside his suit jacket. "You look tired, Kate."

"I am," she admitted.

On this late afternoon of day four of the trial her gray jacket and pants felt as grimy as their color. And she still had a meeting with Linda Foster before this day would end. Shifting her hips on the hard plastic chair, resenting more than usual the polite small talk necessary before she could state her business, she said, "Every time I take a homicide case to court, I wish I knew a better way to prepare and stay on top of the mountain of detail."

Rubbing two fingers across a jaw lightly pitted with acne scars, he looked at her with narrowed dark eyes. "Yeah, and this is a rough case, Kate."

"No problems in being ready, though," she assured him, uncomfortable under his scrutiny. How much did he suspect of the conflict between her and Taylor? She didn't know Mike Bodwin very well, but she did not mind this craggy-faced, slightly portentous officer, one of many officers she had worked under in her police career. In his first year at Wilshire Division he had dispensed a minimum of supervision; whether this was due to his own uncertainties as a supervisor or a reasoned decision to allow her performance to speak for itself, she did not know, and had not cared about knowing, until now.

She said, "We're well prepared for court, Lieutenant. But my work on this case wasn't as timely as it should have been." She sat up in her chair, anger again rising with the memory of Stacey Conlin's testimony. That a key witness had to be inserted into a trial at virtually the last minute might make for good television drama, but it was damned poor police work.

Bodwin said drily, "Carrying this case by yourself might have something to do with it."

She looked at him. "Ed's talked to you, then."

He shook his head. "The case file talked — all those reports with just your signature. And I'm not quite as dumb as I look." He took his cold pipe from the ashtray, knocked out the ash, set it back down. "You run your own show, no problem, you and Ed are pros." He picked up a gold Cross pen. "Then you work a major case by yourself, you formally request an appointment for the first time since I've been in the department, you come in and close my door." He grinned. "Looks like serious shit to me."

Disarmed by his grin, she smiled back. "I've always appreciated your confidence in me, Lieutenant. And you're right — the reason I'm here is the Teddie Crawford case." She continued soberly, "Going solo on a major death investigation is something I don't want to do again, there's too much risk of error. But any death investigation Ed Taylor and I handle could turn out to be another Teddie Crawford case."

"Listen Kate, it's tough." He continued carefully, "These are changing times, it's tough as hell keeping up with all the shit we have to do to please everybody. But I damn well expect anybody who wears a badge to do their job the best way they know how. If somebody has trouble with that, I need to know it. But I can't solve any problem unless I'm clear on what it is. What are you telling me about you and Ed?"

She released a breath. "Only that I request another partner."

Bodwin's face did not change. He tapped his pen on his blotter. "Want to tell me about it?"

"No, sir."

Lacing his pen through his fingers, he was silent. It occurred to Kate that Bodwin had chosen not to smoke his pipe in her presence. She was irritated by the absurdity of it, and that she could not very well tell him to go ahead and smoke in his own office.

He said, "You and Ed, seven good years. What would it take to patch this up?"

"At this point," Kate ventured, "a new partner would probably be good for us both."

He grinned faintly. "A new partner for Ed would mean he'd have to work."

She did not respond, unsure whether he was joking or probing.

"Like I said, Kate, I'm not as dumb as I look. I know how much water he rows. We both know Ed's got his twenty years in, he can pull the pin any time. We put him with another partner . . ."

He sighed. "He's a fixture in this office. And you're the best homicide cop I've got. I've often been tempted — but, well, you and Ed have worked so well together, nobody really wants to disturb a good thing."

He put the pen down and steepled his fingers. "You really want to do this, Kate?"

She said firmly, "I have to."

He sighed again. "Well, right now I want you to focus on this case, finish it up. When do you testify?"

"Tomorrow morning."

He consulted his calendar. "I'll sit in." Looking at her, he frowned. "Some problem with that?"

"No sir," she said.

"How's the case look?"

She managed a smile. "You know how these things are — the homicide could be on film and still be touch and go with a jury. But we've got an excellent prosecutor." She got to her feet. She had to see that prosecutor now — one final difficulty on this difficult day.

Bodwin said, "I'll get back to you, Kate. But I want you to think on this some more."

"Yes, sir," she said.

Leaving his office, looking around the familiar, crowded confines of the Detectives Squad Room, she felt a sense of disorientation, of displacement. Her police career had moved into uncharted waters.

Linda Foster, her suit jacket tossed over a file cabinet, sat at her desk immersed in a legal brief, the sleeves of her white silk blouse pushed up above the elbows. Casting a glance at Kate, she jerked her head at the Farberware coffee pot. "Be useful, get us some coffee." Focused again on her reading, she groped for her coffee mug and handed it to Kate.

Kate did as she was instructed and then sat

across from Foster. Foster finally put down the brief, took off her glasses and tossed them on top of it, massaged her temples. "God, am I pooped."

"Tell me about it," Kate said.

Foster grinned, animation lighting the gray-green eyes. "But it's going okay. Considering the meat of the case is still to come."

"Yes. We'll know a lot more when we see Jensen on the stand."

"Him, yeah." Foster waved a hand. "I was thinking about your testimony."

Kate took a deep breath. "I need to talk to you about that. Beyond just going over the questions you'll ask on the stand."

"Sure." Cradling her coffee mug in both hands, Foster looked at her inquiringly.

"You don't want any surprises. So thore's something I need to tell you."

Foster started to say something. Looking into Kate's face, she nodded instead, holding her mug very still.

Kate said, "Remember I told you I knew Kenneth Pritchard from before? I never did know him all that well. But a woman I . . . lived with knew him very well. She died six years ago." Her gaze fixed on Linda Foster, she said evenly, "Pritchard knows the personal circumstances of my life with her."

Foster looked down, turning her mug in her hands, looking into its contents. "Okay. Am I stupid? I don't get how that's connected with your testimony tomorrow."

Kate said quietly, "I believe he'll try to bring out

my private life when I'm on the stand. To make the
point to the jury that I'm prejudiced in my
investigation of the death of a gay man."

Foster closed her eyes. "Fuck." Again she looked
into her coffee mug. "Yeah. He seems enough of a
slime to do that. And it shouldn't fly a foot.
But . . ."

"But it might," Kate finished for her.

"No, I really don't think it'll fly. It shouldn't get
past the objection stage. But the jury will hear the
question. And that's all Pritchard really wants."

"My lieutenant will be in court tomorrow."

"Double fuck." Foster put down her mug. "Kate, I
can't prevent Pritchard from asking the question."

"I know that. You're certain Judge Hawkins will
disallow it?"

"Reasonably certain. She *should* disallow it. But I
can't guarantee it."

"If she does allow it —"

"Say no more." Foster held up a hand. "I
appreciate your telling me. If lightning strikes a part
of Hawkins' brain, and she overrules my objection, I
don't need to know how you'll answer Pritchard."

Kate nodded.

"I have to tell you this, Kate. The way I read it,
the way I read him, he may hold off, not ask the
question on cross-examination. He may really set it
up — not cross-examine you at all, but reserve his
right to question you later, and then call you as a
defense witness."

Kate sat perfectly still. "Triple fuck," she said.

Linda Foster chuckled. After a moment, Kate
joined her. Their laughter filled the office, reaching
frenzied heights.

"This case," Foster gasped, wiping her eyes. "This case is a wonder. I'll tell you one crazy thing, Kate. I found out I can really get into doing what I do."

"I'll tell you one thing, Linda — you're very good at it."

Foster's eyes, still wet from laughter, met Kate's. "Thanks. That means a lot to me."

There was a sudden, awkward silence. Acutely mindful that what she had revealed lay between them, Kate felt excruciatingly self-conscious. She had never before admitted her sexual identity to a heterosexual person.

"I . . ." Foster cleared her throat, tapped a finger on her desk calendar. "This time of year's always been tough for me. April thirtieth, my daughter would have been ten."

"I'm so sorry," Kate said, taken aback. "What . . ."

"Angie was the brightest two-year-old you can imagine. She managed to get into the garage, found some turpentine."

"Oh my God, Linda," Kate uttered.

"Jack and I were real careful about the blame. But they say most marriages don't survive the death of a child. Ours sure didn't. I won't ever get married again, I know I can't replace Angie. But I'm glad to have the partner I'm with, I'm glad to have my seven-year-old — David's real special to me."

"I'm sure he is." Numbly, Kate searched for something else to say, piercingly aware of what had occurred between herself and this woman she had just come out to, this woman who had in turn disclosed the most painful moment in her life as payment in kind.

"Okay, enough of this having fun," Foster said briskly. "Let me get you some more coffee, let's get to work." Reaching for Kate's mug, she said, "I'll tell you something, my friend. There's one fact Pritchard can't do a thing about. His son of a bitch client is *guilty*. And I'm gonna put him in jail if it kills me. I'm gonna put him in jail till his ass mildews."

— 15—

"The People call Detective Kate Delafield."

Kate took the oath from the court clerk, and settled herself in the witness chair behind the microphone. She had chosen carefully her gray and white houndstooth jacket, gray pants, white turtleneck blouse — conservative clothes, not too sober but appropriate to the gravity of the proceedings, quality clothing that looked good on her and was so simply styled that she would not have to think about adjusting it.

Turning slightly toward the jury, she

concentrated on keeping her posture erect but not stiff. In the arena that was this courtroom, every aspect of her would be magnified and scrutinized, tallied and judged irrevocably. Her competence, and most of all, her credibility, would be assessed each time she spoke: what she said, how she said it, how she looked when she said it. All her months of work on this homicide case would be distilled into the next few intense hours of testimony as she recounted all her actions in the process that had led to the arrest and prosecution of Kyle Jensen.

Lieutenant Bodwin was not as yet present; Kate expected him perhaps mid-morning after she had finished the more routine phase of her testimony. From an angle of vision she could see Kyle Jensen, arms crossed, staring at her; Kenneth Pritchard, neatly attired in a dark blue suit, was doodling with the pen he would use to take notes for his cross-examination.

His cross-examination. She would not think about Kenneth Pritchard and what he would ask. There was no point. From the moment she had walked into that scene of murder at Tradition, events had been set into motion that seemed, at this moment, inexorable.

Do the best you can for Teddie Crawford, she told herself. You're all he has.

You're all he has. She would use it as a mantra.

Linda Foster, smartly turned out in a long maroon jacket over a black skirt, approached Kate with barely subdued eagerness. She loves this, Kate thought. The clash, the contest, the risk. This woman was born to be a high stakes player.

Foster addressed Kate firmly: "Would you please

state your name and rank, where you work and how long you have worked there."

And so it began.

As Linda Foster paused to leaf back in her pages of notes, juror number four put her face down into her PARIS sweater. Her face had been in her chest during Kate's first two hours on the stand, while Kate had testified to each item of evidence she had collected and why, where she had collected it, when she had conveyed it to the crime lab, its property tag number and item number, and the corresponding crime lab number. But juror number four had focused on Kate during the recounting of Jensen's statements, her eyes squinting in concentration behind her glasses, a forefinger absently combing the ends of her straight blonde hair. And the three note-taking jurors had been constantly busy, especially juror number eight, the older woman who remained Kate's choice as probable jury foreperson.

"Detective Delafield," Foster said, finding the note she sought. "In his statement at the hospital and at Wilshire Division about how he cut his hands, the defendant said that he cut them on a ham can in the rear of his apartment building, is that correct?"

"Yes, that's what he told me," Kate said.

"We have offered in evidence the photographs of the search area for that ham can. A can which was never found, is that correct?"

"That's right."

"Nor did you find any blood whatsoever at the rear of the defendant's residence."

"No I did not."

"So the defendant was lying. In his statement about what he stole from the victim's body, the defendant said that he had, and I quote, 'Tossed it. An alley. Don't ask me where. I just tossed it.' Is that correct?"

"That's correct." Foster, Kate thought, was bringing to a skillful and effective conclusion all these hours of testimony . . .

"So the defendant was lying. When you asked the defendant whether he had ever been in a bar named Malone's, or knew the bartender, he denied it — is that correct?"

"Yes, that's correct."

"So the defendant was lying. In the defendant's statement about his whereabouts on the night of the murder, he stated he was with Shirley Johnson. Is that correct?"

"That's correct."

"So the defendant was lying. In the defendant's statement about who helped him remove his blood-soaked clothing, he claimed it was Shirley Johnson when it was actually Burt Dayton. Is that correct?"

"That's correct."

"So the defendant was lying. This defendant lied again and again. All this defendant did was lie —"

"Objection!" Kenneth Pritchard barked.

"Sustained," Judge Hawkins said.

Foster looked into Kate's face. She gave Kate an almost imperceptible grin. A thumbs-up sign of encouragement, Kate knew.

"I have no further questions. Thank you, Detective." Foster strode back to the counsel table.

Kenneth Pritchard rose in leisurely fashion, left his note pad on the counsel table, and approached the witness stand, hands in his pockets. Kate tensed, remembered her body language, and leaned back.

"Detective Delafield." Her name, spoken softly, seemed almost musical in the courtroom.

Kate held his gaze with difficulty, chilled by his easy assurance. She kept her own face expressionless.

"Detective Delafield, when you entered the crime scene on the morning of February fourth, did you see signs of disturbance anywhere except in the kitchen?"

"No, I did not," she said, extending her answer beyond a simple "no" to show her firmness of tone to Pritchard and to the jury.

"Did you see blood anywhere except in the kitchen?"

"No."

"Now, you have enumerated objects collected in evidence which you contend my client took from the defendant — a watch, a ring, and a wallet, is that correct?"

"Correct."

"There was money in Mr. Crawford's wallet when you collected it in evidence, in the amount of sixty-seven dollars. Is that correct?"

"That's correct."

"Money which had not been taken out of the wallet by my client. Correct?"

"Yes."

"Is there a cash register in the dining room of Tradition?"

"Yes."

"Was that cash register disturbed in any way?"

"No, it was not."

"Was the cash drawer open?"

"No."

"Was there blood anywhere on the cash register?"

"No."

"Detective, isn't it true that there was, in fact, money in that cash register?"

"Yes, there was."

"Thank you, Detective," he said softly. Again he smiled at her. "No further questions."

Sagging in relief, the tension emptying out of her, she flashed a glance at Linda Foster. Foster, her lips thinned, her nostrils flared, was glaring at Pritchard as he walked back to the counsel table.

What was Pritchard doing? Why had he not asked her the question she knew he would ask? Why had he not even reserved his right to recall her as a witness? And beyond that, how to explain the sum total of his cross-examination, after her four hours of testimony?

"Redirect?" Judge Hawkins inquired of Linda Foster. If the judge was surprised by Pritchard's conduct, her smooth dark face did not reveal it.

"Yes, your honor." Her face composed, Foster rose to her feet at the counsel table. "Detective, you have just testified that no money was taken from the victim's wallet or from the cash register."

"That's correct," Kate said obediently.

"Wouldn't the condition of the defendant's hands make it imposs —"

"Objection!" shouted Kenneth Pritchard. "Speculation."

"Sustained," Judge Hawkins said impassively. "The jury will disregard the question."

"No further questions," Linda Foster said.

"Do you have anything further of this witness, Mr. Pritchard?" Judge Hawkins asked.

"No, your honor."

"The witness may step down." She looked inquiringly at Linda Foster.

"Your honor," Foster said, "the State rests."

Judge Hawkins nodded, then glanced at the courtroom clock. "Court is in recess until two o'clock."

Only then did Kate think to look out beyond the courtroom railing. To meet the warm, smiling gaze of Aimee. Surprised, nonplussed, Kate managed a grin.

Seated in the back row of the courtroom, Aimee touched her index finger to her lips and blew a surreptitious kiss, then got to her feet and made her unobtrusive way from the courtroom. Kate mentally shook herself, realizing that her tension had been so great, her focus on her testimony so intense, that she had not seen Aimee come in, nor Lieutenant Bodwin, who sat in the front row staring in bafflement at Kenneth Pritchard.

Kate pulled herself to her feet and left the witness stand, passing the counsel table without looking at Kenneth Pritchard or Kyle Jensen.

"Fine job," Bodwin greeted her in the outer court. He jerked his head at Pritchard, who was taking a document from his briefcase. "The look on your face when he said no more questions —" He chuckled. "That's the strangest, most piss-poor cross-examination I've ever seen."

She shrugged. "I have to believe he's got something else up his sleeve."

"Maybe so," Bodwin said indifferently. "Kate, if you haven't changed your mind, I'll be talking to Ed. About our conversation yesterday," he added as Linda Foster came through the railing gate and over to them.

"Go ahead," she told him. "Lieutenant, may I present Linda Foster. Linda, Lieutenant Bodwin."

"Fine job, counselor," he said, nodding to her. "You've got this one in the bag."

"Not hardly, Lieutenant," she answered, her face closed and hard. "But your detective here did an outstanding job."

"We both agree on that." He shook Foster's hand and took his leave.

Kate said in a low tone, "What the hell's Pritchard doing?"

"Fucking theatrics," Foster hissed. "He'll —" She broke off as Pritchard opened the railing gate and came up to them.

"Kate," he said, "I thought I'd serve this on you personally." Smiling, he handed her the document he had taken from his briefcase, and sauntered off.

She looked down at a formal subpoena to appear as a witness for the defense.

"Playing it to the max," Linda Foster snorted. "The slimy little prick."

— 16 —

Ferris Sweency had been relaxed in the witness box ever since Linda Foster had risen to state courteously that the People would not challenge Kenneth Pritchard's qualification of him as an expert witness in the area of drug and alcohol abuse.

A fiftyish man with thin gray hair combed straight back and a sparse gray moustache, he wore a tweed sport jacket with patches at the elbows. He had been answering Kenneth Pritchard's questions with calm authority.

"So, Mr. Sweeney," Pritchard said, leaning on the

witness stand, "what you've told us here today is that in your years of work with victims of drug abuse, you have determined definite behavior patterns common to users of cocaine."

"Yes, that's right."

"And that cocaine intoxication can result in impairment of judgment."

"Very definitely."

"In *severe* impairment of judgment."

"Indeed," Sweeny said regretfully. "Depending on the amount ingested and the pattern of abuse."

"Can cocaine ingestion result in loss of emotional control?"

"Yes."

"Can it result in uncontrollable behavior?"

"Yes."

"In violent behavior?"

"Yes."

"In homicidal behavior?"

"Yes."

"Thank you," Pritchard said. "No further questions."

Linda Foster rose and moved to the witness stand. "Mr. Sweeney," she said politely, "about cocaine, amounts of cocaine, impairment from cocaine, and all the statements you've made today about this substance. On what controlled scientific laboratory tests do you base your statements?"

He looked disappointed in her. "My observations are empirical of course," he replied. "Based on years of experience in working with alcohol and drug abusers."

Foster looked astonished. "You have no laboratory

source material on which to base any of your claims?"

Sweeney bristled. "In the current political climate in this country, the lack of funded laboratory studies of drugs and drug users is a fact. And a disgrace."

"Mr. Sweeney," Foster said, "have you yourself ever taken or experimented with a controlled substance?"

"No. No, I never have."

"Then your statements are based entirely on your experience in drug abuse programs with chronic drug abusers, is that correct?"

"Yes, that's right."

Foster pointed to the jury and said in an incredulous tone, "So you have come here today to appear before this jury and claim knowledge based not on scientific evidence, but on statements made to you by dope addicts."

Ferris looked even more disappointed in her. "That is a gross —"

She turned to Judge Hawkins and said disdainfully, "I have no further questions of this witness."

Kate, grinning in delight, watched juror number four cross her arms over her PARIS sweater and look scornfully at Ferris Sweeney.

Judge Hawkins impassively asked, "Redirect, Mr. Pritchard?"

Pritchard looked unperturbed. "I have nothing further."

"The witness may step down."

"Your honor, let's get right down to it," Pritchard said. "The defense calls Kyle Jensen."

* * * * *

Kate remembered Taylor's summation of Kyle Jensen's chances at trial: "He could even get off. A jury's looking at this red-blooded normal guy, they'll figure he freaked out and just lost it, that's all."

Jensen's moustache had been freshly trimmed, his blond hair barbered; for his appearance on the stand he had donned a maroon V-neck sweater, navy blue pants and a white shirt with a blue tie. Red, white and blue, American as apple pie, Kate reflected sardonically, watching the faces of the jury and their agreeable evaluation of him. Just your normal blue-eyed, clean-cut, good-looking American boy.

Pritchard, one hand clasping a notebook, the other in his jacket pocket, approached the witness stand, casually elegant in his dark blue suit. He asked without ceremony, "How old are you, Kyle?"

"Twenty-seven."

"What do you do for a living?"

"Before all this went down," he said steadily, "I worked for Green Haven Landscapers."

"And where are you from?"

"Pittsburgh. Been out here about a year."

Jensen's high-pitched huskiness seemed to be playing well in the courtroom, Kate estimated. Masculinity was so often a matter of packaging . . . She remembered one night when she had awakened out of a doze to a high-pitched male voice emanating from the TV, to discover that the voice belonged to Clark Gable.

Pritchard said, "Your father is deceased, is that correct?"

"Yeah, that's right," Jensen said, his face immediately clouding.

An effective opening, Kate conceded. Exploiting the soft spot in Jensen about his father opened Jensen to the jury, won him immediate sympathy.

"He was a veteran of the Korean War, wasn't he?"

"A decorated vet," Jensen corrected him.

"Quite badly wounded, was he not?"

"Yeah, he got shot up pretty bad."

"Your mother is living?"

"Yeah, she can't be here, she's real sick."

Sure, Kate thought, remembering Jensen's contempt for his mother. Pritchard was doing a good job manufacturing all-American credentials for Jensen.

"Do you have brothers or sisters?"

"Objection, your honor," Linda Foster said curtly. "This episode of *The Waltons* is irrelevant."

Kenneth Pritchard spoke angrily into the laughter in the courtroom. "Your honor, this testimony is directly relevant to my client's background and character."

"Objection overruled," Judge Hawkins said disapprovingly to Foster. Kate was delighted by the grins on the faces of the jurors, by Foster's puncturing of the mood in the courtroom.

"Do you have brothers and sisters?" Pritchard repeated.

"No, sir."

"Kyle, I want to move now to the events of February fourth. You were at Malone's Bar on that Friday night." Pritchard waited.

"Yes, sir."

"What were you doing there?"

"Drinking beer. I just stopped in."

"Describe for us your meeting with Mr. Crawford."

Jensen shifted in the witness chair. He already needs a cigarette, Kate thought.

"I'm at the bar drinking my beer. He comes in with this woman and another guy —"

"Why did you notice him?"

"I'm sitting with my back turned to the bar, kind of eyeballing the place and whoever came in the door. Next thing I know he's at the bar getting some beers . . ."

Seated in her usual place in the courtroom, notebook in her lap, Kate listened acutely to the recounting of Jensen's meeting and conversation with Teddie Crawford. She would add her own nuances to Linda's notes of discrepancies between what Jensen had said in Kate's interviews with him and what he was saying now with quiet earnestness to the jury. She remembered how convincing he had been in his hospital room, until she had begun dissecting the truth.

"How many beers did you have at Malone's?"

"Four."

"Who paid for your drinks?"

"Me. I did."

"All right. Now, did you go anywhere in the bar itself with Mr. Crawford?"

"Yeah, the john. The restroom."

"For what purpose?"

"To do some coke."

"Who supplied the coke?"

"We both had some."

Kate made a note and circled it. Jensen had previously claimed that all the cocaine had been supplied by Teddie Crawford.

"How many lines of cocaine did you ingest?"

"Two."

"When you went to the restaurant, how many lines of cocaine did you ingest at the restaurant?"

"Four."

"Whose cocaine?"

"Some his, some mine."

"Kyle, why did you tell the police it was all Mr. Crawford's cocaine?"

"Because I was in deep sh . . . I was in deep enough without getting busted for possession or dealing or God knows what."

"All right. So you're at Tradition. Describe what happened."

"I did the coke, I'm really sailing. He shows me around his restaurant. Then . . ."

Jensen clasped his hands together on the railing of the witness box. He really wants a cigarette bad, Kate speculated.

"Then what happened, Kyle?"

He flicked a quick glance at the jury. "He groped me."

Pritchard moved to stand directly in front of Jensen. "Describe what he did, Kyle," Pritchard said gently, persuasively, like a priest in a confessional eliciting details of a sin.

"Ran his hand across my chest. I stepped away. "Then —"

"How did you feel about that?" Pritchard interrupted. "When he did that?"

"Like I was shot in the back. No damn way did I expect that."

"Up to this point, Kyle, did you have any inkling that Mr. Crawford was a homosexual?"

"Not a clue."

At a high-pitched comment of "Oh Mary, please," and several other snorts of derision in the courtroom — Kate recognized Gloria Gomez's voice — Judge Hawkins rapped her gavel sharply.

Unruffled, Pritchard said, "There was testimony from a 7-Eleven clerk about conversation between her and Mr. Crawford. What do you remember about that?"

Jensen said forcefully, "I went in the place to get cigarettes. He went in with me, paid before I could get my money out." He said more heatedly, "I remember he talked to this brassy-looking clerk, I didn't pay attention, what did I care what he had to say to some clerk?"

"All right. At the restaurant, he showed you around the place. Then what did he do?"

Jensen fixed his gaze on Pritchard. He cleared his throat. "Skimmed his hand down over my crotch. Said I . . . said he liked the look of my basket."

"Meaning what?"

"Meaning . . . he liked . . . what he saw between my legs."

"How did you feel about this comment about your genitals?"

Jensen's voice rose. "Freaked, totally freaked. I told him right away I'm not gay. I mean, I was freaked."

"When you told him you weren't gay, what did he say to that?"

"He just laughed. He says maybe I need to do more coke."

Kate listened in chilled triumph to this new information, a scenario similar to what she had envisioned the night she had gone alone to Tradition to reconstruct the murder.

Pritchard said, "How did you feel about his remarks?"

Jensen shifted his shoulders, adjusted the tie in the V of his sweater. "Freaked. Totally freaked he said that." The diamond-shaped eyes narrowed, glittered. "Totally freaked he thought coke could make me into somebody like him. Like for even a *second* I could be *anything* like *him*."

"Okay, Kyle. What did you do?"

He clasped the railing of the witness box. "I'm cool. I tell him again I'm not gay. So he laughs and says okay, have it any way I want, come on in the kitchen. So I go in there with him."

"Why? Why did you do what he said?"

"The front door's locked, the kitchen's the way outta there. Besides, my leather jacket's in there."

"Okay, take this one step at a time. So you go into the kitchen. Did you try to leave?"

"Yeah. Yeah, and he gropes me again, he says . . ." He hesitated, flicked his eyes toward the jury, back to Pritchard. "He says I don't have to do anything to him, just let him suck my cock."

Pritchard took several moments to look into his notebook, allowing the words to hang in the courtroom. Kate scanned the solemn faces of the jury, then made a note that Jensen had omitted the coke he had previously mentioned ingesting in the kitchen.

Pritchard asked quietly, "How did you feel when he suggested that sex act, Kyle?"

"I could of vomited on him."

Kate noted that in the interview Jensen had made the identical comment, but in relation to seeing Teddie Crawford with the knife, not in reaction to anything Teddie had said.

"What did you say to him, Kyle?"

"I pick up my jacket, tell him I'm getting the hell out of there."

"Then what?"

"He yanks a big knife out of a rack, holds it up. I say 'Easy, easy.' I figure he's doing it because I'm bigger than he is, it's the only way this fai — this guy's got of making me stay."

A very key ad lib onto his confession, Kate thought, circling her note.

"What did he say to you then, Kyle?" Pritchard asked.

"He says he wants to do me, that's all, and I'll really like it."

Kate flashed a glance over the jury, the twelve as immobile as statues, the six men especially stone-faced. Even one vote for acquittal could result in a hung jury . . .

Pritchard asked Jensen, "What did you say?"

"Nothing. I turn to lay down my jacket, figuring I can get him to relax a little so I can take the knife away. Then I make a quick grab for his wrist." Jensen snaked out his right hand in demonstration for the jury. "But he jerks the knife so I catch it in my hand. So then I go after the knife, I see I got to get it away from him right now or he'll really cut me. So I grab at it with my other hand —" Again

he demonstrated. "I knee him and we both go down
on the floor. He's still got the knife and he's fighting
like an animal, all of a sudden we're fighting like
crazy . . ."

Pritchard let silence accumulate. "Then what,
Kyle?"

Staring out over the courtroom, he shook his
head. "I dunno. I don't remember after that. I just
lost it, man. I just fu . . . I just plain lost it. I don't
remember after that."

"All right, Kyle. The *last* thing you remember is
you're fighting with him like crazy. What's the very
next thing you remember?"

"Him stopping. He finally stopped fighting me. I
see the blood all over the place, all over me, my
hands bleeding."

"Then what?"

"I freaked out. All I knew was I had to get the
hell out of there. I grabbed paper towels, they
soaked right through, I tried to wash up, saw how
bad I was cut. So I got some dish towels . . ." He
trailed off, looking uncertainly at Pritchard.

Pritchard repeated, "You freaked out."

"Yeah. Yeah, the coke, you know, I was smashed
as hell on the coke."

"Kyle." Pritchard lowered his voice. "Kyle, why
did you take Mr. Crawford's wallet and jewelry?"

"I was scared spitless, I knew I was in real bad
trouble, I figured nobody'd believe what happened,
I'd be in the gas chamber for sure. I thought about
my fingerprints, I started throwing everything I'd
put my hands on into a plastic bag. I took his stuff
thinking I could make it look like a robbery."

Kate thought: I may gag.

Pritchard asked, "If you were trying to make it look like robbery, why didn't you go through the cash register?"

"Never thought about it, I couldn't think straight —"

Pritchard repeated, "You couldn't think straight."

"Yeah. Yeah, the coke, I was smashed as hell on the coke."

The second time Pritchard had prompted him on the smashed-on-coke business, Kate thought.

"Then what, Kyle?"

"I got outta there. Wrapped my hands good as I could in towels and climbed on my bike and split."

"Why did you tell the detectives that Shirley Johnson had helped you out of your clothes?"

"Who wouldn't? The guy I got messed up with was a fa— was gay, I didn't want anybody on the cops getting the idea I was gay too. Especially when I share a place with a guy."

Pritchard nodded. "But Shirley Johnson did take you to the hospital."

"Yeah. I didn't want to go, she said all this stuff about infection, said my hands were cut too bad not to go."

"Why did you agree to go to Wilshire Division to be questioned?"

Jensen said angrily, "The woman cop lied to me. Said they had to do some kind of report because my cuts were so bad."

Kate barely smothered a grin.

"I believed her," Jensen said aggrievedly. "I didn't know shit about my rights. I figured I'd really get into hot sh— uh, water if I said no, they'd suspect something funny for sure. I really believed her, I

figured I'd just go and get it over with. I was
scared, I wasn't thinking too good."

"Were you taking medication for your hands?"

"Yeah."

"At the hospital when they first questioned you?"

"Yeah."

"At Wilshire Division?"

"Yeah. My head wasn't any too clear."

"Kyle, the fact is that on February fourth a man
died. How do you feel about that?"

"Terrible. I wish to God I could change what
happened." His face, his voice, were earnest. "I never
had a clue what happened that night could ever
happen." He focused his blue eyes on the jury. "I
just hope you believe me, I didn't mean for it to
happen."

You didn't mean to get caught, Kate thought,
looking at him in cold vituperation.

"No further questions," Kenneth Pritchard said.

Linda Foster rose.

Judge Hawkins glanced at the courtroom clock.
"In view of the hour, shall we commence
cross-examination tomorrow?"

Foster nodded. "That's quite acceptable, your
honor."

— 17 —

"So, Jensen's story — discrepancies up the kazoo." Linda Foster tapped her notebook as if it were a fat bank account. "Pritchard already knows cross-examination will be hell. And Jensen — when I'm through with that bastard he's gonna think he's a McDonald's hamburger."

Kate grinned. She sat relaxed, drinking coffee, in Linda's office upstairs in the Criminal Courts Building.

Foster looked intently at her. "But Kate, I keep thinking about those cuts on Jensen's hands, about

you going to Tradition that night to feel what
happened, to know in your bones how it went down
with Teddie. So, I think it would help if I did what
you did."

She's talking confident, Kate thought, but she's
worried. She said, "Why don't we both go."

"Good," Foster said with alacrity. "Can we meet
around eleven? Is that okay?"

Kate said, "If you get there first, stay in your car
and wait."

Foster grinned at her. "Yes, Officer."

Kate let herself into her apartment.

Aimee came out of the kitchen and embraced her.
Stepping quickly back, she stuffed her hands in the
back pockets of her shorts and said with a touch of
diffidence, "I made spaghetti, I didn't know when
you'd be here."

"Smells wonderful." Shrugging out of her jacket,
Kate savored both the aroma in the apartment and
the sight of Aimee in white shorts and a tank top.
She took off her gun belt, laid it and the jacket
across a chair. "I need to meet Linda in a couple of
hours." She turned back to Aimee and said warmly,
"It was such a surprise to see you there today. It
was good."

"I'm glad." Then Aimee said in a rush, "I decided
this morning to call in sick and go see you but I
wanted to do that since this trial began, I wanted to
ask if it would be okay, you've been so preoccupied I
thought you might be upset if I said anything —"

"I can see that," Kate said contritely, pierced by

the defenselessness in Aimee's face. She had come to
understand that Aimee's assertive ways camouflaged
a precarious confidence. "I get completely involved in
a homicide trial." Much less this one, she thought.
She remembered Anne's good-humored exasperation
at her absences, physical and mental, when a case
was in trial.

Aimee said, "Today I thought I'd just look in the
courtroom and see this Linda Foster, see you on the
stand . . . But there was something about how you
looked — I just had to stay there, be there with
you."

Kate said simply, "I'm very glad you were."

"I was proud of you." Aimee placed her hands for
a moment on Kate's shoulders. "You're so good at
your work, the jury believed every word you said."

Kate captured her hands. "I hope you're right. I
don't know if I could've concentrated as much if I'd
known you were in the room. All I know is how
good it was to see you afterward."

"I'd like to think . . . you need me for
something."

"I do," Kate said in surprise. "I feel so very lucky
about you —"

"I want to be more than that to you. Mostly I
feel like . . . just some kid who sort of stumbled
into your life."

"You're much, much more." She spoke this truth
in wonder. Maggie had said, *The way you are with
this young woman — holding back — you're still
lonely.* Until now she had not been able to see how
desolate her lonely life raft of self-sufficiency had
been.

She squeezed Aimee's hands. "Tomorrow will be

. . . a very hard day for me." For now she could not tell her more. "Could you . . . maybe call in sick again?"

Aimee grinned. "I feel a relapse coming on." She moved toward the kitchen. "Come have dinner before you have to go see this other woman in your life."

Tradition was closed, its front door padlocked. Francisco Caldera had closed the restaurant permanently the day the trial began. Kate led Linda Foster from the alley into the kitchen and flipped the lights on to a room unchanged from her memory; yet she felt an indefinable, terminal alteration in its atmosphere. Like Teddie Crawford, Tradition, also, was gone. Tradition, also, had bled to death. She looked around with poignant regret, with mourning.

Foster placed her briefcase on the counter. Gesturing Kate to silence, she paced the kitchen, arms crossed over her cotton knit sweater, grimly looking at the pristine floor and walls. She walked into the restaurant; Kate knew not to follow. Instead she emptied her own briefcase, spreading photos and drawings across the table.

Several minutes later Foster came back into the kitchen, head down, hands shoved into the pockets of her black denim pants. Again she paced back and forth, the only sound an occasional squeak from her tennis shoes on the tile floor.

She finally muttered, "I'm goosebumps from this place, fucking goosebumps."

Kate picked up the photograph given to her by Gloria Gomez, an image of a dark-haired young man

in three-quarter profile, smiling, his brown eyes
lighted with eagerness. She had looked at this photo
many times, but now she said thickly, through a
throat filling with tears, "Teddie had so much life in
him, he had so much guts . . ."

"Especially compared to the shit who killed him."
Foster yanked open her briefcase and dumped out its
contents — documents, a notebook, a plywood model
of a knife — and said with fierce impatience, "So,
you're convinced Teddie never had the knife. Jensen's
cuts say different, his cuts are the defense's big
weapon. Let's brainstorm a scenario I can attack
with."

Kate pointed to a set of drawings, the emergency
room surgeon's sketches of the wounds in Jensen's
hands. "We'll start with Jensen's claim of how
Teddie was holding the knife, see if there's any
possible way his cuts could have happened that
way." She picked up the plywood knife. "Okay, I'll be
Teddie . . ."

Half an hour later, having traded roles, having
tried every variation on a knife fight she could think
of, Foster said in frustration, "Jensen's cuts make no
damn sense at all, Kate. Okay, granting there's some
way he could slice his thumb and the palm of each
hand — how could he get all those cuts on his
fingers at the same time from a single-edge blade?
How did he even *get* those little cuts? You grab a
knife that's coming at you with your hand, not your
fingers. And how in hell did he manage to get cut
on the *outside* edge of his right palm? Strong as he
is, how could he get so *many* cuts — and get his
thumb cut through to the bone before he kneed
Teddie and got him down and took the knife away?"

"I've been asking myself all those things for months," Kate said.

"Kate, this is a serious question. Do you think the wounds could be self-inflicted?"

"I've considered that. It would explain the cuts on the fingers. But why would he almost amputate his thumb? Why would he cut the outside edge of his palm?"

"Maybe he was too wiped out on cocaine to know how he cut himself."

"Do you believe that?"

"Not for a fucking minute." Foster tossed down the plywood knife and with a grimace picked up the crime lab photograph of the murder weapon. "Of all the photos," she said, "this is the hardest one to look at. For me."

"Me too," Kate said. "It's the dried blood from top to bottom. It . . ." She trailed off.

"Yeah," Foster said. "You can't help but see the slick, gory mess it was when Jensen was finished."

"Linda." Kate reached to Foster. "Give me that photo."

After a single confirming glance, Kate put the photo down, picked up the plywood knife, balanced it in both hands. "Now it all makes sense," she whispered, staring at the knife. "How he was cut. And why. The blood spatter on the wall. Oh God, Linda, I know what he did."

— 18 —

"Mr. Jensen," Linda Foster opened her cross-examination, "why were you in a place like Malone's?" Her tone was polite, curious.

He looked at her without expression. "I was having some beers."

"Yes, that we understand. But why were you drinking at a bar frequented by gay men?"

"Objection," Kenneth Pritchard said. "No foundation for such an assertion."

"Objection sustained," Judge Hawkins said.

Foster said, "Mr. Jensen, there must be dozens and dozens of bars between where you live and Malone's. What was the attraction of this particular bar?"

Kate, delighted by Foster's immediate aggressiveness, observed the slight rise of Jensen's chest as he bolstered himself to answer. He was well-turned out again today, in navy blue pants, a white shirt and gray tie under a gray vest sweater. "I found the place, that's all," he declared. "I made a delivery near there. I liked it. If fags — if gays hang out there I didn't know it."

"The bar is in West Hollywood, Mr. Jensen. That never gave you a clue about its possible clientele?"

Judge Hawkins gaveled down a ripple of amusement in the courtroom. Jensen answered with irritation, "I didn't know where it was. I could of cared less where it was."

"Mr. Jensen, would you say you had a good memory?" Foster's tone had become polite again.

"Well . . . yeah." He seemed disconcerted by this new direction of questioning. "Yeah I do," he added emphatically.

"Given that good memory, is it fair to say that you'd tend to remember things less well today than you did right after they happened?"

Jensen hesitated, searching for Foster's angle, inspecting the question for some moments. Kate looked at the jury. No one was taking notes; all twelve, including PARIS, were keenly watching the everything-at-stake battle forming into shape before them.

"Yeah," Jensen finally concluded, "I'd have to say that's fair."

"Is it fair to say there are even things you would remember right after they happened that you would no longer remember today?"

Again he reflected. "Maybe. Well, yeah, anybody'd have to forget a few things."

"So it is then fair to say that your memory is more clouded today than it was the day after Mr. Crawford's death?"

He looked at her with grim suspicion. "I dunno, maybe a little bit."

"But you do agree that you remembered things better immediately after his death than you would remember them today."

"Okay, I'd have to say that's fair."

"All right. I want to ask you some questions about the statement you gave to the police the very evening of the day Mr. Crawford died."

Gotcha, Kate thought. Foster had set him up.

"You testified yesterday that you did two lines of cocaine at Malone's. How much cocaine did Teddie Crawford do?"

He shrugged. "I didn't pay that much attention. I was doing my own thing."

"You testified yesterday that you had four lines of cocaine at Tradition. How much did Teddie Crawford do?"

"I didn't notice."

"How very odd, Mr. Jensen," Foster said. She moved unhurriedly to the counsel table and consulted a sheaf of papers, its individual pages tagged with colored paper clips. She picked up a page marked with an orange clip. "In the statement you gave to the police, you said Mr. Crawford had done two lines at Malone's and three lines at Tradition. You said he was really wasted."

"I don't know what I said. I was scared of the cops," he declared.

"And you're not scared right now?" Foster asked with only a trace of sarcasm.

He pointed to the jury. "I figure I got twelve people who'll be fair."

"I'm certain they will be. Mr. Jensen, you've been sitting in this courtroom listening to scientific testimony from the crime lab and the pathologist that blood and tissue samples from the victim's body showed only traces of alcohol and ingestion of no more than a line of cocaine. Could that have had something to do with the change in your testimony?"

He said combatively, "No, it's just like I said."

"Yesterday you twice testified that you were, quote, smashed as hell on coke, unquote." Adjusting her glasses, she picked up a page marked with a green clip. "In your statement to the police, you volunteered about Mr. Crawford's state of intoxication, quote, Yeah, he was really wasted, unquote. In reply to their question, quote, And you? Were you wasted? you replied, quote, Nah, I was high, that's all, unquote. What about that, Mr. Jensen?"

"Anything I said to the cops I said because I was scared."

"And you're not scared right now?"

Jensen fixed a wide, blue-eyed gaze on the jury. "I feel okay here."

Enlisting their aid, Kate thought. It might work on one of them — and all he needs is one.

Foster said, "Refresh my memory on a point, Mr. Jensen. When was it during your association with Mr. Crawford that you wanted to vomit all over him?"

Again Judge Hawkins gaveled down laughter in the courtroom. Kate grinned. Jensen answered testily, "When he groped me."

"I see." She selected a page with a yellow clip. "In your statement to the police you said it was when the victim picked up the knife. Yesterday you said it was when the victim proposed an act of fellatio. Today it's something else altogether."

"What difference does it make?" he snapped. "The whole thing made me want to vomit."

She picked up a page with a white clip. "According to your statement to the police, after the victim expressed sexual interest in you, you went back into the kitchen with the victim and did another line of cocaine. Did you, or did you not do that?"

Jensen cast a glance at his lawyer. But Pritchard's gaze, Kate noted, was fixated on Foster's sheaf of paper-clipped pages. "Yeah," Jensen said. "Okay, I did a line in the kitchen."

"So, appalled though you were by what Mr. Crawford had just proposed, you chose to do more cocaine rather than leave."

"Hey, it wasn't like that, there was a line left on the glass, that's all, it was my coke —" He broke off.

"Yes, it wouldn't do to waste cocaine, would it?"

"Objection," Pritchard complained. "The State is badgering the witness."

"Sustained," Judge Hawkins said. "Careful, Ms. Foster."

"Yes, your honor." Foster picked up a page with a blue clip. "In your statement to the police, you said that when Mr. Crawford was holding the knife you leaned over to pick up your jacket to distract him. Is that what you did?"

"No, it was like I said yesterday, I was putting *down* the jacket."

"I see. And yesterday when you described Mr. Crawford picking up the knife, you informed us, quote, I figure he's doing it because I'm bigger than he is, it's the only way he's got of making me stay. Unquote. It's the first time you've mentioned this assessment, Mr. Jensen. Why is that?"

"I finally added it up, that's all."

"Or did you realize how ludicrous it was to claim that a man as attractive as the victim would need to threaten someone at knife-point for sex?"

"Objection," Pritchard barked.

"Objection sustained."

Jensen said belligerently, "He'd need to stick the damn knife in me for sex."

"Would he indeed," Foster said. She asked almost casually, "When you finished stabbing the victim, was he dead?"

Casting his gaze downward, Jensen said softly, "He wasn't moving."

She picked up a page with a red clip. "That's not what I asked you. In the statement you gave the police the day Mr. Crawford died you said you could hear some sound from him."

"I wasn't sure if I heard anything."

"But maybe you did."

"I can't say."

"Did it occur to you to get help for this dying man now that he was no longer a threat to you?"

"I just wanted out of there."

"I'm sure. Where were you when you finished stabbing the victim?"

"What do you mean? I just remember kneeling there, holding the knife."

"With him between your legs?"

Jensen's body jerked toward her. "What the hell do you mean?"

"Weren't you straddling his body, Mr. Jensen?"

He said vehemently, "I'm telling you I don't remember."

"You said you thought about your fingerprints, you started throwing everything you'd put your hands on into a plastic bag. Is that right?"

"Yeah, right."

"You've testified that you were smashed as hell on cocaine, yet you had the presence of mind to try and make it look like a robbery — isn't that right?"

"I was confused. Messed up as hell."

"In point of fact, no fingerprint of yours was found at the murder scene. You've testified that you were smashed as hell on cocaine, yet you had the presence of mind to remove every source of your fingerprints from the scene — isn't that right?"

"Hey, I wasn't there very long, I didn't touch all that much stuff."

"You've testified that you were smashed as hell on cocaine, yet you managed to ride your motorcycle —" Foster consulted her notebook — "four miles through the city with your hands bundled in makeshift bandages — isn't that right?"

He gripped the railing with both hands. "Hey, what happened at that restaurant would sober anybody up."

"Yesterday you complained about being questioned by the police after the surgery on your hands, that your head wasn't any too clear." She asked sarcastically, "Were you smashed as hell on pain pills, Mr. Jensen?"

"Nothing like the coke, but my head was fuzzy."

"Is your head fuzzy right now?"

He looked at her warily. "No."

"Then let me test your memory." She picked up a page with a violet clip. "When you were questioned at Wilshire Division, didn't the detectives ask what your situation was with pain medication, whether you felt well enough to talk to them?"

"Well, yeah, but I didn't think I could say no."

"Do you remember telling the police that the medical treatment to your hands was not exactly brain surgery?"

"Yeah. But I was trying to get it over with and get outta there."

"Mr. Jensen, let me again test your memory." She picked up a page with a pink paper clip. "Do you remember being informed of your rights when you were at Wilshire Division?"

"I didn't understand what it all meant."

"You were informed of your rights, Mr. Jensen. You said, and I quote, what bullshit, unquote. Remember that?"

"I was just trying for . . . an attitude."

"The officers who questioned you tried again to carefully explain your rights to you and you made your bullshit remark again, Mr. Jensen. Do you remember that?"

"Hey." He shook his head. "It was all like TV stuff to me."

"In this courtroom yesterday you accused the police of misleading you, you said that you quote, didn't know shit about your rights, unquote. Don't you think you bear some responsibility for that?"

"Objection your honor," Pritchard complained. "The State is again badgering the witness."

"It hardly seems so, Mr. Pritchard," Judge Hawkins said. "Overruled."

But Foster did not give Jensen a chance to answer the question. "Shirley Johnson," she said. "Who is she to you?"

"A girl I like a lot."

"Is she your girlfriend?"

"No." He managed a slight grin. "Not yet."

Foster picked up a page with a brown clip. "Why did you tell the police that she was?"

"No big deal. I didn't want them thinking I was a fag — I mean, gay."

"It seems very important that people not think you're gay."

He said belligerently, "Wouldn't it be to you?"

She smiled. "I'm not the one who's here to answer questions, Mr. Jensen, but it would be no big deal to me. Let's talk about you and the victim and the knife. Would you take us through the scenario again of what happened in the kitchen when you claim he picked up the knife?"

"I turned to lay down my jacket, to distract him so I can take the knife away. I grab at his wrist —" He demonstrated as he spoke, "— but he jerks the knife and I get it in my hand, he cuts me. I grab at it with my other hand, I knee him and we both go down on the floor. That's it."

Kate admired Foster's self-control. She had to be elated as Kate that Jensen had again physically demonstrated Teddie Crawford's so-called act just as he had on direct examination. But Foster's face had not changed.

Foster said, "When he held the knife toward you, was the cutting edge up or down?"

"Up."

"Are you sure?"

"Yeah." He held up hands criss-crossed with red scars. "He cut me. What more do you need?"

You'll see, Kate thought. You're set up but good, you lying bastard.

Foster said, "You've got real problems with your powers of observation, Mr. Jensen. Correct me if I'm wrong on any of these points. You did not observe that Malone's Bar was in West Hollywood. Even though you were standing next to the victim, you did not hear any of his conversation with Stacey Conlin, the clerk at the 7-Eleven store. You did not observe how much coke the victim ingested. After you finished stabbing him, you did not observe whether you were straddling him. You did not observe whether the dying man was alive after you finished stabbing him. And you did not observe what is patently clear to everyone else in the universe: that the man you killed was a gay man."

"Objection, last statement draws a conclusion."

"Sustained, the jury will disregard the last statement."

Foster scarcely waited until the judge finished speaking. Standing in front of Kyle Jensen she demanded, "Why were you in Malone's Bar?"

He squared his shoulders to confront her. "I told you, to have some beer."

"You claim you did not know Mr. Crawford was gay."

"I didn't."

"Then what attracted him to you?"

"I wasn't attracted to him, goddammit. He was just a guy."

"If you were not attracted to Mr. Crawford's attributes as a gay man, then were you attracted to the jewelry he wore, the jewelry you took from his mutilated body?"

"Objection!"

"Your honor, I am trying to determine a reason why the defendant accompanied a gay man to a private place at two o'clock in the morning."

"Objection overruled. The witness will answer."

"I just wanted to have a good time. I took the dude back to his restaurant, that's all there was to it."

"Except after you took him there you killed him."

"I never meant to. I never meant for any of it to happen."

Linda Foster marched back to the counsel table and picked up the sheaf of papers with their bright paper clips. "A lie, Mr. Jensen, like the rest of your testimony. Lies which will soon —"

"Objection!"

"Sustained. Strike that from the record, the jury will disregard." Judge Hawkins added reprovingly, "Ms. Foster —"

"My apologies, your honor. I have no further questions for this witness. At this time."

Kate sat on her hands to keep from applauding.

Kenneth Pritchard stood beside Kyle Jensen for redirect examination, facing the jury. "Kyle," he asked his client, "how long have you been in Los Angeles?"

"About a year."

"Are you familiar with the geographic divisions in Los Angeles, its various communities?"

"No, sir."

"Would you know, for example, where West Hollywood left off and where Hollywood began?"

"No, sir."

"On any occasion when you were in Malone's Bar, were there women in the bar?"

"Yes, sir. All the time."

"Would you say that it's unusual to run into a gay man in a straight bar in Los Angeles?"

"No, sir. Why would it be? Everybody knows the town's full of bars and gays."

"Kyle," Pritchard said gently, "have you ever been arrested?"

"No, sir."

"Ever had to give a statement to the police?"

"No sir."

"Ever been in police custody for any reason?"

"No sir."

"How did you feel when you were being questioned at Wilshire Division?"

"Scared. Scared spitless. I didn't know what they could do to me. The whole thing was a nightmare." He added, "And it's like it's never ended."

"Kyle," Pritchard said intensely, "I want you to tell this jury exactly why you went to Tradition that night with Mr. Crawford."

"Because he was a nice guy, I liked him, his place seemed a good quiet spot to do coke in and have a good time. That's all. I swear it."

"No further questions," Pritchard said.

"I have nothing further at this time," Linda Foster said.

"The witness may step down," Judge Hawkins said.

"Your honor," Kenneth Pritchard said, standing erect beside the counsel table, "the defense calls Detective Kate Delafield."

— 19 —

Glancing at the twelve faces turned to her, the familiar yet enigmatic faces she had so exactingly scrutinized over the past days, Kate wondered what these twelve must think about her taking the stand as a witness for the defense. Did they imagine her a Janus-like creature who would offer contradiction to her previous testimony? Kate met Aimee's puzzled eyes and gave the slightest of nods to reassure her.

Now that she had reached this day, this moment, she felt calm. The answer to the question Kenneth Pritchard would ask was within her, and what

225

mattered was understanding how she would answer and why, not whether or not Judge Hawkins would allow the question.

Pritchard walked to the witness box and stood gracefully balanced on the balls of his feet, hands in the pockets of his trousers. "Detective Delafield, are you familiar with the West Hollywood area?"

So this was his lead-in. "Somewhat," she answered. She would not give him an excess word. Nor would she take her eyes off him.

"What can you tell us about it?"

"Objection," Linda Foster said mildly, "irrelevant."

"Your honor." Kenneth Pritchard's tone managed to convey both surprise and disappointment. "The State itself has brought the West Hollywood area under discussion."

"Your honor," Linda Foster countered, "the People focused on a narrow and relevant field of inquiry."

"By all means let me rephrase the question to suit the State's specifications," Pritchard said, adding an ironic little bow toward Linda Foster. "Detective Delafield, do you have a professional connection with the city of West Hollywood?"

To blunt Pritchard's game-playing, Kate answered soberly, drily, "West Hollywood is policed by the Sheriff's Department. All police departments interface with each other."

"Detective, can you give us an explanation of why West Hollywood is known as a gay city?"

"Objection, irrelevant."

Pritchard turned indignantly to the bench. "The People have repeatedly emphasized Mr. Crawford's sexual preference. I fail to understand an objection to questions relevant to that issue."

"Objection overruled, the witness may answer."

"Let me repeat the question, Detective," Pritchard said. "Can you explain why West Hollywood is known as a gay city?"

He's enjoying this, Kate thought. "I don't know that it's considered a gay city by everyone," she replied. "It has a significant gay population, its city council has several openly gay and lesbian members."

"Are you familiar with gay bars in West Hollywood?"

"Some are known to me, yes."

"Any particular reason why they're known to you?"

"Yes," she said quickly, before Linda Foster could object. "Most police professionals are familiar with major features of their own Division or an adjacent territory — and West Hollywood is an adjacent territory."

"Is Malone's Bar known as a gay bar?"

"I wouldn't know how it's known."

Pritchard's smile was tolerant; she was quarry he would inevitably corner. "Detective, do *you* know it as a gay bar?"

"Not by the definition of a gay bar as a bar that's exclusively gay."

"But is Malone's a bar that gays frequent?"

"Its owner has described it as such a bar."

"Well then," Pritchard asked with a resigned air, "is it known as a gay bar within the gay community?"

"Objection, calls for hearsay."

"Objection sustained."

Pritchard indicated with a good-humored shrug that he would abandon this unavailing trail.

"Detective, from your knowledge of West Hollywood, is it true that it has a Gay Pride march each year?"

"Yes."

"Are you familiar with the West Hollywood march?"

"Objection, your honor. Irrelevant."

Judge Hawkins contemplated Kenneth Pritchard, then said to Kate, "You may answer this question, Detective."

Pritchard repeated, "Are you familiar with the West Hollywood march?"

"Yes."

"Have you been to that march?"

"Objection," Linda Foster insisted. "The People object to this entire line of questioning."

"Objection sustained. The jury will disregard the last question. Counsel, get yourself off this patch of ice right now."

"Yes, your honor. Detective, would it be fair to say you worked very hard on this case?"

Pritchard's dark eyes picked up sheen as Kate did not answer immediately. But she had paused only to formulate an answer. "I don't think anybody should receive more, or less, justice than anyone else," she said. "I work hard on every case I'm involved in."

She was pleased by the dispassionate mask that replaced the confidence on Kenneth Pritchard's face.

"A noble ideal," he said. "Like so many of the so-called ideals of police work. But isn't the truth of the matter that you put inordinate effort into this particular case?"

"Objection —"

"Your honor," Pritchard interrupted Foster, his voice rising, "this line of questioning goes directly to the propriety of the investigation of this —"

Judge Hawkins' voice rose over his: "The objection is sustained, the question is to be stricken from the record, the jury will disregard it. Counsel, you will desist, the foundation for such a line of questioning is totally improper."

Even knowing that Pritchard was accomplishing his objective, Kate was gratified by Judge Alicia Hawkins. That she was clearly provoked by Pritchard's tactic, that her ire was visible, would have an ameliorating effect on the jury.

"Your honor," Pritchard persisted, "it seems only proper that I be allowed to pursue whether a police officer took an inordinate personal —"

"Objection!"

"— and lacked professional objectivity —"

Judge Hawkins gaveled down all further interchange. "Not another word, either of you. Members of the jury, you will disregard. Mr. Pritchard, your remarks will be stricken from the record, you are displaying contempt for this court. Approach the bench, both of you."

Kate watched the jury; they were rapt, held by the electricity of the drama. Juror number four stared in open-mouthed fascination, hands clutched over the PARIS letters on her sweater, as Hawkins, Pritchard, Foster, and the court reporter assembled into a tight knot at the far end of the bench.

Out of an angry buzz of discourse Pritchard's voice rose. Kate clearly heard, ". . . if she's a *lesbian* . . ." countered by Foster's furious,

". . . Latino officer? Black officer?" and Judge Hawkins' order, "*Lower* your voices, Mr. Pritchard not *another* word . . ."

A minute later, the conference broke up. Foster and Pritchard looked flushed — Foster with outrage, and Pritchard, Kate surmised, with victory.

Judge Hawkins resumed her seat on the bench and said coldly to Pritchard, "You may proceed."

"I have no further questions," Pritchard said.

Kate thought: Of course not, you turd.

"I have no questions, your honor," Linda Foster said, looking at Kenneth Pritchard with loathing.

"The witness may step down," Judge Hawkins said.

Kate walked through the inner court, her gaze fixed on Aimee's stunned face, trying to soothe her with her eyes. As she passed the jury box she put thumb and forefinger together in a surreptitious *it's okay* sign to Aimee. She took her usual place in the first row of benches behind the counsel table.

The answer she had been prepared to give she would explain to Aimee, she would share with Aimee this entire case. But her answer, so crucial to her, had never even mattered to Kenneth Pritchard. He had achieved his end — that the jury clearly hear him try to ask the question. Now the next question was, how would it all play with this jury?

Kate glanced up to meet the stare of juror number eight. The woman's gray-eyed gaze immediately slid away.

"Your honor," Kenneth Pritchard said, "the defense rests."

With effort, Kate resisted any further analysis of

what had just transpired. She needed her full
concentration for what would now occur.

Linda Foster rose. "Your honor, the People have
a rebuttal witness." Her voice contained echoes of
her anger. "The People submit as evidence sketches
of the surgically repaired wounds to the defendant's
hands, to be marked as People's exhibits fifty-nine
and sixty."

"Objection —" Pritchard began.

"Your honor," Linda Foster snapped, "the
defendant raised his hands while he was on the
stand, the defendant has already shown his own
scarred hands to this jury."

"Objection overruled," Judge Hawkins said crisply.
"The sketches will be designated People's exhibits
fifty-nine and sixty."

Foster handed the two sketches to Kenneth
Pritchard who glanced at them and assented, "As
stipulated."

Linda Foster announced, "The People call Dr.
Henry Mercer."

— 20 —

Henry Mercer, Kate thought, looked scarcely less rumpled in his baggy gray suit than he had in his hospital greens. And his air of bristling impatience was as ill-concealed here as it had been in the emergency room at Hollywood Presbyterian Hospital. Yet in this courtroom, like an ER, the impatience seemed to confer on him a mantle of authority.

Mercer sat in the witness chair rubbing the long slender fingers of his left hand back and forth over his close-trimmed beard, casting restless glances over the jury and courtroom as Linda Foster organized

several pages of notes. He fastened his intense gaze
on her as she moved toward the witness stand,
sketches in hand.

"Dr. Mercer, I draw your attention to People's
exhibits fifty-nine and sixty. Are these sketches of
the wounds you treated in the hands of defendant
Kyle Jensen?"

He leaned forward to examine them. "Yes,
February fourth." The answer was swift, the tone
abrupt.

Foster took the sketches over to the jury box. At
the counsel table she removed the plywood model of
the murder knife from her briefcase and displayed it
to Kenneth Pritchard, then addressed Judge
Hawkins. "Your honor, this is a model of People's
exhibit thirteen. We will be using this duplicate of
the recovered knife in demonstration."

Foster again approached the witness stand. "Dr.
Mercer, the wounds you treated in the defendant's
hands consisted, in general, of severe lacerations, is
that correct?"

"Correct."

"Would you describe in layman's terms the
wounds to the defendant's right hand."

He traced a fingertip on his own right hand. "In
layman's terms, the major wound was to the web
between the thumb and forefinger. Incised to the
bone, with some evidence of tearing. Also a minor
cut to the outside of the palm. Minor cuts to all the
fingers."

"And to the left hand?"

"A simple cut across the palm, another inside the
thumb. Minor cuts to all the fingers."

"Thank you. Now, using this knife in

demonstration, I'm going to set up a hypothetical situation."

"Objection," Pritchard protested. "Objection to this entire fishing expedition."

"Your honor," Foster said, "the People have called this witness to support their charge of first degree murder."

Kate smiled. Pritchard had to regret an objection that had harvested so dramatic a response.

Judge Hawkins picked up her half-glasses and peered through them at Foster. "Proceed," she said. "Preferably with a minimum of theatrics."

"Dr. Mercer," Foster said, standing beside the witness box and facing the jury, "assume a man is holding a knife in both hands." She gripped the handle of the demonstration knife in both hands. "Assume this man has been stabbing another man repeatedly." She lifted the knife over her head and brought it down.

"Objection, this is deliberately inflammatory, this is pure speculation."

"Your honor," Foster repeated, "the People have called this witness to support their charge of first degree murder. I am laying the foundation."

"Proceed," Judge Hawkins ordered.

Foster handed the plywood knife to Mercer. He turned it gracefully in his fingers as if evaluating it as a surgical tool. She walked over to the evidence table. "Let the record show that People's exhibit number thirteen, the actual recovered knife, is being shown to the jury." Foster displayed an open-top box containing a bloodstained knife held down by wires.

"Objection. Your honor, this is entirely inflammatory."

"Overruled, the recovered knife is in evidence."

"Dr. Mercer, assume that the knife you hold, identical in size and shape to the one shown here in People's exhibit thirteen, has become covered, coated, slick with the stabbed man's blood."

Kate's gaze swung to Kyle Jensen, who sat immobile, staring at Mercer, and then to the engrossed jury, then to Kenneth Pritchard, who was scribbling rapidly on his legal pad.

"Dr. Mercer, assume that the knife has become so slick that the attacking man's hands slip and slide on the knife as he stabs his victim."

Pritchard's pen froze over his pad, his head jerked up. "Objection! Objection to this entire blue-sky speculation."

"Your honor," Foster said implacably, "the People have called this witness to support their charge of first degree murder."

"Objection overruled," Judge Hawkins said curtly. "Proceed."

Kate watched with savage enjoyment. Pritchard had to object, she exulted — Foster was attacking his only real defense — but every time he objected, Foster could repeat her phrase, and emphasize the importance of this witness and his evidence.

"Dr. Mercer, this is my question. Given this scenario, could the wounds on the hands of such an attacker correspond with the wounds you treated on the defendant's hands?"

"Your scenario could account exactly for the wounds I treated."

Judge Hawkins gaveled insistently against the wave of sound in the courtroom. Kyle Jensen, staring down at the counsel table, was shaking his head.

Foster waited for quiet, and a few moments beyond that. Then she said, "Would you explain for the jury."

Mercer gripped the knife handle, placing his left hand on top of his right. "First of all, blood's very slippery stuff, like oil. So as the knife picks up gore, the hands begin to slide, the bottom or right hand would slide over the haft. That would open the minor cut to the outside edge of the palm."

His intense dark eyes had narrowed, as if he were unravelling an interesting but not too complicated problem. "Then the bottom hand slips over the haft, onto the blade."

Kate watched the jury carefully. All the faces were alert with comprehension.

"As the stabbing continues —" Mercer demonstrated with the knife, "— with each stab there's an up and down sawing action on the web of flesh between the thumb and the index finger, and the haft would help tear open the wound. A heavy sharp knife like this one, it wouldn't take much to saw and tear the web open to the bone."

"Objection, your honor." Pritchard's voice was quietly emphatic. "This is inflammatory speculation."

"Your honor," Foster countered, "the witness is speaking entirely in his area of expertise."

"Overruled. You may proceed," Judge Hawkins said to Mercer.

Mercer had been looking at Pritchard with annoyance. "Now for the left hand," he continued, and again demonstrated with the knife. "The left hand would slide down as well but would receive far less trauma, it would be cut across the palm and up inside the thumb. And the fingers of both hands would acquire cuts from the twisting and shimmying of the blade."

Ostensibly checking a note in her notebook, Foster finally said into utter silence in the courtroom, "Doctor, wounds such as these would produce copious bleeding, would they not?"

"Indeed they would."

"Previous testimony has established that two arcs of the defendant's blood on the wall were cast off in the act of stabbing."

"Only two? With hands this badly cut, if they'd been cut *before* the stabbing began, there'd have been lots of arcs on the wall, blood would have been thrown with every act of stabbing. So those two arcs had to land at the end of the stabbing, not the beginning. Further proof of the scenario."

Pritchard had not objected, and Kate looked at him in astonishment, as did Judge Hawkins. He had to be completely stunned, Kate thought. He had allowed Mercer to answer Foster's last question, to testify in an area clearly outside his expertise.

"Thank you, Doctor," Linda Foster said, her voice brimming with satisfaction. She took the knife from him, returned to the counsel table. "No further questions."

Pritchard got to his feet, moved slowly, thoughtfully to the witness box. Kate was amused to see both Pritchard and Mercer rubbing their chins as they contemplated each other.

"Dr. Mercer," Pritchard said in a respectful tone, "would you answer me a question about the wounds to the hands of my client?" He moved back to the

counsel table, picked up the demonstration knife.
Gripping the knife, he returned to the stand. "With
the kind of wounds you describe in my client's right
hand, wouldn't those wounds be compressed by the
act of holding a knife?"

"Yes," Mercer said. "So?"

Poor Pritchard, Kate thought in amusement. To
add to his difficulties, Mercer obviously felt that he
had said his piece clearly and definitively, and he
now would be churlish over being challenged or
having to retill the same ground.

"Wouldn't compression on the wounds affect
them? Staunch and control the amount of blood
flowing from them?"

"So? It's why you've got only two arcs on the
wall instead of more."

"Or perhaps there's another explanation
altogether, Doctor," Pritchard snapped. "You and the
district attorney have constructed a scenario to fit
her convenient theory of Mr. Crawford's —"

"Objection!"

"Sustained. Mr. Pritchard —"

"I'll rephrase, your honor."

"I haven't constructed any scenario," Mercer
barked.

"Move to strike," Pritchard said quietly.

"Motion granted, the jury will disregard. Dr.
Mercer, please wait until you're asked a question."

Mercer's bony shoulders moved in a disdainful
shrug.

Pritchard said, "The district attorney has
reviewed with you a scenario surrounding Mr.
Crawford's death. But isn't it entirely possible, isn't
it just as likely, Dr. Mercer, that the wounds to Mr.

Jensen's hands could result from some other scenario?"

"Give me the knife." Mercer peremptorily held out his hand.

"I beg your pardon?"

"You want me to answer your question, give me the knife."

Dubious, then suddenly eager, Pritchard handed it over. Foster looked worried, and Kate watched with concern. Mercer could demolish his own testimony.

"Okay. Your man could maybe ward off a blow and get a slash on the outside of his palm. He could maybe twist his hand some weird way and get the web cut, get his palm cut, whatever. Same with the other hand. Or . . ." Mercer held the knife in both hands and began a stabbing motion. "Or he could very simply stab somebody using both hands on a very bloody knife and get the exact wounds that he's got. Now what makes more sense?"

Linda Foster was beaming at Henry Mercer. What a wonderful witness, Kate thought joyfully.

Pritchard said sternly, "Dr. Mercer, please. Just answer this question. *Is* another explanation possible?" His voice rose. "*Is* it possible, Dr. Mercer?"

"Of course it's possible," Mercer said contemptuously. "Anything is possible."

Pritchard deliberately turned his back on Mercer. "No further questions."

"I have nothing further," Foster said in triumph.

"The witness may step down."

Linda Foster rose. "Your honor, the People have no further witnesses."

Pritchard nodded acknowledgment.

Kate watched Pritchard sit down at the counsel table and confer with Kyle Jensen. The defense had been dealt a body blow, but she knew with every instinct in her that Kenneth Pritchard was not nearly finished.

— 21 —

"Ladies and gentlemen," Linda Foster began her closing address to the jury, "certain facts in this case are not in dispute."

Kate sat quietly watching the jury, thinking that their faces seemed more unreadable to her than any jury she had ever observed — probably, she conceded, because never had she felt so enmeshed in a case.

On this, the last day of the trial, Foster would make her closing address; Pritchard would follow. Kate was certain that Pritchard had saved a major weapon for his summation, and she could guess the nature of the weapon. But since the prosecution bore the burden of proof, Foster would be allowed a rebuttal to Pritchard's closing statement. Then the case would go to this enigma of a jury.

The courtroom benches were nearly filled. Of the people in the room known to Kate, Gloria Gomez and Francisco Caldera sat behind her, along with Jimmy Malone, who had closed his bar until the verdict came in. At the back of the room were Aimee, and Carl Jacoby, Teddie Crawford's ex-lover — who did not know that he was sitting next to Kate's own lover. The press was also present — correspondents from the *Advocate*, the *Lesbian News* and *Frontiers*, a reporter and photographer from the *Los Angeles Times*. Burt Dayton sat with the blonde, gum-chewing Shirley Johnson. Stacey Conlin from the 7-Eleven, wearing jeans, high heels and a white fake-fur jacket, had edged in shyly, taking the seat nearest the door. Margaret and Joe Crawford had called Linda Foster or Kate each day of the trial, but they had not been able to bring themselves to come to court.

Foster's simple, dark gray suit and high-collared white blouse were perfect attire, Kate thought, for this final proceeding on this final day. Foster stood slim and straight at the podium, a sheaf of notes in front of her as she continued her address to the jury.

"We know for a fact that twenty-three-year-old Teddie Crawford met defendant Kyle Jensen at a bar frequented by gay men. We know for a fact that Teddie Crawford invited the defendant to his restaurant, that they went there on the defendant's motorbike, stopping on the way at a 7-Eleven store. And we know that at the restaurant, defendant Kyle Jensen killed Teddie Crawford."

Without looking, Foster pointed behind her, toward Kyle Jensen. "From here on, we have this defendant's fuzzy, inconsistent, contradictory story as to how and why he killed his victim. In his statement to the police, the defendant claimed that Teddie Crawford was quote, really wasted on coke, unquote, while stating that he himself was merely high. Then, hearing in this courtroom test results on the victim's body that clearly refuted his claim, he changed his story to tell us that he hadn't noticed how much cocaine the victim had taken. And the defendant decided that he himself had been quote, smashed as hell, unquote. His hope, ladies and gentlemen, is that you will accept his claim of drug intoxication as an explanation for his despicable crime."

Kate looked at Jensen. He sat immobile, staring into his hands which were loosely clasped on the counsel table. Pritchard appeared relaxed beside him, making notes with a thick black fountain pen.

"Next we have the defendant's story of the so-called sexual advance." Foster's tone became more sarcastic. "The defendant says about the victim, quote, I wanted to vomit all over him, unquote. First he tells us this impulse swept over him when the victim picked up a knife. Then he tells us no, it was when the victim proposed an act of fellatio. Then he says no, it's when the victim groped him. This defendant claims to be so appalled by the victim's

behavior that he wanted to vomit all over him —
yet it was more important to him to snort cocaine in
the kitchen than to leave the victim's restaurant."

Foster picked up a note marked with a yellow
paper clip. Smart to use the paper clips again, Kate
thought. Remind the jury of all Jensen's lies.

"In his testimony this defendant said that Teddie
Crawford picked up a knife because, quote, I'm
bigger than he is, it's the only way he's got of
making me stay, unquote." Foster tossed the
paper-clipped note onto the podium. "Ladies and
gentlemen, examine this statement. This defendant
claims that Teddie Crawford wanted to perform an
act of fellatio on him. Aside from the ludicrous idea
that Teddie Crawford, a vital and handsome young
man, would need to demand sex at knife-point —
how is it that Teddie Crawford would manage to
perform such an act at knife-point?"

Judge Hawkins gaveled against the wave of
laughter that gathered strength in the courtroom.
Linda Foster seemed startled by the sound. Kate
well understood. Foster was focused on the jury,
nothing existed for her except the jury.

As the courtroom noise subsided Foster continued,
"You have listened to testimony from people who
knew Teddie Crawford. You now know that Teddie
Crawford did not, for a moment, hide his sexuality
in a closet. Stacey Conlin, the clerk at the 7-Eleven
store, openly teased him about being a queen — the
most flamboyant sort of gay man — right in front of
the defendant. This defendant tells you he wasn't
listening. This defendant tells you he didn't notice
that his victim was gay. This defendant actually

thinks you're going to believe he didn't know that this conspicuously gay man was gay."

Kyle Jensen, still staring down at his hands, was slowly shaking his head.

"And then we have the defendant's account of the murder itself," Foster said derisively. "Teddie Crawford came at him with a knife, the defendant tells us. As we now know, ladies and gentlemen, this is hogwash. We know the victim never had that knife. We have expert testimony from the surgeon who repaired the defendant's hands as to the actual source of those wounds. This testimony only brings into focus other facts about the gory scene of murder at Tradition."

Foster picked up a page flagged by a red paper clip. "Blood from the defendant was found *only* in these places: On the murder weapon. In the cast-off pattern on the wall. On the counter top and the taps and in the drain of the sink where the defendant attempted to clean himself up after the murder."

She placed the page on top of her notes, leaned over the podium. "Equally significant, ladies and gentlemen, is where *no* blood from the defendant was found. Blood spatter expert Charlotte Mead testified that she had tested all areas of the victim's shirt, and found no trace of any blood from the defendant — not even on the front of the shirt. Consider what this means. If the cuts to the defendant's hands were defense wounds as he claims, how would he not get his own blood on the victim's shirt while he was stabbing him? He never got any blood on the victim because he was not cut until he cut *himself* in his final thrusts into Teddie Crawford's body."

Foster's hand gestured in an arc. "We have the cast-off blood on the wall. Two patterns, belonging solely to the defendant. If the defendant had cut his hands defending himself as he claims, how could he slash and stab the victim thirty-nine times and have only two arcs of blood on that wall? The truth is that the defendant cut his own hands in the act of murdering Teddie Crawford, and he threw those arcs as he came to the end of his murderous rampage."

Foster took the demonstration knife from the shelf of the podium. "The defendant has convicted himself with his own demonstration of what happened at Tradition, and, ladies and gentlemen, you saw it. You saw him sit right there in the witness chair and demonstrate how Teddie Crawford came at him with a knife. In both his interview with the police and here in this courtroom he was asked if the cutting edge of the knife was up or down. Both times he said it was up. You heard me ask if he was sure. He said that he was."

Foster pointed the knife toward the jury. "But if the victim was holding the knife like this, with the cutting edge facing *up,* and if the defendant reached *up* for the knife as he demonstrated with his own hand, then how could he have been cut between the thumb and index finger?"

Foster held the knife in position for a long moment, waiting, Kate knew, for this dramatic disclosure to sink in.

"The wounds to the *victim's* hands are the true defense wounds, ladies and gentlemen. The victim, five feet-eight to the defendant's five-eleven, one hundred and forty-two pounds to the defendant's one hundred and eighty-five — had his own hands slashed and a finger almost severed in his desperate and futile attempt to defend himself from this pitiless killer."

Foster put the knife away and selected a page with a yellow paper clip. "The defendant says he left Malone's Bar with the victim quote, Because he was a nice guy, I liked him, his place seemed a good quiet spot to do coke in and have a good time, unquote." She laid the paper down. "But the fact is, Teddie Crawford had only a minor amount of cocaine in his body. And the truth is, the defendant came to Tradition knowing exactly what he would do when he cornered this young gay man."

Jensen sat staring at his hands, still shaking his head.

"This defendant told you in the most sincere tones that he never meant for his crime to happen. Yet this defendant stated here in this courtroom that he did not know if his victim was dead when he finished stabbing him. This defendant made absolutely no attempt to get help for a man he claims he did not mean to kill. This defendant stripped jewelry from his victim's bleeding body and left a scene of horror not knowing if his victim was alive or dead, slipping and sliding through his victim's blood as he walked away."

Foster's gaze moved slowly over the jury. "By every definition, this defendant has committed first degree premeditated murder. This defendant has laid claim to the cuts in his hands as proof of self-defense. But in actuality they have been proven to be a grisly part of a vicious act of premeditated

murder. Ladies and gentlemen, the People ask for
justice: the People ask that you find this defendant
guilty of murder in the first degree."

Linda Foster gathered up her notes. "Thank you,
ladies and gentlemen of the jury."

Rocking slightly on the thin soles of his highly
polished shoes, Kenneth Pritchard stood at the
podium, hands resting on a leather folder of notes.
He looked distinguished, Kate admitted — even
imposing in his power colors: black suit, snow-white
shirt, a tie with a striped pattern of subtle blues
and grays.

"Ladies and gentlemen," Pritchard began, his tone
soft, almost gentle, "I'd like you to remember back to
when we began these proceedings."

Pritchard paused but did not look around as the
courtroom door opened. Kate turned, and was jolted
to see Taylor. He nodded to her, made a thumbs-up
sign to the bailiff, glanced at Stacey Conlin and
rolled his eyes, then seated himself beside her.

Why was Taylor here? Curiosity about the
outcome of her solo performance on this case? Or
had Bodwin talked to him? Kate turned back to the
inner courtroom, pushing away thoughts of Taylor;
she needed all of her focus on Kenneth Pritchard.

"If you recall," Pritchard was saying to the jury,
"I promised lots of drama from the district attorney.
I promised you she would fill this room with as
much fog —" Pritchard's hands began to sculpture
clouds, "— as a special effects man in an old time

movie. And I asked you to keep an open mind. Do you remember that?"

Several jurors rewarded him with nods — juror number two, Robert Baldwin, number six, Dion Franklin, number seven, Victor Chen, and Eugenia Lowe, the older woman who was juror number eight.

"I told you that when all was said and done, this would turn out to be a very sad and very simple story. I told you that *why* Mr. Crawford died was the actual issue before us — and, ladies and gentlemen, it remains as the central issue the twelve of you must decide."

Pritchard leaned over the podium. "The State has laid passionate claim to this case as first degree, premeditated murder. *Passionate* claim, ladies and gentlemen, because they bear the burden of proof — beyond a reasonable doubt and to a moral certainty. And the State would like you to accept emotion in place of proof."

He raised both hands. "Yes, the State maintains it *has* proof. The State offers *claims* of proof. *Allegations* of proof. *Theories* of proof. What the State actually offers is a *veneer* of proof — the scenery they've painted to fit their case, like a salesman inventing virtues to sell his product."

Pritchard stepped out from behind the podium to stand before the jury box. "The State has made all kinds of claims about where blood is and where it isn't, they've trotted out their blood expert for your edification. An expert who described the scene where Mr. Crawford died as a massive pool of blood, yet who also tossed off opinions to a scientific certainty as to where blood from Mr. Jensen was and wasn't.

Ladies and gentlemen, use your good common sense. In a massive pool, blood from my client could be anywhere, masked by sheer quantity."

Pritchard extended his fine, supple hands, palms up. "The State makes much of the wounds to my client's hands, whether or not they're defense wounds. Two men were present at that scene of what has been aptly called a nightmare. No one else. One of those men is dead. My client has testified that in the altercation, in his words, he lost it. He doesn't know what happened. And that, I submit to you, ladies and gentlemen, is the simple truth of it."

Pritchard paced, stopped. "How did my client receive the wounds to his hands? My client says that Mr. Crawford came at him with a knife, its cutting edge up. The State has leaped on this as proof positive of his guilt. I for one believe my client, I have no problem that Mr. Jensen may have received initial wounds to his fingers instead of his palm as he reached up to try to disarm Mr. Crawford — and that those other wounds opened up as the entire incident escalated. Mr. Crawford may even have inflicted all those wounds on Mr. Jensen before my client got the knife away from him."

Pritchard nodded. "Yes, Mr. Crawford was the smaller man. But who can speak for his strength under such circumstances? We all know the story of the woman lifting a car off the body of her child."

Again Pritchard paced, stopped. "The State claims to know precisely what happened. But the State can only speculate. Ladies and gentlemen, all of us can only speculate. No one can say with certainty exactly what happened at Tradition, only the two men who were there. The State's own medical expert admitted that anything was possible."

Pritchard gestured in an arc. "The State has used two patterns of blood on the wall — what they mean, what they don't mean — to chart its version of the entire incident, like someone would use a poll to determine an election. Well, I for one believe in election results, not polls."

He pointed to where Kyle Jensen sat at the counsel table attentively watching. "The State has entertained itself by picking apart the statements of my client. But it's not difficult at all to understand the contradictions between Mr. Jensen's statement to the police and his testimony here. Kyle Jensen has never been in trouble, never been arrested. Never been in police custody. Never been in a police interrogation room. He did what most normal people would do in a situation that had turned into a living nightmare — he tried to protect himself. Ask yourself how you would behave in such a circumstance."

He turned back to the jury. "The State has also made great stock out of Mr. Jensen's statement about wanting to vomit all over Mr. Crawford and exactly when that particular emotion came over him. Mr. Jensen has been in Los Angeles less than a year. We who live here are accustomed to the diversity and tolerance for lifestyle in this city. We lose sight of the fact that others do not share our cosmopolitan sophistication. Sexual diversity may seem commonplace to us. Regardless of our opinions about it, we may have come to accept and even take it for granted. But it can be very foreign, frightening, intimidating, repugnant to someone else.

"The State trumpets that there was no reason for the young, good-looking Mr. Crawford to pull a knife. But why should anyone assume that Mr. Crawford, by any definition not a conventional man, was without a pathological side to him? Why is it less likely for Mr. Crawford to behave in a pathological fashion than it is for Mr. Jensen? Serial killer Ted Bundy was a good-looking young man. Why must we conclude that just because Mr. Crawford was good-looking, he was not pathological?

"At Wilshire Division and in this courtroom, Kyle Jensen was asked to remember a scene of horror. No, he didn't get all the details right. Kyle Jensen is a frightened young man. He was frightened then, he is frightened now."

Extending both hands, Pritchard said in a rising voice, "How could Kyle Jensen not know that Teddie Crawford was homosexual, the State thunders. Well, Mr. Jensen was brought up in a normal, conservative household. His father fought and nearly died for this country in Korea. Mr. Jensen has been brought up like most of us — taught that homosexuality is one of society's deepest taboos. I ask you to imagine yourself in his place. Here he is a stranger in Los Angeles, confronted by a man who embodies everything he has been taught to abhor. A man who makes an abhorrent sexual proposition — and backs it up with a knife. Need I mention the specter of AIDS?"

Kenneth Pritchard walked over to stand in front of juror number two, Robert Baldwin. "The violence of the incident at Tradition comes out of two elements: Mr. Jensen's drug intoxication and his revulsion. We are all products of our culture and upbringing. In the same situation, how much control would you have? If you were confronted by a coiled snake, aside from its threat to you, wouldn't you lash out at that snake from sheer, natural revulsion?"

A low, growling, angry murmur began in the courtroom; Judge Hawkins gaveled it down.

Kenneth Pritchard said quietly, "I said at the beginning of these proceedings that we all bear responsibility for our acts. If my client, Kyle Jensen, accepts that responsibility, so too, ladies and gentlemen, must the dead young man himself."

He stood back to address the entire jury. "The State bears the burden of proof — beyond a reasonable doubt and to a moral certainty. Clearly, the State has failed to prove its case. We cannot give young Teddie Crawford back his life. But we can give this young man . . ." He gestured to Kyle Jensen. "We can allow this young man, who will carry the scars of this incident his entire life, to go on with his life."

Kenneth Pritchard strode to the podium, picked up his leather folder. "Ladies and gentlemen, I ask you to find Mr. Crawford's death a justifiable homicide. I ask you for a verdict of not guilty."

* * * * *

As Kenneth Pritchard sat down at the counsel table beside a pleased-looking Kyle Jensen, Linda Foster ripped a page of notes from her pad and strode over to the jury box, disdaining the podium.

Kate, sickened by Pritchard's closing, forgot her nausea. *She's out of control.*

"Ladies and gentlemen," Foster said, and noisily cleared her throat. Juror number four looked at her in wonder. All the jurors looked disconcerted.

Kate watched in rising apprehension. *She's too angry, she's out of control, she'll blow the whole case.*

"The defense has correctly identified the nature of Teddie Crawford's death." Foster's voice was vibrating, her body rigid with fury. "Sexual diversity, the defense tells us, can be —" She jabbed a finger at the page of notes in her hand, "— quote, foreign, frightening, intimidating, repugnant. Unquote." Glaring down at her notes, she cleared her throat again. "Quote, If you were confronted by a coiled snake, aside from its threat to you, wouldn't you lash out at that snake from sheer, natural revulsion? Unquote. There is a word for this, ladies and gentlemen. The word is homophobia."

Foster slapped the paper with the back of a hand. "The defense claims the violence at Tradition came out of the defendant's drug intoxication and his revulsion. There is a word for violence coming out of homophobia, a word we haven't used yet in this courtroom. The word is gaybashing."

"Objection, your honor," Kenneth Pritchard said quietly.

"Your basis, Mr. Pritchard?" Judge Hawkins inquired.

"Inflammatory terminology. Drawing a conclusion without foundation."

Facing Pritchard, waving her notes, Linda Foster retorted, "The defense itself has established the foundation."

Judge Hawkins peered down at Pritchard through her half-glasses. "I must concur, Mr. Pritchard. Objection overruled. Proceed."

"The defendant," Linda Foster said, turning her back squarely on Pritchard and addressing the completely attentive jury, "is not the only gaybasher in this room."

Pritchard leaped to his feet. "Objection!"

Judge Hawkins looked at him expectantly.

"Your honor, I object!"

"Yes, Mr. Pritchard," Judge Hawkins said, "I heard your objection. I am waiting to hear your grounds."

Kate watched in pure joy. Pritchard was trapped. To explain his objection was to admit that Foster's statement applied to him. To not object meant that he accepted the statement without challenge.

Pritchard sank slowly back into his chair.

Kate thought: If we go on to lose this case, this may be our best moment.

"Mr. Pritchard," Judge Hawkins said, "are you withdrawing the objection?"

Kate thought: I love this woman.

Pritchard muttered, "Yes, your honor."

"Proceed, Ms. Foster."

Let it go now, Linda. You've made the point, don't dilute it.

Foster walked closer to the jury box, yanking off her glasses as if they were a barrier separating her from the jury. "Ladies and gentlemen, this crime is not, as the defense terms it, an *incident*. It is a *crime*. The crime of murder. Teddie Crawford made no bones about the fact that he was gay, and he died for it." She waved the glasses toward Kyle Jensen. "This defendant knew Teddie Crawford was gay. This defendant is so filled with the fear of being thought homosexual that he lied about who undressed him, he lied about having a girlfriend."

Vigorously shaking his head, Kyle Jensen glared at Linda Foster. Pritchard put a hand on his arm; Jensen shook it off.

"The defense says this trial is like an election and the evidence the People have offered is a poll," Foster said wrathfully. "This is a court proceeding about a man who is *dead*. The People have presented concrete evidence of first degree homicide to a reasonable scientific certainty. The defense wants you to ignore qualified experts and take the word of the defendant. If we could accept the word of murderers about their crimes, we wouldn't need experts."

Foster's body was no less rigid, but her voice had calmed. "No, this defendant has never been arrested. This defendant walked into the casino and went right to the big game — and the defense says we should all forgive him for it." Foster continued bitingly, "The defense says we should just let him have this one little murder."

Foster punctuated her words with shakes of her

glasses. "The People have proved their case beyond a reasonable doubt — so much so that the only avenue left to the defense is to scoff at the wall of evidence around this defendant. The defense has asked you to use your good common sense. The People ask you the same thing. Because your good common sense will tell you the defense wants you to ignore evidence of first degree murder."

Foster heedlessly stuffed her glasses and her page of notes into her jacket pocket. "The victim's body was mutilated by thirty-nine knife wounds. The People have demonstrated conclusively that the defendant did not act in self-defense — there was no blood from the defendant on the victim, the defendant cut himself in the act of killing the victim. There was not another mark on the defendant — not a bruise, not a scratch, nothing. But the victim was stabbed thirty-nine times. Thirty-nine times, ladies and gentlemen. Consider an act of homicide in which someone is stabbed thirty-nine times."

Foster lifted an imaginary knife in both hands and brought it down viciously, again and again:

"*One* . . .

"*Two* . . .

"*Three* . . .

"*Four* . . .

"*Five* . . .

"*Six* . . .

"*Seven* . . ."

Foster finally stopped her demonstration. "*Thirty-nine times.* This defendant stabbed his victim *thirty-nine times.*"

She turned and looked directly into Kyle Jensen's blue-eyed rage. "This defendant has said he wishes he could change what happened. This defendant has said he never meant for any of it to happen. When did we hear this defendant say he was sorry Teddie Crawford is dead?"

Foster turned her back to him. Fishing her page of notes from her pocket and waving it, she said scornfully, "The defense claims other cities don't share our tolerance for diversity of lifestyle, our cosmopolitan sophistication. The people in the defendant's hometown of Pittsburgh will be interested to know they live in such a cultural backwater. Similar cities may be interested to know their citizens have a license to come to Los Angeles and kill gay people."

Linda Foster's voice rang in the courtroom. "The defense says the defendant has been taught that homosexuality is one of society's deepest taboos. If you agree with the taboo, then you avoid the taboo. You don't go into a bar gay men frequent. You don't stalk a gay man. You don't take that gay man to a secluded place and kill him in the most hideous possible way, you don't strip jewelry off his bleeding body. The defense says we're all products of our culture and upbringing. The People ask you: what kind of world do you want to live in?

"We complain about our society, we complain we're powerless to change anything. You have the power to change something. You have the power to tell this court, to tell the people who mourn young

Teddie Crawford, what kind of a world he had a right to live in."

Linda Foster crumpled her page of notes. "You can find this defendant guilty of murder in the first degree. Because he is guilty. And because it is right. I ask you for that verdict."

— 22 —

"Lots of fireworks," Taylor said, inclining his head toward the closed courtroom door.

Kate, still reverberating from Linda Foster's rebuttal closing, managed a smile at the understatement. Her entire life had merely been passing before her eyes in that room. Yet at her core she felt an indifference to Taylor and his remark that was separate from their conflict over this case.

At Taylor's signal she had come out into the hallway while Judge Hawkins read the jury

instructions. She knew Taylor might have important
information on one of the open homicides in their
caseload. But, looking into his broad, slightly flushed
face, she saw his purpose.

Taylor said, "Bodwin told me not to talk to you
till he did — he's waiting till you finish up here.
Screw him, we're partners, Kate."

He moved to sit on one of the benches built into
the wall. The corridor was active with traffic —
participants in other cases in other courtrooms. Kate
joined him, wondering what Bodwin had said to
Taylor.

"He calls me in," Taylor said heavily, "says we're
getting all kinds of new people in the department,
and he's gonna talk to you about working with
different partners as a kind of training detective."

"Really," Kate said. She added in a more cautious
tone, "I haven't heard a thing about it." She liked
the idea. She hoped Bodwin had not invented it as a
convenient explanation for Taylor.

"You couldn't pay me to work with a rookie,"
Taylor grunted. "Takes too fucking long to learn how
to be a good homicide cop."

"It does take a long time," Kate agreed. Her
investigative instincts had been honed over many
years and many crime scenes.

"Bodwin says even if you're not interested, he's
gonna give us new partners. It's fucking crazy, Kate.
I mean, for chrissakes if it ain't broke, why fix it?"

Kate did not reply.

Taylor said, "I ask why and he just says it's
time. It's time," he repeated in a sarcastic falsetto.
"Must be the latest dipshit management theory."

He did not seem to notice that she had scarcely
reacted to his news. He picked at the crease in his
trousers. "I don't want a new partner, Kate. I don't
need the hassle. Me and Marie, we talked last
night." He looked up at her, his brown eyes
suddenly soft. "There's this place we've been looking
at in Fillmore . . . You're the first to know, Kate. I
really am gonna go raise some avocados."

"I'm glad for you, Ed," she said, nodding. "You've
been talking about it a long time."

He grinned. "I'll tell you something else, partner.
I feel good about it." Then he looked away, down the
hallway. "But all those years . . . there's a lot of
water over the dam."

She said sympathetically, "You're still part of the
police family, Ed — you know that. Once a cop,
always a cop."

He nodded. "We've had some good times together,
Kate."

"Yes, we have, Ed." She turned at an indefinable
sound from the courtroom. She belonged in there,
she needed to be back in there.

Taylor got up. "So I'll see you at the retirement
party." Injury was mixed in with his flippancy. He
had obviously noticed her divided attention. "Good
luck with your fag case," he said. "Looks like you'll
need it."

Reaching for the courtroom door, she paused to
observe his huffy march down the hallway. He had
pulled her out of proceedings on the major homicide
case on which he had forced her to go solo, had not
so much as inquired into her own feelings about
Bodwin's reassignment plans, had again maligned

her community. She thought: Go grow your stupid goddamn avocados.

Linda Foster picked up her briefcase and came out of the inner court as the courtroom emptied of spectators.

Kate said, "Wonderful job, Linda, the best."

"It's the best I could do, Kate." Her gaze was fixed on the men and women slowly filing into the jury room to begin their deliberations.

Kate beckoned to Aimee, who waved and began to thread her way through the benches. Kate watched with enjoyment the heavy swing of her dark hair, the sensuous grace of her body, the blue-violet of her eyes made more vivid by the royal blue of her silky blouse.

"Linda," Kate said, "I'd like you to meet Aimee Grant. My partner."

Ignoring the hand extended to her, Aimee reached to Linda Foster and hugged her. "You were fantastic."

Foster looked abashed, but pleased. "I hope I was fantastic enough." Inspecting Aimee in frank admiration, she said, "You two women have very good taste."

Kate said, "I think so too." Aimee grinned.

Foster glanced at her watch. "So. Let's get something to eat at the cafeteria, go on up to my office. The jury should be out a long time. I hope."

"Why do you hope so?" Aimee asked. "He's so obviously guilty."

"You're so obviously objective," Foster joked as they walked from the courtroom. "I've learned one thing from being a trial attorney — objectivity is a sometime thing with juries."

"Too true," Kate said.

"The longer they're out," Foster said, "the more chance they can work their way through their homophobia and get to a decent verdict."

The three women had settled themselves in Linda Foster's office. The Farberware coffee pot chuffed away, barely keeping up with their coffee consumption.

"Tell me something," Aimee said to Kate. "When that creep called you as a witness for the defense — if Judge Hawkins had allowed his questions, how would you have answered?"

"Kate may not want to answer that in front of me," Linda Foster said quickly.

"No problem, Linda," Kate said. "Police officers from any other minority group would never be asked such a question, never be challenged about their objectivity toward someone of their own culture — so why should gay or lesbian officers? Since no black or Latino or Asian officer would answer such a question, I decided I wouldn't either. I decided I'd refuse to answer."

"Right, absolutely right," Aimee declared.

"And absolutely the point I made to Hawkins," Foster said.

"Yes. I heard you."

"She was furious with Pritchard," Foster said

with a chuckle. "She was probably imagining her own judicial objectivity as a black woman judge being questioned."

Aimee mused, "Another judge maybe would have ordered you to answer, Kate. Sent you to jail for not answering."

"Yes," Kate said.

Foster nodded. "And I'd have —"

Her phone rang.

Foster looked at the instrument as if it had acquired unwelcome life. Gingerly, she plucked up the receiver.

"Linda Foster speaking." She listened for a moment. "Yes. Thank you." She hung up. "We have a verdict." She took a deep breath. "Fuck."

Kate looked at her watch. The jury had been out two hours and five minutes.

Cameras had been set up on tripods at the rear of the courtroom; a cameraman from KTLA waited near the door, a minicam on his shoulder. The room was crowded to capacity with spectators.

The jury filed in solemnly, looking at no one. Kate had taken her usual place, in the first row behind the counsel table; Linda Foster was studying the twelve grim faces, her own face tight with tension. Kyle Jensen sat rubbing his palms over his knees and staring at the jury. Kenneth Pritchard was leaning casually back in his chair, but he too watched the jury.

Looking regal in her judicial robes, Judge Alicia Hawkins waited for the jurors to settle themselves, then adjusted her half-glasses on her nose and asked evenly, "Ladies and gentlemen of the jury, have you reached a verdict?"

The jury foreperson, Eugenia Lowe, rose. "We have, your honor," she said in a firm voice.

The clerk, a studious-looking, plump young man, took the folded piece of paper from Eugenia Lowe, brought it over to the bench, handed it to Judge Hawkins. She unfolded it, looked at it, handed it back to the clerk.

"The defendant will rise."

Kyle Jensen and Kenneth Pritchard stood; Jensen's hands were clenched at his sides.

Amid the ritual of this ancient ceremony, Kate felt as if she too were standing to receive this verdict, that it would be as much a pronouncement over her as it would be over Kyle Jensen.

"The clerk will read the verdict."

Kate felt, rather than heard, a ringing in her head.

The clerk read in an uninflected voice, *"We the jury find the defendant, Kyle Thomas Jensen, in the above entitled action —"*

The ringing became a painful buzzing.

"— guilty of a felony, section one-eighty-seven of the penal code —"

Kate was dizzy with the ringing-buzzing.

"— murder in the first degree."

In the tumult of the courtroom Linda Foster sat frozen, then whirled to Kate; their gazes fused. Unable to speak or move, Kate watched Foster's eyes, her face, illuminate with joy, with triumph.

Kyle Jensen had sunk into his chair. Pritchard remained standing, leaning over, both hands flat on the counsel table. Foster turned back to the bench as Judge Hawkins gaveled and demanded order in her court.

In the explosion of flashbulbs and the continuing clamor, Kate looked around blindly, to see Carl Jacoby, his face granite-hard, stalking from the courtroom. Francisco Caldera and Gloria Gomez were sobbing in each other's arms. Aimee was standing, along with a sizeable contingent of the audience, arms raised in exultation.

Kate's gaze settled on the jury. Juror number four's face was again down in her PARIS sweater; she was sobbing. Juror number three took her hand. Eugenia Lowe met Kate's eyes with a swift, gray-eyed glance, then took the hand of juror number seven, Victor Chen, whose face streamed with tears; he reached for juror number six, Dion Franklin. All the jurors linked hands.

— Epilogue —

As Kate and Aimee pushed their way through a jam-packed Nightwood Bar toward Maggie Schaeffer, Kate noticed a forest of identical brown beer bottles on all the tables.

Maggie leaned across the bar. "Everybody, I mean everybody's ordering the same thing tonight." She winked at Kate. "Good thing I thought to get a lot of it stocked." She reached into a tub, opened two bottles of beer, and slid them across the bar.

Kate picked one up, and grinned delightedly at the label: Foster's.

Patton pushed her way through to the bar, salaamed to Kate and winked at Aimee. Kate pointed at the bottle of beer tucked into the belt of Patton's low-slung jeans and said incredulously, "You're actually contaminating the temple of your body with alcohol?"

"Shit no. This is just solidarity with my sisters. I'd as soon drink horse piss."

"This is real good horse piss, Patton." Tora, slinging an arm around Patton's shoulder, took a swig from her bottle, and waved it in salute to Kate and Aimee. "This fine horse piss came all the way from Australia."

Laughing, Maggie punched a button on the VCR behind the bar. "Hey, Kate," she exulted, and gestured with a flourish at the television screen. To deafening cheers in the bar, Linda Foster appeared, being interviewed by a KTLA reporter in the corridor of the Criminal Courts Building.

"The case is opening doors for her," Kate said, raising her voice above the din. "She's already been assigned another homicide case. And there's talk about forming a special hate-crimes unit in the DA's office."

"Is she interested?" Maggie asked.

Kate laughed. "She's told them she'll run it."

"I *love* that woman's style," Tora crowed. She flung her arms around Audie and Raney, who had made their way through the crush and up to the bar. "And I love *these* women."

"This is all great and everything," Patton said sternly, "but you know what we're celebrating?" She answered her own question. "That a guy got what he deserved for killing one of our brothers."

"It's more than Atticus Finch could do for Tom Robinson," Audie pointed out. She explained to Aimee, "That's the lawyer who defended the black man in *To Kill a Mockingbird,* honey."

"I *know* Audie," Aimee groaned. "I know how to read."

"Why, child," Raney said, "a beautiful sweet child like you knows how to *read?*"

And a number of other quite sophisticated things, Kate thought, grinning as the women teased and flirted with Aimee. Kate's gaze strayed over the swell of Aimee's thighs outlined in the tight denim of her faded jeans. Last evening had been filled with intimate conversation as Kate unburdened herself of all the anguish of this case; the intense evening had been followed by a night of intense lovemaking, its lingering memory filling her with hunger for the night to come. Had she ever — even at first — wanted Anne this much? Surely she must have . . .

Anne. She was still disturbed with Anne — disturbed that Anne was not here to explain her friendship with Kenneth Pritchard. But perhaps the explanation lay simply in the nature of the closed-in life she and Anne had led as lesbians in those days. Perhaps Anne, in her isolation and loneliness — and naivete — had confused prurient interest from Pritchard for sympathetic friendship.

The women were still bantering with Aimee, whose good-natured comebacks were picking up edges of impatience. Kate said, "I talked to some of the jury."

The women eagerly crowded around. Kate continued, "After they elected Eugenia Lowe, they spent a lot of time going over the jury instructions, making sure everybody understood them. Then they took the first ballot, just to see where everybody was about guilty or not guilty. The first vote was unanimous."

Kate reached into her shoulder bag. "Eugenia Lowe saved one of those ballots." She spread the small white square of paper on the leather cover of her notebook and held it up so that all the women could see the drawing: a stick-like figure, a hand held up, standing in front of a tank. On the body of the tank was printed GUILTY.

"Tian An Men Square," breathed Audie.

"I bet this was Victor Chen's ballot," Aimee said.

"Probably," Kate said, "but . . . who knows for sure?"

"Would you let me have it?" Maggie asked. "I'll frame it, hang it in the bar."

"A fine place for it," Kate said, handing it over.

Watching Maggie enfold the ballot in a napkin, Kate continued, "So then they had a discussion to be clear about the difference between first degree murder and voluntary manslaughter."

"What a conscientious jury," Audie said.

Kate nodded. "Having a leader like Eugenia Lowe had to make a difference. Then they took a second ballot — it was unanimous, too."

"Did they say anything at all about the why of all this?" Patton asked, hands on her hips.

"They mentioned various things. The evidence about the blood especially — Charlotte Mead's testimony. Mercer's explanation about the wounds on Jensen's hands was key. Stacey Conlin's conversation with Teddie. And Linda Foster," Kate said. "Mostly Linda Foster. Her anger." She shrugged. "They thought Linda Foster was a good person, they were all really impressed with how angry she was."

"God," said Patton. "What if she hadn't been angry enough."

"Linda says it's gay people who aren't angry enough," Kate said.

"I think some toasts are in order." Maggie reached for her own bottle of beer from under the bar.

"Do me a favor," Patton said, pulling her bottle out of her belt. "Let's propose all the toasts so I only have to take one sip of this horse piss. And I get the first toast." She raised her bottle. "To Kate Delafield. The best. Except at pool."

"We'll see about that, my friend," Kate said, touching her beer bottle to Patton's.

Maggie lifted her Foster's. "To Linda Foster — and good people who get angry."

Holding her own bottle aloft, Kate gazed into the caring faces surrounding her. "To Teddie Crawford," she said.

"A brother," Aimee added, looking at Kate, "who did not die in vain."

A few of the publications of
THE NAIAD PRESS, INC.
P.O. Box 10543 • Tallahassee, Florida 32302
Phone (904) 539-5965
Toll-Free Order Number: 1-800-533-1973
Mail orders welcome. Please include 15% postage.
Write or call for our free catalog which also features an
incredible selection of lesbian videos.

BABY, IT'S COLD by Jaye Maiman. 256 pp. 5th Robin Miller
Mystery. ISBN 1-56280-141-4 $19.95

WILD THINGS by Karin Kallmaker. 240 pp. By the undisputed
mistress of lesbian romance. ISBN 1-56280-139-2 10.95

THE GIRL NEXT DOOR by Mindy Kaplan. 208 pp. Just what
you'd expect. ISBN 1-56280-140-6 10.95

NOW AND THEN by Penny Hayes. 240 pp. Romance on the
westward journey. ISBN 1-56280-121-X 10.95

HEART ON FIRE by Diana Simmonds. 176 pp. The romantic and
erotic rival of *Curious Wine*. ISBN 1-56280-152-X 10.95

DEATH AT LAVENDER BAY by Lauren Wright Douglas. 208 pp.
1st Allison O'Neil Mystery. ISBN 1-56280-085-X 10.95

YES I SAID YES I WILL by Judith McDaniel. 272 pp. Hot
romance by famous author. ISBN 1-56280-138-4 10.95

FORBIDDEN FIRES by Margaret C. Anderson. Edited by Mathilda
Hills. 176 pp. Famous author's "unpublished" Lesbian romance.
ISBN 1-56280-123-6 21.95

SIDE TRACKS by Teresa Stores. 160 pp. Gender-bending
Lesbians on the road. ISBN 1-56280-122-8 10.95

HOODED MURDER by Annette Van Dyke. 176 pp. 1st Jessie
Batelle Mystery. ISBN 1-56280-134-1 10.95

WILDWOOD FLOWERS by Julia Watts. 208 pp. Hilarious and
heart-warming tale of true love. ISBN 1-56280-127-9 10.95

NEVER SAY NEVER by Linda Hill. 224 pp. Rule #1: Never get involved
with . . . ISBN 1-56280-126-0 10.95

THE SEARCH by Melanie McAllester. 240 pp. Exciting top cop
Tenny Mendoza case. ISBN 1-56280-150-3 10.95

THE WISH LIST by Saxon Bennett. 192 pp. Romance through
the years. ISBN 1-56280-125-2 10.95

FIRST IMPRESSIONS by Kate Calloway. 208 pp. P.I. Cassidy
James' first case.   ISBN 1-56280-133-3   10.95

OUT OF THE NIGHT by Kris Bruyer. 192 pp. Spine-tingling
thriller.   ISBN 1-56280-120-1   10.95

NORTHERN BLUE by Tracey Richardson. 224 pp. Police recruits
Miki & Miranda — passion in the line of fire. ISBN 1-56280-118-X 10.95

LOVE'S HARVEST by Peggy J. Herring. 176 pp. by the author of
Once More With Feeling.   ISBN 1-56280-117-1   10.95

THE COLOR OF WINTER by Lisa Shapiro. 208 pp. Romantic
love beyond your wildest dreams.   ISBN 1-56280-116-3   10.95

FAMILY SECRETS by Laura DeHart Young. 208 pp. Enthralling
romance and suspense.   ISBN 1-56280-119-8   10.95

INLAND PASSAGE by Jane Rule. 288 pp. Tales exploring conventional & unconventional relationships.   ISBN 0-930044-56-8   10.95

DOUBLE BLUFF by Claire McNab. 208 pp. 7th Detective Carol
Ashton Mystery.   ISBN 1-56280-096-5   10.95

BAR GIRLS by Lauran Hoffman. 176 pp. See the movie, read
the book!   ISBN 1-56280-115-5   10.95

THE FIRST TIME EVER edited by Barbara Grier & Christine
Cassidy. 272 pp. Love stories by Naiad Press authors.
                                         ISBN 1-56280-086-8   14.95

MISS PETTIBONE AND MISS McGRAW by Brenda Weathers.
208 pp. A charming ghostly love story.   ISBN 1-56280-151-1   10.95

CHANGES by Jackie Calhoun. 208 pp. Involved romance and
relationships.   ISBN 1-56280-083-3   10.95

FAIR PLAY by Rose Beecham. 256 pp. 3rd Amanda Valentine
Mystery.   ISBN 1-56280-081-7   10.95

PAXTON COURT by Diane Salvatore. 256 pp. Erotic and wickedly
funny contemporary tale about the business of learning to live
together.   ISBN 1-56280-109-0   21.95

PAYBACK by Celia Cohen. 176 pp. A gripping thriller of romance,
revenge and betrayal.   ISBN 1-56280-084-1   10.95

THE BEACH AFFAIR by Barbara Johnson. 224 pp. Sizzling
summer romance/mystery/intrigue.   ISBN 1-56280-090-6   10.95

GETTING THERE by Robbi Sommers. 192 pp. Nobody does it
like Robbi!   ISBN 1-56280-099-X   10.95

FINAL CUT by Lisa Haddock. 208 pp. 2nd Carmen Ramirez
Mystery.   ISBN 1-56280-088-4   10.95

FLASHPOINT by Katherine V. Forrest. 256 pp. A Lesbian
blockbuster!   ISBN 1-56280-079-5   10.95

CLAIRE OF THE MOON by Nicole Conn. Audio Book —Read
by Marianne Hyatt.   ISBN 1-56280-113-9   16.95

FOR LOVE AND FOR LIFE: INTIMATE PORTRAITS OF
LESBIAN COUPLES by Susan Johnson. 224 pp.
ISBN 1-56280-091-4   14.95

DEVOTION by Mindy Kaplan. 192 pp. See the movie — read
the book!   ISBN 1-56280-093-0   10.95

SOMEONE TO WATCH by Jaye Maiman. 272 pp. 4th Robin
Miller Mystery.   ISBN 1-56280-095-7   10.95

GREENER THAN GRASS by Jennifer Fulton. 208 pp. A young
woman — a stranger in her bed.   ISBN 1-56280-092-2   10.95

TRAVELS WITH DIANA HUNTER by Regine Sands. Erotic
lesbian romp. Audio Book (2 cassettes)   ISBN 1-56280-107-4   16.95

CABIN FEVER by Carol Schmidt. 256 pp. Sizzling suspense
and passion.   ISBN 1-56280-089-1   10.95

THERE WILL BE NO GOODBYES by Laura DeHart Young. 192
pp. Romantic love, strength, and friendship.   ISBN 1-56280-103-1   10.95

FAULTLINE by Sheila Ortiz Taylor. 144 pp. Joyous comic
lesbian novel.   ISBN 1-56280-108-2   9.95

OPEN HOUSE by Pat Welch. 176 pp. 4th Helen Black Mystery.
ISBN 1-56280-102-3   10.95

ONCE MORE WITH FEELING by Peggy J. Herring. 240 pp.
Lighthearted, loving romantic adventure.   ISBN 1-56280-089-2   10.95

FOREVER by Evelyn Kennedy. 224 pp. Passionate romance — love
overcoming all obstacles.   ISBN 1-56280-094-9   10.95

WHISPERS by Kris Bruyer. 176 pp. Romantic ghost story
ISBN 1-56280-082-5   10.95

NIGHT SONGS by Penny Mickelbury. 224 pp. 2nd Gianna Maglione
Mystery.   ISBN 1-56280-097-3   10.95 — 2

GETTING TO THE POINT by Teresa Stores. 256 pp. Classic
southern Lesbian novel.   ISBN 1-56280-100-7   10.95

PAINTED MOON by Karin Kallmaker. 224 pp. Delicious
Kallmaker romance.   ISBN 1-56280-075-2   10.95

THE MYSTERIOUS NAIAD edited by Katherine V. Forrest &
Barbara Grier. 320 pp. Love stories by Naiad Press authors.
ISBN 1-56280-074-4   14.95

DAUGHTERS OF A CORAL DAWN by Katherine V. Forrest.
240 pp. Tenth Anniversay Edition.   ISBN 1-56280-104-X   10.95

BODY GUARD by Claire McNab. 208 pp. 6th Carol Ashton
Mystery.   ISBN 1-56280-073-6   10.95 — 6

CACTUS LOVE by Lee Lynch. 192 pp. Stories by the beloved
storyteller.   ISBN 1-56280-071-X   9.95

SECOND GUESS by Rose Beecham. 216 pp. 2nd Amanda Valentine
Mystery.   ISBN 1-56280-069-8   9.95 — 2

THE SURE THING by Melissa Hartman. 208 pp. L.A. earthquake
romance.   ISBN 1-56280-078-7   9.95

A RAGE OF MAIDENS by Lauren Wright Douglas. 240 pp. 6th Caitlin
Reece Mystery.   ISBN 1-56280-068-X   10.95

TRIPLE EXPOSURE by Jackie Calhoun. 224 pp. Romantic drama
involving many characters.   ISBN 1-56280-067-1   10.95

UP, UP AND AWAY by Catherine Ennis. 192 pp. Delightful
romance.   ISBN 1-56280-065-5   9.95

PERSONAL ADS by Robbi Sommers. 176 pp. Sizzling short
stories.   ISBN 1-56280-059-0   10.95

FLASHPOINT by Katherine V. Forrest. 256 pp. Lesbian
blockbuster!   ISBN 1-56280-043-4   22.95

CROSSWORDS by Penny Sumner. 256 pp. 2nd Victoria Cross
Mystery.   ISBN 1-56280-064-7   9.95

SWEET CHERRY WINE by Carol Schmidt. 224 pp. A novel of
suspense.   ISBN 1-56280-063-9   9.95

CERTAIN SMILES by Dorothy Tell. 160 pp. Erotic short stories.
                                            ISBN 1-56280-066-3   9.95

EDITED OUT by Lisa Haddock. 224 pp. 1st Carmen Ramirez
Mystery.   ISBN 1-56280-077-9   9.95

WEDNESDAY NIGHTS by Camarin Grae. 288 pp. Sexy
adventure.   ISBN 1-56280-060-4   10.95

SMOKEY O by Celia Cohen. 176 pp. Relationships on the
playing field.   ISBN 1-56280-057-4   9.95

KATHLEEN O'DONALD by Penny Hayes. 256 pp. Rose and
Kathleen find each other and employment in 1909 NYC.
                                            ISBN 1-56280-070-1   9.95

STAYING HOME by Elisabeth Nonas. 256 pp. Molly and Alix
want a baby . . . or do they?   ISBN 1-56280-076-0   10.95

TRUE LOVE by Jennifer Fulton. 240 pp. Six lesbians searching
for love in all the "right" places.   ISBN 1-56280-035-3   10.95

GARDENIAS WHERE THERE ARE NONE by Molleen Zanger.
176 pp. Why is Melanie inextricably drawn to the old house?
                                            ISBN 1-56280-056-6   9.95

KEEPING SECRETS by Penny Mickelbury. 208 pp. 1st Gianna
Maglione Mystery.   ISBN 1-56280-052-3   9.95

THE ROMANTIC NAIAD edited by Katherine V. Forrest &
Barbara Grier. 336 pp. Love stories by Naiad Press authors.
                                            ISBN 1-56280-054-X   14.95

UNDER MY SKIN by Jaye Maiman. 336 pp. 3rd Robin Miller
Mystery.   ISBN 1-56280-049-3.   10.95

CAR POOL by Karin Kallmaker. 272pp. Lesbians on wheels
and then some! ISBN 1-56280-048-5 10.95

NOT TELLING MOTHER: STORIES FROM A LIFE by Diane
Salvatore. 176 pp. Her 3rd novel. ISBN 1-56280-044-2 9.95

GOBLIN MARKET by Lauren Wright Douglas. 240pp. 5th Caitlin
Reece Mystery. ISBN 1-56280-047-7 10.95

LONG GOODBYES by Nikki Baker. 256 pp. 3rd Virginia Kelly
Mystery. ISBN 1-56280-042-6 9.95

FRIENDS AND LOVERS by Jackie Calhoun. 224 pp. Mid-
western Lesbian lives and loves. ISBN 1-56280-041-8 10.95

THE CAT CAME BACK by Hilary Mullins. 208 pp. Highly
praised Lesbian novel. ISBN 1-56280-040-X 9.95

BEHIND CLOSED DOORS by Robbi Sommers. 192 pp. Hot,
erotic short stories. ISBN 1-56280-039-6 9.95

CLAIRE OF THE MOON by Nicole Conn. 192 pp. See the
movie — read the book! ISBN 1-56280-038-8 10.95

SILENT HEART by Claire McNab. 192 pp. Exotic Lesbian
romance. ISBN 1-56280-036-1 10.95

HAPPY ENDINGS by Kate Brandt. 272 pp. Intimate conversations
with Lesbian authors. ISBN 1-56280-050-7 10.95

THE SPY IN QUESTION by Amanda Kyle Williams. 256 pp.
4th Madison McGuire Mystery. ISBN 1-56280-037-X 9.95

SAVING GRACE by Jennifer Fulton. 240 pp. Adventure and
romantic entanglement. ISBN 1-56280-051-5 9.95

THE YEAR SEVEN by Molleen Zanger. 208 pp. Women surviving
in a new world. ISBN 1-56280-034-5 9.95

CURIOUS WINE by Katherine V. Forrest. 176 pp. Tenth Anniver-
sary Edition. The most popular contemporary Lesbian love story.
ISBN 1-56280-053-1 10.95
Audio Book (2 cassettes) ISBN 1-56280-105-8 16.95

CHAUTAUQUA by Catherine Ennis. 192 pp. Exciting, romantic
adventure. ISBN 1-56280-032-9 9.95

A PROPER BURIAL by Pat Welch. 192 pp. 3rd Helen Black
Mystery. ISBN 1-56280-033-7 9.95

SILVERLAKE HEAT: A Novel of Suspense by Carol Schmidt.
240 pp. Rhonda is as hot as Laney's dreams. ISBN 1-56280-031-0 9.95

LOVE, ZENA BETH by Diane Salvatore. 224 pp. The most talked
about lesbian novel of the nineties! ISBN 1-56280-030-2 10.95

A DOORYARD FULL OF FLOWERS by Isabel Miller. 160 pp.
Stories incl. 2 sequels to *Patience and Sarah.* ISBN 1-56280-029-9 9.95

MURDER BY TRADITION by Katherine V. Forrest. 288 pp. 4th
Kate Delafield Mystery. ISBN 1-56280-002-7 10.95

THE EROTIC NAIAD edited by Katherine V. Forrest & Barbara Grier. 224 pp. Love stories by Naiad Press authors.
ISBN 1-56280-026-4   14.95

DEAD CERTAIN by Claire McNab. 224 pp. 5th Carol Ashton Mystery.
ISBN 1-56280-027-2   9.95

CRAZY FOR LOVING by Jaye Maiman. 320 pp. 2nd Robin Miller Mystery.
ISBN 1-56280-025-6   9.95

STONEHURST by Barbara Johnson. 176 pp. Passionate regency romance.
ISBN 1-56280-024-8   9.95

INTRODUCING AMANDA VALENTINE by Rose Beecham. 256 pp. 1st Amanda Valentine Mystery.
ISBN 1-56280-021-3   10.95

UNCERTAIN COMPANIONS by Robbi Sommers. 204 pp. Steamy, erotic novel.
ISBN 1-56280-017-5   9.95

A TIGER'S HEART by Lauren W. Douglas. 240 pp. 4th Caitlin Reece Mystery.
ISBN 1-56280-018-3   9.95

PAPERBACK ROMANCE by Karin Kallmaker. 256 pp. A delicious romance.
ISBN 1-56280-019-1   10.95

MORTON RIVER VALLEY by Lee Lynch. 304 pp. Lee Lynch at her best!
ISBN 1-56280-016-7   9.95

THE LAVENDER HOUSE MURDER by Nikki Baker. 224 pp. 2nd Virginia Kelly Mystery.
ISBN 1-56280-012-4   9.95

PASSION BAY by Jennifer Fulton. 224 pp. Passionate romance, virgin beaches, tropical skies.
ISBN 1-56280-028-0   10.95

STICKS AND STONES by Jackie Calhoun. 208 pp. Contemporary lesbian lives and loves.
ISBN 1-56280-020-5   9.95
Audio Book (2 cassettes)
ISBN 1-56280-106-6   16.95

DELIA IRONFOOT by Jeane Harris. 192 pp. Adventure for Delia and Beth in the Utah mountains.
ISBN 1-56280-014-0   9.95

UNDER THE SOUTHERN CROSS by Claire McNab. 192 pp. Romantic nights Down Under.
ISBN 1-56280-011-6   9.95

GRASSY FLATS by Penny Hayes. 256 pp. Lesbian romance in the '30s.
ISBN 1-56280-010-8   9.95

A SINGULAR SPY by Amanda K. Williams. 192 pp. 3rd Madison McGuire Mystery.
ISBN 1-56280-008-6   8.95

THE END OF APRIL by Penny Sumner. 240 pp. 1st Victoria Cross Mystery.
ISBN 1-56280-007-8   8.95

HOUSTON TOWN by Deborah Powell. 208 pp. A Hollis Carpenter Mystery.
ISBN 1-56280-006-X   8.95

KISS AND TELL by Robbi Sommers. 192 pp. Scorching stories by the author of *Pleasures*.
ISBN 1-56280-005-1   10.95

STILL WATERS by Pat Welch. 208 pp. 2nd Helen Black Mystery.
ISBN 0-941483-97-5   9.95

TO LOVE AGAIN by Evelyn Kennedy. 208 pp. Wildly romantic
love story.   ISBN 0-941483-85-1   9.95 —

IN THE GAME by Nikki Baker. 192 pp. 1st Virginia Kelly
Mystery.   ISBN 1-56280-004-3   9.95

AVALON by Mary Jane Jones. 256 pp. A Lesbian Arthurian
romance.   ISBN 0-941483-96-7   9.95

STRANDED by Camarin Grae. 320 pp. Entertaining, riveting
adventure.   ISBN 0-941483-99-1   9.95

THE DAUGHTERS OF ARTEMIS by Lauren Wright Douglas.
240 pp. 3rd Caitlin Reece Mystery.   ISBN 0-941483-95-9   9.95 — 3 ⊛

CLEARWATER by Catherine Ennis. 176 pp. Romantic secrets
of a small Louisiana town.   ISBN 0-941483-65-7   8.95

THE HALLELUJAH MURDERS by Dorothy Tell. 176 pp. 2nd
Poppy Dillworth Mystery.   ISBN 0-941483-88-6   8.95

SECOND CHANCE by Jackie Calhoun. 256 pp. Contemporary
Lesbian lives and loves.   ISBN 0-941483-93-2   9.95

BENEDICTION by Diane Salvatore. 272 pp. Striking, contemporary romantic novel.   ISBN 0 941483 90 8   9.95

BLACK IRIS by Jeane Harris. 192 pp. Caroline's hidden past . . .
                                          ISBN 0-941483-68-1   8.95

TOUCHWOOD by Karin Kallmaker. 240 pp. Loving, May/
December romance.   ISBN 0-941483-76-2   9.95

COP OUT by Claire McNab. 208 pp. 4th Carol Ashton Mystery.
                                          ISBN 0-941483-84-3   9.95 — 4

THE BEVERLY MALIBU by Katherine V. Forrest. 288 pp. 3rd
Kate Delafield Mystery.   ISBN 0-941483-48-7   10.95

THAT OLD STUDEBAKER by Lee Lynch. 272 pp. Andy's affair
with Regina and her attachment to her beloved car.
                                          ISBN 0-941483-82-7   9.95

PASSION'S LEGACY by Lori Paige. 224 pp. Sarah is swept into
the arms of Augusta Pym in this delightful historical romance.
                                          ISBN 0-941483-81-9   8.95

THE PROVIDENCE FILE by Amanda Kyle Williams. 256 pp.
2nd Madison McGuire Mystery.   ISBN 0-941483-92-4   8.95

I LEFT MY HEART by Jaye Maiman. 320 pp. 1st Robin Miller
Mystery.   ISBN 0-941483-72-X   10.95

THE PRICE OF SALT by Patricia Highsmith (writing as Claire
Morgan). 288 pp. Classic lesbian novel, first issued in 1952 . . .
acknowledged by its author under her own, very famous, name.
                                          ISBN 1-56280-003-5   9.95

SIDE BY SIDE by Isabel Miller. 256 pp. From beloved author of
Patience and Sarah.   ISBN 0-941483-77-0   9.95

STAYING POWER: LONG TERM LESBIAN COUPLES by
Susan E. Johnson. 352 pp. Joys of coupledom. ISBN 0-941-483-75-4   14.95

SLICK by Camarin Grae. 304 pp. Exotic, erotic adventure.
ISBN 0-941483-74-6   9.95

NINTH LIFE by Lauren Wright Douglas. 256 pp. 2nd Caitlin
Reece Mystery.   ISBN 0-941483-50-9   8.95

PLAYERS by Robbi Sommers. 192 pp. Sizzling, erotic novel.
ISBN 0-941483-73-8   9.95

MURDER AT RED ROOK RANCH by Dorothy Tell. 224 pp.
1st Poppy Dillworth Mystery.   ISBN 0-941483-80-0   8.95

A ROOM FULL OF WOMEN by Elisabeth Nonas. 256 pp.
Contemporary Lesbian lives.   ISBN 0-941483-69-X   9.95

THEME FOR DIVERSE INSTRUMENTS by Jane Rule. 208 pp.
Powerful romantic lesbian stories. ISBN 0-941483-63-0   8.95

CLUB 12 by Amanda Kyle Williams. 288 pp. Espionage thriller
featuring a lesbian agent!   ISBN 0-941483-64-9   8.95

DEATH DOWN UNDER by Claire McNab. 240 pp. 3rd Carol
Ashton Mystery.   ISBN 0-941483-39-8   9.95

MONTANA FEATHERS by Penny Hayes. 256 pp. Vivian and
Elizabeth find love in frontier Montana.   ISBN 0-941483-61-4   8.95

LIFESTYLES by Jackie Calhoun. 224 pp. Contemporary Lesbian
lives and loves.   ISBN 0-941483-57-6   10.95

WILDERNESS TREK by Dorothy Tell. 192 pp. Six women on
vacation learning ''new'' skills.   ISBN 0-941483-60-6   8.95

MURDER BY THE BOOK by Pat Welch. 256 pp. 1st Helen
Black Mystery.   ISBN 0-941483-59-2   9.95

THERE'S SOMETHING I'VE BEEN MEANING TO TELL YOU
Ed. by Loralee MacPike. 288 pp. Gay men and lesbians coming out
to their children.   ISBN 0-941483-44-4   9.95

LIFTING BELLY by Gertrude Stein. Ed. by Rebecca Mark. 104 pp.
Erotic poetry.   ISBN 0-941483-51-7   10.95

AFTER THE FIRE by Jane Rule. 256 pp. Warm, human novel by
this incomparable author.   ISBN 0-941483-45-2   8.95

PLEASURES by Robbi Sommers. 204 pp. Unprecedented
eroticism.   ISBN 0-941483-49-5   8.95

These are just a few of the many Naiad Press titles — we are the oldest and
largest lesbian/feminist publishing company in the world. We also offer an
enormous selection of lesbian video products. Please request a complete
catalog. We offer personal service; we encourage and welcome direct mail
orders from individuals who have limited access to bookstores carrying our
publications.

MAXIMIZING STUDY ABROAD

A Students' Guide to Strategies for Language
and Culture Learning and Use

MAXIMIZING
STUDY ABROAD

A Students' Guide to Strategies for Language
and Culture Learning and Use

R. Michael Paige

Andrew D. Cohen

Barbara Kappler

Julie C. Chi

James P. Lassegard

Center for Advanced Research
on Language Acquisition

UNIVERSITY OF MINNESOTA

STUDY ABROAD:

Guide to Strategies for Language and Culture Learning and Use

roduced by
Center for Advanced Research on Language Acquisition
University of Minnesota
619 Heller Hall
271 - 19th Avenue South
Minneapolis, MN 55455

ISBN: 0-9722545-0-1

First Edition, Second Printing
Printed in the United States of America

Background

As with all successful collaborative efforts, the development of the *Maximizing Study Abroad* series has a long history and has involved the participation of many people. In 1999 the Center for Advanced Research on Language Acquisition (CARLA) at the University of Minnesota received funding from the U.S. Department of Education's Language Resource Center program to create a set of user-friendly materials on language- and culture-learning strategies designed to maximize students' study abroad experiences. This project was a logical extension of previous work conducted at CARLA on culture and language learning and strategies-based instruction.

During the period 1999-2003 the project leaders created, field-tested, and revised the following set of three guides as part of the *Maximizing Study Abroad* series:

Maximizing Study Abroad: A Students' Guide to Strategies for Language and Culture Learning and Use

Maximizing Study Abroad: A Program Professionals' Guide to Strategies for Language and Culture Learning and Use

Maximizing Study Abroad: A Language Instructors' Guide to Strategies for Language and Culture Learning and Use

Phases of the project

The initial writing phase (1999-2000)

The initial writing phase of this project took place during the 1999-2000 academic year. The writing team was led by Professor Andrew D. Cohen on the language-learning strategies sections and Professor R. Michael Paige on the culture-learning strategies sections. Two graduate research assistants, Julie C. Chi and James P. Lassegard, worked in collaboration with Professors Cohen and Paige throughout the initial development of the guides.

The field-testing and revision phase – part 1 (2000-2001)

The field-testing and revision phase of the project was coordinated by Dr. Barbara Kappler (University of Minnesota International Student and Scholar Services) during the 2000-2001 academic year. The three guides were piloted with volunteer groups of language instructors, students engaged in study abroad programs, and study abroad program professionals and advisers at the University of Minnesota and selected sites throughout the country. Based on the rich feedback received, the guides were extensively reformatted and revised to be more appealing and accessible to end-users.

The field-testing and implementation phase – part 2 (2001-2002)

During the third and final phase of field-testing and development of the guides, prototypes were used to fully explore the range of options in which the materials could be used effectively. The core leadership group (Cohen, Kappler, and Paige) worked with faculty and staff from the Department of Spanish and Portuguese and the Learning Abroad Center at the University of Minnesota to demonstrate how the guides could be used in a wide range of teaching and study abroad contexts. As part of this demonstration phase, Margaret Demmessie, a seasoned instructor of Spanish, taught a special "study abroad" section of beginning third-year Spanish using materials from the instructor and student guides. Each student in this special course section received a copy of the *Students' Guide*. Their response was very positive.

In addition to using the materials in a language course, special workshops were held in fall 2001 and spring 2002 for students planning to study abroad. Dr. Kappler facilitated another round of focus groups with language instructors from various language departments and program professionals from the Learning Abroad Center. In May 2002, CARLA sponsored an intensive workshop on how to use the guides, which attracted more than forty language instructors and study abroad program professionals. Half of the participants were staff and faculty at the University of Minnesota, while the other half came from study abroad programs in Minnesota, Wisconsin, Missouri, Maryland, and Colorado.

By fall 2002, the first edition of the *Students' Guide* and the *Program Professionals' Guide* were published as part of the CARLA working paper series. Both of the guides have been widely circulated to a national audience of leaders in the field of study abroad, and the response from students and professionals has been exciting.

Final development phase for the Instructors' Guide (2002–2003)

The third and final guide in the *Maximizing Study Abroad* series is targeted at the needs of language instructors, and while the materials and philosophy behind the guide are complementary to the first two guides, the needs and focus of the classroom language teacher in using the materials were quite different because not all students in language classrooms are directly preparing for study abroad. Given this difference, the authors and the development team at CARLA thought that it was critical to take additional time to make sure the materials were further tested and revised by practicing language teachers.

In fall 2002 Margaret Demmessie joined the team of authors to help create and revise activities for teachers to use in the classroom and to provide input on writing throughout the guide based on her experience in regularly using the materials in her Spanish classes at the University and with a group of Spanish instructors at a study abroad site in Spain. After another round of major revisions to the guide, another draft was circulated to a group of colleagues at the University of Minnesota, Brigham Young University, and St. Cloud State University who provided in-depth feedback and ideas to make the final guide appropriate for the language-teaching context.

We are pleased to be able to share the full series of *Maximizing Study Abroad* guides nationally to a broad audience of people involved in making the most of study abroad. As we all know, enhancing students' language and culture learning during their study abroad experience is a holistic endeavor that ultimately requires the efforts of the students themselves, study abroad professionals, and language teachers. It is our greatest hope that this series of guides can provide support for the important goal of preparing students to make the most of their study abroad experiences.

Acknowledgments

CARLA wishes to thank the many students, teachers, and study abroad professionals who have contributed to the development of the *Maximizing Study Abroad* series. (Those listed below are from the University of Minnesota unless otherwise noted.)

Maximizing Study Abroad project leaders

The initial vision and the background research for this project came from Professor Andrew Cohen and Professor R. Michael Paige, both leaders in their fields and active members of CARLA since its inception. Cohen's research on styles- and strategies-based language instruction and Paige's work on integrating concepts of intercultural communication into the second language classroom made this project possible. The collaborative scholarship provided both a solid research-based foundation and a framework to synthesize information from both fields into a new body of materials to support study abroad. We are deeply grateful to both for their vision for this project and their continued leadership within the center.

Professors Cohen and Paige were aided greatly in the first year of the project by two graduate students, Julie Chi and James Lassegard. Former graduate assistant Susan J. Weaver also contributed to materials for the very first draft of the guide for language instructors. Chi continued to contribute time and energy to this project beyond the time of her initial work as a graduate student, and Lassegard helped with some final details after he graduated and left the University. After the first drafts of all three guides had been completed, the materials needed to be piloted and revised, and Dr. Barbara Kappler, an assistant director of International Student and Scholar Services, was invited to lead the effort. She gathered and incorporated feedback from students, study abroad program professionals, and language instructors into the final publications. It was a tremendous task to synthesize the volumes of feedback and create more user-friendly texts from an academic framework, especially for the *Students' Guide*. Kappler's in-depth background in intercultural communication, her insights into study abroad experiences, and her skills as both a writer and editor helped transform the guides into a set of lively and informative materials that are engaging for students, program professionals, and language instructors alike.

Students

Many students gave feedback on the development of the *Students' Guide* during workshops, focus groups, and classes held at the University of Minnesota and other local institutions. Special recognition goes to students who, as part of the Undergraduate Research Opportunities Program at the University of Minnesota, used the *Students' Guide* during their own study abroad experience or gave feedback based on previous study abroad experience including Jacob Dick, Kelly Lavin, Tammy Yach, and Molly Zahn.

Study abroad program professionals and program staff

Throughout the process of creating materials, gathering feedback, and revising, many of the staff members in the Learning Abroad Center and other departments at the University of Minnesota assisted in the task of distilling a vast quantity of information into a work that would be read by students. We are grateful to study abroad program professionals Sheila Collins, Sophie Gladding, Holly Zimmerman LeVoir, Heidi Soneson, and Susan Wiese for their willingness to let us "try out" the draft materials on their student audiences and for giving us feedback from their perspectives as program leaders. In addition we are grateful to other staff and students who helped review the guides including Bill Baldus, Michelle Cumming, Joan Brzezinski, Amy Greeley, Joe Hoff, April Knutson, Jodi Malmgren, Gayla Marty, Rachel Sullivan-Nightengale, Barbara Pilling, Gayle Woodruff, and Yelena Yershova. Thanks also to Hanae Tsukada for collecting quotes from international students and for helping to rewrite the section on learning characters. Special recognition goes to Chip Peterson, a veteran in the field of study abroad, for his ongoing support, expertise, and uncanny ability to see both the big picture and the small details at the same time. For their overall support of this project, we express our warmest thanks to Al Balkcum, director of the Learning Abroad Center, and Kay Thomas, director of International Student and Scholar Services.

Language instructors

Specific feedback on all of the guides came from a wide network of language instructors at and around the University of Minnesota. Blair Bateman (Brigham Young University), Eleanora Bertranou, Lucy Carlone, Elaine Fuller Carter (St. Cloud State University), Isabelle Clavel, Kelly Conroy, Francine Klein, Muisi Krosi, Magara Maeda, Patricia Mougel, Allison Spenader, Susan Villar, and Ellen Wormwood gave enormously helpful feedback on the *Language Instructors' Guide* as part of an initial series of focus groups with language instructors. Bateman, Carter, Klein, Wormwood, Villar, María Emilce López, and Kathleen Ganley read the final draft of the *Language Instructors' Guide* during an especially busy time of the year and provided the detailed feedback needed to make the final publication a success. Based on teacher feedback, a new section was added that focused on the intersection between language and culture in foreign language instruction. Klein, who is writing her dissertation on the topic, was the lead author of this new chapter, along with Cohen. Both Bateman and Klein were very helpful in providing important information for the reference section.

Special thanks goes to Charlotte Melin, Patricia Mougel, and Susan Villar for their ongoing help in supporting this work through their language departments and by providing in a set of quotes that helped make connections to the language classroom. We greatly appreciated the enthusiasm and support of faculty and staff of the Department of Spanish and Portuguese for this project including Department Chair Carol Klee, Margaret Demmessie, Kathleen Ganley, and Susan Villar. Special thanks goes to Demmessie who brought many years of experience in language teaching and study abroad program coordination to the challenge of incorporating materials from the guides into her third-year Spanish language course. Her skills, insight, and zeal helped us to do a "real life" test of the materials and gave us a wealth of feedback that was incorporated into each of the guides. We were especially grateful that she chose to join the team of authors in the final phase of writing and revising the guide for language instructors given her experience with the project and her perspective as a language instructor who was in the classroom when she was writing the materials.

Feedback from far and wide

The writing team at CARLA also solicited feedback from experts outside the University of Minnesota. We appreciate the helpful comments received from Anna Uhl Chamot (The George Washington University), Rebecca Oxford and Gloria Park (University of Maryland-College Park), Jonathon Rees (University of Birmingham), and Joan Rubin during various stages of the development of the material.

Behind the scenes

Given the level of truth to the old adage, "the devil is in the details," we wish to thank those working in the CARLA office and in the Office of International Programs whose efforts have proved critical to the success of this project. Special recognition goes to Dan Supalla, a student worker with an incredible eye for proofreading; Jennifer Schulz, who brought her copyediting skills to the project; and Jesse Houchins for his fantastic cover design. Not enough can be said for the contributions of Suzanne Hay, the secretary of CARLA, who brought tremendous skill, background knowledge of study abroad, and good humor to the job of word processing, formatting, and editing through a series of drafts that became too numerous to count.

A final note of thanks goes to our partners in the Office of International Programs, especially Executive Director C. Eugene Allen and Fiscal Officer Elaine Randolph, for their support on a number of fronts to bring the Maximizing Study Abroad project to fruition.

Elaine Tarone   *Karin Larson*
Director   *Coordinator*
CARLA   *CARLA*

December 2003

Table of Contents

Section II: Language-Learning Strategies

Welcome to Study Abroad!

As a study abroad student, you are not going to be just a tourist—you are embarking on something much richer, doing the kinds of things that most tourists can only dream about. You will be with the locals, immersing yourself in the culture and perhaps coming to understand the culture as an insider. Being a tourist is easy—studying abroad takes work to learn the language and the culture of your hosts. And it's rewarding work!

> *My entire trip was the most meaningful, exciting, life-changing four months I have ever had. Every day I learned something new, and I know that sounds a little clichéd, but it's absolutely true. Studying abroad was the best thing I could have done. ~ Seth Lengkeek, England*

> *Study abroad let me finally get a grip on the Spanish language...the only way to learn a language is to speak and hear it. ~ Dan Jakab, Spain*

What does this guide offer?

This guide provides specific strategies for improving your language and culture learning so that your time spent abroad will be as meaningful and productive as you hope. These tools have been developed based on the experience of students and the authors, and solid research in the fields of language acquisition, international education, and intercultural communication.

Why do I need a guide?

While you have probably studied the language and culture of your destination, chances are that you have not been taught strategies that you can use to make the most of study abroad. Quite simply, if language and culture were easy to learn, everyone would be fluent in another language and competent in another culture. Clearly this is not the case. It's hard to do this learning on your own—so this guide is prepared to lead you through the process.

Why this guide?

This guide is unique in linking language- and culture-learning strategies into one workbook. As you know, the two are inseparable. You cannot be competent in another culture without skills in both language and culture.

How do I use this guide?

This guide was not written for you to read cover to cover. Instead, you can use this workbook to go directly to the topic of your particular interest. Begin by taking surveys of your learning styles and language- and culture-learning strategies, starting on page 5. The strategies surveys will guide you to the sections where you can start. In short, the idea is that you will read some before you go, consult the guide while abroad, and check out the suggestions upon returning home for strategies to maintain or improve your language skills.

The guide is long only because it's comprehensive—and if used correctly, it is not time consuming. ~ Jacob Dick, Italy

But a whole guide?

Chances are, you are already stressed out—so much to do, so little time! So why add one more thing to the list? And really, why do this at all? Shouldn't you just jump into the culture? Isn't that why you signed up anyway?

While there is a lot to be said for "just doing it," there are numerous examples of "ugly travelers" (and not just Americans)—those whose lack of cultural sensitivity makes them instantly recognizable in an unpleasant sort of way and, moreover, reflects a lack of respect for their hosts. Why not try to break the mold? Why not take a few moments to learn from those who have traveled before? With a few extra minutes of preparation, you can assure yourself that you are doing all you can to make this the most amazing and meaningful journey of your life!

> *I find the guide to be quite thorough with lots of helpful information. I wish I would have had this guide before I went abroad. ~ Laura Seifert, England*

> *This guide gave me the opportunity to be much more self-reflective while I was studying in Germany. Of course everyone who studies abroad realizes at some level that they are operating in a different environment, facing different challenges and different sources of stress. But the guide works through all these new things in a systematic way, which allowed me to get a better sense of what was really going on. It provides a context larger than simply my own experience for my interactions with a different culture. It also contains a lot of valuable insights about language learning—how to overcome typical frustrations (or: 'Why can't I speak this language yet?'); strategies for improving reading, writing, listening, and speaking skills; and suggestions for ways to practice your skills with the help of native speakers. Not every part of the guide will speak to every student, but it contains much that will be of use to anyone who studies abroad. ~ Molly Zahn, Germany*

Getting Started

1. Take a few minutes to write down on page 4 your goals for study abroad.
2. Complete the language and culture surveys to determine where it's most appropriate for you to focus your time and energy.

    Learning Style Survey, p. 6
    Language Strategy Use Inventory, p. 16
    Culture-Learning Strategies Inventory, p. 23

Terms used in this guide

Host culture: the culture(s) of the country in which you are studying

Target or new language: the language of your host culture

Second language: While you may speak many languages, we may occasionally refer to the target or new language as the "second language."

Second language learner strategies: These encompass both second language learning and second language use strategies. "Taken together, they constitute the steps or actions consciously selected by learners either to improve the learning of a second language, the use of it, or both" (Cohen, 1998).

Setting goals

One of the most important things you can do to help yourself be successful in study abroad is to be aware of what you hope to gain from the experience. Take a few moments to write down your own personal goals for this study abroad trip. Make sure to consider language- and culture-learning goals, as well as personal aspirations.

Note:

1. For the purposes of this guide, *tips, techniques,* and *tactics* are all being used synonymously with *strategy.* No distinction is being made.
2. While we wrote the guide assuming that most readers are native speakers of U.S. English, it can be used by students of any language.

> *Worried that this guide will spoil the experience? Nothing is going to take away the richness of the experience of your study abroad. ~ R. Michael Paige, co-author*

Personal Goals for Study Abroad

Use the space below to list the personal goals you may have for your study abroad experience.

-

-

-

-

-

Discovering Your Styles:
Strategies to Language and Culture Learning

Now is your chance to take three surveys, all intended to give you a better sense of how you learn and how you use specific strategies for culture and language learning. The first survey, the Learning Style Survey, gives you a general overview of your preferences for learning. Understanding your preferences can help you determine your strengths and weaknesses for new learning environments. The second and third surveys give you the chance to consider if you know how to use certain strategies for language and culture learning. If you want more information on specific strategies, you can go directly to the pages indicated in the survey.

The Learning Style Survey

We all have preferences for how we like to learn. Your classmates may have enjoyed how a certain professor lectured, while you craved more visuals. You may feel very uncomfortable with role-playing activities but really enjoy independent research projects. While you may have a general sense of your preferences already, this survey can help you deepen your understanding by comparing and contrasting 11 different learning styles. You will then be better prepared to make the most of your upcoming change—from being in a familiar U.S. classroom where you have spent more than a decade to studying abroad.

Learning-style preferences allow us to understand and organize our learning. Since some aspects of learning are usually out of your control (you may have to take a class where the professor lectures nearly 100 percent of the time), you can improve your learning by understanding your strengths and weaknesses. For example, knowing that you prefer a visual style does not give you free license to demand that professors teach to your style. In fact, it may be absolutely culturally inappropriate to make such a request and might reflect your own hesitancy and reluctance to adapt to the host culture. Instead, knowing that you are a visual learner helps you to understand that you may need to create your own visuals, team with auditory learners, and tap into your own auditory skills that exist but are not fully developed. In short, our goal is to help you "style-stretch" by incorporating approaches that you may have resisted in the past.

Learning Style Survey:
Assessing Your Own Learning Styles

Andrew D. Cohen, Rebecca L. Oxford, and Julie C. Chi

The Learning Style Survey[1] is designed to assess your general approach to learning. It does not predict your behavior in every instance, but it is a clear indication of your overall style preferences. For each item, circle the response that represents your approach. Complete all items. There are eleven major activities representing twelve different aspects of your learning style. When you read the statements, try to think about what you generally do when learning. It generally takes about 30 minutes to complete the survey. Do not spend too much time on any item—indicate your immediate feeling and move on to the next item.

For each item, circle your response:

> 0 = Never
> 1 = Rarely
> 2 = Sometimes
> 3 = Often
> 4 = Always

Part 1: HOW I USE MY PHYSICAL SENSES

1.	I remember something better if I write it down.	0 1 2 ③ 4
2.	I take detailed notes during lectures.	0 1 ② 3 4
3.	When I listen, I visualize pictures, numbers, or words in my head.	0 1 2 ③ 4
4.	I prefer to learn with TV or video rather than other media.	0 1 ② 3 4
5.	I use color-coding to help me as I learn or work.	0 1 ② 3 4
6.	I need written directions for tasks.	0 1 2 ③ 4
7.	I have to look at people to understand what they say.	0 ① 2 3 4
8.	I understand lectures better when professors write on the board.	0 1 ② 3 4
9.	Charts, diagrams, and maps help me understand what someone says.	0 1 2 ③ 4
10.	I remember peoples' faces but not their names.	0 1 2 ③ 4

A - Total _____

24

---

[1] Authors' note: The format of the Learning Style Survey and a number of the dimensions and items are drawn from Oxford, 1995. Other key dimensions and some of the wording of items comes from Ehrman and Leaver (see Ehrman & Leaver, 2003).

11. I remember things better if I discuss them with someone.   0 1 2 3 ④
12. I prefer to learn by listening to a lecture rather than reading.   0 1 ② 3 4
13. I need oral directions for a task.   0 1 ② 3 4
14. Background sound helps me think.   ⓪ 1 2 3 4
15. I like to listen to music when I study or work.   ⓪ 1 2 3 4
16. I can understand what people say even when I cannot see them.   0 1 2 ③ 4
17. I remember peoples' names but not their faces.   0 ① 2 3 4
18. I easily remember jokes that I hear.   0 1 ② 3 4
19. I can identify people by their voices (e.g., on the phone).   0 1 2 3 ④
20. When I turn on the TV, I listen to the sound more than I watch the screen.   ⓪ 1 2 3 4

B - Total   18

21. I'd rather start to do things, rather than pay attention to directions.   0 1 ② 3 4
22. I need frequent breaks when I work or study.   0 1 ② 3 4
23. I need to eat something when I read or study.   0 ① 2 3 4
24. If I have a choice between sitting and standing, I'd rather stand.   0 1 ② 3 4
25. I get nervous when I sit still too long.   0 1 2 ③ 4
26. I think better when I move around (e.g., pacing or tapping my feet).   0 1 2 ③ 4
27. I play with or bite on my pens during lectures.   0 1 2 ③ 4
28. Manipulating objects helps me to remember what someone says.   0 1 ② 3 4
29. I move my hands when I speak.   0 1 2 ③ 4
30. I draw lots of pictures (doodles) in my notebook during lectures.   0 1 ② 3 4

C - Total   23

Part 2: HOW I EXPOSE MYSELF TO LEARNING SITUATIONS

1. I learn better when I work or study with others than by myself.   0 1 2 ③ 4
2. I meet new people easily by jumping into the conversation.   0 1 2 ③ 4
3. I learn better in the classroom than with a private tutor.   0 ① 2 3 4
4. It is easy for me to approach strangers.   0 1 ② 3 4
5. Interacting with lots of people gives me energy.   0 1 2 ③ 4
6. I experience things first and then try to understand them.   0 1 ② 3 4

A - Total   14

7. I am energized by the inner world (what I'm thinking inside).   0 1 2 ③ 4
8. I prefer individual or one-on-one games and activities.   0 ① 2 3 4
9. I have a few interests, and I concentrate deeply on them.   0 ① 2 3 4
10. After working in a large group, I am exhausted.   0 1 2 ③ 4
11. When I am in a large group, I tend to keep silent and listen.   0 1 ② 3 4
12. I want to understand something well before I try it.   0 1 ② 3 4

B - Total   12

Part 3: HOW I HANDLE POSSIBILITIES

1. I have a creative imagination.   0 1 2 ③ 4
2. I try to find many options and possibilities for why something happens.   0 1 2 ③ 4
3. I plan carefully for future events.   0 1 ② 3 4
4. I like to discover things myself rather than have everything explained to me.   0 1 2 ③ 4
5. I add many original ideas during class discussions.   0 1 ② 3 4
6. I am open-minded to new suggestions from my peers.   0 1 2 ③ 4

A - Total   16

7. I focus in on a situation as it is rather than thinking about how it could be.   0 1 ② 3 4
8. I read instruction manuals (e.g., for computers or VCRs) before using the device.   0 ① 2 3 4
9. I trust concrete facts instead of new, untested ideas.   0 1 2 ③ 4
10. I prefer things presented in a step-by-step way.   0 1 ② 3 4
11. I dislike it if my classmate changes the plan for our project.   0 ① 2 3 4
12. I follow directions carefully.   0 1 2 ③ 4

B - Total   12

Part 4: HOW I DEAL WITH AMBIGUITY AND WITH DEADLINES

1. I like to plan language study sessions carefully and do lessons on time or early.   0 ① 2 3 4
2. My notes, handouts, and other school materials are carefully organized.   0 ① 2 3 4
3. I like to be certain about what things mean in a target language.   0 1 2 ③ 4
4. I like to know how rules are applied and why.   0 1 2 ③ 4

A - Total   8

5. I let deadlines slide if I'm involved in other things.   0 ① 2 3 4
6. I let things pile up on my desk to be organized eventually.   0 1 2 3 ④
7. I don't worry about comprehending everything.   0 ① 2 3 4
8. I don't feel the need to come to rapid conclusions about a topic.   0 1 ② 3 4

B - Total   8

Part 5: HOW I RECEIVE INFORMATION

1. I prefer short and simple answers rather than long explanations. 0 1 2 ③ 4
2. I ignore details that do not seem relevant. 0 1 ② 3 4
3. It is easy for me to see the overall plan or big picture. 0 1 2 ③ 4
4. I get the main idea, and that's enough for me. 0 ① 2 3 4
5. When I tell an old story, I tend to forget lots of specific details. 0 1 2 ③ 4

A - Total   12

6. I need very specific examples in order to understand fully. 0 1 2 ③ 4
7. I pay attention to specific facts or information. 0 1 2 ③ 4
8. I'm good at catching new phrases or words when I hear them. 0 1 2 ③ 4
9. I enjoy activities where I fill in the blank with missing words I hear. 0 ① 2 3 4
10. When I try to tell a joke, I remember details but forget the punch line. 0 1 2 ③ 4

B - Total   13

Part 6: HOW I FURTHER PROCESS INFORMATION

1. I can summarize information easily. 0 1 2 ③ 4
2. I can quickly paraphrase what other people say. 0 1 2 ③ 4
3. When I create an outline, I consider the key points first. 0 1 2 ③ 4
4. I enjoy activities where I have to pull ideas together. 0 1 ② 3 4
5. By looking at the whole situation, I can easily understand someone. 0 1 2 ③ 4

A - Total   14

6. I have a hard time understanding when I don't know every word. 0 1 ② 3 4
7. When I tell a story or explain something, it takes a long time. 0 1 ② 3 4
8. I like to focus on grammar rules. 0 1 ② 3 4
9. I'm good at solving complicated mysteries and puzzles. 0 1 2 ③ 4
10. I am good at noticing even the smallest details regarding some task. 0 1 2 ③ 4

B - Total   12

Part 7: HOW I COMMIT MATERIAL TO MEMORY

1. I try to pay attention to all the features of new material as I learn. 0 1 2 ③ 4
2. When I memorize different bits of language material, I can retrieve 0 1 ② 3 4
these bits easily – as if I had stored them in separate slots in my brain.
3. As I learn new material in the target language, I make fine distinctions 0 ① 2 3 4
among speech sounds, grammatical forms, and words and phrases.

A - Total   6

4. When learning new information, I may clump together data by eliminating or reducing differences and focusing on similarities. 0 1 2 ③ 4

5. I ignore distinctions that would make what I say more accurate in the given context. 0 ① 2 3 4

6. Similar memories become blurred in my mind; I merge new learning experiences with previous ones. 0 ① 2 3 4

B - Total _5_

Part 8: HOW I DEAL WITH LANGUAGE RULES

1. I like to go from general patterns to the specific examples in learning a target language. 0 1 2 ③ 4

2. I like to start with rules and theories rather than specific examples. 0 1 2 ③ 4

3. I like to begin with generalizations and then find experiences that relate to those generalizations. 0 1 2 ③ 4

A - Total _9_

4. I like to learn rules of language indirectly by being exposed to examples of grammatical structures and other language features. 0 1 ② 3 4

5. I don't really care if I hear a rule stated since I don't remember rules very well anyway. 0 1 ② 3 4

6. I figure out rules based on the way I see language forms behaving over time. 0 1 ② 3 4

B - Total _6_

Part 9: HOW I DEAL WITH MULTIPLE INPUTS

1. I can separate out the relevant and important information in a given context even when distracting information is present. 0 1 ② 3 4

2. When I produce an oral or written message in the target language, I make sure that all the grammatical structures are in agreement with each other. 0 1 ② 3 4

3. I not only attend to grammar but check for appropriate level of formality and politeness. 0 1 ② 3 4

A - Total _6_

4. When speaking or writing, a focus on grammar would be at the expense of attention to the content of the message. 0 ① 2 3 4

5. It is a challenge for me to both focus on communication in speech or writing while at the same time paying attention to grammatical agreement (e.g., person, number, tense, or gender). 0 1 ② 3 4

6. When I am using lengthy sentences in a target language, I get distracted and neglect aspects of grammar and style. 0 1 ② 3 4

B - Total _5_

Part 10: HOW I DEAL WITH RESPONSE TIME

1. I react quickly in language situations.   0 1 ② 3 4
2. I go with my instincts in the target language.   0 1 ② 3 4
3. I jump in, see what happens, and make corrections if needed.   0 1 ② 3 4

A - Total   6

4. I need to think things through before speaking or writing.   0 1 2 ③ 4
5. I like to look before I leap when determining what   0 1 2 ③ 4
   to say or write in a target language.
6. I attempt to find supporting material in my mind before I   0 1 2 ③ 4
   set about producing language.

B - Total   9

Part 11: HOW LITERALLY I TAKE REALITY

1. I find that building metaphors in my mind helps me deal with   0 1 ② 3 4
   language (e.g., viewing the language like a machine with
   component parts that can be disassembled).
2. I learn things through metaphors and associations with other   0 1 2 3 ④
   things. I find stories and examples help me learn.

A - Total   6

3. I take learning language literally and don't deal in metaphors. 0 ① 2 3 4
4. I take things at face value, so I like language material that says 0 1 ② 3 4
   what it means directly.

B - Total   3

Understanding your totals

Once you have totaled your points, write the results in the blanks below. Circle the higher number in each part (if they are close, circle both). Read about your learning styles on the next page.

Part 1:
A _24_ Visual
B _18_ Auditory
C _23_ Tactile / Kinesthetic

Part 2:
A _14_ Extraverted
B _12_ Introverted

Part 3:
A _10_ Random-Intuitive
B _12_ Concrete-Sequential

Part 4:
A _9_ Closure-Oriented
B _8_ Open

Part 5:
A _12_ Global
B _13_ Particular

Part 6:
A _14_ Synthesizing
B _12_ Analytic

Part 7:
A _6_ Sharpener
B _5_ Leveler

Part 8:
A _9_ Deductive
B _6_ Inductive

Part 9:
A _6_ Field-Independent
B _5_ Field-Dependent

Part 10:
A _6_ Impulsive
B _9_ Reflective

Part 11:
A _6_ Metaphoric
B _3_ Literal

Note:

Before reading the next section, understand that this is only a general description of your learning style preferences. It does not describe you *all of the time*, but gives you an idea of your tendencies when you learn. Note that in some learning situations, you may have one set of style preferences and in a different situation, another set of preferences. Also, there are both advantages and disadvantages to every style preference.

If on the sensory style preferences (visual, auditory, tactile/kinesthetic) you prefer two or all three of these senses (i.e., your totals for the categories are within 5 points or so), you are likely to be flexible enough to enjoy a wide variety of activities in the language classroom. On the other dimensions, although they appear to be in opposition, it is possible for you to have high scores on both, meaning that you do not have a preference one way or the other. Here are three examples: on the extroversion-introversion distinction, you are able to work effectively with others as well as by yourself; on the closure-open distinction, you enjoy the freedom of limited structure yet can still get the task done before the deadline without stress; on the global-particular distinction, you can handle both the gist and the details easily.

Furthermore, learning style preferences change throughout your life, and you can also stretch them, so don't feel that you are constrained to one style.

Part 1: HOW I USE MY PHYSICAL SENSES

If you came out as more visual than auditory, you rely more on the sense of sight, and you learn best through visual means (books, video, charts, pictures). If you are more auditory in preference, you prefer listening and speaking activities (discussions, lectures, audio tapes, role-plays). If you have a tactile/kinesthetic style preference, you benefit from doing projects, working with objects, and moving around (playing games, building models, conducting experiments).

Part 2: HOW I EXPOSE MYSELF TO LEARNING SITUATIONS

If you came out more extraverted on this survey, you probably enjoy a wide range of social, interactive learning tasks (games, conversations, discussions, debates, role-plays, simulations). If you came out more introverted, you probably like to do more independent work (studying or reading by yourself or learning with a computer) or enjoy working with one other person you know well.

Part 3: HOW I HANDLE POSSIBILITIES

If you scored more random-intuitive, you are most likely more future-oriented, prefer what can be over what is, like to speculate about possibilities, enjoy abstract thinking, and tend to disfavor step-by-step instruction. If your style preference was more concrete-sequential, you are likely to be more present-oriented, prefer one-step-at-a-time activities, and want to know where you are going in your learning at every moment.

Part 4: HOW I APPROACH TASKS

If you are more closure-oriented, you probably focus carefully on most or all learning tasks, strive to meet deadlines, plan ahead for assignments, and want explicit directions. If you are more open in your orientation, you enjoy discovery learning (in which you pick up information naturally) and prefer to relax and enjoy your learning without concern for deadlines or rules.

Part 5: HOW I RECEIVE INFORMATION

If you have a more global style preference, you enjoy getting the gist or main idea and are comfortable communicating even if you don't know all the words or concepts. If you are more particular in preference, you focus more on details and remember specific information about a topic well.

Part 6: HOW I FURTHER PROCESS INFORMATION

If you are a synthesizing person, you can summarize material well, enjoy guessing meanings and predicting outcomes, and notice similarities quickly. If you are analytic, you can pull ideas apart and do well on logical analysis and contrast tasks, and you tend to focus on grammar rules.

Part 7: HOW I COMMIT MATERIAL TO MEMORY

If you are a sharpener, you tend to notice differences and seek distinctions among items as you commit material to memory. You like to distinguish small differences and to separate memory of prior experiences from memory of current ones. You can easily retrieve the different items because you store them separately. You like to make fine distinctions among speech sounds, grammatical forms, and meaningful elements of language (words and phrases). If you are a leveler, you are likely to clump material together in order to remember it, by eliminating or reducing differences, and by focusing almost exclusively on similarities. You are likely to blur similar memories and to merge new experiences readily with previous ones. If you are concerned about accuracy and getting it all right, then the sharpener approach is perhaps preferable. If you are concerned about expediency, then being a leveler may be the key to communication.

Part 8: HOW I DEAL WITH LANGUAGE RULES

If you are a more deductive learner, you like to go from the general to the specific, to apply generalizations to experience, and to start with rules and theories rather than with specific examples. If you are a more inductive learner, you like to go from specific to general and prefer to begin with examples rather than rules or theories.

Part 9: HOW I DEAL WITH MULTIPLE INPUTS

If you are more field-independent in style preference, you like to separate or abstract material from within a given context, even in the presence of distractions. You may, however, have less facility dealing with information holistically. If you are more field-dependent in preference, you tend to deal with information in a more holistic or "gestalt" way. Consequently you may have greater difficulty in separating or abstracting material from its context. You work best without distractions.

Part 10: HOW I DEAL WITH RESPONSE TIME

If you are a more impulsive learner, you react quickly in acting or speaking without thinking the situation through. For you, thought often follows action. If you are a more reflective learner, you think things through before taking action and often do not trust your gut reactions. In your case, action usually follows thought.

Part 11: HOW LITERALLY I TAKE REALITY

If you are a metaphoric learner, you learn material more effectively if you conceptualize aspects of it, such as the grammar system, in metaphorical terms. You make the material more comprehensible by developing and applying an extended metaphor to it (e.g., visualizing the grammar system of a given language as an engine that can be assembled and disassembled). If you are a literal learner, you prefer a relatively literal representation of concepts and like to work with language material more or less as it is on the surface.

Tips for the learner

Each style preference offers significant strengths in learning and working. Recognize your strengths to take advantage of ways you learn best. Also, enhance your learning and working power by being aware of and developing the style areas that you do *not* normally use. Tasks that do not seem quite as suited to your style preferences will help you stretch beyond your ordinary comfort zone, expanding your learning and working potential.

For example, if you are a highly global person, you might need to learn to pay more attention to detail in order to learn more effectively. If you are an extremely detail-oriented person, you might be missing out on some useful global characteristics, like getting the main idea quickly. You can develop such qualities in yourself through practice. You won't lose your basic strengths by trying something new; you will simply develop another side of yourself that is likely to be very helpful to your language learning.

If you aren't sure how to attempt new behaviors that go *beyond* your favored style, then ask your colleagues, friends, or teachers to give you a hand. Talk with someone who has a different style from yours and see how that person does it. Improve your learning or working situation by stretching your style!

Language Strategy Use Inventory

Andrew D. Cohen and Julie C. Chi

The purpose of this inventory is to find out more about yourself as a language learner and to help you discover strategies that can help you master a new language. Check the box that describes your use of each listed strategy. The categories are: *I use this strategy and like it; I have tried this strategy and would use it again; I've never used this strategy but am interested in it*; and *This strategy doesn't fit for me*. By referring to the page numbers at the end of each section, you can use this inventory as an index to find out more about the strategies that interest you. Please note that "target" language refers to the new language you are learning.

Listening Strategy Use

Strategies to increase my exposure to the target language:

1. Attend out-of-class events where the new language is spoken.
2. Listen to talk shows on the radio, watch TV shows, or see movies in the target language.
3. Listen to the language in a restaurant or store where the staff speak the target language.
4. Listen in on people who are having conversations in the target language to try to catch the gist of what they are saying.

Strategies to become more familiar with the sounds in the target language:

5. Practice sounds in the target language that are very different from sounds in my own language to become comfortable with them.
6. Look for associations between the sound of a word or phrase in the new language with the sound of a familiar word.
7. Imitate the way native speakers talk.
8. Ask a native speaker about unfamiliar sounds that I hear.

Strategies to prepare to listen to conversation in the target language:

9. Pay special attention to specific aspects of the language; for example, the way the speaker pronounces certain sounds.
10. Try to predict what the other person is going to say based on what has been said so far.
11. Prepare for talks and performances I will hear in the target language by reading some background materials beforehand.

Strategies to listen to conversation in the target language:

	I use this strategy and like it	I have tried this strategy and would use it again	I've never used this strategy, but am interested in it	This strategy doesn't fit for me
12. Listen for key words that seem to carry the bulk of the meaning.	☐	☐	☐	☐
13. Listen for word and sentence stress to see what native speakers emphasize when they speak.	☐	☐	☐	☐
14. Pay attention to when and how long people tend to pause.	☐	☐	☐	☐
15. Pay attention to the rise and fall of speech by native speakers—the "music" of it.	☐	☐	☐	☐
16. Practice "skim listening" by paying attention to some parts and ignoring others.	☐	☐	☐	☐
17. Try to understand what I hear without translating it word-for-word.	☐	☐	☐	☐
18. Focus on the context of what people are saying.	☐	☐	☐	☐
19. Listen for specific details to see whether I can understand them.	☐	☐	☐	☐

Strategies for when I do not understand some or most of what someone says in the target language:

	I use this strategy and like it	I have tried this strategy and would use it again	I've never used this strategy, but am interested in it	This strategy doesn't fit for me
20. Ask speakers to repeat what they said if it wasn't clear to me.	☐	☐	☐	☐
21. Ask speakers to slow down if they are speaking too fast.	☐	☐	☐	☐
22. Ask for clarification if I don't understand it the first time around.	☐	☐	☐	☐
23. Use the speakers' tone of voice as a clue to the meaning of what they are saying.	☐	☐	☐	☐
24. Make educated guesses about the topic based on what has already been said.	☐	☐	☐	☐
25. Draw on my general background knowledge to get the main idea.	☐	☐	☐	☐
26. Watch speakers' gestures and general body language to help me figure out the meaning of what they are saying.	☐	☐	☐	☐

For more information on listening strategies, see pages 165-179.

Vocabulary Strategy Use

Column headers (checkboxes) for each item:
- I use this strategy and like it
- I have tried this strategy and would use it again
- I've never used this strategy but am interested in it
- This strategy doesn't fit for me

Strategies to learn new words:

27. Pay attention to the structure of the new word. ☐ ☐ ☐ ☐
28. Break the word into parts that I can identify. ☐ ☐ ☐ ☐
29. Group words according to parts of speech (e.g., nouns, verbs). ☐ ☐ ☐ ☐
30. Associate the sound of the new word with the sound of a word that is familiar to me. ☐ ☐ ☐ ☐
31. Use rhyming to remember new words. ☐ ☐ ☐ ☐
32. Make a mental image of new words. ☐ ☐ ☐ ☐
33. List new words with other words that are related to it. ☐ ☐ ☐ ☐
34. Write out new words in meaningful sentences. ☐ ☐ ☐ ☐
35. Practice new action verbs by acting them out. ☐ ☐ ☐ ☐
36. Use flash cards in a systematic way to learn new words. ☐ ☐ ☐ ☐

Strategies to review vocabulary:

37. Go over new words often when I first learn them to help me remember them. ☐ ☐ ☐ ☐
38. Review words periodically so I don't forget them. ☐ ☐ ☐ ☐

Strategies to recall vocabulary:

39. Look at meaningful parts of the word (e.g., the prefix or the suffix) to remind me of the meaning of the word. ☐ ☐ ☐ ☐
40. Make an effort to remember the situation where I first heard or saw the word or remember the page or sign where I saw it written. ☐ ☐ ☐ ☐
41. Visualize the spelling of new words in my mind. ☐ ☐ ☐ ☐

Strategies to make use of new vocabulary:

42. Try using new words in a variety of ways. ☐ ☐ ☐ ☐
43. Practice using familiar words in different ways. ☐ ☐ ☐ ☐
44. Make an effort to use idiomatic expressions in the new language. ☐ ☐ ☐ ☐

For more information on vocabulary strategies, see pages 181-195.

Speaking Strategy Use

Strategies to practice speaking:

45. Practice saying new expressions to myself. ☐ ☐ ☐ ☐
46. Practice new grammatical structures in different situations to build my confidence level in using them. ☐ ☐ ☐ ☐
47. Think about how a native speaker might say something and practice saying it that way. ☐ ☐ ☐ ☐

Strategies to engage in conversations:

48. Regularly seek out opportunities to talk with native speakers. ☐ ☐ ☐ ☐
49. Initiate conversations in the target language as often as possible. ☐ ☐ ☐ ☐
50. Direct the conversation to familiar topics. ☐ ☐ ☐ ☐
51. Plan out in advance what I want to say. ☐ ☐ ☐ ☐
52. Ask questions as a way to be involved in the conversation. ☐ ☐ ☐ ☐
53. Anticipate what will be said based on what has been said so far. ☐ ☐ ☐ ☐
54. Try topics even when they aren't familiar to me. ☐ ☐ ☐ ☐
55. Encourage others to correct errors in my speaking. ☐ ☐ ☐ ☐
56. Try to figure out and model native speakers' language patterns when requesting, apologizing, or complaining. ☐ ☐ ☐ ☐

Strategies for when I can't think of a word or expression:

57. Ask for help from my conversational partner. ☐ ☐ ☐ ☐
58. Look for a different way to express the idea, like using a synonym. ☐ ☐ ☐ ☐
59. Use words from my own language, but say it in a way that sounds like words in the target language. ☐ ☐ ☐ ☐
60. Make up new words or guess if I don't know the right ones to use. ☐ ☐ ☐ ☐
61. Use gestures as a way to try and get my meaning across. ☐ ☐ ☐ ☐
62. Switch back to my own language momentarily if I know that the person I'm talking to can understand what is being said.

For more information on speaking strategies, see pages 197-214.

Reading Strategy Use

Strategies to improve my reading ability:

63. Read as much as possible in the target language. ☐ ☐ ☐ ☐
64. Try to find things to read for pleasure in the target language. ☐ ☐ ☐ ☐
65. Find reading material that is at or near my level. ☐ ☐ ☐ ☐
66. Plan out in advance how I'm going to read the text, monitor to see how I'm doing, and then check to see how much I understand. ☐ ☐ ☐ ☐
67. Skim an academic text first to get the main idea and then go back and read it more carefully. ☐ ☐ ☐ ☐
68. Read a story or dialogue several times until I understand it. ☐ ☐ ☐ ☐
69. Pay attention to the organization of the text, especially headings and subheadings. ☐ ☐ ☐ ☐
70. Make ongoing summaries of the reading either in my mind or in the margins of the text. ☐ ☐ ☐ ☐
71. Make predictions as to what will happen next. ☐ ☐ ☐ ☐

Strategies for when words and grammatical structures are not understood:

72. Guess the approximate meaning by using clues from the context of the reading material. ☐ ☐ ☐ ☐
73. Use a dictionary to get a detailed sense of what individual words mean. ☐ ☐ ☐ ☐

For more information on reading strategies, see pages 215-221.

Writing Strategy Use

	I use this strategy and like it	I have tried this strategy and would use it again	I've never used this strategy but am interested in it	This strategy doesn't fit for me

Strategies for basic writing:

75. Practice writing the alphabet and/or new words in the target language. ☐ ☐ ☐ ☐

76. Plan out in advance how to write academic papers, monitor how my writing is going, and check to see how well my writing reflects what I want to say. ☐ ☐ ☐ ☐

77. Try writing different kinds of texts in the target language (e.g., personal notes, messages, letters, and course papers). ☐ ☐ ☐ ☐

78. Take class notes in the target language as much as I'm able. ☐ ☐ ☐ ☐

Strategies for writing an essay or academic paper:

79. Find a different way to express the idea when I don't know the correct expression (e.g., use a synonym or describe the idea). ☐ ☐ ☐ ☐

80. Review what I have already written before continuing to write more. ☐ ☐ ☐ ☐

81. Use reference materials such as a glossary, a dictionary, or a thesaurus to help find or verify words in the target language. ☐ ☐ ☐ ☐

82. Wait to edit my writing until all my ideas are down on paper. ☐ ☐ ☐ ☐

Strategies to use after writing a draft of an essay or paper:

83. Revise my writing once or twice to improve the language and content. ☐ ☐ ☐ ☐

84. Try to get feedback from others, especially native speakers of the language. ☐ ☐ ☐ ☐

For more information on writing strategies, see pages 223-230.

Translation Strategy Use

Strategies for translation:	I use this strategy and like it	I have tried this strategy and would use it again	I've never used this strategy but am interested in it	This strategy doesn't fit for me
85. Plan out what to say or write in my own language and then translate it into the target language.	☐	☐	☐	☐
86. Translate in my head while I am reading to help me understand the text.	☐	☐	☐	☐
87. Translate parts of a conversation into my own language to help me remember the conversation.	☐	☐	☐	☐

Strategies for working directly in the target language as much as possible:				
88. Put my own language out of mind and think only in the target language as much as possible.	☐	☐	☐	☐
89. Try to understand what has been heard or read without translating it word-for-word into my own language.	☐	☐	☐	☐
90. Use caution when directly transferring words and ideas from my own language into the target language.	☐	☐	☐	☐

For more information on translation strategies, see pages 231-234.

Culture-Learning Strategies Inventory

R. M. Paige, J. Rong, W. Zheng, and B. Kappler

The purpose of this inventory is to find out more about yourself as a culture learner and to help you discover strategies that can help you adapt to cultures that are different from your own. Check the box that describes your use of each listed strategy. The categories are: *I use this strategy and like it; I have tried this strategy and would use it again; I've never used this strategy but am interested in it*; and *This strategy doesn't fit for me*. By referring to the page numbers at the end of each section, you can use this inventory as an index to find out more about the strategies that interest you.

Pre-Departure Strategies

Strategies for when I am in surroundings that are culturally different from what I am used to:

	I use this strategy and like it	I have tried this strategy and would use it again	I've never used this strategy but am interested in it	This strategy doesn't fit for me
1. Consider ways in which different cultures might view things in different ways (e.g., how different cultures value "alone time" or independence).	☐	☐	☐	☐
2. Figure out what cultural values might be involved when I encounter a conflict or something goes wrong.	☐	☐	☐	☐
3. Think about different cross-cultural perspectives to examine situations in which I seem to offend someone or do something wrong.	☐	☐	☐	☐
4. Use generalizations instead of stereotypes when I make statements about people who are different from me.	☐	☐	☐	☐
5. Counter stereotypes others use about people from my country by using generalizations and cultural values instead.	☐	☐	☐	☐
6. Make distinctions between behavior that is personal (unique to the person), cultural (representative of the person's culture), and universal (a shared human concern).	☐	☐	☐	☐
7. Look at similarities as well as differences between people of different backgrounds.	☐	☐	☐	☐

For more information on pre-departure strategies, see pages 39-73.

This portion of the Culture-Learning Strategies Inventory looks at the culture-learning strategies you think you will use once you are in the country of your study abroad experience, referred to in this inventory as your "host country." If you have studied abroad before, you may want to complete this inventory before you depart for your next study abroad experience. Or you can fill it out by indicating which strategies you think you *will likely* use in a variety of situations.

In-Country Strategies

Strategies I (will likely) use to adjust to a new culture and cope with culture shock:

	I use this strategy and like it	I have tried this strategy and would use it again	I've never used this strategy but am interested in it	This strategy doesn't fit for me
8. Explain my cross-cultural experiences (the good *and* the difficult) to my family and friends at home.	☐	☐	☐	☐
9. Consider what my friends living in the host country say about people from my own culture, using what I know about cultural bias.	☐	☐	☐	☐
10. Strive to keep myself physically healthy.	☐	☐	☐	☐
11. Assume that some moments of "culture shock" are normal culture learning experiences and not worry about them too much.	☐	☐	☐	☐
12. Use a variety of coping strategies when I feel I have "culture shock overload."	☐	☐	☐	☐
13. Keep reasonable expectations of my ability to adjust to the new culture given the amount of time of my stay and my particular study abroad program.	☐	☐	☐	☐

For more information on strategies for cross-cultural adjustment and culture shock, see pages 83-99.

Strategies for dealing with difficult times in the new culture:

14. Keep in touch with friends and family back home by writing letters and e-mails.
15. Keep a journal or a diary about my experiences.
16. Participate in sports and other activities while abroad.
17. Find someone from my own culture to talk to about my cultural experiences
18. Relax when I'm stressed out in my host country by doing what I normally do back home to make myself comfortable.

For more information on strategies for dealing with difficult times in the new culture, see pages 83-99.

Strategies for making judgments about another culture:

19. Observe the behavior of people from my host country very carefully.
20. Analyze things that happen in my host country that seem strange to me from as many perspectives as I can.
21. Consider my own cultural biases when trying to understand another culture.
22. Refrain from making quick judgments about another culture.

For more information on strategies for making cultural judgments, see pages 59-68, 69-73, and 101-113.

Strategies for communicating with people from another culture:

23. Don't assume that everyone from the same culture is the same.
24. Investigate common areas of miscommunication between people from my host culture and my own culture through books and by talking to other people who know the two cultures well.
25. Read local newspapers to better understand the current political and social issues in my host country.
26. Build relations with local people by finding opportunities to spend time with them.
27. Help people in my host country understand me by explaining my behaviors and attitudes in terms of my personality and culture.

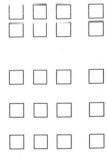

For more information on strategies for communicating with people from other cultures, see pages 121-127.

Strategies to deal with different communication styles:

28. Consider using different types of communication styles when talking with someone from a different culture. ☐ ☐ ☐ ☐

29. Try a different approach when my communication style doesn't seem to be working well. ☐ ☐ ☐ ☐

30. Listen to whether my conversation partners are indirect or direct in their communication styles. ☐ ☐ ☐ ☐

31. Mirror the communication style of my conversation partners (i.e., if they are always indirect, I try to be indirect too). ☐ ☐ ☐ ☐

32. Respect the way people from other cultures express their emotions. ☐ ☐ ☐ ☐

33. Refrain from disagreeing right away so that I have a chance to listen to what others are trying to communicate. ☐ ☐ ☐ ☐

For more information on strategies to deal with different communication styles, see pages 121-127.

Strategies to understand nonverbal communication in another culture:

34. Learn about the ways in which people in my host country use nonverbal communication. ☐ ☐ ☐ ☐

35. Examine how my own nonverbal communication is influenced by my culture. ☐ ☐ ☐ ☐

36. Observe which nonverbal communication differences are most difficult for me to adjust to in my host country. ☐ ☐ ☐ ☐

37. Practice using a variety of different nonverbal communication patterns. ☐ ☐ ☐ ☐

38. Figure out how far people stand from each other in my host country and try to keep the "right" distance from others. ☐ ☐ ☐ ☐

39. Observe the gestures that people use in my host country. ☐ ☐ ☐ ☐

40. Ask friends in my host country to explain the meaning of different gestures to me. ☐ ☐ ☐ ☐

41. Try to use eye contact in a way that is appropriate in my host country. ☐ ☐ ☐ ☐

For more information on strategies for nonverbal communication, see pages 129-138.

Strategies to interact with people in the host culture:

The column headers (right side):
- I use this strategy and like it
- I have tried this strategy and would use it again
- I've never used this strategy but am interested in it
- This strategy doesn't fit for me

42. Join clubs or organizations of people who have interests like mine. ☐ ☐ ☐ ☐
43. Ask people in my host country about their perceptions of my country and culture. ☐ ☐ ☐ ☐
44. Go to the market in my host country and interact with people in the shops. ☐ ☐ ☐ ☐
45. Hold back on making judgments of other people based on my first impressions. ☐ ☐ ☐ ☐

For more information on strategies for interacting with hosts, see pages 75-82.

Strategies to use with my homestay family:

46. Find out from my homestay family what I can do to help around the house. ☐ ☐ ☐ ☐
47. Ask my homestay family about smoking rules in the house and observe those rules if I smoke or invite over friends who smoke. ☐ ☐ ☐ ☐
48. Get permission before bringing someone to my homestay family's house. ☐ ☐ ☐ ☐
49. Share pictures of my own family with my homestay family. ☐ ☐ ☐ ☐
50. Teach games common in my own country to my homestay family. ☐ ☐ ☐ ☐
51. Enlist the help of a friend in my host country when I have a conflict with my homestay family to help me understand the situation. ☐ ☐ ☐ ☐
52. Figure out the "rules of the house" for eating, using the bathroom, dressing around the house, and helping out by observing and asking questions. ☐ ☐ ☐ ☐
53. Ask my host family about their views on privacy and being alone rather than assume that we share the same views. ☐ ☐ ☐ ☐

For more information on strategies for interacting with homestay families, see pages 75-82.

Post-Study-Abroad

Strategies to use when I return home:

I use this strategy and like it

I have tried this strategy and would use it again

I've never used this strategy but am interested in it

This strategy doesn't fit for me

54. Find a group of people who have had similar study abroad experiences to talk to and share experiences. ☐ ☐ ☐ ☐

55. Participate in activities sponsored by study abroad and international groups back home. ☐ ☐ ☐ ☐

56. Take a language class that will help me keep up with the language of the country I studied in (if appropriate) and/or take classes on subjects I became interested in during my study abroad adventure. ☐ ☐ ☐ ☐

57. Volunteer for an international organization or work with international students. ☐ ☐ ☐ ☐

58. Share my feelings and experiences with friends and family, without expecting that they will relate to all that I say. ☐ ☐ ☐ ☐

59. Try to keep connected with friends I made while studying abroad. ☐ ☐ ☐ ☐

60. Give myself time to readjust to my own country. ☐ ☐ ☐ ☐

For more information on strategies for returning home, see pages 143-159.

General Departure Tips

Six easy things to do before you go

1. Buy a dictionary and train yourself on how to use it effectively. Consider your skill level and determine if you should have a monolingual dictionary (e.g., Spanish-Spanish) or a bilingual dictionary (Spanish-English).

2. Start a journal.

3. Set goals. Identify your current level of language proficiency. Write down your goals for where you want your language skills to be by the end of your time abroad. Put these goals on the front page of your journal or on the flap of your dictionary. If you are new to the language, you probably have dreams of carrying on a conversation at a basic level and making friends. If you are an experienced language learner, you undoubtedly want to increase your comprehension and speak more "like a native."

> I knew I had achieved successful competence in German when natives in both Germany and Austria started telling me: 'Mensch Leo, du kannst reden!' ('Gee Leo, you can converse!'). This distinction between 'speaking' a language and 'conversing' in that language is very important.
> -- Leo Papademetre, Germany

4. Make a list of things you would like to learn while abroad. Write these in your journal or notebook.

5. Collect photos and/or postcards of your school, friends, family, home, favorite vacation spot, etc., to share with new friends and hosts while studying abroad.

6. Define for yourself what "survival" skills you personally will need:

   - Do you have special dietary needs (kosher, halal, vegetarian, dairy- or wheat-free)? Do you know how to ask for these things in ways that are culturally appropriate?
   - Do you have any critical health issues or medication needs? Do you know how to explain them?
   - Will you be engaging in any hobbies that you will need to get equipment or supplies for while you are abroad (e.g., photography equipment, paints, batteries, etc.)?

What does it take to be successful in study abroad?

Here is what hundreds of students and teachers who have gone before you say it takes to be successful in a new culture. Check which of these general skills you already possess and turn to the corresponding sections in the guide for areas you would like to explore further.

☐ **Awareness of how you learn a language**

It's not enough to want to learn a language. Understand the strategies you use and should use to maximize language learning.

☐ **Clear goals**

You've considered it at least 20 times: Why do you want to study abroad? Take time to consider your top three goals—not for the purpose of a scholarship or study abroad application, just in terms of what you really want to get out of your time overseas.

☐ **Awareness of the importance of language and culture**

Don't view language and cultural differences as obstacles or as insignificant. Be willing to understand the ways that people differ, including differences within a cultural group.

☐ **Eagerness to learn**

This includes a willingness to learn more about yourself and possibly see dramatic changes in how you view yourself. In addition, it means being open to learning about the differences and similarities you are about to experience while you are abroad.

☐ **Readiness to give and receive**

How willing are you to initiate conversations between you and the people in your host country? Consider what you have to share and what you would like to receive from the people with whom you interact.

☐ **Willingness to reduce expectations**

Are you able to lower your expectations? You may need to adapt your ideas about what you can accomplish on a daily basis. This goes for language acquisition as well as the extent to which you'll feel comfortable in the host culture. Enjoy the alternatives and take advantage of the opportunities the new surroundings offer.

☐ **Tolerance for ambiguity**

Are you willing to accept the unexpected? You may encounter some things in the language and the culture you find strange or even uncomfortable. "Going with the flow" is critical in study abroad.

☐ **Capacity for empathy**

Empathy is truly a cross-cultural skill in which you make efforts toward understanding how other people in the situation feel and how they see the situation. Actively seek to understand the situation from another point of view.

☐ **Understanding of your own cultural background**

Who are you? In what ways are you similar to and different from people from your own country? Consider socioeconomic differences, as well (e.g., traveling to another country is, by world standards, a luxury).

(Adapted by Kappler and Nokken from Hess, 1997.)

Re-Entry Tips – Before You Go!

1. Invite your family and friends to save your e-mails, letters, and postcards so that you can have these all when you return home.
2. Try to come back a few days before returning to school and work. It's overwhelming to move, get things from storage, register for classes, go back to work, see friends and family, and catch up on jet lag in a few hours.
3. Look for courses related to your study abroad. For example, one author found that by using her study abroad credits toward electives in communication, she was able to double major in economics and communications—a combination that was much more rewarding to her than economics alone.
4. Watch out for deadlines while you are gone. Your university will have special procedures on how you can legally give rights to someone on campus to have them register you for courses, sign up for housing, etc.

The world is a great book, of which they who never stir from home read only a page.
~ St. Augustine

Section I

Culture-Learning Strategies

INTRODUCTION:
CULTURE-LEARNING STRATEGIES

Living abroad has certainly expanded my perspective of the world. By trying to get comfortable in other cultures, trying to learn other ways of doing everything, I have learned much more about myself. Also, by being exposed to new beliefs, ideas, and values, and by analyzing many aspects of my own culture under a new and richer light, I have broadened my viewpoint on many issues. Furthermore, I have acquired the recognition that in international affairs, language is not enough – that for the synergy of business and cultural relations to take place, deep intercultural understanding is required. My international experience is a source of richness that sets me apart from many people and has been a continuous benefit to my career. ~ Antonella Corsi-Bunker; Switzerland, Italy, and France

For some, the ability to learn how to get along in a host culture comes naturally and fairly easily. For most of us, though, it does not. The following sections have been designed to provide you with a wide variety of culture-learning strategies (i.e., ways to help you effectively learn about the host culture).

In learning about cultures, there seem to be two main pieces of advice that are polar opposites:
- Jump in and just go with the flow.
- Wait until you understand what's going on around you.

We suggest a balanced approach. If you go solely for immersion, you run the risk of repeatedly being an "ugly American" and perhaps worse, you run the risk of not really understanding the culture because others are simply constantly adapting to you. On the other hand, waiting until you have gathered everything you need to know will lead you to feel too anxious and your time may run out before you feel ready. In order to learn about the host culture, you need to be immersed in it *and* you need to take time to reflect upon your experiences in order to really understand the host culture. This section of the guide helps you keep this balance.

There are a number of culture-related activities throughout this section to help you prepare for your study abroad experience, with suggested answers provided for each activity. These answers are not meant to be definitive, and for many of the activities there are no "right" or "wrong" answers. It may very well be that you disagree with some of the suggested answers, which may spur you on to examine how issues of culture can vary from person to person. The answers, like the exercises themselves, are intended to be used as food for thought and to stimulate further discussion.

Coming home story: Beginning at the end

April 28th was the day I chose. I don't even know why. I knew I had to return to Minnesota sometime, so I picked an unimportant date. I had lived in Mexico for four months and, although I didn't consider it home, it just felt more like my home than Minnesota. In the week before I left, I continued my life in Mexico as normal except for packing a little and buying some gifts. I spent my last Saturday, my last Sunday, my last Monday, Tuesday, Wednesday, and Thursday in Cuernavaca. And then Friday, April 28th, arrived. I wasn't excited. I wasn't scared. I wasn't sad. I was just numb, in total disbelief.

I decided not to tell anyone when I was coming home. My mother would ask and I would say, 'Oh, sometime at the end of April or early May.' I finished classes at the beginning of April and since then, my friends were wondering when I was coming home so they could meet me at the airport. I pictured the scene: my mom almost crying with happiness when she sees me, a stern hug from my dad, a quick 'welcome home roughing up' from my brothers, friends giving hugs and asking how the trip was, etc.

The whole idea scared me to death. I haven't seen these people in four months, and they want to come together in one place and bombard me the moment I get off the plane? No way! So I decided to tell only two friends when my flight came in—Matt and Carlos are the two people who I knew would not stress me out.

The morning of the 28th I took a taxi to the bus station and a bus to the airport in Mexico City with my friend Alberto. We got to the airport with about 15 minutes before I had to board the plane and nervously talked. He and I had become really good friends, and I think we were nervous about saying goodbye. About seven minutes before I boarded the plane it hit me. I was leaving. I didn't want to leave Mexico. I didn't want to leave this wonderful culture and beautiful language. I didn't want to leave my friends. And I didn't want to leave the new 'me' that I had discovered. I started to cry. Alberto gave me a hug, we said goodbye, and I walked to the gate. I knew that if I looked back at him I would just walk back to him and say, 'Let's go back to Cuernavaca. I can't leave!' Instead I walked to my gate and boarded the plane.

I had a layover in Houston, and it was terrible. I walked off the plane and was surrounded by white people. Everyone was speaking English. I hadn't seen so many people like me in so long. It seems like I should have been fine with it, but I was very uncomfortable. I kept thinking about Alberto and my other Mexican friends, and I kept thinking about all the places I had seen every day that I may never see again. My 40-minute layover seemed to last forever.

My plane ride to Minneapolis was uneventful except for my thoughts of how I didn't want to be going there. I stepped off the plane and saw Matt and Carlos and almost started to cry. I wanted to cry because no matter how great it was to see them, I didn't want to see them. I wanted to be in Mexico.
~ Susie Peltzman, Mexico

We all come home at some point. And that is often when we begin to realize just how much we have learned about ourselves, about living in another culture and speaking a second language, about profound cultural differences and wonderful human commonalities, and about the pain of leaving our new home and the mixed emotions about returning to our old one. It is quite a journey, as Susie's story suggests.

The purpose of this guide is to be a companion and a help along the way. The learning is always going to be uniquely yours. Our hope is that the strategies and ideas presented here will enhance your experience.

The Culture-Learning Strategies portion of this guide is divided into three major sections: Pre-Departure, In-Country, and Post-Study-Abroad (also referred to as re-entry).

YOU AS A CULTURALLY DIVERSE PERSON

Most of us are not aware we have a culture until we step outside of it.
~ Jacob Dick, Italy

You are embarking on study abroad to meet real people from other countries. You'll want to learn as much as you can about them—their cultural background, their personality, their likes and dislikes. In exchange, they'll want to know about you. This next activity helps you reflect upon the cultural groups and categories to which you belong. All of our experiences growing up have contributed to who we are today, particularly in terms of what we value, what we believe, what we know, and how we behave.

Discovering your cultural diversity

Take a few minutes to complete this diagram. In as many circles as you can, write a word you feel describes you or is a significant part of who you are or how you choose to identify yourself to others (e.g., sister, student, African-American, Christian, Democrat).

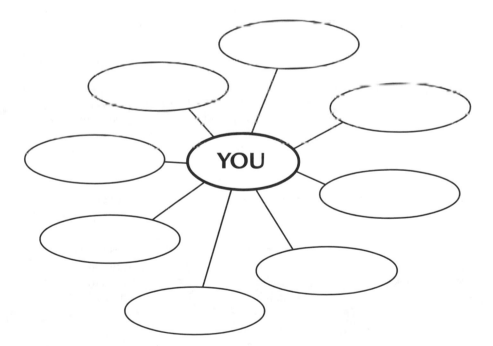

Reflection questions

- If you had to pick just one circle, which would it be? Two circles? Why are these the most important parts of your cultural identity?

- Did you have difficulty filling in eight circles? Did you find eight was not enough? What insights have you gained about yourself from this exercise? Is there an identity that others don't readily recognize in you? Is this OK? Or is it frustrating?

- Go back to the diagram and add some of the values you attribute to the circles. For example, values from being a student might be "independence," "respect for knowledge," or "question authority." Are there places where the values conflict?

- How might these circles change when you are abroad? For example, did you list your nationality in one of the circles? Your social class? Did you list the languages you speak? How might it feel to be seen as just one or another circle—such as U.S. American?

- How might the roles you play in the U.S. be similar and different in your host country?

(Adapted from Gardenswartz and Rowe, 1994.)

The various roles that we play in life impact our identity, shaping our sense of who and what we are. Below are some of the identities given by three study abroad students who filled out a personal culture diagram, followed by the reactions they had to this activity.

Student #1
- Hispanic
- woman
- writer
- activist
- lover of books
- cat owner
- photographer

Student #2
- black
- male
- math major
- student
- brother
- waiter
- biker
- Democrat

Student #3
- parent/mom
- sister
- Irish heritage
- Catholic
- pre-law student
- friend

Student #1

My number one identity is Chicana. It shapes everything I do, and I'm very proud of this. However, my identity is also very tied up with being a woman, specifically a woman of color. Culture and gender are huge issues for me because they've had to be. It's impossible to be a minority woman in this country and not confront these identifiers as a part of life because that's how everyone else sees me.

Student #2

People always ask me if I play sports. Sports are not part of my identity, but their asking shows that they're stereotyping me. I had a hard time selecting one circle. All of these circles really affect me. Being black is important, but I socialize with people from all different backgrounds. It's important to get along with everyone.

Student #3

I've never spent much time thinking about my identity. I say I'm Irish, but if I picked one or two circles, it would never be that. I'm really an American, and I didn't even put that as one of my circles. Now that I am a mom, I realize how much this shapes me and brings out my values. I suppose I'm also middle class, but because I'm a student paying my own tuition, I always feel so poor!

Although you know the many cultures that you belong to, others you meet will not automatically know this about you. One challenge about studying abroad is that you may feel as if you are seen only as a U.S. American, rich, female, etc. Similarly, it is important to realize that all people are complex and have multiple layers of identity so that you don't fall into the trap of limiting them to one identity, just as you don't think of yourself as being just U.S. American. One strategy is to try to learn at least eight aspects of your host's identity.

What IS Culture, Anyway?

We live it. We are surrounded by it. What is it?

> *Culture refers to values, beliefs, attitudes, preferences, customs, learning styles, communication styles, history/historical interpretations, achievements/accomplishments, technology, the arts, literature, etc.—the sum total of what a particular group of people has created together, share, and transmit.* ~ R. Michael Paige, co-author

Understanding culture does not simply mean knowing a list of values that a culture "has." Culture is a system, meaning you cannot say, "U.S. Americans value time and don't value relationships." We value both. There are times when relationships are going to be the most important thing to a U.S. American. And there are times when being on time to work, being independent, and being practical are going to come first. The key to understanding another culture is understanding the system of decision making—what value or rule comes out on top in specific situations. One strategy for learning this system is to understand the iceberg concept of culture.

Becoming Familiar with Culture:
The Iceberg Analogy

Culture shock in Sydney didn't hit me when the meat tasted slimy or even when every other sentence was 'no worries mate.' It hit when I went to register for classes and spent an entire day trying not to rip out all of my hair due to the process that was so slow it was painful. I took registration on the Internet for granted. No longer will I do that. ~ Elizabeth Hook, Australia

My first bit of advice would be patience. You are no longer in the land of instant gratification. France, for the foreigner, is an acquired taste. ~ Joy Wiltermuth, France

You know there will be differences and similarities. But how do you recognize and understand these when you are face-to-face with these similarities and differences?

During the third week of my 15-week stay in Venezuela, it became time to iron some of my clothes. Upon doing so, the iron fell off the ironing board and onto the tile floor. The piece designed to make the iron stand up had broken off, so I decided I had better tell my host mother what had happened. It wasn't easy, but with body language, showing her the iron, and my beginning-level Spanish, she understood what I had done. I could not help but notice she looked somewhat agitated and concerned. She fidgeted around with the iron for awhile and left the room and went about her business. I, thinking it was not a big deal, went to class and forgot about the incident.

However, the next day I woke up to an empty house and a note addressed to me lying on the kitchen table. After an hour of using my Spanish-English dictionary, I figured out what it said. My mother, using many kind and genial words, was asking me to go into town to buy the super glue that would repair the broken iron. This involved a great deal of uncertainty for me. In the beginning, I hated going anywhere in the city alone, so I called every person I knew and either nobody was home or they could not go with me. Not wanting to disappoint my host mom, I set out alone to find the glue.

On the note were the directions to get to the carpenter's shop, so basically I knew where I was going. I needed to take the bus because it was too far to walk, and besides, I had been avoiding the bus as much as possible; therefore, I felt it necessary to overcome my fear. However, as soon as I stepped onto the bus I knew I was going to have a problem because I got pushed to the back of the bus, which meant I was going to have to shout 'Por la parada, por favor' at the top of my lungs to get off the bus. It is one thing to speak in Spanish, but it is an entirely different thing to shout in Spanish. ~ Joshua Bleskan, Venezuela

Joshua and the iceberg

Joshua faces a number of challenges in this situation. To help sort through these, the analogy of an iceberg is helpful. The tip of the iceberg represents the pieces of culture that we can see. The area below the water line represents deeper cultural meaning.

1. What do you see happening in Joshua's example? Place these items on the iceberg above the line.
2. What might be some deeper cultural differences that lie below the surface? Place these items on the iceberg as well.

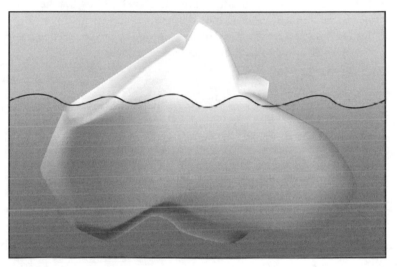

Other students who have looked at this incident have placed the following items above the line on the iceberg as the observable elements of culture:

- *Language* – his host is using Spanish, his Spanish is limited
- *Indirect communication* – his host did not directly discuss the incident with him
- *Formal and polite communication* – his host's note
- *Yelling on the bus* – people in the back yell to get off the bus

The tricky part is, of course, what lies beneath the surface. Notice that the portion of the iceberg beneath the water is much greater. The portion that is *invisible* includes peoples' values, norms, and belief systems. Here's a look at what other students have said were some of the deeper cultural differences Joshua encountered:

- His own culture's emphasis on independence and individualism
- His assumption that nothing being said on the day of the accident meant that nothing was wrong; the absence of words can mean no conflict or no problem
- His host country's rules of behavior in public places

Here's a bit of an explanation of these differences:

- Joshua's culture emphasizes independence. His language inadequacy and unfamiliarity with public transportation made him feel uneasy and dependent on others. He experienced frustration that he felt dependent on his friends, but finding none available, he was determined to go out on his own and find the glue. Joshua experienced a desire to be independent, a strong U.S. American value. In this sense, Joshua's clash with cultures was not directly with Venezuela, but with himself. In the end, it is also the value that helped him through the situation.
- When the host mother did not immediately tell Joshua that he needed to fix the iron, he assumed it was not a big deal. But as Joshua himself later realized, the iron needed to be fixed. The note was not just a way to communicate but potentially a sign of a preferred way to communicate because it's a way to save face.
- To Joshua, yelling in public places may be considered very inappropriate. But in Venezuela it was apparently OK in one public place—a crowded bus—so he experienced a different norm for behavior in a public place.
- Joshua's willingness to step outside of his comfort zone and understand the elements underneath the iceberg helped him be successful in this situation. In addition, he and his host mom had something in common. They both held the belief that people are responsible for their own actions.

Why do you think Joshua's host mother wrote the note? Write your responses below the line of the iceberg.

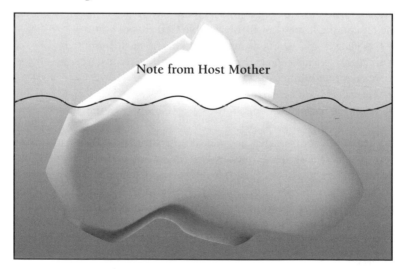

Here is what people who have been to Venezuela had to say about the note:

- *Perhaps she is being sensitive to his limited language skills, and so she wrote a note to help him.*
- *This may not have much to do with culture, but more to do with social class—this may be an issue of money and income. This family may not have the money to fix or replace the item, so it is important that Joshua take care of it.*
- *There may be a value difference here. The perception of Venezuelans may be that U.S. Americans are wasteful. Perhaps she has had U.S. American students in the past, and when incidents like this have occurred they have bought new things instead of having them fixed. She may be trying to teach him that it's OK to fix the iron instead of replacing it.*
- *For Venezuelans and his host mom it may be more appropriate to give messages indirectly, especially when you are at the beginning of a relationship. It is a way to save face and not embarrass Joshua.*
- *As a Venezuelan, I can see that the note is written not necessarily to avoid conflict, but to emphasize that in taking care of things you are taking care of your relationships with other people, and that is the most important thing. He needs to fix the iron not because it's an iron, but because it will show that he cares for her.*

Here's what Joshua had to say about this:

Because of the success I had with the iron incident, my host mother gained a lot of confidence in me and we became the best of friends. So when I shattered the sink during my 10th week, there was no longer a need to write me a note to fix it. She told me that she would pay for half if I paid for the other half. Now, had I not done what at the time seemed like a rather insignificant thing—go to the store and buy some glue—breaking the sink could have been a very uncomfortable situation. Fortunately, I did what I was politely asked, and it benefited me greatly in the future. For this reason, I believe there is nothing more detrimental in cultural adaptation than avoiding the uncomfortable. What is the worst that can happen? More times than not, the worst that can happen comes from the avoidance.

The iceberg analogy has some key points for learning about a culture:

- The things we observe almost always have deeper meaning, that is, they represent a more fundamental cultural value. Although the iceberg separates culture into visible and invisible elements, these are almost always interrelated (such as the written note being a sign of a deeper communication pattern in the culture).
- What we think we see is not always what is going on. Even trickier is how a visible aspect of culture, something so seemingly obvious such as laughing, can have very different meanings in different cultures. For example, laughing can mean "that's funny" or "I'm embarrassed."
- We interpret what we see in the host culture as we would in our own, but the actual meaning may be quite different.

I like this iceberg strategy. It's an easy-to-use mental image. ~ Jacob Dick, Italy

Identifying aspects of culture

What are the kinds of things that typically lie above or below the surface? Take a look at these sample items and place them on the iceberg—the more visible elements going above the waterline and the less visible below.

_____ clothing	_____ methods of worship	_____ rules of politeness
_____ views on equality	_____ time management	_____ relationship with nature
_____ religious beliefs	_____ tipping customs	_____ attitudes toward sexuality
_____ personal distance	_____ gestures	_____ degree of eye contact
_____ works of art	_____ concept of beauty	_____ food

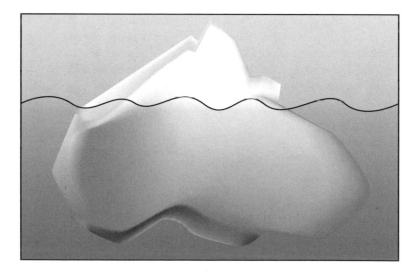

Reflection questions

- Did you place some items both above and below? If so, why?

- Were some items difficult to place?

- Where did you place methods of worship? If you don't have any visible signs of worship (like going to a public place of worship), what does that mean? How would someone come to learn about your own religious beliefs?

- Most would place "views on equality" in the deep aspects of culture. What might be visible signs that you are a feminist or support gender equality among men and women? Are there signs in the way you dress? Speak? What visible signs are there about equity among social classes?

Suggested answers

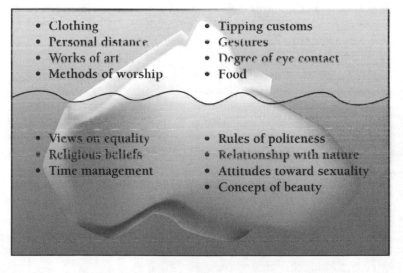

- Clothing
- Personal distance
- Works of art
- Methods of worship

- Tipping customs
- Gestures
- Degree of eye contact
- Food

- Views on equality
- Religious beliefs
- Time management

- Rules of politeness
- Relationship with nature
- Attitudes toward sexuality
- Concept of beauty

Examining the connections between surface and deep aspects of culture is a critical strategy for being effective in crossing cultures. For example, certain gestures may be signs of religious beliefs such as some Muslim women not shaking hands with men when they greet each other. And, in the case with Joshua, understanding the note as a way to maintain the relationship and a preference for indirect communication was critical to Joshua's success with his host. Of course, some visible signs may not be connected to a deeper meaning—it may just be the way things are!

Culture-Specific and Culture-General Learning

Imagine students preparing to come study in the U.S. There would be some *culture-specific* things that would be helpful to know—common greetings, what expectations teachers have of students, and maybe something about patterns of friendship. Of course, you say, but there are so many variations, how would we prepare the students for these? We could do so by helping them understand the ways cultures can differ, so when they encounter a visible difference they can better get at what's underneath this difference. They would be learning the culture from an insider's perspective, and they could begin thinking about how to adapt. This is *culture-general* learning (i.e., principles that apply regardless of the setting). In your own preparation, you'll need a balance of culture-specific and culture-general learning.

Differentiating Cultural from Personal and Universal

> *It was really hard to tell in the beginning if something was cultural or just personal. I remember one time asking my host parents out to dinner at what for me was kind of an expensive restaurant. When we were getting ready to go I was a little frustrated when I saw my host father's brother and his family had arrived to join us. I didn't say anything because I know family is important in Mexico and what would I say anyway?*
>
> *When the bill came I figured that my host father would help out—after all, he was the one who invited his brother and his brother's family. As it turns out, I got stuck with the bill and felt really taken advantage of. I had found Mexicans to be so generous and then this really made me think my host father was a jerk. ~ Kelly Lavin, Mexico*

Kelly's experience brings up an issue that can be challenging: How do you sort out what's normal cultural behavior and what's not. In this case, is the host father really a "jerk," or is he following some cultural rule or norm? How can you figure this out?

Let's start with some definitions from the *Peace Corps Cross-Cultural Workbook*:

Cultural: refers to what a group of people have in common with each other and how they are different from other groups

Personal: refers to ways in which each person is different from everyone else, including those in the same group

Universal: refers to ways in which all people in all groups are basically the same

(Storti and Bennhold Samaan, 1997.)

Some important points to remember

- Personal preferences exist everywhere. Oftentimes a preference may very well have cultural and historical roots. The longer you are in the country the better you can distinguish between what is cultural and what is more personal.
- When something is cultural, this means there is a recognizable pattern of behavior. When you have learned the patterns, then you know when something is out of the norm. You'll be better able to know, for example, when someone is being unusually friendly.
- Awareness of cultural patterns also helps you figure out your own perceptions of events and your adaptation strategies.

Kelly found out several weeks later that an invitation to one family member is, in fact, an invitation to other family members who know about the upcoming event. This became clear when she saw her host father in a similar situation when people who she knew hadn't been directly invited showed up to the restaurant, and he paid the bill for everyone.

She also learned something important about distinguishing between a universal (in this case, hosting a social event) and culturally specific patterns—the details that differ between cultures during such events.

Differentiate cultural from personal and universal

Read the list of behaviors below. Indicate if you think the behavior is universal, cultural, or personal. If you feel that there is more than one answer, think of some examples to show how this may be true (you don't have to write these down).

U = Universal
C = Cultural
P = Personal

1. _____ Eating with chopsticks
2. _____ Women walking five steps behind men
3. _____ Walking rather than riding the bus
4. _____ Feeling sorry after accidentally stepping on someone's foot
5. _____ Respecting your elders
6. _____ Making a slurping sound when eating soup or noodles
7. _____ Wearing warmer clothing when it is cold
8. _____ Being depressed after the death of a loved one
9. _____ Sleeping with a light on
10. _____ Shaking hands with someone you first meet

(Adapted from Storti and Bennhold Samaan, 1997).

Suggested answers

Cultural

1. Eating with chopsticks
2. Women walking five steps behind men
5. Respecting your elders
6. Making a slurping sound when eating soup or noodles
10. Shaking hands with someone you first meet

These statements are considered to be cultural because there are places in the world where a majority of the people would engage in the behavior. While it can also be true that these are personal behaviors, there are often rules regarding the behaviors—suggesting personal variation is the exception, not the rule. For example, in the U.S. Midwest, some may make a slurping sound when eating soup or noodles; however, by general Midwest standards, it is considered to be improper etiquette.

Universal

4. Feeling sorry after accidentally stepping on someone's foot
5. Respecting your elders
7. Wearing warmer clothing when it is cold
8. Being depressed after the death of a loved one

The above represent behaviors and beliefs found in all cultures. Of course, this does not mean that you respond exactly the same way in each culture—you may apologize profusely in one culture for stepping on someone's foot and in another you simply say "excuse me" or nothing at all. Notice that "Respecting your elders" is on both the cultural and universal list because while this belief is common throughout cultures, the extent to which respect is shown varies so greatly that it can seem to differ across cultures.

Personal

3. Walking rather than riding the bus
9. Sleeping with a light on

These reflect individual preferences, rather than cultural norms. Of course, there are some cultures where riding the bus is the only realistic option given distances between sites. Whether one walks or rides the bus may still be a matter of choice.

Some Strategies for Culture-Specific Learning

Learn about and try to understand the culture that you'll be going to. Learn about the history and politics of the country and how they have affected the present-day culture. Also, try to understand your own culture as this will help you to better understand another. ~ Jessica Novotny, Spain

How to learn about your host culture

Don't wait until you are overseas to learn about the host culture(s) of your study abroad country. Why not? A little bit of knowledge can go a long way to establish good relations. Should you bring a gift? If so, what's appropriate? How formal should you be with your hosts? What should you expect in terms of how to register for your classes? What are some major political issues facing the country? Knowing the answers to these questions will help you get off to a good start and will build your confidence. Also, many find themselves intimidated by the knowledge people from other countries have not only about their own politics, history, and culture, but also about U.S. American politics and culture. Feeling insecure, it's easy to shut yourself off from these conversations, further preventing you from gaining the knowledge you seek! We're not suggesting you "know everything," but, rather, prepare yourself with a few key pieces of information.

Here are a few suggestions for getting prepared. Of course, you can't do all these before you go. Select areas most interesting or most challenging to you.

People from the country and culture you are visiting:
- Check out the international organizations or university groups at your college
- Find out if there are professional organizations in your area with an international exchange focus (e.g., Rotary International, AFS/Youth for Understanding)
- Visit with other students who have studied abroad in your country. Ask your campus study abroad office about how you can meet returnees
- Meet with returned volunteers from the Peace Corps or other agencies

Literature:
- Check out books—novels, short stories, poetry, etc. Learn about the major literary figures and their works
- Discover the Intercultural Press (a wonderful resource for intercultural and culture-specific books, both fiction and nonfiction)
- Explore language readers and textbooks for cultural information
- Read non-fiction books on history, geography, politics, etc.
- Seek out travel writing

- Look for CulturGrams, publications produced by Brigham Young University, outlining key cultural information on more than 170 countries and cultures of the world; available on the Internet and through public libraries

Film:
- Rent videos from the international section of the video store or the public library
- Watch film festival listings for movies made about or in your host country

Newspapers and magazines:
- Check out your school's special collections for newspapers and magazines from the host country
- Pay attention to cultural trends and hot topics, such as:
  - What societal issues are considered important to the people?
  - What sports teams does the country have? What is their record?
  - What artists or musicians are currently popular?

Internet:
- Read online newspapers
- Listen to online radio
- Search the Internet for country-specific information about topics of interest (If you enjoy cooking, Rollerblading, or pottery, find organizations related to these interests. You could even start up dialogues with people before you leave.)
- Look up maps of the country. Have an understanding of where the major cities and other important geographical areas are located

Much of the above could be considered required knowledge before you leave for your study abroad. You can think of it as a great way to expand upon your cultural literacy of the target country without a huge expenditure of time.

Basic things you should know before you go

Activity

It's strategic to have some basic facts about your host country at your fingertips. This helps you to get into conversations and shows your respect for the culture. Take some time to investigate the following topics—use the Internet, foreign newspapers, and magazines or ask a person from your host country.

- Names of political leaders
- Names of political parties
- Major religion(s)/spiritual beliefs and their effect on the host country
- Hot topics of the day (e.g., government scandals)
- Recent conflicts and the role of the U.S. in those conflicts
- Type of government
- Year of independence and circumstances
- Economic conditions
- Cultural diversity (immigration and refugee populations, etc.)
- Class structure (e.g., what will your status as a student be in this country? What percentage of students in your host country go to college?)
- U.S. role in local economy, politics, culture, etc.
- Types of gifts, if any, that will be appropriate to bring to host families, new friends, etc.

When in Rome, Do as the Romans Do... But What's a Roman?

Did you ever hear anyone say:
- The French are rude.
- Mexicans are lazy.
- Spaniards love their siestas.
- Brits have a wonderful, dry sense of humor.
- U.S. Americans are self-centered.
- U.S. Americans are friendly.
- Asian students are good in science and math.

Are these statements always true? Of course not; they are ***stereotypes***—*the automatic application of information we have about a country or culture group, both positive and negative, to every individual in it.* This information is often based on limited experience with the culture, so it is incomplete at best and downright wrong at worst. If you consider only stereotypes when learning about a culture, you limit your understanding of the host culture and can make serious mistakes.

What's the alternative? A *generalization*. This means *using initial ideas about a group to form hypotheses*. For example, you've been watching British television and note the dry sense of humor that forms the basis for several sitcoms. Then you meet several Brits who also have a dry sense of humor. You begin to form a hypothesis about British humor.

Generalizing recognizes that there may be a tendency for people within a culture group to share certain values, beliefs, and behaviors. Generalizations can also be based on incomplete or false information, but you are less likely to get into trouble with a generalization because you are using that information with caution, you are constantly testing and revising your ideas, and while you are searching for general patterns in the culture, you never assume that every person will act in the same way.

Differentiating stereotypes and generalizations

This exercise gives you some practice in differentiating between stereotypes and generalizations. Read each statement below and decide whether you think it is a stereotype or generalization.

S = Stereotype
G = Generalization

1. _____ "Many Latinos cherish their family life, so it's not surprising that Rosa still lives at home."
2. _____ "The Japanese are xenophobic, which is understandable because they live on an island country, separate from other countries."
3. _____ "It figures that Boris likes to go out drinking, since alcoholism is widespread in Russia."
4. _____ "I don't understand how Huang could do so poorly on the tests. Asians are supposed to be good at math."
5. _____ "The French have a deep respect for their language and culture, and they usually prefer that foreigners speak in French when they visit."
6. _____ "In Italy, when a man approaches a women, he's only interested in one thing."
7. _____ "In Japan, the man typically is the breadwinner of the family, and he will often value the company he works for more than his family life."
8. _____ "America is a violent country. Everyone carries a gun."
9. _____ "I can't imagine that Jenny comes from Sweden since she doesn't have light-colored hair and blue eyes."
10. _____ "Germans tend to be very concerned about environmental issues and recycling."

Now check the suggested answers below. While you are reviewing the answers, think about what made some of these generalizations rather than stereotypes. What you see in the generalizations, of course, is the use of qualifying words such as *tend to*, *usually*, *typically*, and *often*. They are not as emphatic and do not imply that everyone in the culture has a certain characteristic.

Suggested answers

1. Generalization (discussed in terms of "many")
2. Stereotype (refers to all Japanese)
3. Stereotype (assuming that alcoholism applies to every person)
4. Stereotype (assuming that good math skills apply to every person)
5. Generalization (discussed in terms of a preference)
6. Stereotype (assuming that every Italian man has a sexual motive)
7. Generalization (discussed in terms of "typically")
8. Stereotype (assuming that every person reacts the same way)
9. Stereotype (assuming that everyone in Sweden looks exactly the same)
10. Generalization (discussed in terms of tendencies)

Additional strategies for making generalizations

You need to take time to explain your generalized statements so that the listener can best understand your point of view. Your desire to learn more about the culture will sound much more authentic if you resist the temptation to exaggerate and stereotype. For example, instead of saying, "Women sure are second class citizens in Japan," you might say, "It doesn't seem that women are treated equally to men in employment; for example, women are often required to make tea because of their gender." Note that the statement includes the observable behavior that led you to the generalization. The extra detail in the generalized statement makes it preferable to the stereotyped statement. You haven't concluded anything yet, but a pattern seems to be emerging from the information you are getting about the country. It also allows your listener to see what the generalization is based on and can lead to further discussion about whether your assumption is accurate or not.

Responding to Stereotypes about You

While you are abroad you are likely to encounter many occasions where the host nationals or other international students will make stereotypical comments about the U.S. and Americans.

How can you respond? One of the things you can do is explain your culture in terms of its general patterns. This assumes that you know what they are, which interestingly is something most of us don't think about very often. The following section will introduce you to the numerous values that underlie the actions and thoughts of most people living in the United States. For example, imagine that your Thai host father has commented on how individualistic U.S. Americans are. They always want to express their own ideas, look after their own welfare rather than their family's, etc. Using generalizations, you can give a cultural overview, saying something like James Lassegard did:

> *Yes, Americans like to be independent and to see themselves as in control of their lives. These values are reflected in the popular song 'I Did It My Way' or in the emphasis on 'self-expression' or 'self-empowerment' in today's society. Of course, this does not mean that all people living in the U.S. value individualism in the same way or to the same extent. It simply means that many, if not most, Americans appear to have this value, and that the culture views this as a positive attribute. ~ James Lassegard, Japan*

The wealthy American?

One challenging stereotype people may have of you is that you are rich. The reality may be that you are going into personal debt to be on this trip or that you have saved for months for the opportunity to study abroad. In either case, you may feel very far removed from wealth and very much like a poor student!

Yet by world standards, you may very well be wealthy. Consider the following:

- Did you have access to a job to save money for study abroad?
- Will you be able to find a job when you return?
- While attending college in the U.S. may not feel like elitism, only 1 in 5 people do. Do you know what the ratio is in your host country?

While these things may not put money directly into your bank account, your access to jobs and education can make you wealthy in comparison to those you might meet in your host country.

In many countries, there exists an image of the United States as a land of limitless wealth and opportunity. For over a century now an idealized image—"where the streets are paved with gold"—has drawn people from around the world to the U.S. and, with the advent of mass media, what is now "known" abroad about the United

States comes via movies, pop music, and television shows. The lives depicted on U.S. soap operas and in most Hollywood movies probably bear little resemblance to your own, and it may seem laughable that those depictions would be accepted as reality *anywhere*. However, there are often few alternative images to counterbalance the impact of shows like *Baywatch* or *As the World Turns*. (Try to imagine the scenes from a movie about your life, if you are an average college student: purchasing a month's supply of ramen noodles in the grocery store or moving your aunt's avocado-and-rust colored plaid couch, circa 1973, up four flights of narrow stairs into your apartment. Not exactly a lifestyle that translates easily into international blockbuster material.) With the imbalance of superstars, pop singers, and multimillionaire athletes versus ordinary U.S. citizens represented in the media, it is not surprising that there is the stereotype of U.S. Americans as rich and materialistic, and by extension, greedy, shallow, and wasteful. Depending on your host country, you may find a strange mix of curiosity and antipathy directed toward you because of these stereotypes about the U.S.

As a U.S. American, you may hold strong views about this country. Some of you may feel that the United States is the land of opportunity, a special place in the world where those who work hard can achieve unlimited personal success. Others of you may feel that this is a country riddled with social problems and gross inequalities. Still others of you may not have given these issues much consideration up to this point, and you just accept the United States as it is. Regardless of your opinions about the U.S., it will be worthwhile to pay attention to the differences in wealth and personal opportunities that you notice between your host country and your home country. Some differences may be overt and some may be subtle, so look closely. Write down what you see and hear and observe, and talk with your friends and host family if you can. In the end, the point is not to come away with a definitive answer or opinion, or to define which value system is "right" and which is "wrong." Hopefully you will discover what you feel is valuable in both cultures and ultimately have a greater understanding of what you have in the U.S., both in terms of physical possessions as well as opportunities.

And here is final advice from another traveler about being a U.S. American abroad:

> *I remember feeling as though people judged me unfairly because of my nationality while traveling in eastern Europe. I was with a group of kids about my age while in Slovakia, and I felt that they were overly critical of me as an individual because of my government's actions recently in Belgrade. The anger I felt toward them for judging me actually helped me. It is very important to remember the golden rule of intercultural interaction: Don't judge a person completely because of cultural stereotypes if you don't want them to be equally critical of you. I now realize that no one is responsible for their government. We are all individuals and deserve to be evaluated on our own merits, not those of our elected officials.*
> ~ Dan Jakab, Spain

PRE-DEPARTURE CULTURE STRATEGIES PART II:
UNDERSTANDING THE WAYS CULTURES CAN DIFFER IN VALUES

Before studying in England, I had not traveled much. I really did not know if I was a 'typical' American or not. I was just me. And I expected to find my British family to be a British family—whatever that would be. I was not expecting to find major differences and in many ways, I did not. What I did find was that they saw me as very different from them. I was an American. Through their eyes and reactions to me, I learned much more about myself than I was able to learn about them. ~ Barbara Kappler, England

Self Discovery

You've heard this before: going to a foreign country leads people to "discover themselves." Of course, you don't need to travel thousands of miles to encounter differences and make such discoveries. But this experience will undoubtedly be different because, as a foreign student traveling to another country, you are immersed in the host culture. Often, you become essentially a minority. Your next-door neighbors, fellow students, and hosts will probably share some, but certainly not all or even very many, of your values and beliefs. Confronting and experiencing these value differences is what leads to the exciting—and sometimes challenging—opportunity to get to know yourself.

Making sense of value differences is not easy. Before you can fully understand another culture and often yourself, it is important to become familiar with the basic ways that cultures can differ and your own values and beliefs. In this section, you will have the opportunity to learn about some of the predominant value and belief orientations for U.S. Americans and to examine and reflect upon your own. First, a few reminders:

1. Our observations about U.S. American culture are generalizations, not stereotypes. They are ideas about the **cultural patterns** that prevail in the U.S. Not everybody fits these patterns, but almost everyone knows of them. Also, there are many culture groups in the U.S., each with its own values and beliefs.

2. A value system does not tell people exactly how they should behave, but it does set the standard by which they are judged. Most of the time, these standards are not written down; they are simply understood by most people in the culture—especially when the system comes into conflict with another system.

Predominant U.S. American Cultural Patterns

"Hey, how's it going?"

The language we speak reveals much about our cultural values and belief systems by offering us clues into our own and other cultures. In your study of the new language, you may have instinctively picked up the subtle nuances of your host culture. But how much have you thought about the language that you speak here in the U.S.? Often idiomatic phrases, sayings, and proverbs that we have heard since we were small children reveal much about us and U.S. American culture.

Interpreting culture through popular sayings

Take a look at the popular sayings listed below. What might they suggest about U.S. American values and beliefs? Write your answer next to the statement on the right.

Popular Saying or Expression	What value(s) is being emphasized?
1. "If at first you don't succeed, try, try again."	
2. "Make lemons into lemonade."	
3. "Make yourself at home."	
4. "Don't blame me!"	
5. "The squeaky wheel gets the grease."	
6. "Where there's a will there's a way."	
7. "Talk is cheap."	
8. "It's no big deal."	
9. "What's the bottom line?"	
10. "What's up?"	

Suggested answers

Popular Saying or Expression	What value(s) is being emphasized?
1. "If at first you don't succeed, try, try again."	*Productivity, stick-to-it approach.*
2. "Make lemons into lemonade."	*Staying positive is important. You are responsible for making the best out of a negative situation. Similar saying is "Look for the silver lining."*
3. "Make yourself at home."	*Informality, equality. Note that many internationals comment that when they hear this phrase, they don't really know what it means or how they should act.*
4. "Don't blame me!"	*While we may emphasize individual responsibility, we are also skilled at finding another source of the problem and are able to articulate "why it's not me!"*
5. "The squeaky wheel gets the grease."	*It's good to complain and to point out problems. This helps to improve the world we live in and the products we use. Improvement and change are often highly valued. At a personal level, it means that the one who complains will get attention and help and if you are quiet and accommodating, you won't get helped.*
6. "Where there's a will there's a way."	*Persistence is important. Individuals can accomplish enormous feats, if they are willing to work hard.*
7. "Talk is cheap."	*What's important is action. Another saying related to this one is "we could sit around and talk about this all day," which is a negative way to say "let's get moving!"*
8. "It's no big deal."	*Emphasis on downplaying problems and avoiding conflict. This varies greatly by region in the U.S.*
9. "What's the bottom line?"	*Focus on results and most often on money.*
10. "What's up?"	*Informality. Also the importance of recognizing people as you see them or "run into them."*

These suggested activities can further help prepare you for your upcoming experience:

- Take a moment to think about the expressions you find yourself and those around you using most frequently. What might they tell you about underlying U.S. American values?

- Now imagine how people in your host country might interpret some of these expressions. Trying to translate directly from one language to another is when you realize that the particular concept or value you wish to convey may not be as important in the host culture as it is in your culture of origin. Or it may be that the value is relatively unique to your cultural community.

- Can you find some sayings in common? For example, a student from Bishkek, Krygyzstan, explained that instead of saying, "It's no big deal" or "Don't make a mountain out of a molehill," Krygis people say, "Don't make an elephant out of a mosquito!"

International perspectives on U.S. Americans

Another way to learn about our own culture is to study how others view us. Before you go, it is helpful to become more aware of how non-Americans generally view Americans.

In the previous activity, in order to begin exploring U.S. American culture, you were asked to identify values associated with popular sayings and expressions. Another way to get a glimpse of U.S. values and cultures is to see what internationals have to say about their experiences in the U.S. We asked some international students to comment on their first impressions of life in the U.S. This will give you a sense of what "outsiders" notice about life in the U.S. and how they may view you, knowing you are a U.S. American.

Uzbekistan

My fellow Uzbek friends say that Americans are 'freedom-lovers,' 'free to express themselves,' and 'open-minded.' To that I can add that Americans adore their country and are real patriots of their native land. They do not know limits. For example, a 46-year-old can decide to go to college to get a bachelor's degree. They also love money and spend most of their time earning and saving. At the same time, they like recreational activities a lot, such as sports, travel, etc. Also, they are into the 'political correctness' thing a lot. Americans are very 'environmentally conscious,' meaning they care about the environment and ecology a lot and enforce environmentally friendly practices such as reuse/recycle.

Japan

Americans have high self-esteem and respect others' individuality.

One of the things that I found interesting or odd about U.S. Americans after I came to the United States is that they seem to be busy all the time and proud to tell people how busy they are. I sometimes felt as if they were implying that they were too busy with other things to be bothered with me. They seem to be very friendly and easy-going, but you have to make an appointment for whatever you do with them, even going out for coffee with friends sometimes. Otherwise, people would leave you saying, 'I gotta go.' It took awhile for me to get used to it.

Kyrgyzstan

Many people from former Soviet Union countries would say, 'People in the USA are very friendly, but they hardly be real friends' or 'Americans are very busy people and hardly have time for socialization with each other.'

Mongolia

I have very positive thoughts about U.S. Americans. First of all, they are very friendly. Even if they are in a bad mood, they do their best to be friendly. Second, I think U.S. Americans are very good communicators. Talking with others and sharing information all the time seems to be important for them; however, they are forgetful. They ask you a question and you give them the answer, but when you see them again, they ask you the same question again. Third, Americans are very good at timing and planning things ahead of time. I have always been so amazed at how they plan events and activities of all types including their work and vacations. Once they plan to do something they do it no matter what. Moreover, they are good at meeting deadlines and doing things on time.

Iceland

Of all the things I thought of Americans before I came, two issues have remained as still true. They are incredibly loud and take up a lot of space in public places. The sound level at an American restaurant is as high as a cliff full of birds in my country of Iceland. It is hard to pass Americans on the sidewalk because they usually take up half the space themselves just by the way they walk and swing their arms. Every time I go home to Iceland, I'm stopped by someone who tells me I'm taking up too much space on the sidewalk!

Hong Kong

I have noticed the following differences in friendship:
- *Americans talk about politics and sports with their friends whereas we talk with our friends about deeper subject matters such as ideas, beliefs, and our goals in life.*
- *There is a deeper commitment among friends in my culture. I can expect my friends to be there for me even when we are far apart or vice versa.*

Korea

Americans are individual-oriented. Each individual's opinion, perspective, and way of living are considered to be unique in the society. Americans are polite to strangers in general; however, that politeness is often superficial. In other words, they act politely for the sake of politeness (meaning that they act politely not necessarily because they respect others but because they know that they ought to be polite). Americans love food…lots of food. They love eating out. Restaurants are serving more than enough food to the customers and wasting more than what is needed to feed the starved people in extremely poor countries.

Germany

Americans are very patriotic, almost nationalistic. Americans are convinced that theirs is the best country and that other nations need to learn and absorb the American belief system. There is little if any introspection and reflection of what can be learned from others. Even though the U.S. stands for freedom of speech, liberty, and the pursuit of happiness, its core values continue to reflect the white, male, Christian thinking of the Founding Fathers.

Reflection questions

- Were you surprised at any of the comments?

- Many of us grew up with adults trying to teach us the golden rule ("Do unto others as you would have them do unto you"). While this works pretty well with people from the same cultural group, it does not necessarily work well in crossing cultures. Instead, consider the Platinum Rule in which you "do unto others as they themselves would have done unto them" (M. Bennett, 1999, p. 213). How might you go about discovering how people in your host culture would like to be treated?

Comparing Cultural Attitudes and Viewpoints

The culture of people living in the United States is often thought to be *individualistic*. U.S. Americans generally enjoy a great deal of freedom to do what they want, and much attention is paid to the self as opposed to the group. For example, you probably decided your own field of study, rather than having your family decide for you. And when you started to take classes, you probably faced a great deal of choice about exactly what courses to take. This system of educational choice and independence is relatively unusual in other parts of the world.

And just think about all the words containing the word "self" that are commonly used by Americans: self-help, self-righteous, self-esteem, self-awareness, self-empowerment. Even this guide is considered to be self-access and assumes motivation on the part of the student to work independently.

The problem with saying that U.S. Americans are individualistic is that we will not really understand how individualistic we are unless we attempt to compare ourselves with other cultures. U.S. Americans are indeed individualistic, but relative to which other countries? Mexico? China? Germany? Furthermore, what does this individualism really mean for what U.S. Americans value or how they tend to interact with others? This chapter explores some of the predominant values, beliefs, and orientations held by many U.S. Americans and encourages you to contrast them with those of your host culture.

Contrasting U.S. American views with the host country

In this exercise familiarize yourself with what is considered the typical U.S. American view for each category. Then find out what people in your host country think about the same concept or belief, and describe their views in writing. This is not an easy task. First of all, it requires you to recognize that there are some cultural characteristics that are common enough to be labeled "American." Secondly, it requires you to have some familiarity with the host culture. Throughout this section it is recommended that you talk to others about the cultural attitudes and viewpoints presented here. It is also highly recommended that if you have access to one or more persons from the country in which you plan to study, you should check out some of your preconceptions with them.

1. Activity

U.S. American views:	Host country views:
• Taking action is more important than just talking about it.	
• Considering the most practical way to get something done is important.	
• "So, what do you do?" is one of the first questions you are asked when you meet someone for the first time.	
• You feel like you should be doing something on a weekday afternoon rather than relaxing at home.	
• You get together to do something with your friends more than just to hang out. You also schedule the activity to take place at a certain time (Friday at 8 p.m.).	
• "I have to work" is considered an acceptable excuse not to attend an important social activity like family gatherings or even a wedding or graduation.	

2. Change and taking risks

U.S. American views:	Host country views:
• Change is good. • You can always pick up, move, and start over somewhere else. • It's important to reinvent yourself. • If something is old or broken, it's OK to buy a new one and donate the old one to charity.	

3. Fate and destiny

U.S. American views:	Host country views:
• You control your own destiny. • Success is due to hard work and talent, more than luck. • You are responsible for your successes or failures. • If at first you don't succeed, try, try again.	

4. Human nature

U.S. American views:	Host country views:
• People are basically good. • You are innocent until proven guilty. • To err is human. • People can usually be trusted to do the right thing.	

5. Equality

U.S. American views:	Host country views:
• We are all equal under the law. • It is acceptable and expected to "level the playing field" to make things more equal. • People should all have the same opportunities for success.	

6. Age

U.S. American views:	Host country views:
• The ability to be productive is valued more than seniority. • Youth culture is pervasive in fashion, art, and the media. • Respect is based more upon tangible achievements than on seniority or experience. • It's not unusual for a family to place an aging member into a nursing home where the person receives good care and the family can continue to be somewhat independent.	

7. Misery and misfortune

U.S. American views:	Host country views:
• Don't let it get you down. • If you're depressed you need to do something about it. • Always look on the bright side. • Make lemons into lemonade. • Cheer up, there's always tomorrow. • Don't worry, be happy.	

8. Saving face

U.S. American views:	Host country views:
• If I make a mistake or embarrass myself, there are always second chances to rectify the situation. • Being open and honest is essential, even if it makes others uncomfortable. • Accidents will happen; forgive and forget.	

9. Formality

U.S. American views:	Host country views:
• Make yourself at home. • Formality is associated with unnecessary stuffiness and isn't conducive to good relations. • First-name basis in the office is common, even for people who are superior in rank. • Come as you are.	

Reflection points

- Were there some U.S. values you disagreed with? If in reading some of the statements about U.S. Americans you found yourself saying, "That's not me!" or "That's not true!" you may have discovered a value where you differ from the mainstream. Think about why this might be. Are there certain groups (political, ethnic, class) that you feel a part of that may help explain this difference?

- Were you able to write down anything for the host culture? If you are unsure of the host culture's view, it would be easy to make the mistake of assuming that things are probably pretty similar. Keep this list handy and record what you find as time goes on in your study abroad experience.

- If you were thinking, "This isn't how it is anymore," you are right to a degree. Cultures change, of course, but the rate of change is often slower than we think. And, perhaps just as important, your hosts may expect you to behave as a "typical" U.S. American. Hence, the image they form of you may or may not be a true reflection because they are seeing you through their own value lens.

(Adapted from Storti and Bennhold-Samaan, 1997.)

When traveling to England, I certainly learned about myself—who I was as a person. I also learned who I was—and wasn't—as a U.S. American.
~ Barbara Kappler, England

UNDERSTANDING YOURSELF AS A MEMBER OF A CULTURE OR CULTURES

To realize it takes all sorts to make a world, one must have seen a certain number of the sorts with one's own eyes. There is all the difference in the world between believing academically, with the intellect, and believing personally, with the whole self. ~ "Jesting Pilate," Aldous Huxley

I forgot about the 'me' part. What's important to me? I was at first frustrated they were asking about me. I was so focused on learning about them.
~ Tresa River, Ireland

Turn back to the diagram of the "culturally diverse you" in the first section of this chapter (p. 39). What did membership in various organizations and groups tell you about what you value or believe? For example, did a certain youth group encourage you to be independent? Did your family emphasize how important it was to take care of each other? Clearly, even within the same country or culture, we can find great diversity in values and beliefs. Here is a chance for you to explore more fully your own values and belief systems. This exercise is especially helpful if you did not fully believe that the values in the previous chapter reflected your own values.

The values chart – How I rate myself

In the previous exercises, you were asked to come up with values underlying U.S. popular sayings and to compare and contrast possible U.S. values with those of your host country. Now you will have a chance to focus on who you are in terms of your own values. Since little about humans can be thought of as either/or choices, we have placed each of these values on a continuum. While chances are you are relatively high in one contrasting value and low in another, you may be high in both, even if they are frequently viewed as opposites. Read each description of these values, think about the continuums, and then fill in the circle where you feel you rank in regard to these various values and beliefs.

The Individual	The Group
While you may seek input from others, you are ultimately responsible for your own decisions regarding where you live, what your major is, and where you decide to study abroad. You have a sense of pride in being responsible for yourself and know that others expect you to be independent.	You believe the primary group is the smallest unit of survival. Looking out for others protects one's self. Group harmony is the greatest good. Children are taught to depend on others, who in turn can always depend on them. Identity is a function of one's membership or role in a primary group.

Low ← — — — — — → High

The Individual	☐	☐	☐	☐	☐	☐	☐
The Group	☐	☐	☐	☐	☐	☐	☐

Equality
You believe you have a great deal to contribute to your own education and enjoy courses in which there are discussions and independent projects. You prefer to be on a first-name basis with your instructors, boss, and co-workers.

Hierarchy
You believe that instructors are the experts and, given their status, should be referred to by their titles. You prefer course assignments in which you demonstrate through exams or papers that you understand the material the instructor presented.

Low ← → High

Equality	☐	☐	☐	☐	☐	☐	☐
Hierarchy	☐	☐	☐	☐	☐	☐	☐

Time is flexible
You feel that following a clock is artificial. Promising to meet someone at a certain time is not a commitment set in stone. Rather, appointments and social gatherings happen when the time is right.

Time is tangible
You take great care to plan your day to make sure you arrive to class, work, and meetings with friends and family on time.

Low ← → High

Time is flexible	☐	☐	☐	☐	☐	☐	☐
Time is tangible	☐	☐	☐	☐	☐	☐	☐

Meritocracy
You believe that it is important to get things done by yourself and that what is fair for one is fair for all. You know that when you graduate, the jobs you get will be because you have earned them.

Associations
You believe that while what you accomplish on your own is important, you know that it's "who you know" in your life that will make the biggest impact in where you attend school and what jobs you get after graduation.

Low ← → High

Meritocracy	☐	☐	☐	☐	☐	☐	☐
Associations	☐	☐	☐	☐	☐	☐	☐

Activity
Your day is scheduled with a number of activities including work, studying, and social time with friends. When planning to get together with family and friends, you focus on an activity, like playing a sport or going to a movie.

People
Who you are with is more important than what you are doing. Rather than schedule specific activities, you are most likely just to hang out with your friends and family.

Low ← → High

Activity	☐	☐	☐	☐	☐	☐	☐
People	☐	☐	☐	☐	☐	☐	☐

Change
You know that almost everything around you will change – even the friends you have throughout your lifetime. You look forward to change and view that it brings many positives to your life. You may change something just for the sake of change.

Tradition
You feel it's important to keep traditions in the world around you because these bring a positive and expected rhythm to your life. The friends that you have had since you were very small will be the most important friends you have throughout your entire life.

Low ← → High

Change	☐	☐	☐	☐	☐	☐	☐
Tradition	☐	☐	☐	☐	☐	☐	☐

Reflection questions

Now that you have filled out the values chart for yourself, take some time to reflect upon your responses. If possible, get together with another student going abroad to share and discuss your responses.

- Do you have any marks on the far ends (either the highest or lowest circle) of the value continuums? If so, that means you have a strong value orientation in those particular areas. Think about how this might be a source of strength for you. But also consider how your values can be a challenge in the host culture.
- Were there certain values where you felt strongly about both sides of the continuum? Sometimes, the situations we are in require us to behave in different ways, for example, being very focused on activities at times but focused on people at others. How might this be a source of strength for you in the host culture?
- Try to discuss your answers with another study abroad student and then consider these questions:
  - How did your answers compare?
  - What were the similarities and what were the differences?
  - Can you pinpoint aspects of your backgrounds and personal histories that may have influenced your system of values and beliefs?
  - Ask each other where you think the average U.S. American would be on these value dimensions and then look at how close you are to the average.

To compare further, find someone who is from the host country or has spent a lot of time there. Discuss the values chart together and plot out the "average person" from that country. Where do the main similarities and differences lie for the two countries? Where do the main similarities and differences lie for you, in particular, and the host country?

How will my host country rate on the values chart?

Take a different color pen and try to guess where your host culture might fall on these continuums. Also, consider various groups within the country and how their values may differ (for example, university students versus host families, upper class versus lower or middle class, etc.).

Also, take a look at the quotes below and see what they suggest about value differences between these students and their hosts?

- *I was so surprised to find out that my host mom would come into my room every day and clean things up. While I knew she was being helpful, it just really bugged me that she was in my space.*

- *Eating out was a very social activity—you almost never saw anyone dining alone or even drinking a cup of coffee alone at a café. Also, when you went out to a restaurant, the expectation was that you would sit and enjoy the meal and then linger, possibly for several hours, with your companions. At first this seemed slow and inefficient to me, but gradually I came to really enjoy not feeling rushed.*

- *I went overseas pretty open-minded. I knew there were differences in how men and women were treated. But no matter how hard I tried, I could not get used to men calling out to me and whistling. I know it wasn't just me —they did it to the women from the country as well.*

- *I knew I'd have to make a difficult decision to be open about being gay. I was prepared for that—and expected people to be pretty homophobic. What I was not prepared for was that nobody talked about gays at all. It was like they wanted to pretend we did not even exist. The silence was unbearable.*

- *I wanted to travel every weekend. Paris, the sea—everything was just a few hours away. I also wanted to get to know my family better. I tried to spend time with them during the week so that I would not feel bad about leaving them on the weekend. It seemed to work OK.*

What do these quotes reflect about the following set of value differences? Think about the contrast of values, where your values fit compared with the host country, and how these may impact your stay.
- High privacy norm vs. low privacy norm (including an expectation of privacy in public places—no one will whistle when you walk by)
- High personal independence vs. low personal independence
- Strict gender roles vs. open gender roles
- Liberal sexual orientation vs. conservative sexual orientation
- Strong family commitment vs. weak family commitment

A few key points to wrap up the chapter:
- The ability to recognize values and beliefs that are culturally based improves with practice, familiarity with the culture, and increased contact with members of that culture.
- Understanding the predominant values and beliefs of your own culture and those of others provides the foundation for much of intercultural learning.
- Again, the point here is not to overly emphasize differences that exist between cultural groups, but to recognize them as they are and be aware of the impact they have on a given individual's behaviors and actions.
- Recognizing, accepting, and even appreciating the cultural differences in others can be steps on the path toward becoming interculturally competent and will provide opportunities for further culture learning.

Conclusion to the Pre-Departure Section

Congratulations! You have completed a critical part of your study abroad journey. Getting to know a bit more about yourself and your hosts will be sure to make your experience an even greater one.

> *Many people think that the study abroad experience begins the day you step off of the plane, but it really begins before you go, during the time that you are preparing to go. There are many questions running through your head that are important. Only if you are aware of these can you help yourself.*
> *~ A. J. Fleming, Spain*

IN-COUNTRY CULTURE STRATEGIES PART I:
STRATEGIES FOR SOCIAL RELATIONS:
INTERACTING WITH HOSTS

Khoo Ah Au liked Americans. Above all he found their personal relationships easy to read. His own people were always very careful not to give themselves away, to expose crude feelings about one another. Americans seemed not to care how much was understood by strangers. It was almost as if they enjoyed being transparent. ~ *"Passage of Arms," Eric Ambler*

Khoo Ah Au was able to learn what he liked about U.S. Americans because he spent time with them. In studying abroad, there can be real obstacles to spending time with locals. One obstacle is the tendency for students to form tight groups comprised entirely of fellow international students or home country students. Having the opportunity to get together and talk gives you a way to provide fellowship and support for each other. However, it isn't recommended that you use these groups exclusively for support and friendship to the extent that you neglect opportunities to interact with the host culture. Finding ways to immerse yourself in the culture while periodically taking time out to be with your home country friends will provide you with a much more enriching study abroad experience.

A second obstacle is anxiety about meeting and talking with people. The ironic thing is that the best cure for anxiety is meeting and talking with people!

A third obstacle is that there may be a limited number of options for you to meet host nationals in your program. You need to be the one to initiate the opportunities. The following outlines some tips from fellow travelers

Ideas for interaction

The following are some suggestions from fellow travelers about means of increasing your contact with the hosts in your area and of dramatically increasing your international and intercultural learning experience. Some options may not be available where you are situated, but if there is a need for such a program you might want to make efforts toward its creation.

- What are you interested in? Soccer? Classical music? Juggling? Find a local group, club, or society comprised of locals who have similar interests.

- Start or join a study group to study the language or for a cultural exchange.

- Make a meal for some fellow students or your hosts. One author of this text made tacos in Malaysia—it was tricky finding the ingredients but well worth the effort. Another made chocolate chip cookies with a friend in Taiwan and sold them at a local market!

Section I: Culture-Learning Strategies **75**

- School clubs. There usually is an international student organization on campus. What a great way to meet local students who are interested in you!

- Give presentations to local schools, community organizations, and businesses. Often the university or school where you belong will have opportunities, whether volunteer or paid, for foreign students to give short presentations about their home countries. Here's your chance to deepen the locals' cultural knowledge of the U.S. and to de-bunk stereotypes in the process!

- Join in political activities. However, be careful: some countries discourage or even prohibit foreign students from engaging in these activities. Check with your study abroad program administrators before joining.

- Attend religious/spiritual activities. Just because you are in a foreign country doesn't mean you have to stop being spiritual. You may or may not find a place to worship of the same denomination to which you belong, but you can be adventurous and explore the spiritual and religious beliefs of the locals.

- *Adjust your expectations about what you can get done. In the U.S. I am constantly on the go, and I can get a lot done in a day. However, I remember taking a two-hour train trip to Halkis from Athens, conducting a 45-minute interview in Greek (which I was not fluent in), and then returning home on the train. It was only 2 p.m., but that was it for the day. The language, the traveling, the heat of summer—I was wiped out, physically and mentally. ~ Suzanne Hay, Greece*

- *At the beginning of my stay, I never wore a watch, so I was forced to ask people on the bus or on the street what time it was. This built my confidence and helped me meet people. ~ A. J. Fleming, Spain*

- *Try to develop a routine that integrates you into the culture. With repetition, that is, frequenting a certain restaurant or café, locals will become comfortable seeing you and you might make new acquaintances. ~ Julie Radmar, France*

Making the Most of Homestays and Host Families

Many study abroad programs offer homestay opportunities. Some programs require that students stay in a homestay. For others it is optional. A homestay can provide you with a learning experience like no other: the opportunity to gain first-hand knowledge of what family life is like in the target culture and to use the language in an informal setting. Homestays also provide you with the chance to get to know the host nationals on a much deeper level than you would in your daily encounters. An additional benefit is that a host family can be a wonderful support network for a foreign student. You could make lifelong friends!

It is a good idea to take some time to think about the homestay in terms of your own expectations, particularly before you meet your host family. Take some time to answer the questions below.

Activity

Homestay expectations

What are my expectations for the homestay? What do I hope to gain from my homestay? (Rank from 1 to 5)

_____ Get support in adjusting to the culture
_____ Improve my language skills
_____ Participate in family life and learn the culture
_____ Make new friends
_____ Other._____

What will be my responsibilities as part of the homestay? Although this will vary, typically you will be expected to engage in the activities of the family and to abide by the rules of the household. This could include respecting any curfews and family chores that may be expected of you. A few questions that you might ask yourself are:

- Is the homestay smoking or non-smoking?

- Am I prepared to adjust my diet to accommodate the homestay family?

- Will I be expected to help take care of small children in the family?

- How will my gender affect my host family's expectations of me?

- How will my family's social status affect me?

- Will I be expected to pay for things I took for granted at home (such as telephone bills, groceries, etc.)?

- Will I be encouraged to treat any household staff with respect and distance?

Potential Homestay Conflicts

My friend from the U.S. and I were assigned to the same host family. My friend did not like the arrangement because we were so far from school (a 20-minute walk and then a 40-minute bus ride). She moved closer to school and lived with other students. I decided to stay. I came to cherish my time on the double decker buses of London and going home for evening meals. These were great opportunities to be involved in daily life in London. My friend was equally happy to be close to school and to meet other internationals and students from all over the U.S. She ended up traveling in Europe with these newfound friends. We both knew what we wanted going into the experience, and this helped us decide what was the best living arrangement for us.
~ Barbara Kappler, England

As you might anticipate, any number of conflicts can occur during your homestay. Problems could arise due to cultural differences or personal differences between the homestay family and student. In some cases you will be in a position where you can decide what kind of homestay you prefer. Although the homestay is bound to be an incredibly enriching learning experience, you are going to be confronted first-hand with the culture on a daily basis. Having reasonable expectations of your homestay is one way of easing the adjustment to your new surroundings. Finding out as much as possible about how the host nationals live before you get to your country is another way.

What if your homestay isn't working out? For example, what do you do if the family simply ignores you? How do you respond if you are served food that you tried but absolutely cannot eat? What if you are required to do more than what you would consider a reasonable quantity of chores? Since conflicts can occur because of culture or personal characteristics, it may be very difficult for you to figure out whether something is happening because you're not used to the culture yet or just because this family is not a good match. Your relationship with your homestay family is likely to affect your attitudes toward the host country in general. For problematic homestays, you might want to try the following:

Give the homestay some time

- Finding common ground and interests and developing relationships does not happen overnight.
- Talk to other students to see how their homestay experiences compare with yours.
- Ask for help from program staff or faculty in interpreting things in the homestay that puzzle you or in developing strategies to deal with conflict or problems.

Explore the alternatives

- Is there the chance to change homestays? What are the consequences of doing so?
- Are other forms of housing available to students in the area, such as dormitories or private accommodations?

If your first homestay doesn't work out for one reason or another, try not to take it personally or let it detract from your overall study abroad experience. A successful homestay will have a positive effect on your attitude and view of the country, while a negative experience could have the opposite effect. What is important is to keep an open mind, have reasonable expectations, and to give the homestay a decent try. In most cases you will discover that the rewards are well worth the effort.

Strategies for Interacting with Your Hosts

Whether or not you have a homestay, you will probably have an opportunity to visit the home of a local person or family during your travels. While you may have some experience that will help you know what to expect, we encourage you to consider the following before you spend a great deal of time with your hosts.

Take a mental tour

Before visiting or moving in, imagine bringing a guest to your own home. What are the unwritten rules that this guest might be expected to follow? Is a gift expected? If so, what is appropriate? Does the guest help prepare the meal? Is there assigned seating or chairs that are always reserved for the parents? Is the guest expected to help clean up after the meal? If staying overnight, can the guest help him or herself to breakfast in the morning? If the guest is staying for several weeks, in what ways might this change your expectations?

Understanding unwritten rules you have seen guests follow at your home can help prepare you for the assumptions that you carry with you about visiting in your host country.

Preparing for a visit or homestay

Now that you have had a chance to think about your own personal and cultural expectations of guests, in order to prepare for your homestay or visit, take a few moments to focus on the following items. While some of these things may be very minor, feeling prepared and comfortable will help increase your confidence that you will make fewer mistakes and lessen the chance of offending your hosts. Make sure to consider how your age, status, and the host's experiences internationally and with U.S. Americans may impact the responses to these questions. For those you don't know, get help from a local person.

Greetings and arrival

- What is the expected greeting? A handshake, hug, bow, or simply words?
- What is an appropriate time to arrive? At exactly the invited time, early, a few minutes after the stated time, or hours after the stated time?
- Should you take your shoes off at the door? If so, are you expected to bring indoor shoes to wear? Go barefoot? Or wear something provided by the host?
- How should you be dressed?

Gift giving

- Is a gift expected? If so, what is appropriate?
- What can you bring from your home culture that would be a nice gift?
- Are certain numbers or colors considered especially good or bad luck?
- Does a gift need to be wrapped? If so, should you encourage your hosts to open the gift in front of you?
- What is the appropriate way to thank someone for a gift?

Food and meals

- If invited for a meal, should you bring something? If so, what is appropriate to bring?
- Are you expected to help prepare for meals?
- Do you sit down or wait to be invited to sit in a certain place?
- What signals the beginning of a meal—an invitation to eat, a saying, a prayer? Are you expected to participate? Initiate?
- Are you supposed to serve yourself or wait to be served?
- Are you expected to eat everything on your plate or to leave something?
- Are there certain rooms or areas where food and drink are not allowed?
- If you are a long-term guest, is it OK for you to buy food for the family? What about food for just yourself?

Toilet, bath, and shower

Our experience is that this one room (or two if the shower/bath is separate from the toilet) can be the biggest source of irritation in a homestay. This misunderstanding is typically centered around how often one bathes (often criticized as too often) and how long one takes in a bath or shower (too long). Spending a few minutes talking to your hosts and others can help you prepare for your hosts' expectations. Consider discussing these questions:

- What is the best time to take a bath or shower?
- How long is it OK to spend in the bath or shower?
- How does the faucet work?
- If the bath is viewed as a family tub or communal place, should you wash up before you get into the bathtub? Are others expected to use the same bath water after you've finished?

Common courtesies

These general questions can help you understand what your role is as an extended guest in someone else's home.

- Will you be asked to follow a curfew?
- Is your room considered private and your own, or can others enter and use your things, even when you are not there?
- Are you expected to be home for all meals? If you are going to miss a meal, what should you do?
- Is it OK to bring your own guest to a meal?
- Does your host family expect to know where you are each day and what you are doing?
- Are there any special rules about using certain areas of the home? For example, an area that is open only to the family? To servants?
- Are there certain items you should ask permission to use, such as the phone or television?

Departure

- How long does a meal last and how long is it appropriate to stay after a meal is completed?
- If you are a long-term guest, are you expected to do something special for your family upon departure, such as give a gift or take the family to dinner or prepare a meal?

Dating

Aside from the obvious benefits of romance and companionship, dating someone from your host country may provide you with a built-in cultural informant, an incentive to learn the language, and perhaps a friendship that lasts beyond your stay in the country.

> *You need to tell people that they can fall in love. And that can have real consequences.* ~ Dan Jakab, Spain (upon reviewing a draft of this guide)

Giving advice on love and dating is a bit tricky in a study abroad guide. Two of the authors are in intercultural marriages. While you would think we would have something valuable to say, we are a bit stumped on giving specifics in writing! However, one author collected a few pieces of advice she has received over the years:

- Trust your instincts. If someone's character seems a bit questionable, question it.
- Don't try to be someone you know you are not—or someone you are not ready to be (like a parent!). While you are overseas, it's a wonderful time for exploring who you really are. Just be careful. Heartache has no mileage limitation.

- Be careful not to send the wrong messages. This means learning the cues for seriousness in a relationship. In some cultures, what is a casual friendship to you might be taken much more seriously. Some cultures also have the stereotype that U.S. Americans are loose and casual about sex, so be aware of how your behavior might be perceived.

And if you are serious:
- Make sure that you both get a chance to visit the other's culture and home before making a commitment.
- Be honest with yourself about whether or not you could live permanently in your partner's culture.

Conclusion

Your study abroad can be the most amazing experience. By thinking carefully how to become involved and interact with people in the host culture, you can actively make a difference in the quality of your stay and in the amount that you learn. Remember it's one thing to be in the vicinity of events and another to actively participate in them.

IN-COUNTRY CULTURE STRATEGIES PART II:
ADJUSTING

I know that I made a lot of mistakes, some I probably did not even realize at the time, but I am sure that others did. Nevertheless, I think the positive thing about this was the way that I reacted to the mistakes I made. I did try and accept them as part of cultural learning. I knew that it was unrealistic to expect myself to do everything correctly or customary the first time I did it. This does not mean that I was always comfortable with making mistakes. At times it became very hard to always have to be watching others and, in a way, to depend on them in order to do things correctly.... These mistakes made me more aware of cultural differences and more motivated to learn about the culture, ways I could adapt to it, and how I could grow as a person from them. ~ Jessica Novotny, Spain

Jessica was effective in crossing cultures because she knew how to learn about culture. People who are effective purposely create learning opportunities, immerse themselves in the culture, and learn from their mistakes and from insiders. Effective travelers have also learned to manage stress and handle their emotions. They are not afraid to take risks and to try out new behaviors. They never think they know it all, because cultures, persons, and situations are always changing. To stay on top of things, effective travelers are always learning and challenging themselves. This section focuses on some common processes of adjusting to the host country so that you can best understand how to manage your stress and emotional reactions in order to make the most of your experience.

Understanding Cross-Cultural Adjustment

When you are overseas, it's exhausting. There needs to be a chapter on naps 'A Guide to Taking Naps Abroad.' ~ Suzanne Hay, Greece

Being able to adjust to the new environment and culture is perhaps one of the most important facets of your experience abroad. Not only will your cross-cultural adjustment help your learning and development in the new country, it will make your international life more rewarding and interesting.

Nearly everybody goes through an adjustment when starting a new job or moving to a new city, so in some ways, adjusting to the host country is like other transitions. Except that when you start your life in a foreign country, for the first time you can encounter many cultural and language differences that you didn't need to contend with when you started a new school or job.

According to anthropologist P. K. Bock (1974), there are three kinds of adjustment that someone who goes into an unfamiliar environment must make: physical, societal, and internal. A well-adjusted traveler should have a pretty good handle on all three.

- **Physical adjustment** involves getting used to the more obvious differences—a new transportation system, the foods that you don't have at home, the system of education at the host university, etc.

- **Social adjustment** involves deeper acknowledgement and acceptance of the host country's values, beliefs, and ways of doing things. Note that it is possible for you to maintain your own belief system while at the same time integrating some of theirs.

- **Internal adjustment** is where you come to terms with your own intercultural identity and are able to incorporate and integrate both cultures with a minimum of discord.

Two kinds of people avoid difficulties with cultural adjustment and culture shock:
1. Those who are naturally comfortable with the above and are extremely flexible (these types of travelers do exist, but they are rare).
2. Those who recreate "home" while abroad. They surround themselves with their native language, foods, and peoples. The question facing these individuals is: Why? Why go to all the work to leave home and then end up taking it with you?

Our advice? Go get a bit of culture shock. Explore and challenge yourself to really learn about the cultures surrounding you.

Understanding Culture Shock and the Stages of Adjustment

The confusion is a cliché; any American, any foreigner, who has lived or worked here will tell you how the cycle goes. Step one, arrival. Step two, This place is so different! Step three, This place is really just like home! Step four, formation of conclusion: 'Now I think I understand this place.' Step five, collapse of confusion; too many exceptions. Step six, repeat from step two. ~ "The Outnation: A Search for the Soul of Japan," Jonathan Rauch

No doubt you've heard of culture shock and you may be thinking, "I know enough about the country so the cultural differences won't present a problem for me." It's true the more you know about your host country, including the language, the easier it will be to adjust. Expecting the differences is helpful, but keep in mind it's the actual cultural confrontation that brings about physical and emotional reactions.

In most cases, culture shock is caused less by one single incident and more by the gradual accumulation of anxiety, frustration, and confusion from living in an unfamiliar environment. Some prefer the terms "culture fatigue" or "culture bumps." And while not everyone experiences some kind of "shock," everyone does go through some adjustment to their environment.

Many people who have been abroad discuss their experience in terms of stages. Often times these stages resemble a "U-curve," which represents the traveler's well being throughout the experience of living abroad (Lysgaard, 1955). Take a minute to acquaint yourself with the four stages of culture shock and the diagram of the U-curve.

The "U" Curve of Culture Shock and Cross-Cultural Adjustment

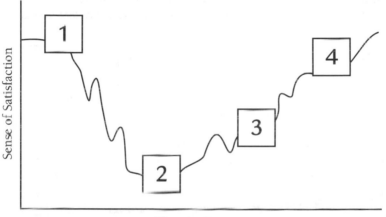

Time in Country

Stage 1: Cultural Euphoria

At the start of your study abroad there is an initial excitement about being in a new culture. This is often called the "honeymoon stage." Everything is new and wonderful, and you are eager to explore it all. This phase seems pleasant enough, but there are some drawbacks involved. You tend to see the culture through rose-colored glasses, and your interpretations aren't necessarily realistic. You also focus more on all the visible aspects of the culture (e.g., food, scenery, clothing) and are ignoring the more complex and less obvious cultural aspects. In addition, you tend to focus on similarities rather than differences in the early stage of the visit. Most tourists who travel for a short period of time remain in this stage for their entire stay.

Stage 2: Cultural Confrontation

In the next stage (typically one third to one half the way through an experience), the initial excitement you felt when you arrived diminishes and the process of cultural adjustment begins. This stage is typically characterized by confusion and frustration and, as such, is the most difficult stage. Your feelings can shift from very positive to extremely negative. You may view both the home and host cultures in unrealistic terms; one is superior while the other is lacking. This is because everything that you used to do with relative ease in your home country appears much more difficult due to the culture and/or the language. Homesickness may also contribute to your feelings of discomfort. You feel discouraged and begin to doubt whether you can learn the language or adjust to the culture. Despite these feelings, you are making critical progress in expanding your cross-cultural awareness and, whether or not you are aware of it, you are developing your own strategies for coping with cultural differences.

> When I was in Malaysia doing an independent research project, I definitely experienced many cultural differences. One was that you bartered for products. No prices were fixed, except the prices of pewter and cultural pewter artifacts, which were fixed by the government. I had my eye on a set of pewter carvings that depicted the various ethnic groups of Malaysia, but they were quite expensive and I was really on a shoe-string budget. One day, the government announced the price of pewter dropped. Thrilled, I went to the local store and asked about the new price. They politely explained that while it is common to barter in Malaysia, one does not barter for pewter. I politely explained that I knew this, but that the government had just reduced the set price. They politely explained again that pewter was not something one bartered for. I did not respond politely and started yelling that I knew this about Malaysia but that the government had lowered prices. Entirely frustrated, I left the store. I had lost it. Yelling is not a normal strategy for me, even when I'm convinced I'm right. However, the stress of always running into new situations got to me. That's culture shock. When the price in the store was lowered several days later to reflect the new government policy, I sent a friend to purchase it. I wish I would have also apologized so the store owners knew that U.S. Americans don't usually do this! ~ Barbara Kappler, Malaysia

Stage 3: Cultural Adjustment

This stage represents the transition out of culture shock into significant cultural adjustment. You feel increasingly comfortable and competent in the culture, and these feelings prevail over the times you have felt frustrated or out of place. Homesickness may still be an issue for you, but you are interacting more effectively with host nationals, leading to an increase in self-confidence. You start to look forward to further interactions in the host country and what you can learn throughout the remainder of your experience.

Stage 4: Cultural Adaptation

In this stage, you have reached a point at which you have a great deal of confidence in your ability to communicate and interact effectively. You have a deeper understanding of the influence culture has in peoples' lives. You have acquired considerable cultural knowledge, but you also recognize that there is much you still don't know or understand. You have integrated many of the values, customs, and behaviors from the new culture into your daily life. You now possess the ability to examine and comprehend a wide range of cultural norms, values, and beliefs.

> *relax. comfort. ride. chill.*
> *After being here and having gotten used to the systems and customs and safety and unwritten rules and street knowledge and language, you know you're adapting well when getting into a matatu isn't a three-hour ordeal. you know you're adapting well when people don't try and cheat you with a high price after you barter with them in kiswahili. you know you're adapting well when you bribe your way into a cricket game for seventy shillings instead of eight hundred. you know you're adapting well when you can eat your food with ugali and chapati using your hands like a pro…you know you're adapting well when you can take down eleven glasses of chai in one day. riding the wave. feeling the rhythm. chilling and hoping that things will stay this way for a bit; but really knowing that they won't, and you will be confronted with new challenges and new opportunities and new feelings of discomfort and alienation and disconnectedness and fear. and the cycle continues—but this time at a different level, with a different understanding, and a different person emerges. and that's the beauty of life. and that's what we are here for —to discover our personalized truths as we find balance and pleasure…in our own struggle to survive… ~ Free Verse by Spencer Cronk, Kenya*

Statements of adjustment

The goal of this activity is to give you the chance to think about adjustment and how you would react or help someone going through the process.

José and Steven are both juniors in college from the United States who meet in the same chemistry class while studying at a foreign university. Their class is taught in the host country's language, and because they are both unfamiliar with the difficult science vocabulary, they begin meeting at a local coffee shop to study together and help each other understand the material. One evening, they find themselves in the midst of several tables of students, all speaking English. As the night winds down, they become immersed in a conversation with six other students around them, all of whom are from the United States. Although everyone is attending the local university, they did not all arrive in the host country at the same time. The amount of time in the host country for each of them falls between one and seven months.

Read the following statements and try to determine how long you think each student has been in the host country and how well you think that student is satisfied with their experience in the host country. Place your answer on the graph below, indicating where you think each student falls.

Kiersten: The people here are so wonderful. I'm having a great time!

José: They always take so long to complete something that could be accomplished much quicker. It's not very efficient.

Steven: Some days I'm frustrated with my language skills, but then I'll have a conversation where I understand everything and I can see how far I've come.

Kurt: I love it here. I can't imagine being anywhere else!

Amira: It doesn't bother me anymore when people stare. I would be curious about the strange-looking foreigner too if I were them.

Maggie: I can't believe I'm eating raw fish. I couldn't stomach it when I first arrived.

Gretchen: I can barely stand the smell of the cafeteria. Give me McDonald's any day.

Martin: I feel like when I return to the U.S. a part of me will remain here in this country.

Satisfaction with the Experience

1 month   2 months   3 months   4 months   5 months   6 months   7 months

Stage 1

Kiersten: "The people here are so wonderful. I'm having a great time!"

Kurt: "I love it here. I can't imagine being anywhere else!"

Stage 2

José: "They always take so long to complete something that could be accomplished much quicker. It's not very efficient."

Gretchen: "I can barely stand the smell of the cafeteria. Give me McDonald's any day".

Stage 4

Amira: "It doesn't bother me anymore when the hosts stare at me. I would be curious about the strange-looking foreigner too if I were them."

Martin: "I feel like when I return to the U.S. a part of me will remain here in this country."

Kurt: "I love it here. I can't imagine being anywhere else!"

Stage 3

Steven: "Some days I'm frustrated with my language skills, but then I'll have a conversation where I understand everything and I can see how far I've come."

Maggie: "I can't believe I'm eating raw fish. I couldn't stomach it when I first arrived."

Satisfaction with the Experience (vertical axis label)

1 month   2 months   3 months   4 months   5 months   6 months   7 months

Reflection questions

- Why is Kurt's comment listed in both stages 1 and 4? (Hint…This was not a mistake; we feel that while overly positive comments are common in stage 1, they can also reflect a deep connection to the culture that is found in stage 4.)
- What advice or reaction would you have to each of the students' comments?
- What does your "U-Curve" look like if your study abroad is two months? One year?
- How has your own emotional experience changed since arrival?

Knowing these eight characters' timelines can be very helpful in understanding how your own experience will change over time and how to recognize when you may be experiencing challenges in cultural adjustment.

Personal highs and lows of study abroad

Think about your own timeline and what issues or events might trigger some low points or create some high points for you during your time abroad. Write those down in the space at the top of the next page. You might want to consider keeping a graph in your journal throughout your study abroad stay to chart your own experience.

Potential Low Points	Potential High Points
•	•
•	•
•	•
•	•
•	•
•	•
•	•

Here are some things other students have shared about their high and low points while studying abroad:

Low Points

- I got on the wrong bus back to my apartment because I misread the sign and ended up on the other side of the city.
- No one here knew it was my birthday —it really made me miss my friends at home.
- My host mother got angry with me for using too much hot water.
- The cash machine wouldn't allow me to access my account, and I ended up yelling at the bank teller because she couldn't understand what I needed.
- I missed my friend's wedding, and she never got the gift that I sent for it.
- My parents cancelled their trip to see me here because it got too expensive.
- My girlfriend from home broke up with me over e-mail.
- My roommates went home for the local holiday, and I ended up in the dorm alone because I couldn't afford to go anywhere.

High Points

- I told a joke to the grouchy fruit vendor at the market and made him laugh. After that, he always smiled and talked to me.
- I dreamed in the language of my host country.
- I went to a holiday festival in another village and learned a traditional dance.
- I traveled alone—something I never would have done before. Because I was by myself, I ended up meeting and becoming friends with travelers from other countries.
- I got invited to a classmate's house for dinner.
- I read the newspaper and discussed an article with my host brother.
- My professor actually liked the essay I wrote on World War II.
- I went on a weekend trip with three new friends to a nearby town.

Some helpful coping strategies

What to do when you are hit with the culture shock blues? Here is some advice from recent returnees:

- **Find ways to relieve stress:** understand your language and culture limits—if things get overwhelming, take a break.
- **Do what you do at home or something close to it:** what worked for you at home when you were feeling down? Reading? Listening to music? Watching a funny movie? Give it a try in the host country as well.
- **Express yourself:** find someone who understands to talk things over—it may be another U.S. American or international student. Singing, playing an instrument, or dancing can also be wonderful means of expression you can do by yourself or with others.
- **Connect with family and friends back home:** write letters home, send e-mails to friends. Writing can be a valuable means of reconnecting when things aren't going so well. But set a limit. Too much time sending e-mail can make you feel you never emotionally left home. And that's not what you want either.
- **Keep a journal** (see p. 115): Writing down your experiences can be a great way to vent and also to process and create a space to gain insights into your experience and the cultures surrounding you.
- **Stay active:** take walks, bike, swim, or engage in other kinds of physical activity. A good workout can be calming and therapeutic.

The above are some examples to get you thinking about what you can do to alleviate the symptoms of culture shock. By now you should be able to come up with a few coping strategies of your own. Think about what normally helps you feel relaxed, valued, and comfortable when you are home. Then adapt these strategies to your new environment in the host country.

My personal coping strategies (list five)

1._____

2._____

3._____

4._____

5._____

Going Beyond Surface Adjustment

Although most study abroad students go through stages of cultural adaptation similar to those just described, there is no set length of time during which each stage occurs. When and how each person goes through the confrontation or adaptation stage, for example, depends largely on the individual, degree of cultural differences, and other situational factors that may be beyond control (poor weather, health, etc.).

Unfortunately, many students during their time abroad do not have the degree of contact with host nationals that is essential for complete cultural adaptation to take place. Students who have adjusted only superficially have not become very involved in the host culture. In short, surface adjustment may be easier for you in the short term, but in the long run you are apt to lose out on opportunities for personal growth and significant intercultural learning. It may require a conscious effort on your part to take advantage of immersion opportunities to participate in the host culture. Other chapters outline some strategies for immersion and for effective interaction with host nationals.

Another thing to remember is that while you are making attempts to adjust to your host culture, the hosts may be making just as much effort to adjust to you and your "peculiar" ways of doing things. In most countries throughout the world, the hosts will have the expectation that people from abroad who come to live in their country for a decent length of time will make an attempt to adjust to the manner, customs, and lifestyle of the country. After all, learning these aspects of the country is one of the reasons you decided to study abroad in the first place, right?

There are some things that you may not be able to change, perhaps certain eating or religious customs. These will need special attention and negotiation skills:

> We hosted a Moroccan student for a few weeks one summer. The first thing he said to us was, 'Hi. I am Rahid. I do not eat pork.' Rahid, as a devout Muslim, had many dietary restrictions—from my point of view. So, I took Rahid to the grocery store with me so he could help me pick out what he could eat. We did try to accommodate his cultural needs so that he could be more comfortable. I also learned a lot about his culture this way. ~ Karin Larson, Coordinator, The Center for Advanced Research on Language Acquisition (CARLA)

Despite our best attempts at adjusting to the new cultural milieu, we still are going to confront differences we don't understand or might upset us, we will still make mistakes in our use of language, and at times we will feel like giving up because we think we aren't making any progress. At these times it's important to stop, give ourselves some positive affirmations, and do something that gets us back into a better frame of mind. The following scenarios will help you consider how to best cope with these challenging moments.

Coping scenarios

A study abroad experience can be the highlight of an academic career. It's an adventure that is anticipated, sometimes for years in advance; a journey we expect will contain few or none of the commonplace problems of day-to-day living in the U.S. It's hard to imagine having normal concerns such as turning a paper in on time or arguing with your roommates about whose turn it is to take out the garbage. Instead you are envisioning yourself walking along the Great Wall of China or witnessing an active volcano on a remote Indonesian island. When planning a study abroad trip, it's easy to envision an experience free from the bureaucracy and small troubles of "ordinary" life.

But just as life in the United States can be occasionally complex and unpleasant, a study abroad experience will contain its fair share of problems and complex issues, some of them unique to the culture where you are studying.

Read the following scenarios from two study abroad students:

Scenario 1

Kerry is a 21-year-old student from the U.S. studying in Slovenia. In mid-November of her year abroad she begins dating Gregor, a fellow student at the university and a native of Hungary. Since she is not going back to the U.S. for winter break, he invites her over to his family's house in Budapest to celebrate the New Year. This would be a large family event and would involve meeting his entire family, including his grandparents, cousins, nieces, and nephews, and spending two days with them. Although she likes Gregor and would enjoy visiting Budapest, she feels anxious that this kind of visit would indicate to his family that she and Gregor are in a more serious relationship than they actually are.

If you were Kerry's friend, what advice would you give her?

Here's some advice other students had for Kerry.

- *Tell Gregor that for you this indicates that the relationship is pretty serious. Ask if he thinks it means the same thing.*
- *Ask Gregor if there is a cultural meaning to this kind of family visit. Explain that you want to know what this may mean to the family and to Gregor before you go.*
- *If you feel funny making a big deal about this with Gregor, get advice from another friend who really knows the culture.*
- *Don't worry so much. Enjoy the experience and don't worry about what Gregor's family thinks. You are only there for a short time and you don't know what the future will bring. Even if there are cultural differences, you cannot control what the family will think.*
- *Ask Gregor what the sleeping arrangements will be. You don't want to be embarrassed in front of the whole family – either way! And you need to know that you'll be comfortable there.*

Scenario 2

Terry is 22 and studying in Bern, Switzerland. Terry is a seasoned traveler and an avid outdoorsman. Part of the reason he chose to study in Switzerland is because he would be centrally located to take long weekend and holiday trips to France, Germany, Italy, and Austria. After his second trip away from Bern, however, his host mother takes him aside and asks him if he is planning on being gone every weekend. She tells him that other host students they have had in the past spent more time with the family and indicates that she would like it if he became more involved with the family. Terry feels torn—he likes his host family well enough, but he already has plans to leave again in two weeks to go hiking and camping with a friend who is studying in Munich. Additionally, there are a number of other trips he'd like to make before his year abroad is over.

If you were Terry's friend, what advice would you give him?

Here's some advice other students had for Terry:
- *You need to think carefully—maybe the host family option is not for you.*
- *Try to plan for the long run. Is it more important to see a great deal of Europe or to form a relationship with the family? Can you maybe come back again to visit friends?*
- *You need to recognize that you cannot have it both ways. You have to decide which is more important—travel or the family.*
- *Will you really get to know Bern and the Swiss if you are spending so much time traveling?*
- *You are only there for a short time. Perhaps you can negotiate with your family and explain that you would like to spend time with them. Be prepared that they may not feel comfortable with you 'scheduling them in' on the weekends you are available. Maybe ask them what would work well. What's the 'ideal' time to be with them? Maybe you could adjust your schedule and spend more time with them during the week in the evenings, for example.*

Some quick tips for going beyond surface adjustment

- Participate in the culture.

- Don't fight the culture; flex with it.

- View culture learning as expanding your skills and knowledge, not an admittance of failure or that you've done something wrong.

- Learn what is most important to the people in the culture.

- Constantly test your own ideas about the culture.

- Don't assume you understand the culture.

- Learn from "experts" (host culture and expatriate friends).

- Occasionally withdraw from the culture to avoid culture fatigue.

- Explain your culture to your hosts; help them understand you.

- Learn from others, but don't become dependent on them.

- Learn from TV, radio, and the press; great for cultural insights.

- When you don't know, ask.

(Adapted from Kappler and Nokken, 1999.)

Be assertive! You need to take responsibility for getting involved and talking with people. ~ Jacob Dick, Italy

Summary

We can't easily control how we feel in response to certain events, but we *can* control how we act upon our feelings. Much of cross-cultural adjustment is about getting used to a number of new and unfamiliar stimuli and understanding them. Part of the reason for studying abroad is because you want differences. Even after you have adjusted somewhat, you may still feel negatively about something in the new culture. But you now are able to understand the cultural basis for it and can accept it for what it is—a difference. Other things that you didn't quite care for when you first arrived you will eventually learn to like and appreciate. This is all part of the process of feeling more at home in your host country.

Study abroad challenged me and reinforced my sense of independence. I found that I was able to do things that normally wouldn't be a big deal, but I did them in a completely different country and a completely different language. Things as simple as buying train tickets, using the phone, and traveling became successes to me. I learned that I was stronger than I thought I was and a very capable person. I now feel that if I were set down anywhere in the world I would be able to make my way and be fine. ~ Sarah Parr, France

Phases of Cultural Awareness

Now that you are in the host country and are surrounded by differences on a daily basis, it's especially important to work on your degree of cultural awareness and how to go about building competence in your new culture.

William Howell (1982) has divided cultural awareness into four categories or levels. These can also be considered developmental phases a traveler goes through when abroad. While you read over the four stages, keep in mind the three different categories of adjustment discussed earlier: physical, societal, and internal. To advance to the next stage of cultural awareness, it is important that progress be made in all of these categories. One of the main goals of this guide is to provide information that helps you make progress through the early stages so you build competence faster and make your experience more rewarding as a result.

I. Unconscious Incompetence

In this phase you may be aware of some cultural differences between you and your host country, but you do not know how this translates into the functioning of society or to how you interact with people in the country. In this stage you are likely to make many mistakes but will be relatively unaffected by them because of your lack of knowledge. This is a difficult stage for someone to discern, since it is very difficult for first-time travelers to know what they do not know. They say that ignorance is bliss, after all.

II. Conscious Incompetence

Although it is not always possible, it might be a good idea to start yourself out consciously thinking of yourself as being in this phase. If you assume that you are likely to make mistakes, you may be more careful about making cultural assumptions or rashly evaluating your surroundings. As a whole, adopting a mindset where you lower your expectations of your abilities in the new culture is probably a very good idea and will ease your relationships with hosts. As you may realize, you are not really incompetent, you just happen to lack knowledge and skills important in the new culture. This tends to be a difficult stage for many, as people are not used to being culturally incompetent until they go abroad. One salvation is to think about how much you are learning and absorbing every day based upon your studies and quality interactions with host nationals. These interactions will take you into the next phase, which may feel more comfortable as you begin to build confidence in your cross-cultural skills.

III. Conscious Competence

In this phase you have reached a certain level of awareness of cultural differences and have discovered a way to understand, accept, and integrate them, although perhaps not fully. You have built up some confidence from numerous successful interactions with hosts, and you are able to shift your behavior so that it is culturally appropriate.

You are still learning and deepening your knowledge of the culture, but now you have a solid basis for how you view and interpret the culture. You are glad to make efforts toward cultural appropriateness because you know that this strategy will be effective for achieving your goals.

IV. Unconscious Competence

The final phase of cultural awareness is one in which you no longer need to think much about cultural differences because you have built up an instinctive understanding, and you know automatically what works and what doesn't in the host culture. How do you know you are in this stage? In certain countries the hosts may stop telling you how good your language ability is, or that you are more "Chinese" than the Chinese. But a better measure is to look at the effectiveness of your interactions with hosts. Are you achieving your goals without cultural-related stress? Are you feeling more comfortable about how the host nationals perceive you and how you perceive your new intercultural identity? If the answers to these questions are "yes" then it's likely you are in this phase of cultural awareness.

Differentiating the phases of cultural awareness

For the following statements, try to determine which phase the traveler is in. Suggested answers are found on the next page.

Chris: *I'm exhausted after I get home everyday. It seems I never can do anything right.*
Phase _____

Elena: *I'm feeling very comfortable in the culture. It's become a second home for me.*
Phase _____

Karenna: *It surprised me to realize that I could have an entire conversation on the phone without getting stressed out.*
Phase _____

Shane: *I notice that the hosts do funny things when they greet one another.*
Phase _____

Ingrid: *It sometimes embarrasses me when other foreigners complain about the culture and act inappropriately. I often feel like I don't want to be associated with them.*
Phase _____

Max: *I feel like the host nationals are watching me all the time. I'm afraid of making mistakes.*
Phase _____

Lia: *Now that I can eat almost anything using chopsticks, it really makes sense to use them as much as the nationals do.*
Phase _____

Jess: *As long as you can speak the language, there will be few problems in navigating the culture.*
Phase _____

Allie: *I am able to learn so much by being able to interact with hosts on their level. I can often understand what they are going to say before they actually say it.*
Phase _____

Answers:

Chris: *I'm exhausted after I get home everyday. It seems I never can do anything right.*
Phase II: very aware of his own cultural inadequacy

Elena: *I'm feeling very comfortable in the culture. It's become a second home for me.*
Phase IV: could also be Phase I if she has no recognition of cultural differences

Karenna: *It surprised me to I realize that I could have an entire conversation on the phone without getting stressed out.*
Phase III: could be Phase IV, but she wouldn't be surprised at her own competence

Shane: *I notice that the hosts do funny things when they greet one another.*
Phase I: finds host behavior unusual, oblivious to his own behavior

Ingrid: *It sometimes embarrasses me when other foreigners complain about the culture and act inappropriately. I often feel like I don't want to be associated with them.*
Phase IV: it can require a lot of patience for a culturally aware traveler to be around those of significantly lower cultural competence

Max: *I feel like the host nationals are watching me all the time. I'm afraid of making mistakes.*
Phase II: expresses more than usual self-consciousness at his own ineffective behavior.

Lia: *Now that I can eat almost anything using chopsticks it really makes sense to use them as much as the nationals do.*
Phase III: expresses awareness of her own competence development

Jess: *As long as you can speak the language there will be few problems in navigating the culture.*
Phase I: attributes all cultural differences to language alone

Allie: *I am able to learn so much by being able to interact with hosts on their level. I can often understand what they are going to say before they actually say it.*

Phase IV: expresses a high level of intuitive cultural empathy and sensitivity

Take a moment and consider which stage describes where you are at today. Which character can you most easily relate to?

As the above exercise demonstrates, where you are in your ability to understand and manage cultural differences is going to have a direct effect on your ability to adjust to the culture and achieve your academic and personal goals. The next section will help you build on these skills by providing ways for you to make sense of the plethora of cultural phenomena you encounter in the host culture.

CULTURE
In-Country

IN-COUNTRY CULTURE STRATEGIES PART III:
STRATEGIES FOR DEVELOPING INTERCULTURAL COMPETENCE

It took me a long time to feel competent in Italy. Certainly I mean my language skills, but I also mean almost a change of attitude—an acceptance that things really run differently here. My hard work and the difficulties I faced did pay off, and I learned to really enjoy the culture at a deeper level. ~ Jacob Dick, Italy

What, you may be asking, is intercultural competence? And when do you know you are competent in the host culture? One way of looking at intercultural competence is the ease at which you are able to adapt and adjust to the culture. Another way is to look at how well you are able to perform tasks that you can do effectively at home.

This section focuses on intercultural competence as the ability or skills that you develop to help you manage differences between cultures. These abilities can be broadly interpreted to include knowledge of culture and where differences lie, feelings and attitudes toward differences, and lastly, how you respond or your behavior when you encounter cultural differences.

Milton J. Bennett's (1993) developmental model of intercultural sensitivity is one way of looking at intercultural competence. Bennett examines the attitudes and degree of awareness toward cultural differences. Intercultural sensitivity is not considered a naturally occurring phenomenon—human beings over the centuries have tended to prefer contact with those with whom they are culturally similar, and societies as a whole are largely ethnocentric. It is only through the process of awareness and understanding of cultural differences that comes through education and experience that people begin to view cultural differences as being positive, interesting, desirable, and having their own internal logic within a certain culture.

A Model of Intercultural Sensitivity

Ethnocentric stages

Chances are that most of us grow up being ethnocentric. We do things the way we do because we believe it's the best way—or we would do it some other way! Ethnocentric has two meanings: *believing your own culture is superior to others* and *the tendency to view other cultures in terms of one's own*. The second meaning, while seemingly more benign, is still potentially damaging. It may seem OK or even natural to view other cultures by comparing to your own, but the danger is that you view your own culture as the central or mainstream culture from which others should be compared and judged (e.g., they are not as modern, they are too liberal). The following stages reflect ethnocentric attitudes toward others.

Denial

People in this stage are not aware that cultural differences actually exist. They also probably only understand culture as visible things (the way people dress, languages) and not as different values or beliefs. Most people in denial have had little contact with people who are culturally different. If they encounter problems in communicating or interacting with people from different cultures, they are likely to think of the cause as having personal reasons rather than cultural. Generally, they interpret these so-called "differences" as being wrong or inappropriate ways of thinking or behaving. People in this stage may say things like, "We should have no trouble interacting in the host culture as long as we can speak the same language." This person is unable to acknowledge cultural differences.

If you identify with this stage of the scale, try these things to move forward:
- Try to make friends with people from the host country and really be open to their points of view.
- Read the local newspaper. Compare the responses in the local newspaper with an international or U.S. newspaper. Do you see different perspectives offered on the same event?

Defense

People in the defense stage also think of cultural differences as being wrong or inappropriate, but they have acknowledged that differences do exist. These people may encounter more difference in their daily lives, but they feel threatened by it and often make efforts toward justifying the correctness and superiority of their own cultural values and beliefs. Statements like, "Why don't they just act more like us?" or blatant stereotyping of groups are indicative of people in defense. Also, statements such as, "When I travel abroad, it makes me realize how much better things are in the U.S." still probably reflect defense because the person is making a blanket statement about the superiority of everything American.

If you identify with this stage of the scale, try these things to move forward:
- Search for common ground. What special events do you have in common with the host country? Maybe it's a sporting event, music concert, holiday, or celebration.
- Challenge yourself to find something, no matter how small, that you prefer in your host country to your home country. Maybe there is a certain saying that you feel captures your feelings in a way that cannot be done in English. Maybe there is a new angle to a topic you've been studying that gives you insights you did not learn in the U.S. Keep adding to this list so that you can enjoy the differences of your new, but temporary, home.
- Explore things from the country—movies, museums, sports. Dig deeper into what is unique about the place.

Minimization

People minimize cultural differences and instead prefer to focus on similarities between groups of people. People in this stage might say something like, "We're all human beings after all" or "Why do we always have to emphasize what makes people different? People are people after all." What makes this minimization is that the person typically views that others are "like me" and does not recognize how others are different. What makes the statement ethnocentric is that the point of reference is "me" or "my culture." The key point is not that we should ignore similarities, but rather that similarities *and* differences need to be understood in order to truly understand the culture.

If you identify with this stage of the scale, try these things to move forward:
- Challenge yourself to get more involved with your host country. Join a club or sports team and notice the similarities and differences in how the group operates compared to teams at home.
- When talking with your new friends from the host country, try to suspend any thoughts such as "yes, that's exactly how I feel" or "yes, it's very similar in the U.S." Instead, try to push those thoughts aside and really listen to your friends' views and make sure that you don't miss key differences.
- Read more local newspapers, books, and magazines to learn how people in the host country really view the world.

Ethnorelative stages

Ethnorelative is a term coined by Milton Bennett when he wanted a word to characterize those who no longer view their own culture as a center from which others should be judged, but rather as a state of mind in which cultures are respected, compared, and contrasted according to the perspective of the cultures involved. Read on to discover more about ethnorelative stages.

Acceptance

This is the first ethnorelative stage, and it involves what might be described as a significant shift in cultural awareness and understanding. In general, people in this stage have ceased looking at cultural differences as negative, but simply as existing. There is a good deal of awareness of cultural differences, and respect is given to groups who are culturally different. There may not be a lot of deep understanding of individual cultures, but there exists the interest and capacity to learn about other cultures. A statement such as, "My life is enriched by my relationships with people from different backgrounds and experiences" signifies acceptance because the person is interested in others from different cultures.

If you identify with this stage of the scale, try these things to move forward:
- As suggested in earlier stages, challenge yourself to get even more involved in the culture. You need to be immersed in conversations to challenge you not only to recognize behavioral and value differences, but also to figure out how to adapt to these new behaviors and values.
- Invite your new friends over for dinner and host a conversation on a timely topic. Give yourself a chance to see your friends relaxed and conversing so that you can learn *and* join in!
- Try out the journaling methods discussed in this guide (p. 115). You can revisit key events—either because they were initially confusing, exciting, or overwhelming—and try to dig deeper into the cultural nuances. You could even try sharing some of your journal entries with others to see if together you can come to a deeper understanding of key behavioral and value differences, as well as sorting out what is personal and what is cultural in any particular incident.

Adaptation and Integration

In this stage, people have incorporated differences in cultures into their own value and belief systems. People in this stage see the value of adjusting their behavior to accommodate cultural norms, and they are more able to empathize with people from other cultures and see things from their perspectives. People in these stages still maintain many of the cultural values of their original culture, but they have integrated others and, more importantly, are able to use at least two different cultural frames of reference for perceiving the world. Lastly, they also may consider themselves bicultural or multicultural. These two statements reflect adaptation and integration: "I usually try to behave appropriately in intercultural situations, but I also can still maintain my values and beliefs" and "When I examine a problem, I usually think about it from more than one cultural point of view."

While this stage is listed as the final point on the continuum, it certainly does not mean that the learning is over. There are always new host cultures and perspectives to explore!

Reflection
- Now that you have had an overview of the Bennett model of intercultural sensitivity, you probably have given some thought to how these stages apply to you. Where do you see yourself on the scale?

- What activities can you do to move yourself forward?

This model is intended to help you become more aware of cultural differences that can lead to deeper learning and the ability to look at things from multiple perspectives. It may sound easy enough, but in reality this type of personal development usually requires a substantial amount of intercultural contact, knowledge, and experience. Identify portions of the in-country section that will help you develop the skills you need.

IN-COUNTRY CULTURE STRATEGIES PART IV:
STRATEGIES FOR MAKING CULTURAL INFERENCES

The American resists describing or judging something in terms of itself or in its own context. Instead, he insists on comparison. He evaluates himself against others like himself; he judges a movie against other movies he has seen; he judges his children against the norm for their age; and then, most naturally, he judges other people against Americans. The evaluation of 'good because' is more naturally rendered as 'good as.' ~ "American Cultural Patterns," Stewart & Bennett (1991)

You didn't sign up for study abroad just to learn about yourself—you signed up to learn about others. As you've come to realize, this can take a bit of work. The fact that you are reading this guide suggests that you are interested in going beyond the simple and judgmental comparisons that Edward Stewart, a Brazilian psychologist, claims U.S. Americans make. This section discusses how to dig deeper into your reactions to come to a more full understanding of your host country.

Cultural Ethnography

To increase our own cultural knowledge of a group of people, we need to "get inside the heads" of the host nationals. Although this is difficult to accomplish, it's not impossible. Whether you are aware of it, you will be making various inferences about the culture and on a certain level you will be engaging in cultural ethnography.

A U.S. American student studying in a European country observed all the other students in a class immediately rise to their feet when the professor entered the room. She guessed that this was a sign of respect. Later, the students explained further the importance of standing when a professor entered the classroom and gave reasons for doing it. Through what they said she made additional inferences about their cultural knowledge.

> *My Estonian boyfriend had not seen his brother for seven years. When they met at the airport, they shook hands. I was a bit surprised because in my family you hug if you haven't seen each other for a week! At first I found myself wondering if they were really close. In talking with my boyfriend and in watching other Estonians, I realized public displays of affection are not usual, and, with the exception of mothers embracing their children and couples hugging each other, this kind of physical contact—even in one's own home— is not all that common. By observing and checking my observations with others, I learned the real reason for the behavior.* ~ Barbara Kappler, Estonia

While in the field, you are constantly making inferences from what people say, from the way they act, and from the objects they use. At first, each cultural inference is only a hypothesis. These hypotheses must then be tested over and over again until you, as the ethnographer, become relatively certain that people share a particular system of cultural meanings. The forming of such hypotheses is a tricky business, similar to the formation of generalizations discussed previously. The next section will provide you with some tools for making sense of cultural experiences and encounters.

Part of gathering information is knowing how to balance insider information with your own observations. A large part of culture consists of tacit, or unspoken, knowledge that host nationals will be aware of but that you, as an outsider, may not. Host nationals know instinctively what subjects they can or cannot talk about or express in direct ways. On the other hand, individual cultural informants may be limited in the type and depth of information they can or will provide because they may never have had to articulate their own cultural rules—they just live by them. Being observant and deducing phenomena on your own, based upon your observations of behavior, artifacts, and language, will enable you to gain valuable insight and information about the host culture.

Enhancing Your Culture Learning

Making sense out of culture

It is important to process fully the cultural information that you gain as a result of your experiences. A way that allows you to accomplish this is often termed "debriefing." Debriefing is a process that facilitates discussing, conceptualizing, clarifying, and summarizing an intercultural experience. The following are some helpful guidelines that can help you to conduct your own debriefing of intercultural encounters and phenomena.

Debriefing in action

John is an on-site academic adviser for an overseas program. Since John began his job eight years ago, he has watched dozens of students go through the program and has witnessed the transition that occurs as students, most of whom have never lived abroad before, experience life in a new culture. Last week during orientation for the new semester, Bob, a new student, walks into John's office. John can tell immediately that he is upset. Bob sits down and begins fidgeting in his chair.

John:	Well, Bob, what can I do for you today?
Bob:	I went to register for classes this morning, but they wouldn't let me. I stood in line for an hour and when I got up to the front of the line they told me I couldn't register.
John:	Do you know if other students were having problems registering?

Bob: No, it was just me. Anyway, I don't know what to do—I'm supposed to start classes on Monday, and now I can't.

John: Did they give you a reason why you couldn't register?

Bob: I don't know, it was some stupid thing about my passport. It's just so dumb —I don't see why I can't register over the Internet like I do at home.

John: What was the problem with your passport?

Bob: Well, I didn't have my passport with me, and the lady behind the desk told me I couldn't register without it. She was really rude about it, too. It was so stupid because I had my student I.D. card from my university at home and my driver's license, so it's not like they couldn't tell who I was. I even had my passport number written down. And she could have been nicer about it.

John: That sounds frustrating; however, you have to remember that those other IDs don't really mean much over here.

Bob: Yeah, but still I don't see why it's such a big deal. And the registration lady wouldn't even listen to me. It would've take me at least an hour to go to my apartment, get my passport, and then go back to campus. Then I would've had to stand in line for another hour. Anyway, what I was hoping was that maybe you could call someone or help me register without having to go through all that again.

John: Well, there's really not much I can do. Although I know it doesn't seem like it should be so difficult, you have to remember that your passport is really the only document that is official internationally, and they need to see the actual passport itself to make sure that it's real. It's important for their security and yours that they check so closely. And, our staff views providing good services as giving you a direct answer. This may seem rude if you are used to staff smiling all the time and letting you down gently.

Bob: I know. It just seems like this wouldn't happen in the States.

John: Well, maybe it wouldn't happen to you since you're a U.S. citizen. However, I think that if you were there as a foreign student you would find a lot of similar issues, what seems like bureaucracy and red tape.

Bob: Yeah, I suppose you're right.

John: So what do you think you should do now?

Bob: I guess I'll go back in tomorrow with my passport and try to register again.

John: Well, Bob, if you aren't able to register again tomorrow, come back and see me. It sounds like having the passport should do the trick though. I hope it does.

Bob: Me too. OK, well thanks, and I'm sorry about being all riled up.

John: Not a problem. Good luck. And stop by and see me again and let me know how things are going.

Bob: OK. Bye, John.

John: Bye, Bob.

Reflection questions

- What are the specific questions that John asks Bob? Do these questions seem to be effective? If so, why?

- How does John go about teaching Bob the cultural rules? In what way does he try to create common ground?

The Description-Interpretation-Evaluation (D-I-E) Model of Debriefing

Without having a lot of experience in the host culture, it is relatively easy to jump to conclusions about what you see, hear, or observe. Since we are looking at the new culture using the same lens or filter we use for back home, it's likely we don't fully understand the reason or rationale behind some cultural practices or norms. The following process of D-I-E can be a helpful tool in coming to a new understanding of the culture.

Step 1: D - Describe

- Describe the object/situation/content in concrete terms.

- What happened in the interaction/experience/situation?

- What was said? What did you see? What did you feel at the time?

Notice that John's question to Bob asked for more description.

Step 2: I - Interpret

- Think of possible explanations for what you observed or experienced.

- What do the words and actions mean to you?

- What adjectives would you use to explain the experience or situation?

- Try to find at least three different interpretations of the interaction or occurrence. What cultural information have you used to produce these interpretations?

Notice that John explained to Bob the reason he needed a passport and why staff may behave differently.

Step 3: E - Evaluate

- Evaluate what you observed or experienced.

- What positive or negative feelings do you have regarding the situation or what you have observed?

- How might you have felt if you were a member of the host culture and held the dominant cultural values and beliefs?

Notice that John tried to help Bob reevaluate his initial negative evaluation by explaining that it is probably similar in the U.S. and why staff behave differently.

The D-I-E model of debriefing can help you consider multiple perspectives and interpretations for intercultural encounters. By listening to and understanding varied interpretations, you will become more open to differing perspectives. You will be able to consider cognitively and switch to alternative perspectives that are required in different cultural settings. D-I-E will also help you to deal more effectively with emotional reactions to differences that often result in a lack of understanding or a rejection of the new experience.

After you have made an evaluation using D-I-E you may recognize that you have to accept certain situations. You may also recognize that you need to act on certain situations. In all, the D-I-E process will help entitle you to your evaluations—positive or negative—because you have taken the time to reason through them

(Adapted from J. M. Bennett and M. J. Bennett, n.d.)

Asking questions using D-I-E

Along with learning the D-I-E process, it's helpful to learn about what kinds of questions to ask. Descriptive questions are usually the best place to start with difficult-to-understand cultural phenomena because they start a dialogue that is free from inputting your own values into the mix. Through descriptive questions you may find out much more information that will assist you in forming interpretations and subsequently evaluating the event. In looking at the following sample questions, notice the great differences in the evaluative, interpretive, and descriptive questions.

Evaluative	Interpretative	Descriptive
Why are these people so rude?	*The people here aren't very trusting of foreigners, are they?*	*Why do so many of the villagers follow me around when I go to the market?*

If you were to start with the evaluative question, you risk offending others or, at the least, revealing that you have been judgmental. The interpretive question, while potentially less offensive, appears to be less of a real question and more of a search for confirming a negative impression you have made. As a result of asking either an evaluative or interpretive question, you may alienate yourself from those you are trying to understand. The third question, from a descriptive approach, is more tangible (you are asking about a specific behavior you've experienced) and more open-minded (you have not, at least in the words selected, and hopefully not in your tone, revealed a negative evaluation of the host culture). Our advice is to use descriptive questions as much as possible to demonstrate you are interested in truly understanding the world around you.

(Adapted from Kappler and Nokken, 1999.)

The Culture-Learning Model of Debriefing

These sample questions below give you an additional tool for culture learning.

1. **Culture-learning questions**
   - How did you discover that the host culture is very age conscious and status-oriented (or some other value or trait)?
   - What other ways could you learn more about the culture?

2. **Culture-specific questions**
   - How do members of the host culture view the roles of men and women?

3. **Culture-general questions**
   - What limitations does your own culture place on your interpretations of other cultures?

4. **Problem-solving questions**
   - How might this situation have been avoided in the first place? What can be done now to help solve the problem?

5. **Affective questions**
   - How do you feel personally about this situation?

(Excerpted from Paige, et al., 1999.)

Activity

Revisiting the iceberg

Now that you are well immersed in your host country, it is likely you have had one or more incidents that have left you scratching your head wondering, "What just happened?" Perhaps you arrived for a party at a friend's house promptly at the designated time of 8:30 p.m., only to find yourself alone with the host for an hour-and-a-half before the other guests arrived. Or perhaps your host brother became angry when you tried to pay for your own meal at a restaurant. Think about your experiences in the country so far, and take one situation that you have had that has left you confused. Write this event in *descriptive* terms above the line. Now think through the possible cultural explanations that may lie below the surface that could help explain this event. Write the possible explanation(s) below the line. Need a refresher on the iceberg? See pages 42-47 of the pre-departure section.

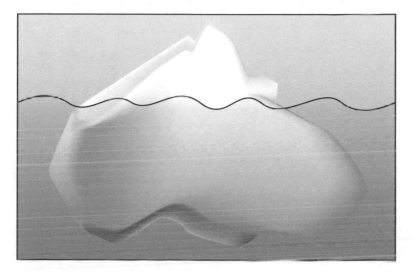

The following chapter on journaling gives even more examples of how to put D-I-E and culture learning into action.

> *Two persons can disagree without one being right and the other wrong—*
> *when their arguments are based on culturally different assumptions.*
> *~ "Culture-centered counseling interventions: Striving for accuracy,"*
> *Pedersen, 1997*

IN-COUNTRY CULTURE STRATEGIES PART V:
STRATEGIES FOR KEEPING A JOURNAL

Keep a journal. It will become a treasure and a link. ~ Joy Wiltermuth, France

The importance of journaling

One of the things many travelers regret most upon their return is that they neglected to keep a journal while they were abroad. As mentioned earlier, one of the most valuable and relatively painless activities you can do to enhance your experience is to keep a journal. No matter how amazing and unforgettable your experience abroad may seem, it doesn't take long before your memories begin to fade…Who was that guy on the bus in Thailand? What was the name of that quaint pension I stayed at in Paris? Keeping a journal can not only help you remember the details of your experience, but it can also help you process and learn the most from it.

What are the functions of a journal?

The journal could have many functions: serve as a record of experiences, provide a reference for culture and language learning and development, or help you cope with feelings and emotions felt while going through cultural adjustment. Journaling may already be a main component of your academic curriculum abroad, in which case your journal entries will already have a specific focus. Whether or not this is the case, the following journaling ideas are intended to assist you to make journal writing a regular part of your study abroad experience.

Keep in mind…

Making periodic entries into your journal will take some time and energy. Whether you make daily entries or write only when the urge hits you will be up to you. Most people find that once they start making regular entries and getting into the journaling habit, it's something they actually look forward to doing.

Two Ways to Keep Journals

The old fashioned way

> *I went to Malaysia for a study abroad research program, and I love to pull my journal off the shelf and go through a few pages, reminiscing about the trip. I have an entry for each day that I was there, and I recorded pretty much the details of, and my reactions to, the day. As I read through, I can close my eyes and feel like I am back there again, even though it was years ago. ~ Barbara Kappler, Malaysia*

A new way to keep a journal

Keeping a journal while you are studying or traveling abroad seems like a good idea at first, but then you get bogged down with the whole experience and most people give up on the idea. And the funny thing is: almost *everyone* regrets not keeping a journal!

What's wrong with the old way?

One of the main reasons people give up on journaling is that they find the process of writing down every detail of their experience overwhelming and sometimes quite boring. Many journal entries go something like this: "We got up in the morning, ready for a day full of sight-seeing. First we went…and then we saw…and then we went…and then we…and then…and then…and then…." This type of journaling stifles your creative juices, does not encourage good writing techniques, and takes too long to regurgitate your entire day on paper.

So what's the answer?

Consider changing the structure of your journal. One avid traveler began keeping a different kind of journal during her third study abroad trip to India and Malaysia.

> *It took a little getting used to at first, and I admit I was a little skeptical, but once I became familiar with the technique I was hooked! Now when I travel or live abroad this is the only type of journaling I do!* ~ Kristi Nokken, India and Malaysia

A new way to journal

This new type of travel journal, developed by Nancy Taylor Nicodemus, involves dividing your journal into four different sections:
- Impressions
- Descriptive
- Narrative
- Expressive

What is unique about this type of journaling is that you do not make chronological entries. Instead, you may make several entries in one day, or none at all (although it is not advisable to go too many days without writing).

You may choose to add other sections to your journal that make sense for you. For example, you can add a "Miscellaneous" section to your journal where you can write entries that don't seem to fit anywhere else. You can also add a "Personal" chapter, which you can use more as a diary to write things that you wouldn't want other people to read.

Impressions section

This is the only section of your journal where entries will be made chronologically. The impressions section is for jotting down the places, people, events, concepts, ideas, smells, signs, and other things you remember. You write words, phrases, or sentences that will spark your memory. Be detailed in this section with dates and the names of people, places, events, cities, etc., because this is the only section where you could recreate your itinerary if you needed to do so.

Look at the following example, given by Kristi Nokken. It is complete gibberish to everyone else, but to her it brings back loads of detailed memories.

> _8 August_   _Universiti Sains Malaysia, Penang, Malaysia_
> _Awies birthday party! Two crazy uncles. A game of lucky draw. Chatting with Winda and her cousin. Dinner with Bernard and Irene. AIESEC meeting with Sow Yee—what a great group of people. Elections—paper everywhere—an environmentalist's nightmare!!! Gloria lost..._

Descriptive section

This section is divided into chapters in which you can write entries that are purely descriptive in nature. You will not elaborate on what you think about what you are writing. Instead, you will use your descriptive abilities to create a vivid picture of what you experienced. Entries in the chapters of this section should be written so that someone who has not visited the culture you are describing would be able to read these entries and create a mental picture of what it was like.

Possible chapter titles: People, Customs, Places, Architecture, Religion, Transportation, Food and Drink, Art, Festivals, Ceremonies, Campus, Life, Stereotypes

Example: Descriptive section, "Religions"

> _13 September_   _Universiti Sains Malaysia, Penang, Malaysia_
> _The women who wear tudungs (which is the head covering worn by some Muslim women) take them extremely seriously! They wear them when they are playing sports; they wear them under baseball hats and graduation caps. I've seen a woman or two swimming—perhaps not with a tudung but at the very least wearing a knitted cap that holds all their hair underneath. Around the dorm, I've seen women covering their hair or head with a towel. They do this when they step outside to collect their laundry from the clothesline. They do it when they go down to make a telephone call even though the telephones are in the dorm—there is a glass door down there, which a man could walk by and quickly peek in._

Narrative section

This section is to satisfy the storyteller in you. There's no doubt you will come home with stories—good, bad, funny, and otherwise. Write about them in this section before you forget.

Possible chapter titles: Good for a Laugh, Stories, Jokes, Embarrassing Moments, Too Good to Be True, They'll Never Believe This at Home

Example: Narrative section, "Stories"

> _30 March   Penang, Malaysia_
> _Naomi and her husband were taking the night bus down to Kuala Lumpur_
> _but made the mistake of going on the night that the World Cup Finals were_
> _playing. When the game started, the bus driver pulled over to the side of the_
> _road and informed everyone that they were stopping so he could watch the_
> _game (most buses have TVs in them). So, for however long the game took, a_
> _whole bus load of people were stuck somewhere between Butterworth and_
> _Penang—just a few miles from where their journey began!_

Expressive section

This is the section where you get to _vent, debate, praise, hypothesize,_ and _evaluate._ Where you may have described an event in one of your descriptive sections, you may then make an entry in this section to record what you thought and felt about that event. In the descriptive example earlier, Kristi Nokken described how careful Muslim women were about wearing their tudungs. In the following example from the expressive section, she talks about tudungs and comes up with an analogy that helped her personally to come to terms with value differences across cultures. It's a good example of the cultural learning process that you may go through while you are studying abroad. This learning process wouldn't necessarily come out in a typical chronological journal because too much time is spent concentrating on daily activities instead of the larger picture.

Possible topic titles: Cultural Adjustment, Religious Awakenings…or Not, Reversals (where you assumed one thing but now realize what it really means to people from the culture), Conclusions, Language Learning, Unanswered Questions, Enigmas, Quotations, Revelations

Example: Expressive section, "Religious awakenings…or not"

> <u>20 October</u>   <u>*Universiti Sains Malaysia, Penang, Malaysia*</u>
> *I've been thinking a lot about women wearing tudungs—or more specifically why some women do wear them and some don't. After all, from everything I've been told and taught about Islam, it is a sin for a woman not to wear one.*
>
> *I think perhaps a good comparision would be to compare the tudung in Islam to birth control in Catholicism. I have many Catholic friends who use birth control. Although their religion strictly says (I believe) that sex is for procreation, many people find this part of their religion outdated and simply choose to ignore it.*
>
> *Perhaps it is the same with the tudung. Some women may simply see the tudung as outdated and simply choose not to wear it (unless in the mosque or during prayers), despite the fact that their religion views it as a sin.*

It may seem a little overwhelming at first, but give it a try. What follows are some tips that will hopefully make it a little less intimidating, a little more managable, and a lot more fun!

(Adapted from Taylor Nicodemus, 1991, and Kappler and Nokken, 1999.)

Tips to keep journaling fun and easy

- Number your pages, and divide your sections early on—preferably before you go.
- Decide which section you probably will be writing in more than others, then divide the rest of the journal somewhat equally among the other categories.
- Give some time and thought to developing the chapters in each section. Think about what interests you most about the culture you are visiting.
- A hardcover book is the best. A loose-leaf binder would work but it's not as sturdy and may not survive your travels.
- Make it your own: tape memorabilia to the cover or inside; attach articles, photographs, or other special mementos.
- Try to write at least one entry every day.
- Carry around a little notebook to write things down that you want to remember—names, places, quotes, descriptive words as they come to mind—and transfer them later into your Impressions section.

IN-COUNTRY CULTURE STRATEGIES PART VI:
STRATEGIES FOR INTERCULTURAL COMMUNICATION

Being in another country provides you with a range of experiences—sometimes boring, exciting, exhausting, confusing, educational, and interesting all within the same morning. Even knowing the host language well may not prepare you for some of the communication issues that you deal with on a daily basis. In the following two chapters we integrate culture and language learning to focus on ways you can become effective intercultural communicators in the host country.

Here are some experiences the authors have had in communicating across cultures:

> It took me months living in Indonesia to figure out if someone was telling me yes or no. Once my wife and I invited an Indonesian friend and his wife to join us for lunch at a nearby restaurant specializing in soto ayam (a delicious chicken soup). When we got to their house to pick them up, it was obvious they weren't expecting us. Talk about a breakdown of communication! I eventually learned that being straightforward wasn't the East Javanese way. Communication was much more subtle. ~ R. Michael Paige, Indonesia

> When I first arrived in Turkey, I couldn't believe how emotional people seemed when they were having a conversation. Half the time I honestly thought they were going to punch each other out. It took me awhile to learn that for Turks, a good conversation is one where people show their feelings. If you're not into it, then people think you're cold and insincere. ~ R. Michael Paige, Turkey

> When my host family told me on the very first day that 'they didn't like Americans' I thought I was in for a terrible experience. It was hard not to take it a bit personally, and their statement was so direct and blunt. It took me awhile to realize that what they did not like was the President and the fact everything was always being portrayed as being better in the U.S. As we got into debates about U.S. politics, I realized I had to work hard not to take things personally. They never meant it that way. They simply wanted to debate and to share their views. In the end, it was a wonderful family stay. ~ Barbara Kappler, England

As these experiences show, communication isn't something we can take for granted. People communicate in many different ways, and it takes awhile to figure out how people are giving and receiving messages. One of the most difficult things about this aspect of communication is that it isn't just about language. Gaining language fluency doesn't automatically mean you have gained communication competence. So in this section, we want to give you an initial understanding about different communication styles.

Styles of Communication

Like many Easterners, Indians don't like to say 'no' outright. Sometimes the lack of an answer is tantamount to a 'no.' In other instances, a 'yes' without a follow-up is a 'no.' ~ "Passport India," Manoj Joshi

Communication style is how we prefer to give and receive information.

When Barbara's co-worker Kristi says, "It's cold in here," what does this mean? Does it literally mean it's cold in here, or is the speaker indirectly asking for the heat to be turned up? If Kristi prefers indirectness, it may mean that she wants the heat turned up. But will Barbara understand the message this way? The odds are higher if Barbara is able to receive the message in the same manner it was sent.

Low-context (direct) and high-context (indirect) communication

Low-context communication

You are probably more familiar with this category of communication since it is likely you've been doing it all your life if you grew up in the United States. This communication tends to be more verbal and more explicit, that is, we tell people what we think they need to know in order to understand us. We fill in the blanks. We write detailed legal contracts. We do not assume that understanding will come automatically from the situation or the context or the person we are speaking with. In the U.S., because people do come from many different cultural or ethnic backgrounds, the tendency is to rely heavily on verbal communication and to be explicit. The goal is clarity of communication. In this communication style, nonverbal communication is important, but the verbal or written message is even more important.

Scenario: You find the room cold and would like someone to turn the temperature up. If you are a low-context communicator, you might say something along the lines of, "It's getting cold in here; could you please turn up the heat?"

High-context communication

In contrast, people from cultures using high-context communication pay a lot of attention to the situation, the environment, and the people with whom they are communicating. Things don't have to be spelled out as much as they are in low-context cultures. You don't have to worry so much about explaining everything since people will have a good understanding just from the context. Perhaps you can think of it as communicating with your family members or friends who know you well— there you don't have to say as much to get your ideas across. In addition, nonverbal cues are much more important in high-context cultures for conveying meaning.

Scenario: You find the room cold and would like someone to turn the temperature up. If you are a high-context communicator, you might wrap your arms around yourself and vigorously rub your upper arms as a way of communicating that you are cold and trying to warm yourself up. You might also say something along the lines of, "Brrrrr. It's a bit chilly in here, isn't it?"

When high meets low and vice versa

What happens if you are a low-context communicator and you go into a high-context culture or environment? It's hard to know what's going on. If you have had a bad day and you come home to your family or roommate, how long does it take for them to figure out you've had a bad day? Only a few seconds! They know how to read the cues from how you say hello, shut the door, or simply how you look without your saying a thing. But what if someone who does not know you well is there? It will take them awhile to figure the clues out. The advantage for low-context communicators is that they often are skilled at asking questions to try to gain more information, and they are very good at processing a great deal of verbal or written information. The challenge is that they may not always know how to read the environment to pick the best time to ask questions.

What happens if someone who is a high-context communicator goes into a low-context culture or environment? This person knows how to read nonverbals in his or her own environment, but how about in the new one? Quite often high-context communicators who are out of their environment feel overloaded with communication cues and can simply shut down in a new environment. Eventually, the skills you have for reading the environment and people will serve as an advantage for sorting out when it is appropriate to ask questions in order to clarify what is happening around them. It is also possible that high-context communicators will feel that they are being treated like children when they are in a low-context environment where everything is so overtly spelled out to them.

Low- and high-context communication

If you are coming from the U.S., chances are you are either a low-context communicator or you are very familiar with this environment. Knowing how to distinguish between high- and low-context messages can therefore help you learn how to "read between the lines"—a skill of high-context communicators. This exercise will help you become more familiar with the differences in low- and high-context communication. For the following ten statements, decide whether the communication is direct/low context or indirect/high context.

L = low or direct context
H = high or indirect context

_____ 1. People have a hard time saying no.
_____ 2. Paying attention to the status of the communicator is as important as the message itself.

_____ 3. The message is more important than the status of who communicated it.

_____ 4. Business is conducted only after enough time is taken for talking about family, your health, important politics, etc.

_____ 5. People get down to business right away and often omit any "small" talk.

_____ 6. It is alright to say "I disagree" to your professor in class.

_____ 7. Use of intermediaries or go-betweens is common.

_____ 8. "I don't understand" is often used to voice disagreement.

_____ 9. If you want something, it's best to come out and ask for it.

_____ 10. Hinting at something is an effective way of getting what you want.

Answers

__H__ 1. People have a hard time saying no.

__H__ 2. Paying attention to the status of the communicator is as important as the message itself.

__L__ 3. The message is more important than the status of who communicated it.

__H__ 4. Business is conducted only after enough time is taken for talking about family, your health, important politics, etc.

__L__ 5. People get down to business right away and often omit any "small" talk.

__L__ 6. It is alright to say "I disagree" to your professor in class.

__H__ 7. Use of intermediaries or go-betweens is common.

__H__ 8. "I don't understand" is often used to voice disagreement.

__L__ 9. If you want something, it's best to come out and ask for it.

__H__ 10. Hinting at something is an effective way of getting what you want.

Specific Communication Styles

Contrast your communication styles with host nationals

In addition to high- and low-context communication, research and experience have uncovered other varieties of communication behaviors. Eight of these styles are discussed in this activity. They are grouped into pairs, each of which represents the end points of a continuum. Between each pair on the line, mark an X to indicate your personal communication style. On the second line place another X for how people generally communicate in your host country. Then, if you wish, indicate on the third line how people in general communicate in your home country. Remember, we are asking you to state generalizations, not stereotypes. Use your interactions with people in the host country as the basis for evaluation or ask a cultural informant.

Direct Communication

Communication is done using explicit verbal statements and represents exactly what the speaker means. There is very little 'beating around the bush' here.

Indirect Communication

Meaning is communicated using indirect means such as suggestions, body language, or pauses. This style often uses other people to resolve conflicts in lieu of direct contact.

You	direct ———————————————————	indirect
Host Country	direct ———————————————————	indirect
Home Country	direct ———————————————————	indirect

Linear Communication

This style is similar to direct communication as it gets to the point without going off on tangents. The communication progresses systematically along a straight line until the point is made. As such it is considered faster and more economical to those who use it.

Circular Communication

In circular communication, the person rarely states the point directly. Instead, a discussion proceeds in a roundabout way and incorporates many details until the point is reached. This way of communicating is similar to how stories are told.

You	linear ———————————————	circular
Host Country	linear ———————————————	circular
Home Country	linear ———————————————	circular

Detached Communication

In detached communication, issues are discussed with calmness and objectivity. Emotion is kept at a minimum, and objectivity is preferred over subjectivity. People who use detached communication may feel that they are just being rational and fair.

Attached Communication

This communication style is characterized with a high level of emotion and feeling. People communicating this way think that they are showing sincerity or personal concern for the topic and the person with whom they are interacting.

You	detached ———————————————————————— attached
Host Country	detached ———————————————————————— attached
Home Country	detached ———————————————————————— attached

Idea-Oriented Communication

In this form of communication, disagreement with ideas is stated directly, with the assumption that only the idea, not the person from whom the idea came, is being attacked. Phrases such as 'no offense, but I don't agree with you,' or 'agree to disagree' are indicative of this style.

Relationship-Oriented Communication

In this communication style, disagreeing with an idea is viewed the same as disagreeing with the person who originated it. Intellectual disagreement in particular is handled more subtly and indirectly. This communication style emphasizes interpersonal harmony and strives to maintain the relationship between people.

You	ideas ———————————————————————— relationships
Host Country	ideas ———————————————————————— relationships
Home Country	ideas ———————————————————————— relationships

(Adapted from Bennett, Bennett, & Allen; 1999.)

Reflection questions

- Did you see any patterns in your responses? Many of these styles can be said to support one another. For example, a direct communication style would support a linear style, as both have a preference for getting to the point quickly. Also, an attached communication style will often coincide with a relationship-oriented style since both emphasize paying attention to the feelings of others.

- Do your own answers change based on the situation you are in? Go back to the diagram and make notes about situations where you might tend to use the opposite style of what you marked here.

- In which styles are you and your target culture most alike? In which are you most different? Do you see how you might have to modify your communicative approach when you interact with people while you are abroad?

IN-COUNTRY CULTURE STRATEGIES PART VII:
NONVERBAL COMMUNICATION

A smile, a simple wave, an affirmative head nod, the universal sign for 'check please' are all examples of gestures that I took for granted before my study abroad experience. Because the motions we use in the States are inherent to me and come automatically, it had not occurred to me that there would be such a difference in the gestures that are used between countries. This was one thing I did not learn much about before my study in France.

One example that came up during my stay in Paris shows the frustration that can develop due to miscommunication because of incorrect gestures. One day I was having a discussion with a native French speaker, so I was trying to take great care with choosing my words since I knew he would be able to pick up my mistakes very quickly. As the discussion continued, it grew into an argument. I was arguing my point and trying to clearly explain my position in French when I slapped the palm of my hand for emphasis on a point. Since I was by no means done talking I continued. Once again, I slapped my hand while debating.

The second time I made this gesture my friend started laughing at me— something you don't want to happen when you're arguing in a foreign language! I started to think, 'What did I say? Am I making no sense?' So I asked him, 'What?! Why are you laughing?' He explained to me that in France when someone slaps their hand as I had done, it means that the conversation is over. He was amused that I had, by his standards, terminated the conversation twice, yet I kept on talking. ~ Tammi Brussegaard, France

According to A. Mehrabian, less than ten percent of the meaning of what you are communicating to someone is from the actual spoken words. How you say something or what your body or face is doing when you say it has meaning too, and this of course is very dependent on culture. The language strategies section on speaking will discuss intonation and the notion that how words are stressed can seriously alter the meaning of what is being said. For example, the nuance of "Is THIS your bag?" is much different from "Is this YOUR bag?"

Similarly, there is in every culture a whole realm of nonverbal communication that consists of things we aren't usually conscious of such as gestures, eye contact, physical distance between people, facial expressions, and touching behavior. As Tammi found out in France, other cultures will often have very different meanings for these nonverbal behaviors from what you are used to.

Communicating Nonverbally

Nonverbal communication is often not discussed in the language classroom, but it is an important aspect of intercultural communication nevertheless. Most of us, if we have not been abroad, will not be very aware of the various ways we gesture with our hands, and we take for granted our facial expressions. Various studies of facial expression have shown that many cultures around the world have similar ways of expressing emotions such as anger, sadness, and joy. But they also show that the same expression can have more than one meaning; for example, in some cultures a smile can mean the person is embarrassed. In addition, the extent to which facial expressions are used varies across cultures. The Japanese, for example, tend to display much less facial expression than people in the U.S. or Latin America.

Most students who go abroad are not going to be aware of all of the nonverbal language of the host culture before they get there. The longer you are in the host country, the more naturally you will be able to use the nonverbal behaviors that are appropriate for various situations.

You can use two basic strategies for picking up the nonverbals more rapidly: *observation* and *practice.*

- **Observe:** Make a conscious effort to watch carefully how people communicate with each other nonverbally. How close do they stand to each other? Do they maintain direct eye contact? Is there a lot of vigorous gesturing when they are speaking? What kind of gestures do they use? Make note also of whether these patterns change between friends versus casual acquaintances.

- **Practice:** Make attempts to perform the nonverbal behavior with groups of host nationals you feel comfortable with and who will let you know tactfully whether or not you are doing the behaviors appropriately.

Both of the above strategies require spending a great deal of time with people in your host country. The second strategy, while very important, may be more difficult than the first. Much of the difficulty of nonverbals is that, even if they are learned and understood, to actually perform them may seem unnatural or uncomfortable to you.

Despite these hurdles, making attempts at using the appropriate nonverbals will be appreciated by people with whom you interact. For example, a student in Japan who does not know to bow slightly when greeting someone of higher status will come off as disrespectful. If you stand too far apart or refuse to touch casually in many Latin American countries, the hosts might think you are cold and unfriendly. To engage in these nonverbals properly demonstrates your sensitivity to the other culture, as well as your willingness to adapt.

Observing gestures and understanding their meanings

These five gestures below are common in many countries throughout the world. This exercise is designed to give you some practice at recognizing nonverbal behavior in both your home and host cultures and to become aware of where the differences lie. It should also help you make interpretations based upon your own observations in the host country. You are asked to interpret the meaning of gestures based upon how most Americans perceive them and what other meanings you think they may have in your host country. Refer to the next page for suggested answers and explanations.

A.	What might this gesture mean to most people in the U.S.?
	What could this gesture mean in your host country?
B.	What might this gesture mean to most people in the U.S.?
	What could this gesture mean in your host country?
C.	What might this gesture mean to most people in the U.S.?
	What could this gesture mean in your host country?
D.	What might this gesture mean to most people in the U.S.?
	What could this gesture mean in your host country?
E.	What might this gesture mean to most people in the U.S.?
	What could this gesture mean in your host country?

(Excerpted from Morris, 1994.)

Suggested answers

A. Although in the U.S. this is typically the sign for "OK," it doesn't mean the same thing in most other countries. In Japan this is the sign for money. In Belgium and France it is interpreted as "zero." And in Greece, Russia, and other countries it could be considered a sexual insult.

B. Most U.S. Americans might interpret this gesture as someone praying or begging someone, as in "I implore you." However, this is a common greeting in India and Thailand and also means thank you in many parts of Asia.

C. To many U.S. Americans this might mean "I don't know" even without the shrug of the shoulders that sometimes accompanies this gesture. In other areas, such as the Middle East and in South America, it is more clearly a sign of trying to show one's sincerity, as in "I swear."

D. This sign, which for most U.S. Americans means "alright!" or "good job!" does have similar use in many other countries. But in Japan, it is used either to indicate the male gender or the number "five."

E. Probably all U.S. Americans have crossed their fingers for good luck at one time. In many Christian countries this has a similar meaning, but this sign is even more commonly interpreted to mean "friendship," except for Italy and Turkey, where it could be understood as "a threat to end friendship."

Summary

The above examples were intended to help you think about the nonverbal communication used in different cultures. The longer you are in your host country and the more you observe, the more you will learn about nonverbal communication in that culture.

Three Important Forms of Nonverbal Communication

Even if you are familiar with many of the physical gestures of your host culture, there is more to nonverbal communication. Gestures are the more obvious forms of nonverbal communication. Learning them is important, but they are not the only ones. We will now look at three other forms of nonverbal communication that exist, but are different, in every culture: eye contact, physical space, and touching norms. Many people may not realize these behaviors actually differ from culture to culture and will not make attempts to modify their own behaviors or to adopt those appropriate to the host culture.

As you read through the following nonverbal trouble spots, note your own preference for the behaviors covered. Take time to jot down how common the behavior is in the country and for which contexts.

1. Eye contact

In the U.S., particularly in the business culture, direct eye contact is standard procedure. While eye contact can imply sincerity and honesty in other cultures just as it does in the U.S., in many Asian countries, including Japan, looking straight into someone's eyes could be considered intimidating or a sign of aggression. The degree of eye contact can also sometimes be based on gender, status, age, and other characteristics of the person. In some cultures, direct eye contact is permissible for members of the same sex but not proper when communicating with the opposite sex.

Eye contact survey

Find out how much eye contact you generally prefer and then think about the different situations listed below. For each situation indicate if you would use *direct, casual, indirect, peripheral (sideways glances)*, or *none*. Then find out the same information for your host country.

Situation	How much eye contact do you prefer?	What is the preferred form of eye contact in your host country?
1. Chatting with friends		
2. Talking with a professor		
3. Interviewing for a job		
4. Giving a presentation		
5. Placing an order with a waiter		
6. Talking to your father		

Did you discover many differences between you and the host country? In which situations are they most pronounced?

2. Sense of personal distance/space

The concept of our own space, or the space between ourselves and others, is another important factor in intercultural communication. Standing too close to people with whom you're interacting may make them uncomfortable, while standing too far away may give the impression that you're cold and unapproachable. Although people have their personal preferences, there is also a cultural basis for the amount of personal space. People from Arab cultures, for example, tend to stand very close to each other when they are talking, while the amount of personal space given to your communication partner is much greater in both the U.S. and Japan.

Personal distance survey

Think about how much personal distance you generally prefer and then think about the different situations listed below. For each situation indicate whether you would prefer to keep the **normal amount of distance, greater than normal,** or **less than normal.** Then find out the same information for your host country.

Situation	How much personal distance do you prefer to use?	How much personal distance would be normal by host country persons?
1. Chatting with friends		
2. Talking with a professor		
3. Interviewing for a job		
4. Speaking to a child		
5. Placing an order with a waiter		
6. Talking to your father		

Did you discover a lot of difference between you and the host country? In which situations are they most pronounced?

3. Touching

As with personal distance, the degree to which people use touch to communicate varies greatly from culture to culture. Even in the United States there are differences based upon ethnicity and cultural background. In many collectivist cultures like India and Thailand, it is considered natural for people of the same sex to touch each other publicly, so you will often see men with their arms around each other or holding hands. But in many other countries physical contact with someone of the opposite sex is considered inappropriate and carries a sexual connotation.

Touching behavior survey

Think about how much touching behavior is appropriate in your culture, under what circumstances, and with whom. Then consider the different situations mentioned below. For each situation indicate whether some kind of touching would be appropriate. Then find out the same information for your host country.

Situation	Is touching appropriate for you in the following situations?	Is touching appropriate in these situations for host country persons?
1. Chatting with friends		
2. Talking with a professor		
3. Meeting with your boss		
4. Speaking to a child		
5. Talking to your father		

Did you discover a lot of difference between you and the host country? In which situations are they most pronounced?

One of the best ways to learn what touching is appropriate for a certain culture is to observe people in how they greet each other. Do they hug or kiss? How many times? In France, people who are close kiss each cheek twice. In Latin America, hugging and sometimes kissing is more common. A handshake is more common in Germany and Northern Europe. In Japan, touching or other public displays of affection, even among close acquaintances, are generally not very common.

Activity

Nonverbals used in host country greetings

Try to figure out what are the most common gestures, including touching, for the following situations. You may have more than one answer. Ask someone from the culture if you're not sure of the answer.

Type of encounter	Common type(s) of nonverbal greeting in the host country
Meeting someone of the same age and sex for the first time	
A man greeting his wife at home	
Two professional women meeting for lunch	
Two adult male friends meeting at a bar	
A brother greeting his sister at the airport	
A child greeting his father as he arrives home from work	
A young woman meeting her boyfriend in the park	
Two women seeing each other at a high school reunion	

Was there a lot of variation in the types of possible greetings based on age, gender, or relationship? What differences do you notice in how people greet each other in the U.S. and in the host country? When you greet someone in the same situation what do *you* tend to do?

Pauses and Silence in Communication

Pauses and silence in communication are other nonverbal patterns that we take for granted and rarely think about. The role that silence has in communication is not often discussed even when we are learning a foreign language. Research has shown, however, that different languages have very different patterns and meanings associated with silence and pauses. Even with English these differences are widely apparent whether the person speaking is from Australia, India, or the southern region of the United States.

In general, U.S. Americans don't have a lot of tolerance for lengthy periods of time during which not much is said. Silence is more often than not considered uncomfortable in the U.S. and should be avoided at all costs. Try it out sometime by pausing in the middle of a conversation, particularly when you are in a group situation, and watch how long it takes before someone else says something. It will rarely be more than a couple of seconds when U.S. Americans are speaking.

In many cultures there is a much higher regard for silence in communicative encounters. The phrase "those who know do not speak; those who speak do not know" is actually a second-century Chinese proverb by which many Asian cultures abide. In these cultures, what is not said is regarded as important, and lulls in conversation are considered restful, friendly, a time for reflection, and appropriate. For those of you going to such cultures, your challenge will be learning to balance verbal expression with silence.

> *A survey of 3,600 Japanese people's attitudes toward speaking obtained data indicating that 82 percent of them agreed with the saying 'out of the mouth comes all evil.' ~ "Skills in Self-Expression," Inagaki, 1985*

Journaling — making sense out of intercultural communication

Previously you covered the materials on participant observation and journaling. Now it's time to practice these skills by observing how people communicate nonverbally with each other in the host country. Select any setting, such as a coffee shop, where you can safely and unobtrusively observe a small group of two or three people. Focus on how they communicate with each other nonverbally rather than only verbally. Use the following questions as a guide and then make entries to your journal using the instructions below

- Is there a lot of gesturing? Who is making them? What sort of gestures are used?

- Is there eye contact? Is it more frequent or infrequent? About how often do people make eye contact?

- Is there touching? At what moment and how often?

- How much time is between when one speaker stops and the other begins?

- How do people show pleasure/agreement vs. displeasure/disagreement?

Journaling questions

- What is the setting?_____
- Who are the speakers (male, female, approximate age)? What can you know or guess about them (e.g., they look like students, businesspersons)?

  Speaker #1:_____

  Speaker #2:_____

  Speaker #3:_____

- Use the chart below to record your observations of their nonverbal behaviors. Watch for gestures, eye contact, physical space, touching, pauses/silence, and paralanguage (tone, pitch, loudness, etc.). One way to organize your observations is to look for patterns or recurring behaviors.

Description of Gesture	Interpretation

- After completing the observation part of this activity, check your interpretations with someone from the host culture.

Additional suggestions for this activity:

- Try this same exercise again at another location with a different group than the first time and see if you notice some commonalities or new patterns in how people communicate.
- Try this activity with another study abroad student and compare the results of your observations.
- Try this in a situation where you can also hear what the people are saying and then make notes on things you noticed about verbal and nonverbal communication together. For example, you can observe what people say and do when they greet each other.

Summary

The last two chapters were intended to give you some insight into the world of intercultural communication where culture, language, and behaviors are combined to affect how we interact with each other. Hopefully you will have developed an appreciation for communicating cross-culturally and have learned some of the cues to pick up when interacting with others who are culturally different from you.

IN-COUNTRY CULTURE STRATEGIES PART VIII:
PREPARING TO RETURN HOME

During the final days in your new country, the last thing on your mind might be taking time to think about "home." These next few pages invite you to do just that—because it can make a world of difference in your entire experience!

I had two very different study abroad experiences and two very different departures for home. The first was in England. My host family had decided to go on a family vacation right at the end of my stay. Since they were not going to be at home for my last days in the country, they took me out for dinner at an Indian restaurant. I can still picture my host mom pleading with her husband Ron not to eat so many hot peppers. After they left, I finished final papers and exams. The last hours were a whirlwind—I was leaving England with just barely enough time to make it home for Christmas. I ran from monument to monument, shop to shop, grabbing mementos to bring home. I stayed up so late the night before I left that with just two hours of sleep, I did not hear my alarm. The taxicab driver luckily pounded on the door, and I finally awoke. I left England in a blur, panicking about catching my flight. When I left Malaysia I was a bit wiser. I walked to my favorite places and sat and absorbed the sights, smells, and sounds of that amazing country. I spent an evening with my Malaysian friends having a relaxing dinner and talking about the past few months. I felt I was just getting to understand this tropical place of contradictions. Even though I was not ready, I left in peace, having said my goodbyes, promising myself and others to return. I have traveled some since these adventures, but interestingly enough—despite my convictions—I have never returned to these places. This is OK, too, as I knew that saying 'I'll be back' was not a replacement for 'goodbye.' ~ Barbara Kappler, England and Malaysia

Leaving the country

You are near the end of your study abroad experience. Your emotions may be ranging from regret, bewilderment at where the time went, excitement about seeing family and friends, numbness, concern about what's next, satisfaction about all you have seen and enjoyed, and a sense of loss. We encourage you to take a moment to record how you feel about leaving your host country:

Acknowledging the range of emotions can help you prepare for saying goodbye to the country, your friends, and the experiences you have come to love (or not) in this new, but temporary, home of yours.

Now think back to Barbara's two very different stories of leaving England and Malaysia. What is *your* ideal way of leaving your new country? You may need to plan carefully as the days before departure can easily become a blur of activity, leaving you little time to soak in and enjoy one last crêpe, lager, or look at the Rhine. Take a minute to record the things you want to experience before departing:

I plan to come back, so I don't really need to say goodbye...

> *Make sure you tell students who read this guide to say their goodbyes.*
> *~ Sarah Sonday, Spain*

Many people do return to the countries in which they studied abroad. But life's unexpected twists and turns leads others, no matter the intentions, to either remain in the U.S. or to explore new destinations. We don't say this to discourage you; we say this because we don't want you to leave the country with a fantasy that you will return and do the things you did not get a chance to do this time. If it's important, do it this time. If that's not realistic due to lack of time or money, still make sure you say your goodbyes in a way you can live with...possibly for the rest of your life.

What's ahead

> *I came back from 4-1/2 months in Mexico and was immediately thrown into a whirlwind of visits with every relative I had ever known as I had missed Christmas at home to experience it in Queretaro. The following week I moved to a new dormitory as school started again. The week after that I moved, again, into an apartment. Life was back to 'normal.' What I wouldn't give to have time to myself to reflect—and breathe! ~ Julie Chi, Mexico*

A thoughtful return

Some of you may experience exactly what Julie did. It's the reality of the fast-paced world in which we live. Since time upon re-entry may be scarce, we encourage you to record here or in your journal your thoughts on these questions to prepare you for returning home:

1. In what ways have I changed?

2. In what ways might my friends and family have changed?

3. How would I like my family and friends to treat me when I return home?

4. What am I looking forward to the most? The least?

5. What are the lessons I have learned that I never want to forget?

6. What are some skills I have learned?

7. Many say that re-entry shock is more challenging than initial culture shock. What are some things I might do to make the transition easier? (See next section for suggestions from other students.)

8. What have been the important things about this study abroad experience that I want to share with family and friends?

9. What do I want to do with the experiences I've had (e.g., continue studying the language)?

Coming home is for many much more of a challenge than going to a foreign culture. Students need to be aware of this. I don't think it is emphasized as much as the culture shock going over, and I think it should be, at least as much if not more so. This is where it all falls into place, or begins to. My suggestion? Keep writing a journal—a lot of reflection is necessary to truly get the most out of it all. ~ A. J. Fleming, Spain

POST-STUDY-ABROAD CULTURE STRATEGIES:
CONTINUE THE LEARNING

If I had culture shock while I was in England, it passed quickly. The same is not true with returning to the U.S.A. There were many things I had to get used to again, like going back to my university and finding a job. However, after six months of being home, I see something now that I cannot get used to —American politics and business. ~ Seth Lengkeek, England

I remember getting off the plane after three months in Malaysia. My family took me to a Mexican restaurant for a long-awaited margarita and a salad. I spent the next four days on the couch. My parents, worried I had contracted some tropical disease, called the doctor in my small town for a house visit. He suggested my parents call the restaurant and find out if food poisoning had been reported. Sure enough. My worst case of illness on this adventure happened after safely returning home. My mom, delivering the news, said, 'Welcome home. Aren't you glad you are sick here and not thousands of miles away?' The irony was that coming home was what made me sick. Yeah, I was glad to be on her couch, but where I really wanted to be was in Kuala Lumpur. I was not delirious enough to tell my mother this. ~ Barbara Kappler, Malaysia

Coming home isn't easy. For some, the return is more difficult than adjusting to the host culture. How could this be? Isn't home what you know best?

Culture shock is the expected confrontation with the unfamiliar; re-entry shock is the unexpected confrontation with the familiar. ~ R. Michael Paige, co-author

"Home" can have a difficult time competing with the thrill—even in it's darkest moments—of the continual adventure and discovery of self and the world of study abroad. As returned student Seth Lengkeek said, "When talking about re-entry, a good subject to discuss is boredom. I found that I had the hardest time dealing with being home when I was bored."

And, moreover, having seen new parts of the world, you have undoubtedly changed. That means that re-entry should *not* be a time simply for getting back into the swing of things. Instead, re-entry is really the time to maximize study abroad. You did not go there to stay. You went knowing you would come home. This chapter is intended to help you make the re-entry experience meaningful for the long term.

You may not want to do this chapter in a linear fashion. So here is a list of topics to choose from:

- Dealing with the emotional challenges of study abroad (see below)
- Examining what you have learned while abroad (p. 147)
    - Seeing the world and the U.S. differently
    - Understanding yourself differently
- Appreciating different styles of successful re-entry (p. 154)
- Study abroad leads to life-long learning (p. 156)
- Strategies for continued learning (p. 157)

Dealing with the Emotional Challenges of Study Abroad

When I first came home my parents had a surprise welcome home party for me and invited all my friends. Some of my friends asked the customary, 'How was Spain?' and didn't ask anything else. They really didn't care…or at least that's how I felt. I noticed that many of my friends I no longer have a relationship with because I feel like I can't relate to them and they can't relate to me. We both changed in different directions while I was gone. ~ Sarah Sonday, Spain

I have found when I've returned from working and studying abroad that each time my family and friends wanted to know how it was, but what they wanted was a bunch of short and funny stories about my experience. I needed time to process my thoughts and feelings about such rich experiences because I came back with lots of contradictory thoughts about my time abroad. When I wasn't able to give my family and friends the short 'sound bite' they seemed to want, they stopped asking questions, and I didn't tell them very much at all about my experiences. It was something that I could only share with others who had also studied abroad and understood the complexity of an experience in a different culture. ~ Karin Larson, studied abroad in France, worked in Taiwan, interned in Malaysia, and worked in Indonesia

Reacting to the changes

Returning to one's home environment isn't easy for a number of reasons, including how much you have changed, how much you understand these changes, and how much your friends and family accept these changes. It's important to take time to consider what the particular frustrations are for you. Either in this guide or in a separate journal, record your reactions to these questions and statements.

1. I know that I have changed as a result of my experience because…

2. My friends do seem to understand_____about me, but they don't understand …

3. My re-entry experience would be better if…

4. Now that I am home, I worry most about…

5. The one thing I know I have learned about myself is…

6. I wish I could explain to my family and friends that…

While home may have remained fairly unchanged in your absence, it's possible that there have been some significant changes—a move, a divorce in the family, or a change to a new university. If you have changed and home has changed, it's almost like you need to learn how to dance together again. Will you vary the music to adapt to the new rhythms of your lives or play the same tune?

Several returnees collaborated to develop the following chart of common emotional challenges encountered and possible strategies for these challenges.

Challenges	Strategies to help you deal with re-entry
Friends and family at home do not seem interested in hearing about aspects of your experience that you feel are important.	• Realize they may be adjusting to changes in you. Give some time for this adjustment. • Plan a special time for you to share photos or food from your experience. • Don't assume the opportunity for meaningful conversation will happen—make room for it to take place. Without a comparable experience, they may have difficulty understanding the depth of your stories. Be patient with them. • Write down your thoughts and feelings. It helps you to be able to process them even if you can't talk about them. • Seek others with similar experiences. • Give presentations to community organizations. Write an article for your local or school newspaper. Be active!
Friends and family may treat you as the same person you were before leaving. You want your relationship to change as a result of your changes.	• They may be feeling uncertain about how you have changed or grown. Discuss your feelings about yourself and others with them. • Encourage positive changes in old relationships. Don't expect your friends to suggest seeing a new international film—especially if they never did before. Take the initiative and invite them. • Seek out relationships with people who are compatible with the new you.
You may be anxious or apprehensive about your academic situation because the subjects you enjoyed studying abroad, including language, appear to have little relevance at home. You might also be confused about your educational future and career plans in light of new or uncertain goals and priorities.	• Take advantage of the wide range of educational opportunities and alternatives available to you by finding informal and nonacademic ways to continue the study of your favorite subjects. • Take time to consider educational and career plans that include your new areas of interest. • Seek out the advice of your counselors and mentors.
If you find that your attitudes and opinions have changed considerably during your stay abroad and are not widely shared in your home community, you may feel highly critical of your home country because you have new perspectives on it. Others might be critical of your "negative attitude."	• Try to keep perspective on your feelings; remember that your opinions and ideas may initially be greatly influenced by the host culture and may not represent your final balanced viewpoint. • Share your feelings with others but carefully choose situations in which to bring up controversial issues. • Continue to foster your ability to look at the world critically by reading and seeking out a diverse range of information, rather than falling into the trap of just thinking of things (politics in particular) negatively.
You may become frustrated because people at home are uninterested in other peoples and cultures. Faced with this lack of concern, you might feel there aren't ways for you to take an active role in helping solve the problems of the world community.	• Attempt to generate local interest in other peoples and their concerns. • Use your special status as an intercultural traveler to educate others through private conversations or by public speeches and presentations. • Look at problems in your own community now that you have a new perspective. Become a change agent.

(Adapted from Kappler and Nokken, 1999.)

Examining What You Have Learned While Abroad

Seeing the world and the U.S. differently

> *I took a class on international management with a Canadian professor. A few of us were joking that when we were overseas and ran into people who did not have a favorable attitude toward U.S. Americans, we would pretend to be Canadians. One even sewed a Canadian flag on her backpack. My instructor's response completely amazed me. He said, 'Why do people have allegiances to countries? The concept of nation-status is an outdated mode.' Years later, I understand the comment. I married someone from another country. It was frightening to have the governments be involved and to have a say in the sanctity of the marriage and in where we might live. I never forgot the Canadian professor's comment. I don't have an alternative, but I now feel I understand this Canadian's view. ~ Barbara Kappler*

Barbara's comments aren't intended to fuel anti-American sentiment or to slander someone for taking pride in one's own country, rather the story's purpose is twofold:

1. To recognize that like many other study abroad students, you may return feeling more aware of U.S. dominance on the world political scene and feel overwhelmed and ashamed—even if you return appreciating toilet paper!
2. Study abroad can result in challenges to core personal or societal beliefs. For example, before studying abroad, the following comments often make little impact. After, they may take on a whole new light:

> *If an extraterrestrial committee of experts in planetary management visited our Earth, they would not believe their eyes. 'You are insane!...You were given one of the most beautiful planets in the cosmos...and look what you have done with it:*

> *'You have divided this planet into 160 separate territorial fragments without rhyme or reason—without geographic, ecological, human, or any other logic. All these fragments are sovereign; i.e., each of them considers itself more important than the planet and the rest of humanity.' ~ Robert Muller, former Assistant Secretary-General of the United Nations*

In short, your view of the U.S. and the world may have changed. For some, this is the most profound experience of study abroad.

> *It's difficult to live overseas and then come back to this country. You carry within you a perpetual ache, a sense that we need to know more, to do more. ~ Jim Malarkey, world traveler*

Specifically in reflecting on the impact of world events surrounding the attacks on the World Trade Center and Pentagon, Malarkey remarked:

> *If I think of myself as primarily an American, then I see the world a certain way. I become concerned about America's enemies. But if I think about myself as a world citizen, then I worry about different things. Then I become concerned about imbalances in the world and about how to fix those imbalances.*

In addition to struggling with notions of world imbalances, a returnee may face contradictions:

> *I thought very differently about the U.S. when I returned from Turkey. People seemed so concerned with things like shopping that seemed quite trivial to me. It was like 'didn't they know there was poverty in the world? How could they consume so much?' And I was also very critical of my government's policies regarding other countries. In retrospect, it seems contradictory because many times when I was abroad I would curiously find myself defending my country's actions. The term contradiction nicely summarizes the conflicting thoughts I had about many things. ~ R. Michael Paige*

And finally, it's OK to appreciate some of the physical and mental comforts of life in the U.S.:

> *I would assume that many returnees come back appreciating much of what the U.S. has to offer. Just take the university setting—toilet paper in the bathrooms, large structures, good heating, ample seating, free daily newspaper, easily available computer terminals, and on and on. We could make a litany of all the wonders of the U.S. This is to counter the somewhat assumed position that things are far better abroad. ~ Andrew Cohen*

Seeing the U.S and the world in a new light

You have probably changed your views on a number of things since you came back. Many students have a new awareness of politics and the interpretations they get from the media of different countries and cultures. Some people feel either more highly critical of their own country or very grateful for the things that they enjoy in their own country—or both. To sort through your changing perspectives, jot down a few ways in which your views have changed. Here are a few questions to get you thinking. Write your responses in the following chart:

1. What new experiences did you have while abroad that shocked or surprised you about the world?
2. How do you feel now about those experiences after returning to the U.S.?
3. Are there certain stereotypes that you have let go of? kept? modified?

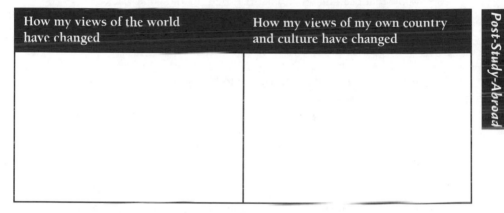

How my views of the world have changed	How my views of my own country and culture have changed

Understanding yourself differently

Positive gains

Re-entry is a transition, and like all transitions it has potential for both pain and growth. Here is a quick list of what some returnees had to say about how they have grown from their experiences:

I now....

- have a new sense of autonomy. If I can figure out the subway in Paris, I can do anything! If I can enroll in a course in Spanish by myself, I can surely tackle my home institution's bureaucracy! If can travel around a tropical island myself and be in a place where I didn't understand all of the language around me, I can be comfortable and confident almost anywhere.
- feel more responsible about my lifestyle choices and their global consequences.

- feel more focused about my career interests.
- feel more self-confident.
- have more concern for international politics.
- have a greater awareness of other eating patterns.
- know that dating can mean different things and know about different patterns of male/female relationships.
- have a genuine feeling of breaking the language barrier by studying a content subject (such as economics) in another language.
- am more in sync with the real world and the harsh reality of life (professors not showing up for class because of societal forces and events)—not the U.S. American "ivory tower" phenomenon.
- have a greater sense of what it is like to watch out for personal security.
- am less consumer-oriented.
- am more interested in social issues.
- know that I can hit emotional rock-bottom and come back up.
- feel connected to people across the world.
- have a new appreciation for the number of opportunities and material things that I enjoy at home and at the same time a keen awareness of how much more I have than people in other countries.
- have a greater sense of connection to family and friends (even if they don't always understand me and my new experiences).
- have a greater view of the possibilities in the world and in my life. It is like the doors and windows to many things were opened.
- feel like a "global citizen" and care more about what happens around the globe.
- am interested in a greater concept of justice and injustice as it is manifested differently in other countries.
- have a higher tolerance for ambiguity in situations. Now I can be in situations in which I don't understand all that is going on and still feel comfortable in trying to communicate.
- am able to suspend judgment about people and their actions because sometimes you just don't have all the cultural and language background that you need.
- have the ability to think more critically about political events and take a look at multiple sides of current issues.

Whew! That's quite a list. Which of the above describe you? Take a moment to write down ways in which you have changed as a result of your study abroad experience:

Possible outcomes of an international experience

This sheet provides a handy reference of skills you may develop as a direct result of your experiences abroad. Use this to spark ideas for creating a resumé, preparing for an interview, and reflecting upon your experiences.

Skills

- Understand cultural differences and similarities
- Adapt to new environments
- Learn through listening and observing
- Establish rapport quickly
- Function with a high level of ambiguity
- Take initiative and risks
- Utilize time management skills
- Identify problems and utilize available resources to solve the problems
- Accept responsibility
- Communicate despite barriers
- Learn quickly
- Handle difficult situations
- Handle stress
- Manage/organize
- Lead others in formal and/or informal groups
- Conduct research despite language and cultural differences
- Cope with rejection

Qualities

- Self-reliance
- High energy level/enthusiasm
- Appreciation of diversity
- Perseverance
- Flexibility
- Open mindedness
- Assertiveness
- Inquisitiveness
- Self-confidence
- Self-knowledge
- Independence

Identity challenges

As mentioned at the beginning of this section, these changes don't always feel good—change can be painful—even if it turns out to be rewarding in the long run.

> *Within four days of arriving back in the U.S. from my first study abroad experience, I turned around and drove 800 miles to spend the summer working as a lifeguard at a resort in the Rocky Mountains. As I crossed over the Iowa border, the song 'Convoy' came on the radio. I burst out crying—sobbing really. I remember driving by myself that day, listening to the radio with tears streaming down my face. 'This is so American,' I thought bitterly. It makes me laugh now—that a '70s pop song about truckers and smokeys and CB radios could have such an intense effect on me.*
>
> *Anyway, the whole idyllic summer that I imagined while I was in Greece turned out to be like that—really charged and emotionally discordant. I didn't know anyone at the resort, and the other staff members from the U.S. all seemed really young and superficial to me. I had a hard time relating to them, so I spent a lot of time alone, taking hikes, and trying to understand why I was feeling so strange. Eventually I became friends with Liza, another lifeguard from Australia, and Stuart, a guy from England, both of whom were working at the resort on student visas. I think because they were also 'international,' I could relate to them on a level that I couldn't with the other staff members.*
>
> *I had heard of culture shock before I went abroad, but I didn't really understand how difficult it would be to return to the U.S. In Greece, my identity had been so thoroughly 'American,' and yet now that I was back in the U.S., I felt so un-American. I knew I hadn't become 'Greek,' but I certainly wasn't the same 'me.' Eventually the struggle abated, but the struggle didn't fit neatly on a curve or a timeline. And, to be honest, there really is no end result. As one of my Greek professors said to me, 'The only thing certain in life is change, and the more you can accept change in your life the happier you will be.' The more experiences I have, the more I realize how true that really is. ~ Suzanne Hay, Greece*

How can leaving home and coming back lead to such struggles? Exposure to different cultures—to different ways of behaving, of problem solving, and of perceiving the world—leads us to question beliefs and values that were once taken for granted. It is almost like trying to sort out two versions of you. This sorting out is a process. The first step in this process is to be aware of the changes that have occurred within you and to embrace your new "intercultural identity." Although this should be a liberating and developmental experience, it may also be accompanied by a sense of loss because you aren't exactly the same person that you were when you left home.

Some who return to the U.S. after study abroad experiences sometimes no longer feel "American" in the same way they did when they first left the country. They also don't feel fully a part of the culture that they just experienced either. In a way they are emotionally in cultural "limbo." This identity conflict can feel overwhelming, and words such as insignificant, lonely, restless, and agitated have been used to describe this internal upset. These feelings are very normal, and the majority of students are able to come to terms with their conflicting identities. Students who feel this way very intensely over a period of time should seek help from counselors, friends, and family.

Some returning study abroad students come back with a very sense of their own unique cultural identity. For example, instead of feeling like they need to be "American" or "French" they can just be themselves…a definite mixture of American and French beliefs, values, experiences, and language. People who are able to integrate their sometimes conflicting sets of experiences can develop a sense that they have found two places to call home.

> *The mark of a successful sojourner is not that he has finally come to*
> *appreciate fully the true meaning of home, or that he may have relinquished*
> *one home for another more suited to him, but that he has found two places*
> *'where he can go out and in.' (Lewis and Jungmar, 1986).*

You may feel in between these two "poles," and for a few months following your return you might experience a feeling of "cultural identity crisis" and might also feel like you are creating a very new identity for yourself. Be patient and also take time to reflect on how you can incorporate all of your cultural identities into your own unique perspective on the world. For now, take a moment to reflect upon these questions:

- What values, beliefs, and behaviors have I learned from my host country that I want to try to maintain while back in the U.S.?

- In what ways might these conflict with U.S. cultures?

- How can I find support for these "new" values?

Keep a journal still. It is a full circle experience—and helps to develop a
more thorough experience. ~ Joy Wildermuth, France

Appreciating Different Styles of Successful Re-entry

Active re-entry

> When I came back from Italy I knew the transition back into my former life would be hard, but I decided that it would be better to be proactive rather than get overwhelmed. Everything that had seemed so familiar before was suddenly completely foreign. But my experience didn't just cause a feeling of alienation; it completely changed me and inspired me. When I got back, I chose activities to participate in that resounded with all that I had now become.

> I gave private Italian lessons, taught a community education course in Italian (I just called and asked if they needed any Italian teachers—they were hesitant, so I said I could volunteer... they said it would be great and gave me the teacher's name. It's not much commitment but gives you good reason to keep up with your language), began a research project on study abroad (the deadline for some funding was close, so I looked for a professor in my area of interest and asked what research he knew of and how I might get involved), got more involved in the Italian department, and started working at a homeless shelter. Through these activities I obviously found plenty of opportunity to strengthen my language skills, but I also was able to see more clearly where Italian was going to fit into my career. The last thing on my mind was whether or not I had some post-study-abroad stress disorder—I just didn't have time to sit home and worry, I was having too much fun. ~ Jacob Dick, Italy

> I found that I had the hardest time dealing with being home when I was bored. Being occupied, whether it be at school or work or just hanging out with friends you have not seen in awhile will help with the re-entry process. ~ Tammi Brussegard, France

Don't just put the experience on the shelf; the experience should not end when you return! Consider some of the following "action steps" to make the most of building on your study abroad experience:
- Join conversational groups to keep up your language skills.
- Volunteer in a community where you can use your new skills in being culturally flexible and, in some cases, where you can use your language skills or be exposed to yet another language.
- Make presentations for school and community groups about the country/countries you were in and the cultures and languages you experienced.
- Select topics on various political, historical, and social aspects of your study abroad experience for papers that you have to write in a variety of classes.
- Sign up for academic or language classes that will build on your experiences.

- Volunteer for any program in which you can address some of the new values that you've adopted as a result of your experience. If you are more aware of hunger in the world, for example, volunteer at a food shelf. If you are now more politically aware, join a political campaign.

Reflective re-entry

If you aren't the kind of person who just wants non-stop action, that is OK. You might want time to reflect on your experience and let it "soak in." For you, purposely reflecting on your experience is sometimes more valuable than a lot of activity that doesn't lead you anywhere. Take a look at what these returnees have to say about taking time to reflect:

> Getting the most from study abroad takes time and reflection. Asking me what I got out of it is like taking a survey in a magazine—the answer is superficial and doesn't really convey the internal shift that's occurred. There's something about being completely out of your normal context that turns everything upside down, and it's both exciting and scary. My experience really did change the concept I have of myself. I am generally a thoughtful, self-aware person, but while I was gone I found myself thinking, 'Who the hell am I?' ~ Suzanne Hay, Greece

> Don't look at things as better or worse. Accept your home culture as an entity that you can look at from an outsider's perspective. This could help cause a harmony from the blending of your two cultural identities. ~ Dan Jakab, Spain

> Re-entry is much more difficult than people anticipate. Many people feel that they can no longer relate to their old life, but people should be warned not to get a condescending attitude toward their old life. ~ Elizabeth Hooh, Australia

> I did not attend the re-entry dinners planned by my study abroad office—I thought they were just for those having problems adjusting. I was fine emotionally, so I did not think I needed to go. However, what I did need and missed out on was a way to connect my coursework in economics and communication to my career interests. I definitely could have made the path a bit easier and more fulfilling—rather than pursuing an initial path that was so clearly wrong for me. ~ Barbara Kappler, England

It's critical to take time to reflect upon your study abroad experience. Stop and ask yourself some questions like:
- How do these experiences fit with my values?

- Are your current activities "in sync" with your new sense of self?

- Do you feel like you are using new skills, making new friends, strengthening former relationships, and gaining new knowledge?

Study Abroad Leads to Life-Long Learning

You've heard it so many times: "Study abroad was the greatest thing I did." This statement typically is not just wistful reminiscing about an adventurous time. Rather, it reflects a turning point, a fork in the road, or a pinpointable moment of a critical life lesson.

I am a big reader of World War II history. When I went to England, I took a history class specifically because it covered World War II. I know it sounds naïve, but I was surprised to learn from my Scottish professor that the U.S. armed forces were not necessarily viewed as coming to the rescue (a view I had read about repeatedly in the U.S.), but rather with some disdain—'Why didn't you come earlier?!' I have never forgotten this lesson—that history has multiple views. ~ Barbara Kappler, England

After I came home from being in Taiwan, I was looking for some kind of volunteer activity to get plugged into here at home. I didn't have a great job and really needed something to make my life more meaningful. Since I had already taught English overseas I decided that it would be interesting to sign up to be a volunteer English tutor with the then very new Hmong refugee population. What I didn't realize was being here in the U.S. with a group of people who had a more radically different culture than even what I experienced in Taiwan would be life-changing. I got drawn into being involved with a number of Hmong families with whom I still have a strong relationship twenty years later. One of my Hmong friends let me stay at her house for a month as my own special 'home stay' here in the U.S. I lived with the family for a month and ate Hmong breakfasts of watery rice, helped with the kids (six of them), and had a birds' eye view of their life in a crime-ridden neighborhood. I can tell you I learned so much in that one month, and that experience helped shape my values and my sense of what is important in life.

I think if I hadn't studied abroad, I would never have had the courage to reach out and try to get to really know people from another culture. Though I learned a lot from being in Taiwan, I think that particular experience was most valuable in preparing me to participate in an even more powerful experience in my life. I think study abroad affects each person so differently and leads them down any number of paths—all worthwhile and mostly more enriching. ~ Karin Larson, Taiwan

I was in the grocery store the other day, and there was a woman at the head of the line whose first language was not English. She was having a lot of difficulty understanding how much money the cashier wanted, and I could tell that the people directly behind her were getting impatient. Eventually she figured it out and gave the cashier the correct amount, but the whole thing made me feel for her. I have a hard time understanding numbers when they are spoken in Greek, and it made me think of all the times I tried to pay for something when I was in Greece but wasn't able to 'hear' how much it cost. One time I tried to buy a bus ticket and, after having the price repeated to me several times and still not getting it, I just stuck out a handful of drachmas for the vendor to take what he needed. It can be embarrassing not to be able to understand such simple things, and it makes you feel very vulnerable, childlike. Anyway, I think that if I could go back and 're-do' my recent experience in the grocery store again, I would make the decision to go up to the woman and try to assist her, even if it meant making the people around me feel uncomfortable for 'disrupting the line.' It's weird to think how rigid our culture can be about certain things, like standing in line, or making sure that things are running quickly and efficiently. We get so worried about time and keeping our 'place' that we become paralyzed to help out those around us.

Although the experience at the grocery store is a tiny example, I think that overall I have a lot more empathy for people who are new to this country and are English as a Second Language learners. My experience abroad continues to make me appreciate what I have in this country, to remember to have patience with others, and to try to extend myself to those around me, strangers or not, when I can. ~ Suzanne Hay, Greece

Strategies for Long-Term Maintenance of Language and Culture Learning

Here are some suggestions from veteran returnees on how to transform your study abroad experience into life-long learning.

Continue your language and intercultural education

Whether through formal or informal instruction, there are many opportunities to continue studying the language and culture of interest after you've returned. Universities and community colleges offer many choices for foreign language instruction, and many offer some of the less commonly taught languages as well. Private language schools also provide opportunities to practice and brush up on language skills through informal classes. Many universities and schools offer language exchange or "tandem" programs that match a native speaker, usually an international student or scholar, with someone interested in that student's home language and culture. In exchange, the partner can tutor them in English.

Involve your friends

Invite your friends to a dinner once in awhile where you have potluck international parties. Use this as a chance to learn not only about the food, but to have your friends share their experiences with other cultures and what they are doing now to keep an international perspective alive. Lots of colleges and universities have student organizations that help get international students and U.S. American students together. And if yours doesn't, you can start one!

Write about your experiences

Magazines and newsletters, both on campus and off, will be interested in reviewing and possibly publishing accounts of your international experiences and the unique perspective you now have. This is an excellent way for you to share with others what it's like living in another country. Most of your audience will not have experienced what you did, so by sharing your stories, intercultural encounters, and travels with them, you allow them to enter into your world—perhaps you may even inspire them to take steps toward their own journey abroad!

Keep the international connections alive

Many returnees report regretting that they did not keep in touch with their new friends after returning home. You will feel torn, like your heart and mind is split between two countries. The good news is that with the Internet, it is easier now more than ever to maintain contact with people halfway around the world. Writing letters and e-mail is also an excellent way to maintain your newly acquired language skills. As more and more nations have Internet connections, the amount as well as the variety of information available via the Web has mushroomed. Online newspapers give you immediate access to news on current events that often are not reported in U.S. newspapers.

Make new international connections

Most universities and colleges have active international student organizations that tend to be organized and attended by both international students and U.S. Americans. Many professional and community organizations exist that have cultural exchange and learning as one of their goals. Find out when the next meeting is and check it out.

Seek out international volunteer and employment opportunities

There are a multitude of opportunities for you to volunteer or find employment that let you utilize your bilingual and bicultural skills:
- Become a homestay family to an international student. Agencies and universities are always looking for suitable homestay families for students, and this is perhaps one of the best means of keeping connected internationally. Be willing to accept a student outside of your own experience and expand your cultural horizons.
- Volunteer or intern in a study abroad office. Your international skills and knowledge about living overseas can be put to valuable use by advising prospective study abroad students and by participating in pre-departure and re-entry orientation programs.

- Volunteer at an office for international students. Offices that work with international students tend to be understaffed and can use volunteers to do a number of vital tasks such as transporting students from the airport, organizing a drive to collect used household goods and winter clothing for international students, or organizing events or volunteering at orientation for new students.
- Become a buddy or tutor for international students. Already knowing how it feels to go through cross-cultural adjustment in a foreign country, you have a unique perspective and can better understand the needs of international students studying in the U.S. Use those cross-cultural skills to help others and, in turn, deepen your own learning and make valuable international connections.
- Seek out volunteer or work positions at international organizations located in your area. You might be surprised at the number and breadth of international linkages that already exist in your area.
- Volunteer to work with refugees or immigrants in your community. The needs and backgrounds of refugees and immigrants in this country vary tremendously, but they typically do not have the kind of resources that international students have. More and more communities around the country have refugee communities that could use the support of culturally sensitive volunteers.
- Act as a tour guide for visitors from your host country. Many companies now have in-house opportunities for bilingual/bicultural translators and interpreters.
- Seek out opportunities through work, school, or other means to go abroad again. Use your cultural and linguistic fluency to accompany a delegation or tour to your country of interest. They do need you and your skills, even if they might not be aware of it yet!
- A wide variety of materials are available dealing with how to find an international job, whether you want to travel abroad again or be based in the U.S.
- There are also many opportunities for interning or volunteering overseas, which may be a great next step for you. Some of these experiences are longer term (1 to 2 years) and some are available for a few months or less.

The above are just a few of the potential volunteer and work-related opportunities where you can use your study abroad experience. Keep in mind that as more and more connections worldwide are formed, there will be even greater need for your international skills and perspectives. Organizations and corporations are realizing that if they want to be successful, having a global perspective and making international linkages is not an option but a fundamental requirement. As someone who has experienced another culture first-hand, you are well equipped to contribute to the growth in international and intercultural awareness happening at home and throughout the world.

Section II
Language-Learning Strategies

INTRODUCTION:
MAXIMIZE YOUR LANGUAGE LEARNING

These strategies give you a new container to put information into.
~ Jacob Dick, Italy

I have been studying Estonian for two years. I sure wish I had learned these
strategies when I first began my language studies! The strategies make me so
much more aware of what works for me—and what doesn't—so I get the most
out of my time studying and learning the language. ~ Barbara Kappler, Estonia

This portion of the guide focuses on strategies for improving your language learning and language use. The readings and activities are intended for skilled learners wanting to hone their skills, novice learners slightly unsure of their skills, and everyone in-between. In short, if you are learning a language, the following pages have something to offer you. To begin, make sure you take the language strategies survey on page 16 to help you focus your learning.

Going to an English-speaking country? Or a country where you have easy access to English? Several educators and students have commented that the following strategies have helped them—even when the hosts spoke English. No matter your destination, unless you will be entirely exposed to native U.S. American speakers, you will need to learn new vocabulary and a new rhythm of speaking.

The following are examples of British English. Write below each one an equivalent sentence in U.S. English. Check your answers on the next page.

1.   Ben had been watching the telly since half five and was starting to feel a bit peckish.

2.   Evan is in a nark. He thought he was going to get a pay rise at work, but instead he was made redundant.

3.   When Alex moved to London all he could afford was a bedsit.

Like any other "foreign" language you are learning, the meaning of a word that you hear or read in the U.K., Australia, Ireland, or other regions such as India and Kenya (where British English is the norm) can often be discerned from its surrounding context. However, the number of new words or expressions, as well as English words that have completely different meanings outside of the U.S., might surprise you. This guide can help you develop strategies for learning this new vocabulary.

Perhaps language learning comes easily for you, and you feel quite confident in your skills. Perhaps you are just beginning your exposure to a new language, and your study abroad experience is going to be a way to really challenge yourself and immerse yourself in the language. Or perhaps you have selected an English-speaking site and are simply interested in strategies to understand different accents and learn some new vocabulary. No matter your situation, you can learn much by becoming aware of the strategies you use for learning language so that you can get the most of your time abroad.

While we often talk about learning a language as if it were just one skill, it's really a number of skills. Thinking in terms of strategies for dealing with different elements of language helps to make language learning a more manageable process. *Language strategies* are the steps or actions consciously selected to improve your ability to learn a second language. Sometimes these strategies are referred to as *techniques*, *tactics*, or *tips*. We also refer to the *target language*, which we consider to be the new language you are learning for your study abroad experience.

The language strategy material is organized according to the following language skills: listening, learning vocabulary, speaking to communicate, reading for comprehension, writing, and translation strategies.

> *The limits of my language are the limits of my world.* ~ Ludwig Wittgenstein

Suggested answers to p. 163

1. Ben had been watching the telly since half five and was starting to feel a bit peckish.
    Ben had been watching television since five-thirty and was starting to get hungry.

2. Evan is in a nark. He thought he was going to get a pay rise at work, but instead he was made redundant.
    Evan is in a bad mood. He thought he was going to get a raise at work, but instead he got fired.

3. When Alex moved to London all he could afford was a bedsit.
    When Alex moved to London all he could afford was an efficiency apartment.

LANGUAGE-LEARNING STYLES AND STRATEGIES:
LISTENING

Pre-Departure Listening Activities

*To me, the number one project for pre-departure would be EXPOSE
YOURSELF TO THE LANGUAGE (which I did not do enough)! Rent
movies. Go to conversation groups. Figure out how to get a host country
radio station over the Internet. Order books-on-tape in the target language
through interlibrary loan. (Or better: ask your language teachers. They
probably have stuff.) I'm sort of ranting because the one aspect of my
German that is the most frustrating is the inability to understand speech.*
~ Molly Zahn, Germany

*In getting ready to go to Malaysia, I had great plans to study the language
before leaving. But working to pay for the trip and studying for the heavy
course load I had were all that I could manage! Before leaving, I did review
some basic grammar and pronunciation. People had told me that I would be
able to get by with English. They were right, I could get by with English. But
even better than getting by, I was also able to learn some Bahasa Malaysian
and some Cantonese from friends I met in-country. Being open to the language
and the basics that I reviewed before departing made a big difference.*
~ Barbara Kappler, Malaysia

1. Listen to radio from your host country over the Internet. You can find good
   sites simply by launching a browser and searching for keywords such as
   "international radio" or the language you are interested in and the word "radio."

2. Form a group to watch foreign films (ones that are not dubbed into English) in
   the target language. Listen to the movies while taking into account the strategies
   suggested in this section.

3. Find tapes or CDs of music recorded in the foreign language and try to understand it
   not only for its words, but also for its meaning. Being familiar with popular music and
   musicians from the country also gives you something to talk about with new friends.

4. If available, go to a local market where they speak your target language and
   eavesdrop on common conversations about the prices of meat or the quality of
   the produce. Listen to the grocer give directions to someone on where to find a
   particular item in the store.

It can be difficult to gauge your skills in some of these areas while still in the U.S. For example, I had NO IDEA how bad my comprehension of conversational-speed German between Germans was until I got here—I had simply never been exposed to it before because, of course, my teachers and classmates at my university didn't talk like that. However, if you begin to recognize your strengths and weaknesses before you go, you can focus on improving your skills. This will make your life drastically easier when you get there! ~ Molly Zahn, Germany

What Does a Competent Listener Do?

In this section we will talk about the skills or abilities that are needed in order to be a successful listener in your host country. You may already have partially developed some of these skills. This section highlights how you can use language strategies to develop your skills, even before you leave for the country or after you've arrived.

Check which of these you feel you can do now when you listen to a native speaker of your target language:

- [ ] 1. Distinguish separate words from a blur of sounds

- [ ] 2. Distinguish one sound from another, like the vowel sounds in the English words sit and seat

- [ ] 3. Comprehend the message without understanding every word

- [ ] 4. Understand the entire message

- [ ] 5. Decipher fast speech

- [ ] 6. Figure out the intention of the speakers

- [ ] 7. Listen to a conversation between two or more people

- [ ] 8. Recognize different types of speech according to the speaker (e.g., age, status, relationship) or setting (e.g., in school, at dinner, at a night club)

Now, go back and circle the ones you would most like to work on. See the following section for specific strategies for developing these skills.

(Adapted from Mendelsohn, 1994.)

Strategies to Become a Better Listener

1. Distinguish separate words from a blur of sounds

Increase your exposure to the language. For example, tape what someone says to you and play the tape over a few times. Or, go on the Web and listen to radio or voice segments in the new language.

Have a friend say a sentence slowly, then quickly. Count the number of words you can identify in each sentence. Try to separate out more words each time you practice.

Visualize. When you hear something said, see in your mind the chunks of language it consists of, perhaps looking for the subject and the verb.

2. Distinguish one sound from another (like the vowels in sit and seat)

Practice aloud. Repeat the major vowel and consonant sounds in that language to yourself.

Practice with a friend. Have the friend repeat challenging sounds and vocabulary for you to identify which sound is being spoken or what word is being used.

3. Comprehend the message without understanding every word

Listen for key words. These are sometimes signaled by stress or by a pause.

Practice "skim listening." Tap into the key topics, and pay particular attention to these while ignoring others.

Play the game of probabilities, inference, and educated guessing. You can use your world knowledge for what is most likely being said, given:
- the topic and your prior knowledge,
- the context,
- who is speaking,
- the speaker's tone of voice and body language, and
- cues from prior spoken words or phrases.

For example, when one of the co-authors, Barbara Kappler, traveled with a friend to Estonia, she could only speak a few phrases of Estonian. However, during the first 10 minutes of visiting friends, she understood the "gist" of what was said because there was a ritual to the conversations: "How was the flight? By what route did you travel? How is your family? Your work?" She understood by hearing *Amsterdamis, Minnesota Ülikool* (University of Minnesota), family member names, etc.

Try to predict what the speaker will say. If you know something about the topic of conversation, take an educated guess depending on the context and the environment.

Listen for words that are borrowed from English. Words like "computer" and brand names like "Coca-Cola" are quite common.

Use both top-down and bottom-up listening strategies. Bottom-up processing involves taking the items heard and putting them together to create meaning. So, for example, you hear: "Yesterday…earthquake…kill 273 people…Kobe," and you conclude that there was an earthquake yesterday in Kobe that killed 273 people. It is because of the adverb "yesterday" that you assign past tense to the verb. In bottom-up listening, you are finding clues by examining the words themselves as fully as you can.

Top-down processing is a more holistic approach where you look for clues to meaning beyond the specific words you hear. You draw on your knowledge of the world and events. For example, you overhear two people talking. One person says the word "earthquake" and you also hear the word "Kobe." From your background knowledge, you know that they are talking about the earthquake that just happened in Kobe.

The advantage of the top-down approach is it allows you to to stay actively involved, especially early on in your language learning. Whereas, the bottom-up approach enables you to modify your interpretation as you collect more information. This approach highlights listening accuracy since you listen more directly to the specific words.

Identify which style you tend to use while watching a movie, attending class, or overhearing a conversation. Pay attention to how you determine the meaning of the conversation. Once you've identified the strategy you use, try to see if you can also use the other.

> *Having previous experience in the same context has definitely helped me understand loads and loads of Korean speech that I never would have understood a few months earlier. This point became clear to me when I was at a Korean restaurant for lunch with my husband, his Korean friends and their daughter, and an English-speaking couple. The waitress, who was speaking Korean, continued on and on about how Korean children learn so much English but tend to forget their Korean very easily. She also told a story about a man she knew who would get upset with his children when they spoke English and insisted that they speak Korean instead.*

I already knew the words for 'Korean,' 'English,' 'daycare,' and 'speak' in Korean, and I had recently started attending the Korean church in my city (giving me many opportunities to witness the concerns of the Korean parents). Using the waitress' tone of voice while she told the story and her nonverbal communication, I easily put the conversation together. Ultimately, I was able to reiterate it to the English-speaking couple without any problems. The others stared in amazement! Even though I didn't have the grammar or vocabulary to repeat it back in full, in the end, I was successful in understanding what the speaker said. ~ Julie Chi

4. Understand the entire message.

Put yourself in a frame of mind to understand the target language. Put aside other thoughts, including what you might want to say in reply, and focus only on what the speaker is saying. Then you should consider your response.

Accept some ambiguity in what you hear, and practice listening.
Remember that it is perfectly normal to encounter speech that you do not completely understand. One hundred percent comprehension, even in your own language, is unrealistic. At your home university, one of your professors may use many words that are new or unfamiliar to you, but you use the surrounding context to understand what the professor is saying. You might be able to get the main idea of what was said, but you probably could not repeat it back word for word.

Try these listening activities:
- Tape a commercial on the radio or TV, and play it back a few times. See how well you can identify the words in the message. When you are unsure of sounds in words, what do you do? Can you understand what is being advertised?
- Record a conversation between two native speakers—ideally, friends of yours—who are talking about a topic you are familiar with. Then play it back to yourself several times. See how much of their interaction you can understand. What strategies do you use to understand the gist of what they are saying to each other?
- While listening or viewing (live or recorded) try to visualize the ideas you understand in your mind—or write them down if that suits your style. As you continue to listen, add new information and update your mental picture or notes on your understanding of what the person is talking about.

5. Decipher fast speech

Reduce your expectations. You may need to be exposed to the language for awhile before you will start to understand fast speech.

Try to stay in the conversation. Don't tune out when you feel the conversation is over your head.

Ask questions. The number one advice from returning students: Ask questions! If you don't understand what you just heard:
- Ask for clarification
- Ask for the statement to be repeated
- Try to paraphrase and see if you are correct

I was in Paris at midnight, in the dark, alone, and lost. I went back to a landmark, the Best Western Hotel, and buzzed the night clerk. I explained, in French, my situation. 'I'm locked out of my apartment, but I'm not really sure where that apartment is. I'm sure it's around here, but I can't remember exactly where. I'm an American student, and I just arrived in the city. I know it's stupid, but I seem to be lost.' He agreed about my stupidity but was kind enough to call my hostess who explained how to get in the building. I made it out of a bad situation by not panicking and not being afraid to ask for help. ~ Tammi Brusegaard, France

Become familiar with ritualized speech. While studying abroad, one of the greatest challenges is that daily life involves so much ritualized language. For example, a student studying in the U.S. talked about how he felt he was doing OK with learning English—then he went to McDonald's. After successfully ordering, he heard the clerk ask "izat fur hearutágo?" Paralyzed, he stood there, only to hear again: "Izat fur hearutágo?" Finally realizing it was a question, he said, "Yes." The frustrated clerk simply threw the meal in the bag. After a few more visits to McDonald's the student said, "Oh! Is that for here or to go!" And proudly said, "Here!"

Unclear word boundaries: When speech is too fast, it can be difficult to distinguish separate words from each other, and, therefore, difficult to understand the meaning or intent of the speaker. Words can sound blended together when spoken quickly.

Weak forms: In English, when a phrase is spoken quickly some vowels become lax, creating words like "gotta" and "gonna," for example. Sometimes initial consonants are deleted in order to make speech more fluid in statements like, "Tell 'em t' meet at the restaurant." You may think of this as "lazy speech," yet this form of language is fast speech and occurs in all languages. You might not be aware of how much you use this sort of abbreviated speech every day in your native language until you try to figure it out in a foreign language!

Suggested activity: Record segments of fast speech (e.g., when friends are using it or from a TV show) and then replay it several times. You will probably find yourself understanding more each time you listen to it. If you still have problems, ask a native speaker to listen to your tape and explain what the speakers are talking about.

6. Figure out the intention of the speakers

Use tone of voice to guess the meaning or intention of what was said. Remember, this is just a guess as the meanings of tone can vary across cultures.

Make yourself aware of nonverbal cues. Look at facial expressions, body language, and hand movements. Again, try to guess the meaning, keeping in mind you may be inaccurate in your interpretation, given cultural differences with nonverbals.

Understand the use of stress. Depending on the language, stressed words may often be more important to the meaning of the sentence than words that are not stressed. Therefore, stress may signal the key words that can help you understand the speaker, especially in skim listening. Consider this sentence in English: "The **grass** is **always greener** on the **other side**." The words in bold are the key words. They are also the stressed words. Say the sentence to yourself. How clearly do you really say or hear the smaller words?

The meaning can change dramatically when people put greater emphasis on the words they stress. Consider the difference in meaning/intention in the following sentences:

- Elena bought a French COOKBOOK. (She bought a cookbook, not a magazine.)
- ELENA bought a French cookbook. (Elena, not someone else, bought it.)
- Elena bought a FRENCH cookbook. (She bought a French, not German, cookbook.)
- Elena BOUGHT a French cookbook. (She bought, rather than sold, a cookbook.)

Determine how people signal the key words in your target language:
- Ask your language teacher.
- Listen to conversations in your target language, and try to note the words that stand out more to you.
- Try reading lyrics to music while you listen to it. Circle or mark the words you heard more clearly.

Learn the stress patterns in your target language. Listen for them while people are speaking, whether in a conversation with you, on the radio, on TV, or in class. Identify when stress might change the meaning, as in the above examples.

Understand intonations. Intonation deals with pitch variation or the rising and falling of the speaker's voice. For example, in English, when the speaker wants to ask a question, the listener will generally hear a rising intonation at the end of the sentence. For a statement, the listener would hear a declining intonation at the end. Emotion is also often expressed through one's intonation.

Be aware that intonation can change the meaning of a message, so you cannot pay attention to the words alone. It is important to check out the role of intonation in your target language to see when it could make a meaningful difference in what you say. For example, what may be intended as an apology, "Well, I am so sorry," may come across in English as a snide comment or even an insult simply if the speaker's intonation falls at the end instead of rising. It is perhaps precisely in these kinds of high-impact communications that you may wish to know how to convey the meaning appropriately through correct intonation! Here are a few suggested activities to help you:

- Take one sentence and try to convey different meanings by changing the intonation.
- Consider the following two conversations. Say them aloud and listen to your rising and falling intonation.

Keon:	Did you like the musical?
Asif:	The cast members were interesting.
Shadeen:	Oh, they sure were unique. I've never seen a group like them before!

Loann:	Hey, guys! What do you think about my new hat?
Aurelio:	Wow! I've got to say, Loann...that's quite a hat!
Micheli:	Yeah. It's really different. Where did you find a hat like that?

7. Listen to interactions between two or more people

Eavesdrop. Expose yourself to a variety of enriching conversations among native speakers. Eavesdropping is easy and generally acceptable on a bus, waiting in line, on the subway or train, etc. Try to get a global understanding of the message.

8. Recognize different types of speech according to the speaker or setting

This may call for getting more involved in the culture so you can be exposed to a variety of speakers (e.g., age, status, relationship) and settings (e.g., at dinner, at a night club). The number one goal for the majority of study abroad students is to increase their language competencies. The number one regret expressed by students is that they did not do so enough.

Why can it be so difficult to learn the language while being surrounded by it? It can be hard to find people to talk to, especially if you are at a beginning level. You need to take charge and take advantage of opportunities to increase your language exposure.

Consider all the opportunities you have for language exposure. You should be able to list at least 15 things.

1. _____

2. _____

3. _____

4. _____

5. _____

6. _____

7. _____

8. _____

9. _____

10. _____

11. _____

12. _____

13. _____

14. _____

15. _____

Here is our list:

1. Watch TV soap operas (the dialogue is often understood by the nonverbal communication).
2. Ask for directions—even when you know where you are going.
3. Watch children's shows.
4. Go to movies.
5. Listen to commercials.
6. Read bulletin boards.
7. Listen to children's radio shows.
8. Read children's books.
9. Read the local newspaper.
10. Read a magazine on your favorite hobby.
11. Ask the grocer how to make a local dish.
12. Talk to the bus driver or a fellow passenger during your commute.
13. Talk to the school librarians about their favorite books.
14. Ask your language instructor for suggestions on novels aimed at your comprehension level.
15. Get a native-speaking conversation partner.
16. Ask questions about items on the menu (move beyond "pointing and nodding" as a way to order food).
17. Go to a museum with written explanations in the native language only.
18. Spend two nights a week with your host family.
19. Eavesdrop on other people's conversations and guess the topic.
20. Search the Internet for sites in the language.
21. Learn the words to the national anthem.
22. Go to a playground and listen to the adults talk to the children.

Make the Most of Your Language Classroom

Many of us don't take full advantage of the language classroom. Why not? It's easy to tune out due to language fatigue, get distracted by an instructor's presentation style, or simply take a mental break from rushing between work and classes.

Here are a few tips to help you get the most out of your classroom time both at home and while in your host country:
- Prepare for classroom lectures. If you have been informed of the topic for the following day, prepare a list of possible questions your instructor might ask you.
- Increase your attention span. Note how long you pay attention and encourage yourself to be more active, such as by answering in your mind the questions asked of other classmates.
- Make sure that you are getting enough sleep, exercise, and healthy food. Learning a language takes a lot of work, and you need to keep up your energy level to do it.

Avoid Faking that You Understand the Conversation

Perhaps you thought you were the only one who ever faked that you understood a conversation? It's actually common and occasionally necessary to save face and time —or simply to look good—but it will slow you down if you use it too much.

Here are ways to avoid faking it:
- Learn culturally appropriate ways to indicate you are not following the conversation. Don't simply keep nodding or maintaining eye contact.
- Ask questions to make sure that you are understanding the conversation.
- When there is in-class reading, focus on the reading of your peers, rather than counting ahead to find the line(s) that you will most likely be asked to read, so as to appear well versed in the material when your turn comes.

Sometimes cover strategies are performed almost instinctively so that you will not be embarrassed in front of the teacher or other learners. Refer to "Strategies for Intercultural Communication" (p. 121) for more information on the impact of culture on communication.

Understand Different Types of Speech

In the U.S., your most frequent exposure to the language is or was probably a foreign language instructor. In your host country, you are likely to hear at least five ways the language is spoken, and you need to be able to maximize your listening to all these types of talk.

- *native-speaker talk:* the language of native speakers speaking to one another with no attempt to simplify, slow down, or repeat for your benefit.
- *teacher talk:* "foreigner talk" that teachers choose to use in the classroom. Sometimes the teacher, perhaps without even being aware of it, may use language that is not exactly grammatically correct just so students will be sure to understand it. Teacher talk can be "sheltered language," because the teacher is making it easier for you to understand and practice using the language. This is one of the main advantages of spending time in a classroom.
- *interlanguage talk:* the version of the target language as spoken by foreign-language learners like yourself when what is said is a version of the target language that is influenced both by the way things are said in the native language and by erroneous hunches about how things are said in the target language.
- *foreigner talk:* the modified language that native speakers use with you in an effort to help you understand what they are saying. It may entail simplifying the verb tense, selecting a more common noun or adjective, or slowing the pace of speech.
- *commentator talk:* the language of TV and radio commentators, which is often read from a prepared text so that there are few false starts and little repetition or redundancy. If you are a beginner in the language, such talk will be most difficult to understand, even if it is in supposedly simplified language.

In the beginning levels of language learning, some forms of language input are difficult and frustrating—such as TV news broadcasts and rapid fire conversations among native speakers. Repeated exposure would eventually lead to comprehension, but such an approach is not a very efficient way to arrive at comprehension. A more efficient way would be through listening to input that is understandable and then gradually increase in complexity.

Understand the influence of culture on your listening

If your classmate asks, "Is that your cell phone?," what would you answer? Would you simply say, "Yes, it's mine," or do you think the speaker is really asking you to turn it off or maybe asking to borrow it for a short call? This is where interpretation comes into play. You could start by thinking about the way the particular culture deals with cell phones, when they are allowed to be turned on, and when/whether borrowing someone else's phone for a call is appropriate. After considering the specific culture, think about the speaker's actual signals. For example, the speaker often gives a variety of nonverbal clues for you to consider. It may be that a given facial expression, a certain gesture, or a particular pause is an indicator of what the speaker intended by asking you, "Is that your cell phone?"

One way to help you understand the cultural rules is to understand if the culture seems to be more low or high context (Hall, 1976). For example, in some movie theaters in the U.S., a message is displayed before the movie starts that asks you to turn off the cell phone. That's low-context, in which the meaning is conveyed directly in written or spoken form. In other high-context situations and cultures, it may be expected that people will just know when it is or is not permitted to have the cell phone on, and there is no need for signs explicitly indicating this. The culture section of this guide also gives you an activity on high and low context in order to practice your understanding of this important idea (p. 122).

Improve your active listening

The strategies you use in your native language to help you listen have probably become second-nature. These strategies are extremely helpful to recall now in order to help you increase your listening comprehension and to practice speaking in the target language (Mendelsohn, 1994). Check to see which of these you are comfortable using in your target language, and challenge yourself to use more of those you are not.

Recall: paraphrase information, putting what you have heard into your own words.
- Revise – change your mind and correct yourself concerning some information that you misunderstood the first time.
- Check – recall information in order to support or verify something that you had already said.

Probe: go beneath the surface of the information presented.
- Analyze the topics – try, by asking questions, to glean more information than has been presented to you.
- Analyze the conventions of language – focus on specific features of the language system such as definitions of words, pronunciation (noting it or practicing it to yourself), and cohesive ties (how words in the second language link up to other words in that context).
- Evaluate the topics – make comments that are judgments or critical assessments concerning information you hear; i.e., contest what you hear based on what you think you know to be the case.

Introspect: focus your attention inward and reflect on your own experiences as a listener.
- Self-evaluate – make comments that show that you are trying to keep track of how well you are doing while engaged in listening (e.g., "This is really too hard for me…" or "I understand that completely, but I think I already knew most of it before she explained it").
- Self-describe – explain how you listen or what you are trying to do as you listen (e.g., "Well I missed this the first time, but now I remember…" or "It all came back to me on the way home…").

Language Shock and Language Fatigue

Some of my worst days abroad were the result of a language barrier.
~ Joshua Bueskan, Venezuela

Experiencing any of these things?
- Getting angry when you can't find a word you know that you know.
- Sleeping or wanting to sleep a great deal more than you did at home.
- Putting on headsets and cranking U.S. American tunes.
- Not putting on headsets and cranking U.S. American tunes.
- Wishing you were in a country where more people spoke English.
- Not caring if you are speaking English to your friends.
- Not caring if you perform rude behaviors according to the host culture.
- Coming home at the end of a day and feeling mad that your host family is home and you have to talk to them.
- Feeling like you are spending hours trying to understand one page of text.

If so, you have language fatigue. And you are not alone. Individuals who immerse themselves day in and day out in another language are bound to get tired physically and emotionally.

Here is what others suggest you do about language fatigue:
- Understand what it is. When you go abroad, you may find that language learning is much different than it was when you studied in your home country. Often study abroad students find that they must do much more independent work than they had to in their own universities. In the host country, you may experience a great amount of stress related to the fact that you do not understand the target language and culture. Sometimes your expectations may be set too high, and you do not recognize the mini-steps you take on a daily basis in your language learning. You might even be surprised to find that learning a language can be as arduous and draining as it is.
- Keep a journal so you realize how far you have come. Ask a trusted friend how you are doing. Seek out support from family and friends.
- Give yourself time away from the learning and use of the language. Read something in your native language, call a friend back home, or take a nap. You may also need time to digest the enormous amount of input you have received during the day.
- Lower your expectations for your language proficiency. Give yourself time to learn at a comfortable pace.
- Praise yourself for the mini-accomplishments you achieve. You are learning much more than you realize.

- And as one student says, "Relax… and maximize the whole language-learning experience."

Here is a quote from a study abroad student about breaking through the "sound barrier":

The Spanish language was fairly new to me when I arrived in Toledo, Spain. I simply took the required Spanish to become eligible for a trip such as this. Upon arrival, I was bombarded with new words, a deep Spanish accent, and conversations at an accelerated speed. How was I to learn to speak Spanish stronger when I feel all I learned was not applicable? Within the first month, after some of the initial language fatigue subsided, I was frustrated because I came to my first plateau. I could depict some words but still had trouble following a conversation. By the time I figured out the sentence my friend or teacher had moved on well past the point I was at. My frustration returned in a more intense way.

At that point, a good friend came over to me while I was struggling to follow a native speaker in a bar. My friend said, 'Justin, relax. I know by now you have the understanding of the Spanish language—you're just trying too hard. Relax, listen, it will come to you—you will be surprised.' From that point, I started to loosen up and follow what I could. Learning a language is a process. The kind words of my friend helped me gain confidence and insight into maximizing the whole language experience. ~ Justin Perlman, Spain

Language shock and culture shock are closely related because of how they both affect your cross-cultural adjustment process. For more information on culture shock and coping strategies, see "Adjusting" (p. 83).

Post-Study-Abroad Listening Activities

Keep the momentum going

Here are some things recent returnees did to keep up their listening skills:

- *I did something I was scared to do before leaving. I was much more confident, so I got a language conversation partner.*
- *Once a week I get together with friends and see a French film, have French food, and speak French.*
- *I got a job at a Mexican restaurant so I can use my Spanish.*
- *I bought CDs—from both the U.S. and my host country—on the Internet.*
- *I stay in touch with friends from there and continue to build my relationships.*
- *I visited again.*

Keep an open mind to opportunities for target language listening, but do proceed respectfully: Approaching a native speaker of the target language back in the U.S. may not be as easy as it had been in the environment of the foreign country. Be cautious about how you approach them, the language you use, and when the right time is to open a conversation.

Do not expect that a native speaker of your target language will want to speak anything other than English. After all, they may be in the U.S. specifically to learn English and the culture of the U.S. Approach them carefully, expressing your interest in their native language and culture; in most cases they will respond favorably.

LANGUAGE LEARNING STYLES AND STRATEGIES:
LEARNING VOCABULARY

Need to learn more vocabulary? Who doesn't! This chapter gives you a variety of techniques for expanding your repertoire.

Let's face it. You have a number of things you want to do while in the host country—see the sights, make new friends, visit neighboring regions and countries, and improve your language skills. This section will help you make the most of your time by identifying vocabulary-learning strategies that work for you.

Pre-Departure Vocabulary Learning Activities

Want to impress your fellow travelers with your language skills? Do you have visions of saying just the right thing when you meet your host family? Or do you just want to know you can keep up your end in a basic conversation? You'll want to brush up on your vocabulary so that when you arrive you won't be groping around for important words. Here are a few things you can do before you go:

- Make a list of the words you expect to need often. Make flash cards or put these in your journal so you can review them every day.
- Purchase sets of ready-made flash cards available at student bookstores and online (just search for the language you want and "flash cards"). Tip: Often the ready-made sets of cards include extra information about the words, such as the forms for the verbs in different tenses.
- Spend time with native speakers and have them provide you with crucial vocabulary you might not know. You will need to tell your partner what situation you need vocabulary for, such as calling a museum to get information about hours. Then your partner will be able to walk you through a mock conversation.
- Make a commitment to learn ten new words a day.
- Discover materials that you can read online. Look for newspapers, magazines, articles about your hobbies, etc. in your target language.
- Think of yourself as a natural topic of conversation and learn how to talk about *you*. People in your host country may be quite curious about you, or the conversation may turn to you simply as a cultural expression of politeness. Either way, it will be helpful, especially when you first arrive, to know some ready statements about yourself. Potential conversation topics may include:
  - **Your basic activities in the host country:** What are you doing there? Studying economics at the local university? Researching the traditional fiber arts of the area? Learn the correct words and phrases needed to express these activities.

- **Your living situation in the host country:** What city or region of the country are you in? Do you have a host family? Are you sharing an apartment with other students? Are you living in a dormitory?
- **Your length of stay in the host country:** When did you arrive? How long will you stay? Will you travel? What do you hope to see or do?
- **Your life in the U.S.:** Where are you from in the U.S.? Are you a student? Do you work full-time? What do you do for recreation/fun in the U.S.?
- **Your family:** Where is your family? Do you have brothers and sisters? Are you married? Do you have children?

Note:

Depending on what country you are staying in, be prepared for some "unusual" questions about yourself ("unusual" in that they may not be considered polite topics of conversation in the U.S.). For example, one study abroad student was asked on several occasions how much she weighed while she was in her host country. Other students have noted being surprised when asked how much they paid for something or how much money they earned. There may be some other topics that you can prepare for before you go with a little research on the host country or with the help of a host country native.

How do you learn vocabulary?

The first step in helping you to improve your vocabulary-learning strategies is to recognize how you actually go about learning new words.

Let's suppose that you are learning the Aymara language, which is spoken in parts of Bolivia and Peru. We picked this language precisely because the odds are small that you are studying Aymara. In the following activity we are asking you to think about what you do to learn new vocabulary and not just recall words you might already know.

The activity involves learning 10 words from Aymara. It may take you 5 to 10 minutes to complete. If you don't have time to learn 10, then try 5—the idea is to practice learning words.

Pretend you have just finished reading about a young man who is hospitalized with an infection in his leg. His new girlfriend brought flowers to his hospital bed but found him sleeping, so she wrote him a note and left quickly.

Learn the words on the following page so when given the English equivalent, you can produce the Aymara word. Pay attention to how you learn each word. After you feel you have put these words to memory, continue reading this section so you separate yourself from the vocabulary for a moment. Do not refer back to this list until asked to do so.

AYMARA	ENGLISH
wayna[1]	young man
usuta	sick
cayu	leg
machaka	new
aca	this
pankara[2]	flower
ucampisa	but
iquiña	to sleep
kellkaña[3]	to write
laka	quickly

The words selected come from Bolivian Aymara and conform more or less to the sound system of Spanish. Aymara belongs to the same language family as Quechua and is spoken by about 600,000 people in Bolivia and Peru.

Much language learning is unconscious or at a low level of consciousness. If you become aware of the actual processes you use, you will gain insights about learning strategies that work for you and those that do not.

For example, you may be a person who thinks that repeating a word over to yourself a number of times will fix the word in your memory, and yet in reality this approach may not work well for you. Remember that just because you have used an approach to vocabulary learning for awhile, it doesn't necessarily mean that it's the best for you or best for learning these particular words. So it may pay to take the time to see what other approaches are out there, for the opportunity to see if something else works better. For example, you may not be aware of how greatly you benefit from seeing a visual image of words or concepts.

Sometimes we use a certain approach to vocabulary learning not because it works, but because we think that we should be able to learn that way. Perhaps we use it because we know it works for someone else, because a teacher once told us to do it that way, or because we did it that way once and it worked then. For instance, you may once have kept an alphabetical listing of target language words and their native language equivalents, not because this listing genuinely contributed to your vocabulary learning, but because it seemed like the appropriate thing to do since other students were doing it.

---

[1] There are three main vowel sounds in Aymara; *a*, *i*, and *u*. The *a* is pronounced like the *a* in "father" as in the Aymara word *laka*. The *I* sound is somewhere in between the *I* in "bit" and the *ee* in "beet." In some Spanish loan words, the *I* can sound more like an *e*, which is pronounced like the *ay* in "hay." The *u* is pronounced somewhere in between the *oo* in "boot" and the *oo* in "look." The *u* can also sound like the *o* in "rope." A common Aymara diphthong is the *ay* like in *cayu* where the *ay* is pronounced like "eye."
[2] In Aymara, *r* is pronounced like the middle consonants in "butter" and is not rolled or trilled.
[3] In Aymara, *c* and *qu* are pronounced like the initial consonant in "kiss" and *k* is pronounced like the initial consonant in "cool."

Now, without looking at the original list, supply the Aymara word:

this	_____
flower	_____
leg	_____
but	_____
young man	_____
to write	_____
new	_____
sick	_____
quickly	_____
to sleep	_____

Note that for this exercise you were asked to perform what is considered to be the more difficult vocabulary learning task—producing a target language word when given the native language equivalent. The intention is to help you see how you learn vocabulary when it is not easy to do so.

Compare with the original list to see how many you got right. Can you retrace the process of how you learned each word?

Below is the list of Aymara words with a choice about how you learned each word. Learning vocabulary by *rote memory* refers to repeating the word orally or writing it down a few times without attempting to link it to something else. *Using an association* refers to any relationship you might have made between the word and something else. For example, *usuta* (sick) could be linked to used up (someone who is sick is used up). Note that it's common to initially assume that rote memory was used, so think carefully about how you really remembered the word.

	Got it Right	Used Rote Memory	Used an Association
wayna (young man)	_____	_____	_____
usuta (sick)	_____	_____	_____
cayu (leg)	_____	_____	_____
machaka (new)	_____	_____	_____
aca (this)	_____	_____	_____
pankara (flower)	_____	_____	_____
ucampisa (but)	_____	_____	_____
iquiña (to sleep)	_____	_____	_____
kellkaña (to write)	_____	_____	_____
laka (quickly)	_____	_____	_____

Now take a look at the Aymara words that you produced correctly. What strategy worked best for you—rote memory or association?

Learning Vocabulary By Association

Associations can be funny—in fact, the funnier or stranger the better because you're more likely to remember it that way. I used to have great ones when I learned Hebrew. My friend and I remembered the Hebrew word likra't, 'against, toward, to meet' with the phrase, 'Licking rats? I'm against it.'
~ Molly Zahn

The energy you use to learn new words is energy well spent. Long-term recall is based on your depth of processing—the more intricate the web you create, the longer you will remember the word. This section helps you understand how to create a more intricate web.

Using *mnemonic* links, or associations, can greatly improve your learning of vocabulary. Here are common associations used by college-level foreign language learners (whose native language was typically English).

Note:
Certainly rote memorization can work, and you need to use whatever strategy works for you. However, research reveals that using an associative technique, particularly using mental images, is more effective for most people than simple rote memory.

Association Techniques

Technique	Description	Example	Explanation
Native Sound	Link to a sound in your native language	Aymara = *pankara* (flower) English = pancake	Think of a pancake-shaped flower
Target Sound	Link to a sound in the target language	Hebrew = *cosher* (aptitude) Hebrew = *kasheh* (difficult)	Something that is difficult takes aptitude
Another Sound	Link to a sound in another language	Korean = *sulsa* (diarrhea) Spanish = *salsa*	*Salsa* sounds like *sulsa* and *salsa* could lead to diarrhea (the goal is to learn; the means can be some novel link)
Meaning of the Parts	Pay attention to the meaning of part of a word	German = *frühstück* (breakfast) German = *früh* (early)	Think that an early meal means breakfast
Structure	Take the word apart and make a connection to a word you already know in that target language	Hebrew = *mithalek* (divides up) Hebrew = *mahlaka* (department)	Dividing up an academic faculty into different departments

Technique	Description	Example	Explanation
Category	Place the word in a topic group in the target language	Hebrew = *mitsta'er* (am sorry) Hebrew = *mevakesh slicha* (ask to be excused) Hebrew = *mitnatsel* (apologize)	Group these three expressions for apologies and then you can compare and contrast their meanings and functions
Visualization	Picture the word in isolation or in written context	Spanish = *ojo* (eye)	👁 👁
Situation Link	Link the word to the situation in which it appeared (e.g., a song or poem you heard it in or some encounter where the word came up)	Korean = *seol-tang* (sugar) English = cappuccino and coffee shop	You remember the word for sugar because you learned it in the coffee shop when there was too much sugar in your cappuccino
Physical Sensation	Associate some physical sensation to the word	French = *triste* (sad) English = feel sad Japanese = *ichi* (one) and *ni* (two) English = *itchy knee*	You feel sad because of the tone of voice with which the word is said Think of an itchy knee. Maybe you even scratch your knee to recall these words
Mental Image	Create a mental image or picture that you associate with the word through the keyword and its meaning	A Korean student remembered "you betcha" in English by thinking of calling someone "cabbage head." *Baechu* = cabbage	Think of agreeing with what that cabbage head has just said
Free Association	Free associations that are specific to your life experiences and reactions to the words	Arabic = *arjuli* (leg) English = your friend, Julie	You think of Julie having long legs in conjuring up the Arabic word, or if you hear the word, it reminds you of Julie and then of her long legs.
Enjoyable Sound	You remember a word simply because you enjoy the sound it makes	Estonian = *rõõma* (joy) Spanish = *pupi lentes* (contact lenses)	One learner enjoys the elongated vowels and loves to say this word One learner remembered this because it sounded silly to her

Learning a language with characters

Learning by association can be very helpful. Studying Japanese and Chinese and the rather complex characters used for reading and writing may well call for the extensive use of associations. In some cases, the ideographs really do depict the concept being expressed. In other cases, it is up to the imagination of the learner. Some *Kanji* (Chinese characters used in Japanese) symbolize shapes of things. The *Kanji* for a tree looks like a branched-out tree. The *Kanji* for "woods" is made up of three *Kanji* for a tree, so the association here is that woods have many trees. You can also create your own associations. For example, take the *Kanji* for "to eat," which looks a bit like a house with a floor in it, and think of someone eating in the house. Then, the Kanji for "to drink" consists of a similar Kanji for "to eat" and another component alongside that looks like a person under a little porch roof. A learner could remember "to drink" by thinking of someone drinking out on the porch.

木	森	食	飲
tree	*woods*	*to eat*	*to drink*

Now let us take another look at the Aymara exercise (p. 182). Check if you used an association and then record which association you used from the previous chart (native sound, target sound, etc.).

	Used an Association	**Which Type?**
wayna	_____	_____
usuta	_____	_____
cayu	_____	_____
machaka	_____	_____
aca	_____	_____
pankara	_____	_____
ucampisa	_____	_____
iquiña	_____	_____
kellkaña	_____	_____
laka	_____	_____

Practicing word association strategies

Select 10 words you want to learn from your target language. Record these and their English equivalent here:

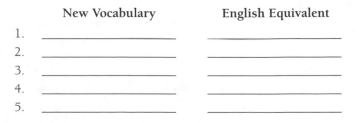

	New Vocabulary	**English Equivalent**
1.	_____	_____
2.	_____	_____
3.	_____	_____
4.	_____	_____
5.	_____	_____

6. _____   _____
7. _____   _____
8. _____   _____
9. _____   _____
10. _____   _____

Jump ahead and write the English word again on the next page, before you start memorization. Scramble the order to make sure you haven't just memorized the words according to their position in the list.

When learning these words, try to use all the association techniques listed in the chart on page 185. Don't get too frustrated if you can't come up with an association; some words are easier than others. After you have learned these words, keep reading as you did in the last exercise. Again, do not look back at this list until told to do so.

Sometimes successful learning strategies are discovered in unusual ways. Here are two examples of language learners remembering new vocabulary using word association:

I had a funny experience when I returned from a weekend in a small city called Fréjus in southern France. Upon returning, I had dinner with my host mother, and she asked me about how my weekend went. I had gone to Fréjus to see a concert of my favorite band and was trying to tell her about it. I told her that there were many people in town and that I had a really good time. She was looking at me strangely and seemed confused. I continued to talk about the concert and suddenly she smiled, stopped me, and explained that I had mispronounced the word 'concert' and was instead saying 'cancer.' The only difference between the two words is in the vowel, and I had not pronounced it correctly. She thought I had been saying there was a lot of cancer in Fréjus and that lots of people were there because of cancer. I was embarrassed about it at first, but we joked about it and I felt a lot better. Of course, now I always remember the word for concert because I link it to the sound of cancer. It's also like using free association because I remember the whole story around learning this word and the correct pronunciation.
~ Sarah Parr, France

When first learning Estonian, I was a bit overwhelmed at needing to remember to add the word 'kas' when I wanted to ask a question. As a result, I found myself a bit obsessed with the word. Instead of asking my future mother-in law, 'kuidas elate' (how are you)? I asked her 'kas elate' (are you alive)? After her response of 'ja' (yes) instead of 'haisti' (fine), I realized my mistake. I now remember 'kas' is not the same as 'kuidas' because I picture myself holding the phone and asking the correct question! I think this free association will stay with me forever! ~ Barbara Kappler, Estonia

Now try to come up with the target language word for the English equivalent.

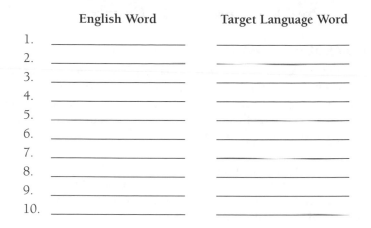

	English Word	Target Language Word
1.	_____	_____
2.	_____	_____
3.	_____	_____
4.	_____	_____
5.	_____	_____
6.	_____	_____
7.	_____	_____
8.	_____	_____
9.	_____	_____
10.	_____	_____

At this point check the original list and see how many of the words you got right. Below, indicate how you went about learning each word. See if there is any pattern to how you used associations.

	Got it Right	Used Rote Memory	Used an Association
1.	_____	_____	_____
2.	_____	_____	_____
3.	_____	_____	_____
4.	_____	_____	_____
5.	_____	_____	_____
6.	_____	_____	_____
7.	_____	_____	_____
8.	_____	_____	_____
9.	_____	_____	_____
10.	_____	_____	_____

Take a minute to answer these questions:
- Note the words, if any, for which you did not come up with mnemonic associations. Is there any pattern to these words?

- What do you now know about how you learn vocabulary?

- Did you use more associations to learn this set of words?

- Did your performance on the memory task improve?

Other Means of Learning Vocabulary:
Pre-Departure and In-Country

1. Take a good look at the words themselves

When looking for clues to meanings of words, you may have been taught to pay attention to parts of words (that is, the word base or root, prefixes, suffixes, or radicals of characters in Japanese or Chinese). Depending on the language you are learning, it may be more effective to look for other clues, including clues in the text surrounding the word you don't know. When in doubt about a word, ask these questions:

- Is it a noun, verb, adjective, etc.?
- What's the relationship between this word and others that accompany it? For example, *Gakusei wa daigaku de sensei to sodan shimashita* ('The student had a consultation with a professor at the university'). Maybe you know the words *gakusei* (student), *daigaku* (university), and *sensei* (professor), but not the word *sodan*. What are some likely choices? Meet? Discuss? The correct word is "consult" but you wouldn't be too far off with the other choices.
- How is the sentence with this unknown word related to other parts of the text? In the example above, the text might go on to indicate what the student got out of the consultation, such as advice about what courses to take.

If there is still doubt as to the meaning of the word, then it may work to break the unknown word into its prefix, root, and suffix, if possible.

2. Use quick and easy cognates

Easy-to-learn vocabulary can be found through *cognates*—words in two languages that are from the same source, look or sound similar, and thus have the same meaning.

- If words are *true cognates* (e.g., "police" in English and *policía* in Spanish), then it will help your vocabulary learning.
- Be wary of *false cognates* (i.e., different meanings in the two languages, such as "macho" in English and *macho* in Spanish, which is how they describe a male animal). Sometimes the existence of false cognates can actually help you remember the meaning of the target language word by remembering the discrepancy in meaning between the words in the two languages.
- *Deceptive cognates* have only partial overlap of meaning and thus you may erroneously interpret the meaning of the word. For example, the word for "education" in Spanish is *educación*, but the Spanish concept of *educación* is broader, more encompassing than the English concept. For another example, the word for "plumber"

in Hebrew is *instalator*. In English, it is possible to refer to a "plumbing installation" but not to an "installer" as a plumber, so there is overlap of meaning between the two words.

The above are excellent points that relate to the fact that in many languages word-for-word direct translation is difficult—if not impossible. There will always be nuances in the original language that don't quite transfer into the language being translated to. Even the many "loan words" borrowed from the English language and used in other languages often mean something very different from their original word. For example, the word "get" has now become popularized in Japan, but its meaning is more narrow than in English. In Japanese, "get" is used as a verb usually with an exclamation mark to mean "to win something" or "to obtain something good or fashionable." It wouldn't be used as in "to get a job," but as in *konsaato no chiketto wa getto shita* or "I got my hands on a ticket to the concert!"

3. Use a dictionary, but not as a crutch

Use a dictionary sparingly. It can provide intermediate or advanced learners with a more finely tuned meaning or set of meanings for a word with which you have some familiarity, but as will be pointed out elsewhere in this guide, it can be overused as a crutch. A good rule of thumb is to keep the dictionary a bit out of reach so that you stretch your mind a little before you stretch your arm! Of course, electronic dictionaries have increased the speed and facility we have at looking up words. This still doesn't mean, however, that we will ultimately benefit much from what we look up. Often, we forget what the dictionary provided us—right after we put it down. Also, we may not look in the right place or may not understand the reference because the choices are not clear, are too technical, include symbols we don't know, and so forth.

4. Use flash cards

Take these great tools anywhere—plane, train, or even just standing in line.

Tips for creating flash cards:
- To assist with long-term memory, the target language word should be defined using your native language and not the target language. Include on the card a minimal amount of context in which the word was heard or read. Write the word in a sentence to help you remember the definition of the word.
- If you have the opportunity, check the cards with a native speaker before you study them to make sure that each word is spelled correctly, that the meanings have been correctly interpreted, and that the words are used correctly in a sentence. Note on the native language side of the card any association technique you created to help remember the word.

Here's an example from Spanish:

> # New word: *fumar*
> ## 'to smoke' (verb)
>
> Association keyword:
> **fumes**
>
> *El está fumando:* "He is smoking."
> "I can smell the fumes from his smoke."

Try these quick tricks when using flash cards:
- When you get a word wrong, don't put it back at the bottom of the pack —place it about six cards from the top, giving you a chance to rely on short-term memory. Then place the word farther back until it is well beyond the reach of short-term memory. Learn ten words at one sitting, reviewing the last two when each new one is learned. Then review the words once the same day and for the next two days.
- Some study abroad students have used Microsoft PowerPoint to create "computer flash cards" that flash characters and vocabulary on the screen.
- For learning nouns, tape flash cards, small signs, or Post-It notes on the objects that correspond with your vocabulary word. Your room can be a visual dictionary with the target language words for desk, lamp, bed, etc.

A note about flash cards: While flash cards can be a great way for you to learn and practice your vocabulary, it is important to try other strategies for learning vocabulary. If you spend all your time making flash cards, you can miss out on more critical opportunities for learning vocabulary.

5. Practice writing your new vocabulary words
To help you remember new vocabulary, practice by writing the words in a variety of different contexts. As mentioned above, creating your own flash cards provides a good opportunity for doing this. For those of you who do not use flash cards, here are some other venues for writing the new words in sentences:
- Experiment with new vocabulary words in e-mail messages or postcards to friends
- Include new words in essays and other class assignments
- Use new vocabulary in a target-language diary you are keeping
- Add the new words along with meaningful sentences to your ongoing vocabulary log

The main thing is to exercise your knowledge of the new words in writing since this helps to fix the words in your mind.

6. Group your vocabulary

Simplify your life. Reduce the number of things you have to learn by grouping like ideas together. Groups can be based on:

- the part of speech – for example, nouns, verbs, adjectives; or function words including those hard-to-guess ones, such as personal pronouns, determiners, auxiliaries, prepositions, and conjunctions
- a theme or topic (e.g., words related to banking, dating, etc.)
- synonyms and antonyms – perhaps within that same theme (e.g., happy, content, joyful, sad, dissatisfied, sorrowful)

7. Create a visual map

You can combine memory strategies through techniques such as semantic mapping. The key concept is highlighted or centralized and is linked with subsidiary concepts, attributes, and so on by means of lines or arrows showing relationships. Here's an example:

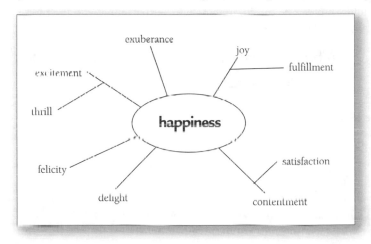

Additional Ideas for Vocabulary Learning

Learning vocabulary can be boring. Here are a few boredom breakers:

- Videotape an interesting television show or movie in the target language, or audiotape your teacher or someone else speaking. Listen to the speakers carefully. Write down any unfamiliar words you hear as best you can and either talk to a native speaker or look up the words yourself. Try to piece together what the speaker was saying, then watch the video or listen to the tape again to verify if your prediction was correct. Later, try to use these new words in conversations.
- Try putting together target-language words into a short, familiar song that you can recall easily like "Frère Jacques," or the music for your favorite commercial or TV theme song. Whenever you need to remember these words you can go back to your "key song."

- Find some music that you like in the target language and try to learn the lyrics and sing along. Note that this is really hard to do if you don't have the words written down, but cassettes and CDs of popular music usually come with an insert that has the lyrics printed. If you don't know the meaning to some of the words, check them out with a dictionary or native speaker. This is a fun way to learn popular words and slang.
- Ask your native-speaking friends or teacher to teach you some tongue twisters, idioms, proverbs, or other language games. Practice these, but also learn the meanings of the words you are playing with.
- Try practicing action verbs by acting them out. You could have a friend give you commands that you need to act out as a way to practice your comprehension or you could describe what you are doing out loud while you are doing it.

These types of activities are especially good for auditory learners and those who learn best by doing, but can be fun for anyone who is struggling with the monotony of memorizing vocabulary.

What Native Speakers Know about the Vocabulary in their Language

You have heard it over and over again: Talk to native speakers. Even if you can't, it's helpful to realize what a native speaker really knows about using the language.
- The frequency of the word in speech and writing and corresponding words (that is, words that can go with it—for example, fruit that is "ripe," "green," or "sweet," but not "stale").
- Limitations as to the use of the word: Is the word stylish, artistic, or out-of-date?
- What is the meaning of the word, and is the word used more in speaking, writing, or both equally?
  - Look at the common dictionary meanings of the word.
  - Look at how can you use it grammatically in a sentence.
- In what part of the country or world is the word used? What is its social role?
  - **By class:** Do people of a certain social status use the word more/less?
  - **By situation:** What is the resulting level of formality conveyed by using the word?
  - **By age:** Is it more common for elders or the young to use this word?
  - **By job or profession:** Is the word restricted to talk within a given profession (e.g., law)?

– **By gender:** Do you use a certain word depending on the gender of the person you are talking to, your gender, or the person or thing you are talking about?

You can see that your host country nationals will know a lot about the words you are needing to learn. By using them as informants, you will be able to pick up tips about the language that you wouldn't be able to in the classroom or by practicing with a non-native speaker.

Post-Study-Abroad Vocabulary Activities

Here are nine tips for continuing to learn new words once back home:
1. Write to friends. Challenge yourself to include two or three new words in each letter.
2. When reading, keep a notebook to write down words you don't know and review the words periodically.
3. Keep using flash cards. Set aside time to use them at least once or twice a week.
4. Learn all the words to a new song.
5. Rent a movie in your target language and learn new words by listening to the soundtrack while comparing with the subtitles.
6. Find a conversation partner who is a speaker of the target language. While you help this person with English vocabulary half of the session, the partner can help you with your vocabulary the other half.
7. Tape commercials from a TV or radio program in the target language and see which words you can understand and what the words reveal about the culture.
8. Volunteer to help in the community with recent immigrants speaking your target language. You may need to think globally here—if your language is French, for example, people from Vietnam, Ivory Coast, and others will often speak French.
9. Get involved with your university's language department, and write an article in your target language for a departmental newsletter.

LANGUAGE-LEARNING STYLES AND STRATEGIES:
SPEAKING TO COMMUNICATE

Pre-Departure Speaking Activities

You may think that it is best to wait until you are safely ensconced in your new environment to worry about really trying to speak the target language. Guess what? It may be less stressful if you start beforehand to "break the language barrier."

Some of you may be lucky enough to be at schools where there are programs designed to help you meet international or local students who speak the language you are learning. Or it may be that you live in an area that has a community of people who are native speakers of the language you are learning. In either case, you have a great opportunity to spend some time before you leave speaking the language with native speakers. Here are some useful suggestions from students who themselves have prepared to study abroad:

- Spend a day with a native speaker or group of speakers of the target language
- Have a regular meeting with a conversational partner over coffee
- Practice the language over the phone if you cannot meet in person
- Offer a language exchange with international students on your campus—the internationals practice their native language with you in exchange for your help in improving their conversational skills in English

If you don't know groups of students who speak the language you are trying to learn, try some of these strategies:

- Contact your school's study abroad office, language departments, or local community groups that are involved with international activities to locate native speakers of the language you are learning
- If you are enrolled in a language class, you could ask if your instructor knows of opportunities outside of class to practice your new language
- At the least, you'll want to speak up in class as much as possible!

The more time that you can spend practicing speaking, the better. Whenever and however you can, try to find opportunities to surround yourself with the target language. When you do this, you are allowing yourself to open up to the new language and lessen the "language shock" may experience when you are in another country. If you don't have any of these opportunities available to you before departure, read on and discover strategies you can use once you have arrived in your host country.

Advice to Help Improve Your Speaking Skills

Overcome the fear to speak

> *The only way to get over fear is to face it—especially with language. The only way to get better is to use it in all situations and to make situations where language skills are pushed to the limit.* ~ Mickie Berg, Italy

Here is Mickie's story on how she pushed herself to the limit:

> *During the five months I spent in Milan, Italy, I not only attended classes but also had an editorial internship at The Italy Daily Newspaper—a four-page section of the International Herald Tribune, a newspaper sold all over Europe.*

> *During the day I had several hours of language class and used my language with my two Italian roommates and at local coffee bars and shops. In the afternoons, I went to the newspaper where many of the employees were English, Australian, or American. We spoke English and the paper was written in English, but the rest of our jobs were in Italian. I translated news from the Italian wire services into English and rewrote the story into correct newspaper style. I helped the other reporters in obtaining information from businesses or whatever else they needed.*

> *I felt comfortable with my language skills in the office with my coworkers or on the telephone. But when I was faced with the prospect of calling strangers in Sicily for interviews on a story, I was terrified. I felt my language skills were not strong enough to go beyond my circle of people who I knew and who cared about me.*

> *I did not do interviews with sources in Sicily, and I did not write the story. However, in the last few weeks of my five-month internship I was forced to do an article of my own for the newspaper. I had story ideas by the dozen through the internship but had too much fear to do the interviews.*

> *Now was the time. I set up interview appointments with the founder of a volunteer civic police. I went to the Stazione Centrale, the location of the story, and hung out, talking comfortably with Italians, Moroccans, police, and homeless. I was shocked to find out that, even though my language skills were not perfect, I was able to communicate. I could understand everything they were saying and was accepted as a respectable journalist.*

> *After I succeeded with the story, I had a twinge of regret for not taking a chance right away and getting out of the office to do more interviews and write more articles. I have regrets but refuse to kick myself for something I didn't do even though my experience would have been better had I not hid behind my poor language skills.* ~ Mickie Berg, Italy

You may read that and think, "Yeah! I can do this!" Or you may think, "There is no way I could work in this language, let alone carry on an interview!" Here's a story for you:

> On my first trip to Japan I was very eager to get in there and use the minimal Japanese I had learned in my college courses. I knew about the propensity for Japanese to want to use English with foreigners and so I requested a homestay that spoke hardly any English. What an ordeal that was! Not only did I have to deal with a language I could barely speak, there were environmental and cultural factors that I was confronting every day that became overwhelming. My first homestay didn't succeed, but my eagerness to learn the language was not diminished. If anything, I wanted to learn more language to see if I could piece together the factors that resulted in my homestay going awry. Even though my second homestay didn't speak any English either, I was able to develop a close relationship with my 'okaasan' (mother) and 'otoosan' (father) that contributed to my language improvement as well as to my motivation for learning about the language and culture.
>
> While I lived in Japan I continued to use a 'Japanese-only policy' with nearly every Japanese I met. Although I met many Japanese who would not recognize I was speaking Japanese to them and who would constantly answer me in English, most Japanese would eventually oblige me by speaking to me in Japanese. Still, this is not an easy task for a Westerner who speaks a language very much 'in demand' by the hosts. It requires some stamina, persistence, and a little stubbornness at times. Nowadays, since I am more comfortable with my language ability, I am more flexible about obliging English conversation. — James Lassegard, Japan

If you need a little push, ask a native-speaking friend to force you to use only the target language when you are together. If your friend is supportive, you will feel even more comfortable speaking the language even if you make errors. Although it may be frustrating, it may be the best way to get past that tongue-tied stage!

Be willing to make mistakes

It is not surprising that errors are made because in order to produce even a single sentence in a target language, you have to perform a mind-boggling series of tasks of planning what to say, figuring out the word order, and then saying it correctly—at the right time! But if you don't make mistakes, what funny stories will you bring home to share with others?

> One day in Venezuela, I was waiting for my American friend to meet me and her host brother. I knew my Spanish language abilities were not that great…but I tried to make conversation anyway with her host brother. It was raining a lot at that moment, so I figured why not talk about the weather. I said, 'Esta llorando mucho,' which I thought was 'it's raining a

LANGUAGE
Speaking

lot.' He looked at me funny and said 'lluviendo?' 'Oh! Yeah, lluviendo,' I said. What I actually said was 'it is crying a lot.' But I was able to joke about it and say it's kinda like someone is crying a lot! Ha, ha, ha! Even if you make mistakes in the target language, usually people will think it is cute and just correct you. They understand you are learning. Have fun with the language.
~ Tammy Yach, Venezuela

Learn when to talk

You may not know where it is appropriate to pause and how to signal that you have not finished. This usually entails some way of filling the pause, which varies from language to language and culture to culture.

In English, we often use fillers like *um…er…you know…*and *like*, which often fill pauses between phrases when we speak. Below are some examples of fillers in other languages. Your goal is to figure out the fillers used in your target language.

There are two common pause fillers in Japanese, *eto* and *ano*. You extend the final "o" sound in pronouncing them and it signals that you are thinking. It is possible to overuse them as well, which is what happened to co-author Andrew Cohen in his efforts to "hold the floor" (to keep talking so you aren't interrupted) in his somewhat rudimentary Japanese. A Japanese language partner politely suggested he could use *ano* a bit less! Another thing is that the Japanese tolerate silent pauses far more than Americans tend to. Cohen had an embarrassing experience of chairing a meeting where a Japanese speaker paused so long before continuing Cohen thought he had finished and led the audience in a round of applause—just to find the speaker still had 10 minutes left of his presentation! He felt so embarrassed he wanted to climb under the table!

In Spanish, *este* will help to hold the floor for the speaker. *Et* will do the same in French. It's important to know how silence is perceived in the culture in order to regulate speech and the use of pause-fillers.

What kind of speaker are you: A planner or a corrector?

There are two groups of speakers among those learning a new language—the *planners* and the *correctors*. Planners prefer to carefully plan their speech in their heads and are often silent or show signs of hesitating. Correctors just jump into the conversation, preferring to produce the speech in whatever form it is in and work on perfecting it after it has been said. These behaviors are also linked to learning-style preferences. As you learned at the beginning of this guide when you took the Learning Style Survey, some learners are more reflective and others are more impulsive. The more reflective ones may like to prepare what they will say carefully before saying it to others. Impulsive learners may be more likely to send it right off and fix it up afterwards, if necessary. One strategy is to be aware of your own preferences and behaviors. A second strategy is to try to use a balance of the two and challenge yourself to take on the opposite approach so you increase your learning of the language.

Communicate more

Not only does speaking more give you a chance to practice your skills, it forces others to speak directly to you, giving you a chance to have more personal conversations.

> I was in a restaurant with my Venezuelan boyfriend, and we were sitting at a table with many other Venezuelans. They were all speaking Spanish, and I understood everything that they were saying. I didn't jump into their conversation because I didn't know any of the other people sitting at the table. So, naturally, I just sat and listened as I would do in the U.S. Well, they ended up asking my boyfriend if I knew how to speak Spanish! I said, 'Sí, hablo Espanol' (Yes, I speak Spanish). And they all looked at me in surprise. I continued to stay quiet and only answer questions directed toward me. And then throughout the conversation they would ask, 'She doesn't understand, does she?' yet I understood every word! I was so frustrated. I had already told them I knew how to speak Spanish and I had been answering their questions, but they continued to believe that I did not understand because I was not speaking! ~ Tammy Yach, Venezuela

Remember that initiating the conversation can seem like a very hard task, but once you do it you'll find that people will be willing to talk with you, even if they have to listen to your broken language.

Keeping the conversations going

Borrow words

Use a word from your native language. For example, you insert the English word *computer*, *taxi*, or *OK* into the target language with the hope that the word will be understood.

Translate literally

You perform word-for-word translation. For example, to tell someone that you are 20 years old in Spanish, you say "*Soy veinte años Viejo*," when the correct form is "*Tengo veinte años*," literally "I have twenty years." While you may not be right, you can often get the point across. Note that *viejo* was capitalized, which means something else (e.g., "Hey, old man, I am 20" or "I am 20 years, I'm old").

"Foreignize" words

Use a word from your native language and fit it into the target language structure or pronunciation. A native Korean speaker may not understand you when you say "ice cream" with American pronunciation, but if you pronounce it "ah-ee-se-ke-lim" in Korean pronunciation, they will know.

> I do this all the time with German verbs (e.g., interpretieren for 'interpret.') For better or for worse, however, these words often really exist in German! (Interpretieren really is one of several words meaning 'interpret.') ~ Molly Zahn, Germany

Co-author Cohen had such an experience in Brazil some years ago. When he kept asking for a "hot dog" at a kiosk in São Paulo, the woman didn't understand at all. When he remembered to say "hachee dogee," the way Brazilians say it, she understood immediately!

Use a simple word if necessary

Use "animal" instead of "deer," "tool" instead of "hammer," or simple words such as "big" for "huge" or "gigantic." You could also attach an intensifier like "very," "a lot," "many," or other descriptive word to achieve a closer approximation.

Use descriptions

If you do not know how to say something the way you wish to, try saying it with the vocabulary and sentence structure you know. For example, one student wanted to thank her host family for driving her to the bus stop. Not knowing how to say, "to drive," she said, "Thank you for your car." Another example would be that if you do not know the past tense very well you could give the consequence instead of describing the action. So, rather than, "Cynthia gave birth to a 6-pound baby boy," you would say, "Cynthia is now the mother of a 6-pound baby boy."

> *I would always need to ask my host mom for more toilet paper when I ran out. I did not know how to say toilet paper so would just ask, 'Hay papel para el baño?' (Is there paper for the bathroom?) ~ Tammy Yach, Venezuela*

Coin a new word

Make up a new word in the target language to communicate the unknown word (you create "air ball" because you do not know "balloon").

Act out or draw the word

When you don't know the word, you may try nonverbal means for getting the idea across. Co-author Andrew Cohen was in a Brazilian supermarket attempting to buy fresh mushrooms without remembering the word. So he drew what he hoped the store clerk would interpret as a mushroom. He was ushered over to the garlic! So he tried to refine his picture. When it looked more mushroom-like, the clerk asked, "*Cogumelo?*" At first, Andrew was slow to understand whether the clerk got the message. First, such a funny-sounding word didn't seem, on the face of it, to mean anything like "mushroom!" And second, the store was out of mushrooms!

> *I had no clue how to say 'alarm clock' in Spanish. The first night I understood my host mom saying, 'Should I wake you up in the morning?' I wanted to say, 'No, I have an alarm clock.' I used the word for watch and added 'but it is not a watch, it's a…' Then I made a square in the air with my fingers and put my hand to my ear, then put my hands together, and laid my head on my hands as if to sleep. 'Oh, un despertador' (an alarm clock), she said!*
> *~ Tammy Yach, Venezuela*

Ask for help

Natives may be more than willing to serve as "experts" on their language and to provide you the word or words you need. They may be flattered that you are so interested.

Abandon certain words

Give up the search for a particular word if it is not really necessary for the conversation.

Don't avoid words or topics

Sometimes you will simply avoid words or topics you don't know. Try to make these into learning situations.

- If you don't know the word for cherries, you can say, "I would like a kilo, please" (pointing to the desired fruit). To improve your language, you could point and ask, "What is the word for cherries?" and then ask for the kilo of cherries.
- You are writing an e-mail to a friend and want to tell about your weekend trip to the mountains. You realize you don't have the necessary vocabulary to say very much, so you just say you had a nice weekend in the mountains. It would be better to use words you do know and to ask for your friend's help.

Learning from Your Mistakes

Establish a relationship with some native speaker that will permit that person to actually correct your mistakes. In some cultures that's hard because people worry you will be offended. I remember that when I was in the Peace Corps in Venezuela it took months before I finally was able to convince one person—a close colleague at my work—that I really did want her to correct every mistake I made. Once she began to do so, she was an invaluable aid to my language learning. ~ Chip Peterson, Venezuela

Correct yourself

You are bound to make mistakes. But did you know that you are capable of correcting about half of your mistakes by yourself? You simply need time to hear just what it was you actually said. If you are in a situation where a teacher or other speaker of the language corrects your errors as soon as you say them, you could:

- Request that they wait until you have had a chance to self-correct
- Ask that they let you finish speaking before they provide the correction

Accept feedback on your errors

For those errors you can't self-correct, you need to be able to digest the corrections that come your way.

Co-author Andrew Cohen tells of missing a bus and consequently arriving late to a language center where he was studying Arabic. Who should greet him in the corridor but one of his Arabic teachers who proceeded to correct his Arabic explanation of how he had missed the bus. Cohen wanted at that moment to be able to hold up a sign saying he was simply in the "communication-of-message" mode while he was explaining being late, and that he wasn't in the "attentive-learner" mode, when he would presumably be more receptive of the corrections his teacher was offering him! However, given that Cohen is an avid language learner and respectful of his instructor's status, he did eventually pay attention to the corrections from his teacher. The point is to be open to being corrected, even when you are focused on another goal.

- To make the most of corrections, write down the correction in a notebook—possibly in a special section for that kind of information (see example under "Feedback on Written Work," p. 224) and verify the correct form with a native speaker of the language (possibly the teacher) at a later time.

Creating Opportunities for Speaking the Language In-Country

The truth is that for many reasons, you may find yourself associating primarily with other English speakers rather than with native speakers. In addition, you may actually be taking most of your courses in English. As a result, your exposure to the language may not be quite what you had expected. What can you do about that?

Gather up your courage and speak to complete strangers

- Seek out elderly people sitting on park benches or at malls, as it's possible they may have time on their hands and may not be in a hurry to cut off your sentences, finish your remarks, or correct your grammar.
- Young children are another resource for casual conversations since they will be less likely to correct your grammar than to focus on the meaning of what you are saying. They may correct your vocabulary, but that could be helpful. Co-author Barbara Kappler found a note she had written to her host family in Britain edited by her 12-year-old host brother! He seemed to enjoy the opportunity to correct her U.S. American English, and it became a weekly ritual for them.

Take advantage of program opportunities

One student, after reading the recommendation about talking to strangers, gave this advice:

> People are chickens, and it is much easier NOT to strike up random conversations with people on park benches—for me, this is VERY difficult. But my language program offered several special opportunities to interact

with native speakers—a visit to a clinic to talk with the patients, special arrangements with a permanent resident of the city, etc. Of course this depends on the program, but it seems many offer such opportunities. The point that needs to be made is that if such opportunities exist, take advantage of them! ~ Molly Zahn, Germany

Become a regular at local establishments

Maybe you don't like to talk to strangers and your program offers few opportunities to meet native speakers. You need to create a way to get to know people over time. Go to the same stores, the same coffee shops or delis, or the same discos so that you can slowly get to know people.

Instead of eating my lunch in the English-speaking cafeteria, I often went to the nearby taco place and ordered, in Spanish, different types of tacos. I didn't know what some of them were, so I asked questions. ~ Julie Chi, Mexico

When I first arrived in Malaysia, I felt a bit timid about going very far so I ended up eating my meals frequently in the same local restaurant. Because I went often, I soon became a regular and ended up having lots of time to get to know the waiters and other restaurant staff. One of the waiters ended up inviting me to go to his village to see a typical Malay wedding—I was amazed that such a great opportunity grew out of hanging out at a local restaurant. ~ Karin Larson, Malaysia

Be careful in choosing housing

Some study abroad programs offer a choice among various types of housing. If yours does, take language into account in making your selection. A homestay, an apartment with native speaking roommates, or some other arrangement that will surround you with the target language daily is preferable to an apartment with U.S. American roommates, a dorm just for foreign students, etc. Think carefully about the goals of your program. While you may lose some freedom in selecting a homestay or give up some familiarity by selecting host nationals for roommates, this decision could have the greatest impact on reaching your language-learning goals.

Be persistent about making new friends

Your stay is temporary. It can be hard for locals to want to befriend you, only to have you leave in a few weeks or months. The burden is upon you to make the extra effort to meet new people. You might notice that these connections lead to others too. And not surprisingly, research has shown that those who date a native speaker show rapid language improvement. More comments about cross-cultural dating are on p. 81.

I dated a native from Venezuela while studying abroad, and since I did not want to speak to total strangers, I could talk to him. This way my Spanish really skyrocketed! I am so glad that I dated him because if I hadn't I would have been like all the other American students there—talking to each other without really learning much Spanish. ~ Tammy Yach, Venezuela

Here's co-author Julie Chi's story on her experience in Seoul, South Korea:

With only a year of formal Korean instruction under her belt, Julie set off for Korea with her husband, a native Korean, to live with her in-laws, whom she had never met.

I knew that in order to make a good impression, I had to be able to make myself understood in Korean. I had my husband, a native Korean, to help me some of the time, but there were many times when I had to make myself communicate in Korean without his help.

I woke up every morning very early to help my mother-in-law cook breakfast for the family. I learned the vocabulary for all the ingredients, and I also learned how to describe the processes for cooking the new foods. Even though it was hard for me to wake up before everyone else because of my exhaustion from speaking Korean the day before, I made myself get up to speak with my mother-in-law.

In addition to helping out in the mornings, Julie also enrolled in a swimming class with her mother-in-law and used this class as an opportunity to have casual "chatty" conversations with her mother-in-law's friends, expanding the topics for discussion as she became more comfortable in Korean. Julie also reconnected with a Korean woman that she had become friends with in the United States, who in turn introduced her to other Korean friends Julie could practice her speaking with.

I made every effort to speak that I could. I even talked with my two-year-old nephew! I made sure to use a lot of gestures and ask a lot of questions like, 'How do you say _____ in Korean?' I made up words, talked around the topic until they understood, and most importantly, I knew when to take a break so as not to burn out. I was very lucky for my experiences, and now that I'm back in the U.S., I continue to practice Korean with a new friend when we meet each week for coffee.

Although Julie had opportunities that you may not, if you are living with a host family you can try to do some of the things Julie did. If you're not, make friends and spend some time with their families or attend some of their activities regularly.

Beyond Knowing the Vocabulary

Have you thought about how you would deal with sensitive situations like apologies or complaints while studying abroad? What about accepting or declining invitations in the target language? Do you know the right kinds of expressions to use? If so, do you know when and how to use them?

Suppose the following things happen to you in the United States:

- You do not want to go to a party thrown by some high school friends. You feel out of touch with many of them and want to spend time with new college friends. What do you say to get out of going to the party?
- You are five minutes late for a doctor's appointment. What do you say to the receptionist? Then, you wait 45 minutes to see the doctor. What do you say to the doctor when you finally get in?
- Your friend meets you for lunch, looking great in a new sweater. What do you say? What if this person is "more than a friend?" What if you don't want the person to think of you as "more than a friend"?

Knowing how to refuse invitations, apologize, complain, make requests, and give compliments in your *own* language requires intricate knowledge of cultural rules and norms.

- For example, while you may value being direct in your communication, you might feel it's a bit rude to tell your high school friends, "I have outgrown our relationship and would rather spend time with my new friends." You may feel it is more polite to explain, "Thanks for the invite, but I can't make it on Thursday—I have other plans."
- In the doctor's office many would make a small apology to the receptionist for being late but would not expect to have the appointment canceled. Most would not expect an apology from the doctor. Making a direct complaint to the doctor may also be considered disrespectful, given the status of the doctor and prior knowledge that doctor's appointments are often behind schedule.
- How do you give a compliment to a friend? Maybe you would say, "Hey, nice sweater." But to impress someone or show that you have a romantic interest, you may emphasize how good your friend looks in the sweater: "Wow, you look really nice today. Great sweater. Is that new?"

Some days, it might be complicated enough to feel competent in your *own* language. How do you do this in a second? The rules that govern the way we say things to get across our intended meaning are so subtle that they are very difficult to decipher by non-native speakers.

The following example is from Hebrew. You want to take a window seat on a bus and need to get by the woman in the aisle seat. You say *sliha*, which you know means "excuse me" in other situations. But this time the woman reacts as if she had just stepped on your foot. You were unaware that in Hebrew *sliha* is a bit rude. In this situation, the means of requesting access to the window seat would more likely be either *Efshar lashevet?* (Is it possible to sit there?) or *Eyfshar la'avor?* (May I get by?).

Have patience. The subtlety of language and culture means it can literally take years to feel confident about how to say these things.

An exercise in 'getting what you want'

The most frustrating situation is often when you need to request something specific from another person. Try your skills out for the following situations in the language and cultural context that you are dealing with:

Situation 1

Your family has decided to visit. There is no easy public transportation from the airport. You need to ask your host (friends or family) for a ride.

What would you say in your home country?	What rules/values/ differences might be involved in the target culture?	What would you say in the target language?

Situation 2

Your friend is often late to meet you to walk to school. You would like to walk together but are arriving late to class and don't feel comfortable. You want to ask your friend to arrive on time.

What would you say in your home country?	What rules/values/ differences might be involved in the target culture?	What would you say in the target language?

Situation 3

You found a cheap airplane ticket to visit friends in a neighboring city. In order to take the trip you need to ask your instructor for an extension on a paper due next week.

What would you say in your home country?	What rules/values/ differences might be involved in the target culture?	What would you say in the target language?

Should you be expected to say things with the same finesse the way a native speaker does? In many cases, the words you say will be accepted even if you violate certain rules. If people recognize that you're a non-native speaker from your accent, they'll be less likely to be offended by the way you say things. In other cases, it may be accepted but would still be inappropriate. In still other cases, it may not be acceptable at all. Take advantage of your time in another country to learn these nuances.

What co-author Clu has done is practice with a friend who isn't offended by what she says but teaches her how to say it better. She asks her friend to tell her whether or not it is appropriate to talk about a certain topic, for example, or how to say something with which she previously had a blundering experience. It's OK to make mistakes, and you can learn from them with some assistance of a friend.

'I'm SO sorry'

Nothing is so simple as an apology, right? Don't you just show you feel bad and say, "I'm sorry?" Well, it's not quite that simple. There are a few things you may want to know about apologies.

You may breeze through your entire study abroad program never offending a soul and never causing a problem. If that's you, skip to the next section. However, if you are like most travelers—including all of us writing this—you will probably need to apologize at some time. And when you do so, given that you've already offended someone or caused a problem, you want to make sure you don't "rub salt in the wound" by apologizing in a manner that makes things worse.

The following chart is a list of strategies for apologizing that apply universally to apologies in any language The trick is knowing which one or ones to use in a given situation in a given language.

Strategies for apologizing

Strategy	Apologizer:	Notes about Use in English
Apology expression	Use a word, expression, or sentence with a verb such as "sorry," "excuse," "forgive," or "apologize."	Can be intensified whenever the apologizer feels the need to do so by adding "really" or "very."
Acknowledge responsibility	Absolute acknowledgment of responsibility ↑ ↓ Rejection of responsibility	**High:** It's my fault. **Middle:** I was confused; you are right. **Low:** I didn't mean to. **Lower:** I was sure I gave you the right information. **Reject:** It was not my fault.
Explanation	Describes what caused the offense (e.g., the bus was late). The explanation is intended to set things right.	Used by the speaker as an indirect way of apologizing.
Offer of repair	Makes a bid to do something or provide payment for damage.	This strategy is only appropriate when tangible damage has occurred.
Promise of non-recurrence	Commits to not having the offense happen again.	

Target Language Phrases	When Appropriate?

(Adapted from Cohen and Olshtain, 1981).

LANGUAGE
Speaking

Note that in some cultures no apology may be effective in rectifying the situation:

I was flying out of Athens, and when we landed I accidentally hit the man behind me in the head with the bag I was getting out of the overhead compartment. I apologized immediately, and he didn't say anything. We had to wait to get off the plane and out of the corner of my eye I could see him touching his head and rubbing it. I felt uncomfortable and guilty, so I turned to him and apologized again. At this point he started yelling at me, going on about how this had happened because I was impatient, and now he was hurt and it was just no good to be so impatient. After a few moments I realized that saying anything more was going to aggravate the situation, so I simply turned and faced forward until the line started moving and I was able to get off the plane.

If the same thing happened in the U.S., my experience has been that the other person would have accepted my apology, especially the second time. In retrospect I should have realized that getting yelled at was a possibility. I spent a year in Greece, and there were a few instances where I personally got 'scolded' by someone in public or witnessed public arguments between strangers. From what I'd seen and experienced, it seemed to be true that when someone yelled at someone else in Greece, the other person didn't automatically apologize but defended themselves by yelling back. In my airplane incident, I don't think anything would have appeased that particular man. Possible alternatives would have been to say nothing at all and act as if I hadn't hit him with my bag or after he started yelling at me, I might have argued back that he was standing too close to me in the first place, and so on. ~ Suzanne Hay, Greece

In contrast to the experience above, co-author Lassegard had the following to say after he and Suzanne Hay compared their respective experiences in Greece and Japan:

If this same incident happened in Japan, a very lengthy apology accompanied by much bowing and expressing of concern for the health of the hapless victim would be warranted. Also, in most cases in Japan, an explanation for a wrong caused by someone comes off as simply an excuse and would never be accepted in lieu of an apology.

The following situation gives an example of how culture impacts the use of language:

You completely forget a crucial meeting with your instructor. An hour later you call her to apologize. The problem is that this is the second time you've forgotten such a meeting. Your instructor gets on the line and asks, "What happened to you?"

If you were an Israeli Hebrew speaker, your culture may support two types of behavior in your reply. First, you would emphasize your explanation. For example, "Well, I had to take my roommate to the doctor and then there was a problem with the landlord..." Second, you would not try to repair the situation by saying something like, "I am so sorry. I'd like to reschedule the meeting whenever it's convenient for you." In the Israeli culture, it is up to the boss (instructor) who determines the next step. It would be presumptuous for the lower status person to suggest what happens next.

Take a look at this example of how cross-cultural misunderstandings can occur:

> At the campus coffee shop, Rebecca, an exchange student from Israel, accidentally bumped into her friend Mary, a U.S. American who is holding a cup of hot coffee. The coffee spills all over Mary, scalding her arm and soaking her clothing. Mary shouts, startled: "Oooh! Ouch!" Rebecca says, "Sorry." Mary glares at her. Rebecca assumes Mary is really mad at her for bumping into her.

What happened? Rebecca, an Israeli Hebrew speaker, directly translated the expression of "sorry" from Hebrew to English. In Israel, it would be understood that she is very sincere in her apology. However, to Mary, a speaker of U.S. English, this does not sound at all like an apology. Mary is expecting an intensifier: "I'm really sorry. Are you OK?" And even possibly an offer of repair: "Oh! Here, let me help get something on that burn and clean up the mess."

Improve your competence

You cannot learn the most appropriate way to say things on your own. It is essential to immerse yourself in the culture and connect with native speakers. However, don't expect to learn these things naturally. You will need to become a language detective and seek answers to specific questions.

Ask native speakers how they would apologize in situations from those involving only a minor offense (e.g., slightly bumping into someone or interrupting their conversation) to those involving a major offense (e.g., hitting their car or hurting them physically). Try to imagine situations you could be in, or those which you have been in, if you have already had experience with native speakers in the past.

Ask a native speaker whether there would be any difference in each of these apologies depending on whether the person being apologized to is:
- of higher status (e.g., a boss or a parent), equal status, or lower status
- a friend/acquaintance or a stranger

Sometimes you may find that specific intensifiers are only used for certain speech acts that are different from the English words "very" or "really." For example, the word *domo* in Japanese can be used to heighten the expression of gratitude or regret, but it is not used to enhance words or phrases in a sentence like "very" is.

We use apologizing in this section as a way to introduce the topic of using language appropriately in different cultural situations. You should also learn how to express yourself in a number of other situations such as:

- giving and receiving compliments
- making requests
- making refusals
- making complaints
- giving directions
- giving advice
- thanking
- greetings

Post-Study-Abroad Speaking Activities

The number one complaint from returnees is that friends and family are not so interested in hearing the details of their experience abroad. What is also frustrating is that you will have fewer opportunities to speak in the target language. You may even feel lost among your fellow Americans. To keep up your language skills and to feel connected to your study abroad experience, you need to find people to talk to.

Where do you find these language informants?

- Locate clubs on campus and in the community that promote your country of interest and target language.
- Use the Internet to find native speakers or people interested in conversational exchange. There are many great Web sites that allow you to have live chats with people living on the other side of the world.
- Check newspapers or the Internet for upcoming cultural events or celebrations of holidays such as the Chinese New Year. Attend other activities like foreign films or art exhibits that are specific to your country or region of interest, and actively seek out others with whom you can practice.

LANGUAGE-LEARNING STYLES AND STRATEGIES:
READING FOR COMPREHENSION

Being able to understand the text in another language helped me feel self-sufficient. It allows a freedom from dependency on others.
~ Jon DeVries, world traveler

Like an awakening, there's a point when you realize you're relying more on instinct than a dictionary to breeze through your French novel. Even if fleeting, at that moment I've felt like a cultural insider…as if I might have been born in the wrong place. ~ Kristin Mishra, France

If I can read a local newspaper in a place that I travel, it's empowering, exciting. Feels like another window opens on a different world.
~ Steve Theobald, world traveler

Pre-Departure Reading Activities

Like to read poetry? Science fiction? Cookbooks? Whatever you like to read in English is the best thing to read in your target language before study abroad. Why? Because you'll have the motivation to read it! Here are a few tips for finding resources in your target language:

- Ask your language teachers.
- Check your university or local library's collection for subscriptions to international and national newspapers.
- Search the Internet using your host country's name as your keyword.
- Skim through the phone book for bookstores selling foreign books.
- Talk to a local native speaker for their suggestions
- Ask fellow students, local native speakers, or your language teacher if you can borrow materials.
- Choose a dictionary that's best for you to aid in your reading practice.

  Bilingual dictionaries (English to/from another language) can be misleading because there may not be direct equivalence between the English word and the word in the target language. **Monolingual dictionaries** (single language) can be more helpful in truly understanding the meaning of words, but then you need to be versed enough in the language to understand the definition!

  Monolingual and bilingual dictionaries. There are some dictionaries that are both monolingual and bilingual in the same book, which solves the problem of either/or.

Electronic dictionaries make word retrieval quicker. Many electronic dictionaries allow you to store vocabulary you come across when you are out and about. You can review this vocabulary at your leisure, with the dictionary taking the role of flash cards.

Learner dictionaries. Such dictionaries may be more helpful to low-intermediate learners because they make some effort to use simplified language. Nonetheless, be prepared for them not to be simplified enough at times. A classic case is a learner dictionary of English that defined "to moor" as "to secure or fasten to the dock." The learner didn't know what "secure," "fasten," or "dock" meant, so the definition was useless! In this case, the learner needed also to look up the unknown words in the definition until she finally could understand the word "moor."

Get the Most from Your Reading

Reading in a second language can be like taking a ride on a roller coaster. There's frustration—and sometimes fear and self-doubt—when you feel you're getting nowhere and that you need to look up every word. There's a big thrill of excitement when you can quickly cruise through and know you understand nearly everything. And sometimes it's just hard to keep going as you read the same sentence over and over and over. This section contains strategies for helping you with the ups and downs of reading in another language. These strategies have worked for hundreds of students, and they can work for you too!

Strategies for increasing your comprehension

Decide why you need to read it
You probably feel overwhelmed sometimes because you try to understand every word or idea. Determine if you really need to understand the entire text or just get an idea of what the main topic is. In most contexts, you may only need to get the main idea. Then you know whether to read the material thoroughly or just skim it.

Skim read
Gathering clues about the context is critical in increasing your understanding and retention when reading in another language. Skim reading before you read the text from start to finish helps provide this context. You are probably experienced at skim reading, but here are a few reminders:
- Read through all the headings.
- Jump to the end to see if there is a useful summary, discussion, or conclusion.
- Outline the main sections of the text.

Use both top-down and bottom-up tactics

Just as with listening, you may have preferences for whether you are a "top down" or "bottom up" reader. Ideally, you will be able to use both. *Top down* reading is when you already know something about a topic and apply this to a new reading. For example, you are reading an article about AIDS. Since you already know something about the disease, you expect certain topics to be discussed—such as the number of cases reported and the number of countries affected by the disease. This prior knowledge helps you intuit the meaning of the new article. When you focus exclusively on the words and sentences of the text in front of you and use only those words to assist you in meaning, this is referred to as *bottom-up* reading.

If you are a beginning learner, you may find more success in the top-down approach. Also, if your goal is just to get the main idea, you would still use the top-down approach. However, if you intend to get fine details, or if you know nothing about the topic, you may find that the bottom-up approach is probably more what you need.

Don't overuse your dictionary

A good rule of thumb is to use a dictionary sparingly. Why? Because dictionary use:

- distracts you from the text and takes twice the time.
- may cause errors, especially if you use a bilingual dictionary (i.e., an English/Spanish dictionary) because languages often do not have direct equivalents. In some cases, different countries have different dialects of the language.
- may result in your forgetting the meaning immediately after looking it up anyway!

The following is a comment about bilingual dictionaries from co-author Lassegard, who is currently living in Tokyo:

> Now that I am abroad, I've learned so much language here 'in context' whether written or spoken that I would find it difficult to give English translations unless I really thought about it. I think trying to get a precise English translation (when there isn't one) is one of the biggest obstacles learners have and results in the overuse of dictionaries, which tends to compound the frustration. ~ James Lassegard, Japan

Consequently, it may be most beneficial for you to learn as much vocabulary as possible in context rather than from the dictionary. But if you are going to use the dictionary, you may wish to have some effective system for recording a meaning. It is often the case that learners keep looking up the same words over and over because they forget the entry immediately after finding it. The more effort you use to figure out the word, the more likely you will be to remember it.

Read between the lines

Keep your eyes open to clues in the reading itself. For example, you are reading in a popular magazine about outdated fashion, and the writer tells you not to wear a shirt with a loud pattern. Does this mean that you should not wear a shirt with musical instruments on it or one that plays loud music? No, you know from the context that it means that the pattern is wild and disturbing, so you would not want to offend or disgust other people by wearing it.

Get some background information first

Before reading a new text:

- Ask someone (a friend, native speaker, or someone with more reading proficiency than yourself) to give you an introduction to it, such as an explanation of the topic. This discussion would give you background information for understanding the text.
- This person can help you define difficult vocabulary in advance.

I had a difficult reading to do for one of my Spanish classes in Venezuela. It was on folklore, so I had no clue where the text would be taking me with the different mythical characters and the things that they were engaging in. However, my Venezuelan friend helped me by explaining certain parts of the text to me, and from this I was able to grasp the concept and understand what I would be encountering in the reading. This was a lot faster and easier than using the dictionary, and it also helped me use my target language to help understand the reading. ~ Tammy Yach, Venezuela

Strategies for remembering what you read

Write summaries

Ever feel like you understand each sentence as it goes by and then get to the end and don't remember anything? This is common! The mind has to perform mental gymnastics in order to get at the meaning from a target-language text. What helps is to make ongoing summaries every few lines. This keeps the meaning of previous material fresh while continuing on to new material. To keep your mind thinking in the target language, try to write the summaries in the target language rather than English. Writing them in English only slows you down by forcing your mind to switch back and forth between languages.

I found that making summaries of each Spanish reading was very helpful. I could always refer back to my notes if I was confused or use it as study material for the test. Other students would always ask me for my notes so they could understand the reading. If they had just made their own notes they too would have easily remembered what they read in the beginning of the reading. A foreign language is difficult to learn, thus when reading and retaining what a second language text says, taking notes is necessary for ultimate comprehension. ~ Carrie Borle, Spain

Generate questions

Continually generate questions about the text as you read along.

Make predictions

When the reading feels slow and plodding—even if the topic seems interesting—it's easy to fall asleep or get bored reading in a target language. One way to stay alert and curious is to predict actively what the writer is likely to write about next. Try turning each heading and subheading into a question, using words such as *who, what, when, where, why,* and *how.* Then, predict what the answers will be to each question. While you're reading, notice whether or not your prediction was close to being correct.

For example, you are reading a magazine article with a title that translates to "New Drug Approved." You'll ask yourself, "What is the drug and what is its use? Who created and approved this new drug? Where can one get the drug? How was it created? Should I use this drug?" You might have some possible answers already floating around in your mind, so you read to find out whether or not your predictions were right. You might be surprised that the drug is more (or less) than you expected!

Strategies for getting feedback

How do you know you are doing a good job reading? This can be a bit of a challenge since reading is basically unobservable unless you are reading aloud, which isn't very common unless you are practicing to give an oral reading. In that case you could have someone check your reading for how natural it sounds. Consider meeting with a teacher during office hours to practice, or get paired up with someone who speaks the target language fluently and read it aloud.

When you are doing silent reading, you could ask a native-speaking friend to read a text you had difficulty with or a portion of it and see if the friend has the same understanding of it as you came up with. If it is a popular novel or essay that your friends have read themselves, you could try and summarize it for them and see whether they agree with your summary. The daily newspaper can be a good source of feedback on reading if you can find a friend who reads it. Check whether your interpretation of a lead story is accurate. You can always ask friends to confirm or correct your understanding of given words as well.

> *You know you are doing a good job reading when you can read through the text and understand the general concept. You do not let hard words bog you down or cause you to keep turning to the dictionary. You continue reading and make notes while you read. You can always go back to your notes if you do not understand. ~ Tammy Yach, Venezuela*

During Your Time Abroad

The benefit of being in your study abroad country is the mounds of written information now available to you. The trick is to find material at your level of ability. For example, one of the first challenges you may have is simply doing a bank transaction at an automated window.

> *One of the problems I have currently in Japan is using the ATMs for anything more than withdrawing cash. There are eight selections in kanji (Chinese characters) that are specific to banking transactions that I never quite learned in language class. I know the characters for 'passbook,' so when I want the machine to record my latest transactions on my passbook I just push that button, even though I can't read the other characters. Incidentally, many ATMs have a bilingual English selection, but I only use it as a last resort. ~ James Lassegard, Japan*

The bottom line is that some reading challenges will be insurmountable, at least at first. The important thing is to persevere. Here are some readily available sources for reading:
- Advertisements
- Packaging instructions
- Newspaper headlines
- Maps (When on walks, don't just rely on a better speaker to lead the way. Take out the map and guide the group yourself)
- Instructions at the local ATM machine in the target language—if you have someone to help you in case you have trouble

Reading materials to seek out
- Articles on the Web: After you watch the TV news, go to the Internet and read about one of the interesting headlines you saw on the news (of course in the target language).
- Comic books: The drawings give you clues for understanding the text.
- Children's books: Just remember that nursery rhyme language may not reflect everyday language (for example, while "patty cake, patty cake, baker's man" may still be a popular rhyme in parts of the U.S., the words don't come in handy every day)—but as one language learner said, "It still helps!"
- Subtitles on American movies: You can listen to the actors and at the same time read the local language version.
- Books on tape for foreigners to learn the language.
- Newspapers: Make sure you find one with feature articles or human interest pieces written at a level that you can comprehend. Some countries even have newspapers written especially in learner language!
- Billboards, phrases on T-shirts, bumper stickers.

When I studied English, what helped me was hearing it on a tape and also reading it, so that you get multiple channels. Get a book and audiotape from a library. You improve your vocabulary and you also hear the pronunciation.
~ Tōnu Mikk, Estonian exchange student to the U.S.

Preparing to return home

Before you depart, pick up some books, magazines, newspapers, and other media that you can read when you return. You may even choose to bring home a computer guide or some instructional book written in the target language.

Once you're home

While it may be hard to speak the language frequently once you've returned home, you can keep up on your reading. Here are some suggestions to help you:

- Seek out people who have had similar study abroad experiences and trade reading material so that you aren't limited to what you were able to find on your own. Talk to native speakers of the language and ask them to borrow a novel, a comic book, magazine, or newspaper. They also might have more insight on specific Web sites for your country of interest.
- Start a book club with returnees or students in your language classes.
- Use the Internet because of its interactive nature. Actively seek out pen pals in the target language, even if they are not native speakers.

Co-author Lassegard finds that when he writes in Japanese he gets 10 times more response than when he writes in English. That's a pretty strong motivation to keep reading and writing coherent sentences in the target language. Also, keep in contact with people you met in the host country. E-mail is an easy way to keep in touch. Co author Chi still e-mails her friend in Mexico whom she met more than six years ago! Finally, a recent returnee had this advice to give:

You should make sure that you keep in contact with native speakers from the country you visited. They can write you e-mails…and this is the most effective form of learning. They can help you with your language, and if you have questions, you can ask. They also use language as you would most likely use it in day-to-day conversations. This is the best form of continuing your reading skills and comprehension. I am doing this now that I have come back. ~ Tammy Yach, Venezuela

It is essential to do as much reading as possible in order to become a more fluent reader in the target language. Find different sources, like the ones mentioned above, and others that will supply you with a variety of native writing styles for diverse age and interest groups.

Drink nothing without seeing it; sign nothing without reading it.
~ Spanish Proverb

LANGUAGE-LEARNING STYLES AND STRATEGIES:
WRITING

Pre-Departure Writing Activities

Before you head off to a new world of writing in a second language, you might find it useful to get in a little practice. Who are the first people that you will meet in the new country? Who will you need to interact with the most when you first arrive? Most often, these people are your host family members, a supervisor, or a landlord. What will you say to them when you first meet them? What do you most want to tell them about yourself?

Since you may be very nervous, and a little tongue-tied, you might find it helpful to write a letter of introduction. This way you have the opportunity to tell them exactly what you want to say without leaving out a detail, and you also will be able to use the language correctly. If you are not sure how formal or informal to be in your letter, it may be best to err on the side of more formal. In general, the U.S. has a relaxed writing style (calling people by first name, using contractions, using incorrect grammar). In some languages, writing too informally may send a signal that you are not respectful of the recipient's status, age, etc.

Advice from Writers

The following strategies are from second-language writers, detailing ways that you can improve your writing. Though these suggested strategies apply mainly to the writing of term papers and other academic text, some may also apply to the writing of letters and other shorter pieces, especially when it is important that they be well written.

- **Go back to go forward:** Writing builds on itself. Go back over what you have written to determine what to write next.
- **Repeat key words and phrases:** Good writing is cohesive—the ideas are clearly connected. Going back over your writing helps you to make sure that ideas are linked clearly. To link your ideas, deliberately repeat key words and phrases and use conjunctions (and, but) to guide the reader.
- **Plan out what you are going to write:** Expert writers either have a plan thought out in advance for how to write a text or make workable plans as they go along that draw on their knowledge of effective writing. Inexperienced writers tend to work in small planning units, writing one phrase at a time, and then asking themselves what to say next.

- **Leave a blank for words you don't know:** If words are unknown, leave a blank, perhaps with a circle around it, or write in the English word temporarily. This way you don't unnecessarily distract yourself from the writing process.
- **Edit grammar and mechanics after your ideas are written:** Postpone editing for grammar and mechanics until an appropriate moment because it often distracts you from getting your ideas down. Don't stop the flow; save editing for later.
- **Make major revisions *after* your ideas are written down:** Major revisions should be postponed so as not to interrupt the writing process. For example, if you find a problem, make a quick mental or written note but finish working on the current section before dealing with it. This way, you can revise your writing without disrupting the flow of ideas.
- **Distance yourself from the writing:** Step back from your writing for hours, days, or weeks (if possible). When you are caught up in the text it's hard to see the strengths and weaknesses of your writing.

Feedback on Written Work

One of the biggest mistakes novice writers can make is assuming they have to go it alone. Good writing is often best as a group project. And just like with any other group project, giving careful attention to the feedback of others in your group can be a great help.

Written feedback works when...
- you are interested in feedback on the topic or are particularly concerned about vocabulary.
- you know what to do with the feedback because it is clear and specific.
- you have the knowledge necessary to understand the correction. For example, in a French essay, a female student writes, *J'ai arrivé à Paris il y a trois jours* ("I arrived in Paris three days ago.") The teacher corrects this sentence in her essay as follows: *Je suis arrivée il y a trois jours*. The student is confused because she doesn't really know the rule that certain verbs in French use the "to be" rather than the "to have" verb. The student is also confused that the past participle is inflected for the feminine gender of the writer!
- you record the feedback to help you make improvements for the long run.

For example, if you create your own *learner's log* in a notebook with meaningful definitions, translation equivalents, and examples, each vocabulary correction or suggested alternative could be added to it. If you have included grammar rules in your learner's log, you can also update these based on the feedback that you receive.

A Special Means of Getting Feedback: Using the Reformulation Technique

- Want to sound "more authentic"?
- Frustrated that your writing, while fairly error free, seems unnatural and stylistically awkward?
- Curious about how your writing compares to native writers?

Reformulation…shows exactly what the issues are—what you're doing that is not German but rather English translated into German (or Portuguese, or whatever language), and how you might make it sound more 'authentically' written. ~ Molly Zahn, Germany

Even after spending much time on a piece of writing, you may have the uncomfortable feeling that a native would not have written it that way. Here is one example from a student:

I can write in fairly sophisticated German with relatively few grammatical errors. I don't (usually!) do things like mess up subject-verb agreement or make mistakes with number or gender. The biggest thing I noticed when writing was the way sentences were constructed. In English, I tend to create complex and laborious sentences. (Germans are famous for this, so it shouldn't intrinsically be a problem.) The problem is, my complex sentences in German, although grammatically and, even from a technical point of view, stylistically correct, are structured more like English sentences than German ones. For example, I tried to convert directly into German the following very English sentence:

> Because the first two years at an American University are taken up with general liberal education and because there is no cumulative exam at the end of the degree program, most American students come away from their B.A. programs with merely superficial knowledge of their subject area.

While it is grammatically OK to begin a sentence with 'because' in German, it's not very natural—it doesn't sound so good. Also, the English 'come away with' in the sense of 'gain, receive as a result of an experience' can't really be directly translated. It can, grammatically and everything, but it just isn't something a German would say. The same with 'take up with.' My native speaker restructured the sentence like this:

> In contrast [to the German university system], one studies primarily general topics in the first two years at an American university, and one is not tested on the contents [of his/her degree] upon finishing. Therefore, after the completion of their B.A., most American students have only superficial knowledge in their subject area.

Steps for using the reformulation technique

Reformulation is generally most useful for intermediate and advanced second language writers. It is a method that can be used to improve your ability to write "like a native."

Getting started:

1. Write a short paper (200 to 300 words). Revise until it reflects your thoughts accurately and you self-check for mistakes in grammar and mechanics.
2. Give the paper to a competent native writer at least once for feedback. This writer should go over the paper for vocabulary and grammatical errors.
3. When you receive the native writer's comments, revise your paper based on that feedback. This version is referred to as a reconstruction since it has been corrected to reflect what you meant to say.

Reformulation Tasks

4. Next give the reconstruction to a competent native writer (not your teacher) to rewrite or *reformulate* the entire paper or a portion (say, the first 100 words, since the beginning of the paper is often written with extra attention). It is usually advisable to find someone other than the teacher to do the reformulating because the teacher is perhaps too close to the text already, having gone over it already for correction and other comments. Also, you do not want a reformulation that is too polished. The reformulator's purpose is only to shift the message to a form that is more stylistically similar to that of an average native writer, not a professional.

Once someone has agreed to do the reformulation, he/she should rewrite the paper preserving as many of your ideas as possible while expressing them in his/her own words to make the piece sound more appropriate in the target language. Clearly, it is not always possible to preserve every idea—either because the original idea was not that clear to begin with or because the use of a different word or phrase shifts the meaning to some extent. It is important for your helper to stay as close to the original ideas as possible, to ensure that the writing still reflects your work and not theirs.[4]

5. With the help of a native writer or on your own, compare your original corrected version with the reformulated one. You are encouraged to do this in several steps in the order listed below:

   - **Compare the way things are phrased in your version and the reformulated one.** *How does the native speaker phrase sentences?* Look at the native writer's approach to questioning, defining, hypothesizing, asserting, etc. For example, in your target language, you had written the equivalent of, "I am sorry if I did something wrong." The reformulator wrote with more formality and with a few flourishes: "I wish to apologize sincerely for any inconvenience I may have caused you." These are ritualistic formulas that natives know how to write and which you as a learner may well want to learn! They may come in handy during your stay abroad and beyond.

   - **Compare the means of linking one idea with another and its effect on the clarity of the writing.** *Does it flow? Does it hang together?* Look at ways that the native writer linked together ideas—within and across sentences and paragraphs. Such ties or connectors consist of grammar forms such as *conjunctions*—combining ideas together ("and"), contrasting them ("but"), showing one causes the other ("so"), or giving a time sequence ("then")—and *personal pronouns* ("he," "it," "they," etc.) and *demonstrative pronouns* ("this," "that," "they," etc.). Check to see if the reformulator organized your writing so that it is understandable. For instance, you could check whether he or she identified the topic (or topics) that you are writing about more clearly. You could also see if the native writer changed the order of ideas. The ideas may flow better in a different order in the second language. In addition, you could also see whether any ideas have been enhanced by the addition or elimination of words or phrases.

   - **Compare the selection of vocabulary.** *What vocabulary works best?* Pay attention to whether the native used more precise words, more concise phrases, more/less formal words, and how words can be used together. Pay particular attention to prepositions used with particular verbs, verbs used with particular nouns (e.g., "to *perform* an operation"), and adjectives with nouns (e.g., "the fruit is ripe"). Frequently, the changes that the native writer has made are slight, representing subtleties of vocabulary use.

---

[4]This procedure, then, guards against the likelihood of plagiarism whereby the ideas of the essay—not only vocabulary and structure—would be replaced by those of the reformulator.

- **Compare the choice and ordering of grammatical forms.** *How is the writing structured?* Check whether the native writer has changed some of the grammatical structures—clauses, sentences, or clusters of sentences. If so, note what structures were used in place of the ones in your version. Did the native use more or less complex structures to convey the same meaning? What did the native writer use to avoid repeating the same structure over and over. You will see structures that you already know but haven't used, as well as those that you do not know. Write down new grammatical patterns (in your learner's log) and try to use them in your own writing to help you improve your skills.

What then is reformulation? It is basically a refinement. It is intended to *complement* the feedback that you currently receive regarding your target-language writing, rather than to replace the other forms of feedback.

Example of reformulation

We will now look at an example of reformulation—a four-sentence paragraph from an essay by a university English as a foreign language student:

> One of the severe problems of the social life on campus is the problem of the relationship between Arabs and Jews. It is well known that the mixture of the two cultures causes tension between students, and it especially effects students who live in the dormitories of the university. In my opinion this problem would not have been so severe if unreliable sections from the Students Union did not deliberately wake students to act violently. I therefore suggest that an imediate change of the group which dominates the Students Union will be done by free elections on campus.

The teacher in this case was a teacher of stylistics and thus paid more attention to such matters as well. Her corrections were as follows:

1. "social problems" for "problems of the social life"
2. "better structure than coordination?" – marginal comment regarding the second sentence
3. problem with the word "effects"
4. "university dormitories" instead of "dormitories of the university"
5. "why a past idea 'would not have been'?" – marginal comment regarding the third sentence
6. another word for "sections"
7. deleted the plurals in "Students Union" in both places it appeared
8. comment about tense and choice of verb in "did not deliberately wake" – suggested "provoke"
9. spelling of "immediate"
10. marginal comment, "Structure!" with regard to "will be done" in the last sentence – suggested "to make a change"

The student incorporated the teacher's corrections into a revised version, and the paragraph came out as follows:

> One of the severe social problems on campus is the problem of the relationship between Arabs and Jews. It is well known that because of the mixture of two cultures, tension exists between students, especially those who live in the university dormitories. In my opinion members of the Student Union provoked students and encouraged them to act violently, therefore I suggest that these members must be changed through free elections on campus.

As in the previous example, we see that surface mistakes have been cleaned up. There are now no glaring verb tense errors, for example. But if we look closely, we notice several vocabulary problems—"the mixture of the two cultures" and "these members must be changed." Also, in the first sentence the noun "problem" is repeated, rather than a demonstrative pronoun, producing somewhat awkward cohesion in English.

The following is a reformulated version:

> A serious social problem on the Hebrew University campus is that of relations between Arabs and Jews. It is well known that cultural and political differences between these groups lead to tension and conflict within the student population, especially among those who live in contact with one another in the dormitories. In my opinion, members of the Student Union provoke violence among students. For this reason, I suggest that these members be replaced through new campus-wide elections.

Note that in the last sentence "for this reason" provides a more specific connective marker than "therefore." Also note that the awkward phrases have been replaced: "cultural and political differences between these groups...those who live in contact with one another..." for "the mixture of the two cultures," and "I suggest that these members be replaced" for "these members must be changed." The awkward repetition of the noun "problem" in the first sentence is avoided by use of the demonstrative pronoun "that"—"A serious social problem...is that of..." With regard to syntax, the second sentence is simplified by eliminating a further subordinate clause introduced by "because of" after "It is well know that..."

Practice!

To make this approach to feedback on writing more real for you, we suggest that you write a short essay or select one that you have already written in a target language. If you are required to produce target-language writing in a specialized area, such as business correspondence, medicine, law, culture, or whatever the case may be, you may wish to prepare as an exercise a piece of writing reflecting the field, then go through the step-by-step guide to reformulation.

Writing a Term Paper in the Target Language

You already know a great deal about writing a term paper in your native language, including that organization is key. But what about doing it in your host country's language? You may want to consider some differences in writing style and expectations:

- *Organization* is still crucial but you need to check with your local professors about the expectations *they* have regarding organization, since how papers are organized varies across academic cultures.
- In addition, there are *conventions for writing academic papers.* You can learn about some of these conventions if you have a native writer reformulate some of your term paper for you. In this way, you can see more graphically how they turn phrases in their language—for instance, how to *hedge* when something isn't known to be definitively true (e.g., the equivalent of "it would appear that," "one might assume," "all things being equal," etc.).
- The third major hurdle is to use the appropriate *academic terminology.* Sometimes these terms are evident but other times you need to check with other students, with the professor, with the textbooks, or elsewhere to find out the terms that are used to refer to the concepts you wish to express. In fact, it is sometimes the non-technical terms used technically that cause the most problems in academic writing—terms that take on a technical meaning in a given academic field (e.g., mechanism, process, mode, scheme, etc.).

Post-Study-Abroad Writing Activities

When you return from a sojourn abroad, it may be difficult to continue practicing your writing skills. Here are a few quick ways to keep up your writing:

- Write a letter to your host family every so often—you may also be able to e-mail them.
- Keep a short journal on aspects of your experience abroad that are particularly memorable by using your newly learned language skills.
- Continue writing about how your life has changed since the experience, and try to explain your feelings regarding these changes.
- If you are more fluent in the second language, find a local newspaper that is written in that language and send in an article. Take it through the writing processes and find someone to give you honest feedback on your writing. You might discover a talent you never knew you had!

LANGUAGE-LEARNING STYLES AND STRATEGIES:
TRANSLATION STRATEGIES

We all translate to some degree while learning and using a second language. For example, you may want to know what something means in your native language before going any further. You may go rushing to a dictionary to get the meaning of *cogumelo* in Portuguese (mushroom) before continuing to read a Portuguese text about poisonous *cogumelos*. Very possibly, you already use many of the strategies described in this section, even if you are only somewhat aware that you are doing so. The goal is to raise your awareness about strategies used because once you are aware of them, you can then decide consciously when to employ a certain strategy and whether it might be possible to try a new one.

Choosing between mental and written translation

Choosing between mental and written translation is partly a question of your own learning-style preference.

- You may prefer, for example, to write out or type a translation if you like to take in new language material visually.
- You may also wish to produce a word-for-word translation according to the order that the words appear in the target language.
- On the other hand, you may prefer to keep the material in your head, perhaps focusing on how it sounds, not how it looks.
- Or you may prefer to get the gist of the message, rather than look at each individual word.

Some situations are more appropriate for mental translation (such as in an informal conversation where written translation would be impractical). Other situations would probably call for a written translation no matter what your learning-style preferences are (for example, when you need to produce a written text or give a formal talk). While it may be useful to prepare a written translation of a short target-language passage while reading, translating fully anything of length can be so time-consuming and tiring that you don't learn much of the language at all. The choice between written over mental translation will depend both on what kind of learner you are and what the situation is.

Translating when languages are either very close or very far apart

You may wish to translate a certain type of sentence just because the languages are dramatically different with regard to this pattern. In such cases, translating may help you to accentuate the differences and fix them comfortably in your mind. For example, there may be cases where a verb in a foreign language has two very different meanings and you feel a need to translate out both options to make sure that you do not mistakenly use the wrong one. So, for example, a native speaker of Hebrew uses the same verb, *levaker*, for both 'to visit' and 'to criticize.' It should be clear to the reader how dangerous it might be to use the wrong translation equivalent in an English conversation with a native English-speaking person and find yourself expressing your desire to criticize when that is the farthest thing from your mind!

On the other end of the spectrum are cases where the meaning of a given word is almost the same in two languages, but translation can still help to clarify the range of coverage of a word. So, for example, *sensible* in Spanish means both "sensible" and "sensitive" in English.

Translating idioms, sayings, and expressions

If you are learning a second language, sooner or later you are bound to run across a phrase or a saying whose meaning leaves you baffled. In an attempt to understand it, you may look up each word in the dictionary and double-check your grammar book. It is very possible that, despite these measures, you will find that the meaning of the phrase still eludes you—in fact, it might even seem nonsensical or absurd. If that is the case, chances are likely that you have hit upon an idiom.

Each language has its own set of idioms that act as a lively shorthand to express ideas or describe events. Consider the following:

- If Carlos tries to tell you that he's going to repay you soon, I'd *take it with a grain of salt*.
- "There are always *other fish in the sea*," my mother said after Abby and I broke up.
- We tried to throw a surprise party for Leo, but Erica *let the cat out of the bag* when she was talking to him after work on Friday.
- Donald's *name was dragged through the mud* when he was accused of stealing at work.
- The whole experience with Uncle Bill's inheritance *left a bad taste in my mouth*.

If you are a native speaker of U.S. English, it is almost certain that you immediately understood each sentence without getting bogged down by the literal meaning of the idioms because, really, what does a tiny amount of salt have to do with repayment of a loan? Nothing. Why would letting a feline out of a sack ruin impending party plans? Unless it was eating the birthday cake, it wouldn't. As you can see, it is not the literal meaning that is important but instead the culturally understood sense of the expression, the figurative meaning of the idiom.

Translating idioms from U.S. English to the language of the host country or vice versa can be tricky business. There are a few idioms, such as "to kill two birds with one stone," that have near word-for-word equivalents in a number of different languages. However, for the most part, it is wise to avoid the direct translation of idioms, as they will most likely be confusing at best and offensive at worst.

Learning the idioms and colloquial expressions of your host country will allow you to interact with those around you in a more native-like, natural way, and will move your language learning beyond your textbook into a new, colorful realm. When translating from the language of the host country, our suggestion is to ask a host country native to explain the figurative meaning of the idioms that you run across. If you are translating to the language of the host country, you might want to ask if there are similar idioms in the host country language that would fit what it is you are trying to express.

For example:

It's about the same either way.
- English: It's six of one, half a dozen of the other.
- French: It's cabbage green and green cabbage (*C'est chou vert et vert chou*).

To have the desire to provoke a fight.
- English: To have a chip on your shoulder.
- Italian: To have a fly on your nose. (*Avere las mosca al naso*).

Recently my husband, Keon, and I ate at a nice restaurant. Keon did not like his meal at all and he complained about it the next day saying, 'If I go there again, I will change my name.' I was confused. I didn't know what he meant, so I asked him to explain it for me. He said that it was a Korean expression that meant the food was so bad that he never wants to eat there again. I figured out that he meant, 'I'll change my (last) name before I ever eat there again!' So it's very similar to our expressions like 'when pigs fly' or 'when hell freezes over.' ~ Julie Chi

Translating while speaking

The use of translation strategies in speaking would depend on whether you are speaking informally in everyday conversational contexts or are engaged in the formal sort used when giving a presentation or speech, for which you need to spend time preparing.
- If you are giving a prepared speech, you may wish to jot down translations of specific words or key sentences. These sentences may highlight certain key grammatical features.
- Then while speaking, you could monitor what you are saying by keeping in mind the translation you've jotted down.
- Both for prepared speeches and for informal speaking, you could work back through what you said mentally, translating several items to see if you used the language correctly.

Translating while writing

For some of you, your writing will be better organized and better thought out if you plan first in your native language, simply because you have more tools in the native language and it may be easier for you to see the "big picture" that way—to get a sense of what you want to say. You will also have the vocabulary so you can find workable equivalents in the target language. In any case, when you actually begin to write in the target language, you should find a proper balance between use of your own choice of words, the use of a dictionary, and consultation with a native speaker.

Translating while reading

Be aware that our brains can process and store information a lot quicker and more efficiently in our native language. We can use that to our advantage while reading— and maybe you already do.

> I realized that I [perform mental translation] all the time while I read. I stop at the end of paragraphs and try to form a flash mental image or explanation of the topic of the paragraph. Because this all happens so fast, the main terms are almost always in English. ~ Molly Zahn, Germany

Translating while listening

Listening is the skill where the information stream can be the most relentless—as in movies and TV (where you don't have access to a playback mechanism). In such cases, it is not possible for you to run back the sound a few times until unintelligible gibberish is heard sufficiently well before you can understand any of it. Fortunately, this is usually not a high-stakes situation since no one really cares if you understood everything correctly. In an academic context, however, especially in lectures, the understanding and retention of information may be crucial. You may, in some cases, be able to stop the lecturer for clarification or check with a TA afterwards. But still you will most likely need a method for writing some things down effectively—which will probably call for use of your native language.

In fact, you may translate at the same time you are taking notes on lectures in the target language if it is easier for you to remember the lecture that way and easier to study from the notes. Of course, you may lose more sentences on the way than if you take notes in the target language directly because your mind is busy processing the translation in addition to understanding and organizing the information.

> For me, it's mostly a question of speed. Because what I write down is usually only a summary of what the professor has just said, I sometimes find myself groping for words in German. So I get the thought down in English and then go back to German. There's also the issue that I have my own personal abbreviations and method of taking notes in English that I haven't yet developed for German. That's another reason that taking notes in German is slower. ~ Molly Zahn, Germany

CONCLUSION OF THE
LANGUAGE STRATEGIES SECTION

Throughout the language strategies part of the guide, you have been advised to keep an open mind about trying new strategies for language learning and use. Hopefully you have learned more about your own learning styles and what you can do to improve your language skills, especially in the study abroad context. You have explored a variety of strategies, and you can feel free to adapt them in any way that helps you learn best.

We realize that this guide provides a lot to absorb in one sitting, so take your time and page through it as often as your language needs require. The activities presented are meant to be used as often as you like, depending on your goals, so don't be afraid to try them again at a later time—for example, when your language skills have improved or when you have gained more insight. Again, adapt these activities according to your particular situation and most of all, enjoy them.

In this guide, we have made an effort to combine ideas about language and culture. Since the two concepts are so intertwined, we would like you to be able to use some of the strategies offered in the language and culture sections of the guide together. In many cases, you will find that language and culture come together naturally, so you can take these as opportunities to maximize your entire learning experience in your host country.

Recommended Reading for Language-Learning Styles and Strategies

Brown, H. D. (2002). *Strategies for success*. White Plains, NY: Longman/Pearson Education.

> This is a book for ESL learners, covering the following in short chapters: learning-style preferences, right and left brain, motivation, self-confidence and lowering anxiety, taking risks, language-learning IQ, first-language influence, learning a second culture, learning strategies, group strategies, and test-taking strategies. Every chapter has a questionnaire to help learners get into the issues. Exercises are included for practicing language skills.

Mendelsohn, D. J. (1994). *Learning to listen*. San Diego: Dominie Press.

> This book starts by discussing the theoretical assumptions concerning the learning process, listening process, and listening strategies. The author then makes the case for a strategies-based approach, discusses the essential features and design of a strategies-based course, deals with the linguistic proficiency required to be a competent listener, and gives examples of the strategies-based approach.

Oxford, R. L. (1990). *Language learning strategies: What every teacher should know*. Boston: Heinle & Heinle.

> The most famous of the strategy books, Oxford's text contains two versions of the Strategy Inventory for Language Learning (SILL), which has been translated into several foreign languages and provides learners with a hands-on method to self-diagnose their language learning strategies. The book contains extensive examples of how different strategies can be applied across language skills and tasks. This is a very practical resource for language teachers and strategy teacher-trainers.

Reid, J. (Ed.) (1995). *Learning styles in the ESL/EFL classroom*. Boston: Heinle & Heinle.

> This anthology features the work of authors known in the area of learning styles: Bassano and Christison, Carrell and Monroe, Chapelle, Ely, Oxford, Reid, and others. Included are issues surrounding learning-styles research, classroom activities and curriculum development using learning-styles information, and a look at the relationship between learning-styles research and the classroom. This anthology seeks to define learning styles as opposed to learning strategies. It offers detailed explanations and examples of various aspects of learning styles and includes several assessment tools.

Rubin, J. & Thompson, I. (1994). *How to be a more successful language learner (2nd ed.)*. Boston: Heinle & Heinle.

> This popular and easy-to-read book provides numerous concrete suggestions for how learners can become more independent, effective, and successful in their attempts to learn foreign languages. Divided into two parts, the book introduces learners to the nature of the language-learning process and then provides step-by-step suggestions on how to improve vocabulary, grammar, reading, writing, listening, and speaking skills.

References

Bennett, J. M., Bennett, M. J., & Allen, W. (1999). Developing intercultural competence in the language classroom. In R. M. Paige & D. Lange (Eds.), *Culture as the core: Integrating culture into the language classroom.* Minneapolis, MN: Center for Advanced Research on Language Acquisition, University of Minnesota.

Bennett, M. J. (1993). Towards ethnorelativism: A developmental model of intercultural sensitivity. In R. M. Paige (Ed.), *Education for intercultural experience* (pp. 21-72). Yarmouth, ME: Intercultural Press.

Bennett, M. J. (1999). Overcoming the golden rule: Sympathy and empathy. In M. J. Bennett (Ed.), *Basic concepts: Intercultural communication* (pp. 191-214). Yarmouth, ME: Intercultural Press.

Bennett, M. J., & Bennett, J. M. (n.d). *The D-I-E model of debriefing.* Unpublished materials from the Summer Institute for Intercultural Communication, Intercultural Communication Institute, Portland, OR.

Bock, P. K. (1974). *Modern cultural anthropology: An introduction* (2nd ed.). New York: Alfred A. Knopf.

Cohen, A. D. & Olshtain, E. (1981). Developing a measure of sociocultural competence: The case of apology. *Language Learning,* 31, (1), 113-134.

Cohen, A. D. (1998). *Strategies in learning and using a second language.* Harlow, Essex: Longman.

Ehrman, M. E., & Leaver, B. L. (2003). Cognitive styles in the service of language learning. *System,31:* 393-415.

Gardenswartz, L., & Rowe, A. (1994). *The managing diversity survival guide.* Burr Ridge, IL: Irwin Professional Publishing.

Hall, E. T. (1976). *Beyond culture.* New York: Anchor/Doubleday.

Hess, D. (1997). *Studying abroad/learning abroad: An abridged edition of the whole world guide to culture learning.* Yarmouth, ME: Intercultural Press.

Howell, W. S. (1982). *The empathetic communicator.* Belmont, CA: Wadsworth.

Inagaki, Y. (1985). *Jiko Hyogen no Gijutsu (skills in self-expression).* Tokyo: PHP Institute.

Kappler, B. & Nokken, K. (1999). *Making the most of your time abroad.* Minneapolis, MN: International Student & Scholar Services, University of Minnesota.

Lewis, T. J. & Jungmar, R. E. (Eds.). (1986). *On being foreign: Culture shock in short fiction.* Yarmouth, ME: Intercultural Press.

Lysgaard, S. (1955). Adjustment in a foreign society: Norwegian Fulbright grantees visiting the United States. *International Social Science Bulletin,* 7(1), pp. 45-51.

Mendelsohn, D. J. (1994). *Learning to listen: A strategy-based approach for the second-language learner*. San Diego, California: Dominie Press, Inc.

Morris, D. (1994). *Bodytalk: A world guide to gestures*. London: Jonathan Cape.

Oxford, R. L. (1995). Style Analysis Survey. In J. Reid (Ed.), *Learning styles in the ESL/EFL classroom* (pp. 208-215). Boston: Heinle & Heinle/Thomson International.

Paige, R. M., DeJaeghere J., & Yershova, Y. (1999). *Culture learning in the language classroom: A manual for language instructors*. Minneapolis, MN: The Center for Advanced Research on Language Acquisition, University of Minnesota.

Pedersen, P. (1997). *Culture-centered counseling interventions: Striving for accuracy*. Thousand Oaks, CA: Sage.

Stewart, E. C., & Bennett, M. J. (1991). *American cultural patterns: A cross-cultural perspective* (Rev. ed.). Yarmouth, ME: Intercultural Press.

Storti, C. & Bennhold-Samann, L. (1997). *Culture matters: The Peace Corps cross-cultural workbook*. Washington, DC: Peace Corps Information Collection and Exchange

Taylor Nicodemus, N. (1991). The travel journal: An assessment tool for overseas study. *Occasional Papers on International Education Exchange*, 27. New York: Council on International Educational Exchange.